# JASPER

BOOK TWO OF THE TUDOR TRILOGY

TONY RICHES

# COPYRIGHT

Copyright © Tony Riches

Published by Preseli Press

ISBN-13: 978-1530642625
ISBN-10: 1530642620

BISAC: Fiction / Historical

# ABOUT THE AUTHOR

Tony Riches is a full-time writer and lives with his wife in Pembrokeshire, West Wales, UK. A specialist in the history of the early Tudors, Tony is best known for his Tudor Trilogy. His other international best-sellers include *Warwick ~ The Man Behind the Wars of the Roses* and *The Secret Diary of Eleanor Cobham*.

For more information visit Tony's author website: www.tonyriches.com and his blog at www.tonyriches.co.uk. He can also be found at Tony Riches Author on Facebook and Twitter: @tonyriches.

*For my son*

*Peter*

*"It is true that the records reveal an elusive personality and a man whose movements are often obscure and unfathomable, and yet one who left a deep impression on his generation and not least on the Welsh bards, who supported the cause of Lancaster against York."*

**Professor Thomas Jones Pierce, M.A., F.S.A., Aberystwyth, Wales.**

# 1

## FEBRUARY 1461

He held his breath and shivered as he strained to listen. Sound travelled well in the frosty woodland. The rustle of a blackbird foraging for worms in fallen leaves and the sudden, wooden creak of an old branch, bending in the cold air. He heard the noise again, the heavy scrape of hooves on the stony track, coming his way, hunting him. Too tired to run, he would not be taken prisoner by the men of Edward of York.

Jasper remembered his father's warning. Their proud Welsh army marched over a hundred miles from Pembroke, stopping only at night and starting again each day at dawn, when his outrider returned with grave news. They had sighted York's army camped near Mortimer's Cross, on the old Roman road near the crossing of the River Lugg, directly in their path.

'We should avoid them, head north under cover of darkness,' his father suggested, his voice kept low so the men wouldn't overhear. He had looked his age from their long, cold march across Wales. Too old to fight, his father insisted on riding with them. 'I owe my life to King Henry,' he argued, 'and I owe it to your mother to support him now.'

Jasper recalled his terse reply. 'It's too late.' He saw the pleading in his father's eyes and softened his tone. 'They know we are here, Father. I will try to negotiate terms if we are given the chance, but we must be ready to fight.' In truth he doubted York would be in any mood for talking, since his own father, Richard, Duke of York, was beheaded by over-zealous Lancastrians the previous December.

Then came the news that Sir Richard Neville, Earl of Warwick, and York's right-hand man, had captured King Henry, Jasper's half-brother. He had thought York's soldiers were no match for the men of Wales and the battle-hardened mercenaries who rode with them, but he could not have been more wrong. Their enemy outnumbered them more than two to one and proved to be experienced and well-prepared fighting men.

The salvo of arrows descended without warning in a black cloud of death. One struck deep into the neck of Jasper's horse, which reared with a demented whinny of pain, throwing him from his saddle. He barely managed to scramble to his feet and draw his sword before York's men-at-arms charged, hacking with axes, maces and swords, slashing and killing without mercy.

'Hold firm, men! Stand your ground!' Jasper yelled out as he fought. For a moment he sensed their attackers wavering as men at the front fell dead and wounded. Then the mounted mercenaries behind him turned and galloped away. One after the other, Welshmen threw down their weapons and ran for the safety of the trees, pursued by merciless York soldiers. Their enemy took no prisoners and cut the fleeing men down, flinging their bodies into the slow-flowing, red-running River Lugg.

A knight in gleaming armour, a head taller than those around him, fought with such ferocity he cut a swathe through the Welsh line. Jasper recognised Edward, Earl of March. The new Duke of York could have stayed on his horse and watched the battle from a safe distance. Instead, he had been determined to avenge the death of his father and chose his ground well, driving the Welshmen back towards the river.

Jasper experienced the brutal, savage terror of hand-to-hand fighting when he stormed the castle at Denbigh the year before. Then he had been the attacker, with surprise on his side. Now his own men died around him in the ferocious onslaught by York's trained killers. He drew on every ounce of strength and years of practice as he battled for his life.

Tiring, he parried a scything swipe from a sword and sank to his knees, struck over the head with a murderous blow from a poleaxe. His helmet saved him, but blood flowed into his eyes. Dazed, he staggered to his feet and thrust his sword into the body of one of his attackers. The treasured weapon wrenched from his grip as the man fell writhing in agony.

Jasper cursed with shame at the memory of what he did next. Heads turned at the sound of thundering hooves as York's cavalry, hidden until now, charged around the left flank to surround the Welsh army. He had seen his chance to escape and taken it. He ran like a scared rabbit, sprinting until his lungs strained as if they would burst, abandoning his men and his father to their fate.

Now he must pay the price. His hand fell by habit to his empty scabbard, then to the handle of his dagger, a gift from his father, the cold comfort of the sharp blade now all he carried to protect himself. His helmet and armour lay abandoned in thick undergrowth, together with the bright red, blue and gold quartered royal surcoat he had worn so proudly on their ride through Wales.

Peering from his hiding place Jasper saw the first of the riders and wished for better cover. The man hunched in his saddle, tracking him as he would a wild boar. The horse lowered its head to graze the sparse grasses lining the path, yet the rider made no effort to urge his mount onwards. As Jasper watched, the man slid heavily to the ground, his curse as he hit the hard earth echoing in the silence of the forest.

Like him, the rider had probably fled the battle. He looked badly wounded, but at least he owned a horse. After waiting a moment to be certain they were alone, Jasper cautiously stepped from behind the trees and grabbed the horse's bridle. He saw the man's dark eyes flick from the drying blood on his face to the empty scabbard at his belt, making a judgement but with no sign of recognition.

'Are you for Lancaster or York?' Jasper's grip on his dagger tightened. If he must kill or be killed, he would end the man's life, as he needed the horse.

'I rode with the Earl of Wiltshire.' The man coughed blood.

Jasper knelt closer and studied the wounded man's face. His Irish accent meant he could be one of Wiltshire's mercenaries, paid to strengthen the Welsh army. He guessed the man to be about thirty, his own age. Well built, with the rugged, tanned look of someone who spent his life on the road, a leather cord tied his long dark hair.

Jasper saw the broken stub of the shaft protruding from the blood-soaked cloth of the man's shirt. The arrow had struck deep into his unprotected shoulder, close to the collar bone. There was nothing he could do for him, so he took the dying man's sword. The handle shone from regular use, and the weight of the blade felt well-balanced in his hand.

'I'll be needing my sword.' The man's voice rasped and he took breaths in gasps.

'I'm sorry, but my need is greater.' Jasper wondered if they could both ride the horse then dismissed the idea. 'Can you still ride?'

The man gave a weak smile. 'If you'll help me get a foot in a stirrup?'

He grimaced with pain and swore as Jasper hefted him astride the horse. 'I'll take you to Llanthony Priory, where the monks will tend to your wound.' Jasper peered down the forest track. 'York's men will probably expect us to head for Brecon.'

The man tried to sit upright in the saddle and nodded in agreement. 'I need to lay low for a while.' He gritted his teeth in pain but clung to life with grim determination. Jasper felt a duty to do what he could for him and handed him the reins.

'What name do you go by?'

'Gabriel, after the archangel.' He managed a wry grin. 'I've been a disappointment to my poor late mother, God rest her.'

Jasper decided not to introduce himself. The Irishman hadn't recognised him, and the fewer people who knew his true identity the better. He needed to return to the safety of Pembroke Castle and rebuild his army, yet felt responsible for the dying man.

They set off with Jasper leading at a brisk pace. His throat felt as dry as parchment and his lungs ached from the freezing air, but they must reach the sanctuary of the priory before night fell. His head ached with dull pain from the poleaxe blow and he sensed again the deep, cold shock of shame as he thought how he had failed his men.

If he had listened to his father's counsel they would be riding to join Queen Margaret's army. Instead, he led his loyal followers into York's trap and hundreds, perhaps thousands, died as a consequence of his actions. Worse still, he left his father in command of the left flank, charged by the cavalry. Jasper said a silent prayer for his father, although even the vengeful Edward of York would spare the life of the king's stepfather.

'How much further?'

Jolted from his reverie by the question, Jasper slowed his pace to answer. 'The priory is in the Vale of Ewyas, this side of the Black Mountains,' he glanced up at Gabriel, 'some ten, perhaps fifteen miles from here.' He saw the Irishman nod in understanding. His spirit seemed to be ebbing like the tide and his life now depended on the healing skills of the monks, if he lived long enough to make the journey.

The winter sun, well past its height, threw long, menacing shadows across their path, and the temperature fell sharply. Jasper shivered with the chill seeping through to his bones, despite the exertion of keeping a fast pace. Gabriel rode in silence, and at one point nearly fell from the saddle. Jasper steadied him and realised he must keep him talking, as if he fell from the saddle again, it could be the end of him.

'Where are you from?'

Gabriel continued to ride in determined silence, staring straight ahead, but seemed to be considering the question. Jasper wondered if he should ask again, when at last he spoke, a far away look in his eyes.

'Born and raised in Waterford. God's own country.'

'I've never been there,' Jasper admitted, 'but I've heard Waterford has a fine harbour?'

Gabriel managed a smile. 'Surely does,' he sounded wistful, 'as a boy I'd sit on the harbour wall and watch the ships sail in.' He glanced down at Jasper. 'I wanted to be a sailor, see something of the world.' He lapsed into silence again and closed his eyes as he fought against the pain.

Jasper knew he must keep the man talking. 'How did you end up here as a mercenary?'

'I'm a soldier of fortune not a mercenary.' Gabriel tried to sit straighter in his saddle. 'Worked my passage on a ship bound for Normandy. Ended up helping the English fight the French.'

'You said you rode with Sir James Butler, Earl of Wiltshire?'

He nodded. 'When I found my way home I needed work, so I signed up with Sir James,' he leaned to one side and spat blood on the ground, 'Lord Deputy of Ireland.'

Jasper heard the contempt in Gabriel's voice at the mention of his second-in-command. Handsome and charming, Butler became a favourite of Queen Margaret but remained unpopular with the people. Jasper recalled the ill-fated Battle of St Albans, where he barely escaped with his own life and suffered a wound, defending the king. They said Sir James Butler fled the battlefield, disguised as a monk.

Jasper could never forgive Butler for stealing Lady Eleanor Beaufort from him. He first met Eleanor at a banquet in Windsor Castle and fell deeply in love with her. Born in the same year, they shared much in common. Eleanor's father, Sir Edmund Beaufort, once loved Jasper's mother and almost married her. Jasper never asked his father if she named his brother Edmund after him, although he had heard the gossip.

Lady Eleanor captivated him, like no woman he had ever met. Strikingly beautiful, and fluent in several languages, she had inherited more than a dash of her father's adventurous spirit. A good match, he had hoped to marry her, but after his brother's untimely death he had been obliged to care for Edmund's widow, Eleanor's young cousin Margaret Beaufort, in Pembroke, and act as guardian to his little nephew Henry.

Jasper scowled as he remembered his last meeting with Eleanor. He still longed to know why she had not waited for him, and why she agreed to marry a man like James Butler. He had wanted to hear her say the betrothal had been arranged against her will, although that was not what people told him.

At first she ignored his plea to meet in secret, but the queen allowed him his own tower in Westminster Palace and he persuaded Eleanor to visit him there. He remembered how she kept him waiting for more than an hour past their appointed time. She had seemed unusually reserved when she arrived, and Jasper sensed she felt anxious about their being discovered, so decided to be direct with her.

'Why did you do it, Eleanor?'

'Surely you know?'

'You must forgive me, but the news came as a complete shock. You know I'd hoped...'

'What about my feelings, when everyone talks of how you've fallen for your poor brother's widow?'

He had been aware of talk he had fallen in love with Margaret Beaufort, and thought such rumours the work of his political enemies, making mischief, yet even his father believed the stories and tried to see them wed. Jasper had admired Margaret's faith and courage after all she had suffered, and they spent every moment they could together, so he understood how such rumours started.

'She has remarried, to Sir Henry Stafford.'

'I know she still lives with you, Jasper.'

'As my ward. Lady Margaret is a good, devout woman. I love her as a sister, Eleanor. I give you my word it has never been otherwise.' He had sensed the anger rising in his voice.

She studied him with large, tearful eyes. 'What have I done?'

'The fault is mine, Eleanor.' He had almost choked on the words. 'I should have paid more attention to you, explained why I remained in Wales for so long.'

He remembered the silken feel of her dress, the warmth of her body against his, the sadness on her face, the powerful sense of lost opportunity. The two years since that last meeting passed without him seeing her again, although she had often been in his thoughts. He had to welcome Wiltshire when he arrived at Pembroke Castle with his Breton and Irish mercenaries, yet felt reluctant to appoint him as his second-in-command.

'We need every man we can get, Jasper.' His father was

insistent. 'These mercenaries aren't loyal to you, but they'll follow Wiltshire, so you must give him command.'

His father spoke the truth, although not in the way either of them expected. Jasper fought back a surge of anger and a bitter taste in his mouth at Butler's betrayal. He glanced up at Gabriel, who stared stoically ahead.

'You don't like Sir James Butler?'

Gabriel shook his head. 'The man's a coward. He fled, at the first sign of trouble, without a thought for us.'

Again, Jasper flinched at the unfamiliar pang of shame. He fought for as long as he could, but in the end he had run like a coward, just like James Butler, as to stay would have meant capture or death. He consoled himself with the knowledge neither outcome would have been any use to Queen Margaret, or King Henry. At the same time there would be questions about how he had escaped the battle.

A thought occurred to him. 'You chose not to follow him?'

Gabriel looked at his bloodstained shoulder and the stub of the arrow. 'When I couldn't use my sword there seemed no point staying.' His voice sounded weak and he coughed and spat blood on the ground again. 'They chased me for a while but she's a good horse,' he patted his horse's mane, 'saved my life.'

Jasper stopped to rub the red stain from the earth with his boot. 'No point in making it easy for them to track us.'

'You think they'll bother, this far out?' Gabriel stared back over his shoulder as if expecting to see York men-at-arms following.

'I do.' They would search the dead for him, and someone might have seen his escape. 'Our best hope is they don't expect us to head south.'

'When we reach the priory, will you be taking my horse?' His voice sounded weaker.

'I have to.' Jasper waited while Gabriel considered this.

The horse and his sword were probably the only things the man owned of value but he had to take them both. Still some eighty miles from Carmarthen, it was too far to travel on foot and foolish to do so unarmed.

Gabriel made a decision. 'I owe you my life, so you're welcome to her.'

'I will see the monks tend to your wounds, then I must ride west.' Jasper studied the Irishman, making a judgement. 'I will also need your sword.'

'I told you, I'll need to be keeping my sword.' The Irishman sounded uncompromising.

'You're in no shape to use it, and I will see it's returned, you have my word.'

Gabriel eyed him questioningly. 'And what would your word be worth, now?'

Jasper ignored the slur, although it shocked him to realise others would soon be saying the same. He'd had no choice, but his reputation would suffer as a consequence of his escape. 'I'll send a man, in two weeks, with your sword and your horse. In the meantime I must ask you not to tell anyone what happened.'

'Bad news travels fast enough without help from me.' Gabriel winced at the pain from his wound.

Jasper answered softly, thinking aloud. 'There are people who will take advantage when they learn of our defeat.'

'How do I explain my injury?'

'We shall say bandits attacked us, which is true enough, for they took my horse and my sword. Bands of outlaws haunt the roads through the Black Mountains, so no one will be surprised to learn we've been robbed.'

At last the distinctive silhouette of Llanthony Priory appeared through the trees. Once one of the grandest priories in Wales, its treasures were now lost, pillaged by both sides in the fighting between the followers of Owain Glyndŵr and the

English. Most of the Augustinian monks left for the relative safety of Hereford, but Jasper sheltered from a storm there the previous winter and recalled a warm welcome.

Jasper helped Gabriel dismount before tethering his horse close to a water filled trough. He pushed the stout oak side-door of the priory, which opened onto a square cloister. An elderly friar, dressed in a hooded brown robe, appeared concerned as he saw Gabriel's wounds and the dried blood on Jasper's face and neck. He muttered something Jasper couldn't hear before calling for the others to come and help.

The infirmary was dark and cold, the fastened shutters blocking the light and the empty hearth offering no comfort. Two of the younger monks helped Gabriel lie on a rickety wooden cot while others began lighting tallow candles, filling an iron cauldron with water and preparing a fire in the hearth. The elderly friar answered Jasper's unspoken question.

'We will be late for Vespers but there are few enough of us here now, and your friend needs urgent care.' He turned to Gabriel. 'I shall find our apothecary, who will tend to you.'

'We are grateful for your kindness—and God's providence.'

Jasper shivered in the chill evening air as one of the monks examined the cut on his head. He recalled the shock of the blow, the closest he'd been to death, as once on his knees he made an easy target. He thanked God the blow was deflected by the curved steel of his helmet, long since lost in the woods. He never even saw the man who did it.

'Should have been stitched but you'll survive.' The monk cleaned Jasper's wound, using a damp linen cloth to wipe dried blood from his face and neck. He asked no questions about how it happened and seemed satisfied with the result.

'Thank you.' Jasper lowered his voice. 'What about my companion?'

The monk looked across at Gabriel, patiently watching as

two younger monks cut Gabriel's shirt from around his wound. 'He is in God's hands now, and those of our apothecary.'

The flames of the fire were taking hold, brightening the room and already offering their smoky warmth, when the apothecary arrived. A studious, quietly spoken man, he began laying out a row of instruments to remove the arrowhead. He handed one of the monks a long-handled poker to heat in the fire, and Jasper flinched as he realised they intended to cauterise the wound.

At last he spoke. 'He has been lucky, my lord. The arrow has a bodkin head, still not easy to remove, but a better chance of saving him.'

Jasper nodded. 'I wasn't certain he would make it here.'

'Much longer and it would be too late for my modest skills.'

Before he could reply the friar who first welcomed them caught Jasper's attention. 'You must be hungry after your journey, my lord. Come with me and I'll serve you bread and beer.'

Jasper realised he hadn't eaten a thing all day. He had planned to ride through the night and reach Carmarthen Castle as soon as he could, but after a meal of rye bread and a generous slice of cured ham, washed down with a tankard of weak ale, he closed his eyes to rest.

He dreamed of his father, trying to rally his men as York's cavalry overwhelmed them. As if in slow-motion, he saw the figure of Edward, grinning as he hacked down the Welshmen with his deadly sword. Again, he glimpsed the descending poleaxe at the edge of his vision yet could not see the face of the man who nearly killed him before he surrendered to the blackness,

He woke to the shrill cry of a cockerel to find he had been so exhausted he'd slept well past dawn. He immediately went in search of Gabriel, who he found sleeping in the infirmary, a clean linen bandage bound tightly around his wound. At least he had survived the night. Jasper turned to leave when Gabriel spoke.

'Good morning to you, my lord.'

'You know who I am?'

Gabriel smiled. 'I heard the monks call you that. They told me you are Sir Jasper Tudor, Earl of Pembroke.' He winced in pain but his eyes met Jasper's with gratitude. 'I'm truly in your debt, sir, for saving my life.'

'We live to fight another day, Gabriel—and I will keep good my promise to return your horse and sword.'

'I thank you, sir, as I'll need them if I'm to be in your service?'

Jasper smiled at the hope in Gabriel's voice. 'For now, you must rest, and I must return home, as many lives could depend on it.'

'I wish you well, my lord.' Gabriel raised a hand in farewell.

As Jasper rode through the wintry dawn towards the Black Mountains and home, he allowed himself a smile at the memory of Gabriel's discovery of his true identity. He felt great relief that the Irishman had survived. Helping him cost a lot of time and put them both at risk of discovery, yet at least he had been able to rest. Now he thanked God to be alive, and could begin to plan how to deal with the usurper, Edward, Duke of York.

## 2

## MARCH 1461

Pembroke Castle loomed like a jagged cliff from the grey mists swirling over the river. Jasper found plenty of time on the long ride to think about what he would say about how he had escaped the battle. He could not lie but Lady Margaret would be the only one to hear the whole truth. She read it on his face as soon as she saw him, as clearly as if she knew his most secret thoughts.

She said nothing until they stood alone together in the privacy of the castle chapel, and he watched her light a votive candle and place it on the altar. The beeswax briefly released its honey scent as the yellow flame flickered, then burned brightly, reflecting golden echoes in her all-seeing eyes.

'A prayer for your father, Owen Tudor.' The cold air in the chapel formed a glistening sheen on the single stained-glass window, but her voice sounded warm as she said his father's name.

For once Jasper felt lost for words. He felt closer to Margaret than anyone, yet struggled to tell her of the slow-burning fear that gnawed at his thoughts since he had left the Black Mountains.

'I have failed my father.' Emotion choked his words.

'You were given no choice, Jasper. My prayers are answered by your safe return.'

'I failed my country, Margaret.'

'Our Lord has a purpose for you, Jasper Tudor,' she turned to look into his eyes, 'I know in my heart you are delivered to us for a reason.'

Her words carried a certainty that soothed the fresh wounds of his self-doubt. Lady Margaret could not yet be eighteen years old, yet she spoke with the confident authority of the mother he now remembered only in his prayers. He recalled his father's deep, reassuring voice all those years ago as he knelt at his brother's side in prayer.

'Always remember your mother, boys, and that she was taken by God bringing us your little sister, named Margaret, after my mother.'

Jasper had been barely six years old when she died, and grew up thinking of his mother as an angel, the bright halo around her head his shining light of inspiration. Many years passed before he appreciated how impossible it must have been for her as a young French princess, the daughter of the now-dead, King Charles VI of France. In a desperate attempt to end the latest outbreak of the Hundred Years' War, King Charles agreed to marry her off to King Henry V of England, the conqueror of their country. Soon widowed, she had found herself vulnerable and alone with Henry's child before his father risked everything to marry her.

Lady Margaret waited patiently for his reply. For the first time he noticed she looked like a nun in her black robes and crisp white headdress, a sister of mercy, rather than one of the richest heiresses in the country, her only jewellery a silver crucifix that caught the light as she moved.

'I have been spared to take vengeance on the usurper and

free my father from those Yorkist traitors.' His anger echoed in the low ceilinged chapel.

A frown flashed across Margaret's face. 'Edward of York's father was cruelly murdered, as was his brother. You knew his father well, Jasper. Was he not a good man? Did he ever put himself forward as king, even when poor King Henry was unable to rule?'

Her questions stunned him to silence. She spoke the truth, as ever. Richard, Duke of York had been a noble man and they had almost brokered peace together before the Earl of Warwick stormed their barricades on that fateful day at St Albans. Edward's father deserved better than to have his head on a spike over the Micklegate Bar, mockingly adorned with a paper crown.

'I saw Edward fighting in the battle.' Jasper pictured him as he spoke the words. 'He is in no mood for talking of peace.'

'He is young and needs good men like you—to help him find the right path.' Her voice sounded softer now, and her hand rested lightly on his arm, its gentle warmth a comfort to him.

'I fear it's too late, Margaret. Edward has made me his enemy, and self-serving men like William Herbert will be straining at the leash to profit from our defeat.'

'We must pray for guidance and the safe return of your father.'

As they knelt together Jasper tried to clear his troubled mind, yet the image which returned to his thoughts was of Edward, winter sunlight gleaming from his burnished armour. For a moment, in the heat of the battle, Edward glowered in his direction and he had glimpsed the raw fury in the young man's face. It was too late for talking. The conflict between Lancaster and York which began at St Albans had now become a war.

There was more than enough to keep Jasper occupied at Pembroke Castle, beginning the slow process of trying to rebuild his ravaged army. The best of the fighting men were gone, leaving those too old or young, and worse, those with no appetite to risk their lives fighting in the name of the king.

The only respite came in tranquil moments of prayer with Lady Margaret, who rose to visit the chapel each day at the first light of dawn. Together they prayed for his father, for peace in these troubled times, and for the soul of her late husband. Jasper missed his brother and still questioned the manner of his death. They said he had died of the plague while held captive in Carmarthen Castle, yet Jasper swore to discover if Edmund had been murdered.

His brother never saw his son Henry. Now close to his fourth birthday, the boy beamed a happy welcome whenever he saw Jasper. He had inherited his mother's sparse build yet already showed signs of his father's adventurous character. His latest amusement was to climb the precarious stone steps up the castle walls and shriek with delight as Jasper raced to stop him falling.

Once word of Jasper's return spread, anxious groups of wives, mothers and daughters gathered at the castle gatehouse for news of their menfolk. Jasper sensed the sting of knowing what they must be saying about him. To his face they knew better than to question his actions, yet there was only one way he could have returned alone and uninjured.

He retreated to the sanctuary of his town house in Tenby, a small-windowed, timber-framed former merchant's lodging overlooking the sheltered tidal harbour. In previous years Jasper contributed more than half the cost of improving the fortifications of the seaside town. Now he found comfort within its moated walls, and his lookouts watching in the castle tower high on the hill would give ample warning of enemies approaching by land or sea.

Although he employed a dozen maids and servants at the castle in Pembroke, his only servant in Tenby was his house-keeper, a buxom widow of few words. She tended his fire, cleaned and made sure fresh rushes always covered his floors. His father told everyone about her cooking, particularly her Welsh cawl, a hot stew of lamb and leeks, which he claimed tasted as good as his own mother used to make, although Jasper suspected he remembered little of her.

The cobbles of the narrow roads glistened with frost as he made his way down the hill to the harbour. His regular walk was greatly improved since the civic order banning the throwing of waste into the street. The people now took pride in the little town and cleared away the piles of rotting rubbish, horse dung and worse.

Several new houses graced the high street and the older ones were smartly whitewashed, with brightly painted doors and window shutters. The merchants and traders of the town prospered, although he understood from his good neighbour, wine-merchant Thomas White, that most saw the threat from York as an English problem. Jasper worried what would happen if York's army invaded his remote corner of Wales.

York's spies and informers were said to lurk in the shadows, so once they knew he had returned to Pembroke they would come for him. They could already be on their way, to finish what started that day at Mortimer's Cross. He was troubled by the knowledge that his presence put Lady Margaret and her son Henry in danger, although they would be safe while they remained within the towering walls of Pembroke Castle.

The bracing sea air helped him think about the future, and he leaned against the cold stone of the harbour wall, watching shrieking gulls wheeling over the returning fishing fleet. The fishing boats ploughed steadfastly through the rolling, slate-grey sea, and as they came closer he could see familiar grinning faces, arms raised in recognition. Their holds must be heavy with their catch, the reason the Welsh name for Tenby was *Dinbych-y-pysgod*, the little town of the fish.

He recalled how the Irishman, Gabriel, told him how he had watched the ships come into the harbour as a boy in Waterford. Jasper kept his word and sent two men to Llanthony Priory with the man's horse and sword. They also carried Jasper's letter of invitation to join his personal guard. He doubted Gabriel could read or write, but the monks would read the letter to him and he hoped his offer would be accepted, as he needed every good man he could find.

The thought that Gabriel might be the only other one to escape York's pursuing soldiers troubled him deeply, yet at least he'd helped save one man's life. Jasper sat at his table, struggling with the wording of a letter to the men holding Denbigh Castle, when he heard a sharp knock at his door. He listened as his housekeeper answered, and smiled with relief at the unmistakable voice of a man he thought he would never see again.

Years later, Jasper would tell his half-brother, David Owen, of the day Sir John Scudamore came limping back to West Wales. Mistaken for dead, he'd somehow managed to crawl from the battle and make his way to safety. His friend's face was deeply lined with the look of the bearer of bad news. Jasper ushered him inside and closed the door. He guessed the reason why Sir John would feel obliged to ride all the way to Tenby on such a wet, wintry night, before he said a word.

'You bring news of my father?'

Scudamore's eyes fixed on his wet boots as he struggled to find the right words. 'I'm sorry, Jasper.' His deep voice, usually so full of humour, now barely a whisper. He removed his rain-soaked cape with unnecessary care and sat heavily in the leather chair to one side of Jasper's blazing fire, warming his hands before continuing. He stared into the flames as he spoke in a monotone, as if reciting his prayers.

'Your father was taken to Hereford and executed in the market square, along with my eldest son Henry.'

Jasper closed his eyes as the words echoed in his head. His nails pressed hard into his palm as he fought back tears and waves of anger at the injustice of it all. Edward of York had taken his revenge, an eye for an eye, a father for a father. A thought occurred to him, a slender thread of hope.

'You are certain?'

Sir John continued to stare at wisps of steam slowly rising from his boots as they warmed in the heat from the fire. 'It's the talk of the country, Jasper. I regret I cannot be mistaken.'

'I pray he had a Christian burial.' He recalled the sight of the row of heads left to rot on London Bridge, their sightless eyes pecked by crows, a gruesome warning to others.

'I heard your father was buried at the priory of the Grey Friars. There is no word of what became of my son.'

Jasper realised Sir John suffered an even greater loss, his son and heir, with all his life before him. 'Your Henry was a good man, a credit to you. I will remember him in my prayers.' His words sounded inadequate.

'He planned to marry in the spring, to a pretty girl, from a good family.' Sir John brightened momentarily with the recollection, then slumped in his chair at the enormity of the tragedy.

Jasper poured them both a generous tot of brandy from a wooden cask decorated with silver fleur-de-lis. A gift from Queen Margaret, he had been saving it for a special occasion. He handed a generous tot to Sir John and sat opposite him, looking at the bright flames licking hungrily at a yew log, then broke the long silence.

'I should have insisted my father remained in Pembroke. I could have made him constable. He would have liked that.' He still could not fully comprehend the dreadful news and talked to stop the nightmare images forming in his mind.

'Your father would never have stayed to defend Pembroke Castle. He always was a great adventurer.'

'You're right, John. Nothing would stop him going on the greatest adventure of all, to free the king. I think I've inherited his stubborn streak.' Jasper allowed himself a smile at the memory of the countless times his father refused to consider the possibility he might be wrong.

Sir John took a sip of the precious brandy and gave Jasper a nod of approval as the amber liquid warmed his throat. 'You've heard the queen's men rescued the king?'

'No. I've been laying low since I returned. What happened?'

'The Earl of Warwick tried to block their advance at St Albans, about a week or so ago. They say Exeter routed Warwick's rag-tag army and he ran to save his neck.'

'Henry Holland?'

Sir John nodded. 'The Duke of Exeter has proved he is not a man to be underestimated.'

Jasper frowned as he recalled the cruel way Holland tortured his prisoners on the rack when he became constable of the Tower. Everyone knew the confessions he extracted confirmed whatever Holland wished to hear. Henry Holland was also married to Anne of York, Edward's elder sister. Good money changed hands betting he would be first to desert the House of Lancaster to join York's cause, yet until now no one questioned his leadership or military ability.

'How is the king?' Jasper resisted a creeping suspicion their defeat at Mortimer's Cross could be for nothing. They had set out to join Queen Margaret's army and free the king from Warwick's clutches, yet now it seemed she had done it without him.

Sir John smiled and took another sip of the brandy, which

seemed to be restoring his old self a little. 'I heard they found him sat under a tree, singing songs with the men trusted with guarding him, Lord Bonville and Sir Thomas Kyriell. Apparently they offered no resistance, but it's what happened next that everyone's talking about.'

Jasper crossed the room and poured them both a second tot of brandy. He was starting to realise his mistake in hiding himself away in Tenby at such a crucial time for the country. 'I've not heard, John,' he handed him the brandy, 'tell me what happened?'

'It's impossible to know gossip from truth these days, but I heard Queen Margaret asked her son to decide if the York lords should be spared.'

'He can't be more than seven years old?' Jasper frowned.

'They were both executed—on the boy's order.'

Sir John's words hung in the air like an ominous black cloud on their horizon. Young Edward, Prince of Wales, would one day succeed King Henry. It was a bad omen for the future of the Lancastrian cause, and the future of the country.

'That's an outrage!' Jasper swore at the madness of it all. He stared into the blazing fire as he remembered how Lady Eleanor's father, Edmund Beaufort, always detested Sir Thomas Kyriell. All the same, Kyriell fought at Agincourt at the side of King Henry V and deserved better.

Sir John clearly thought the same. 'Queen Margaret should know this gives York the excuse he needs to do the same with his prisoners.' He shook his head.

'She came to this country as a fifteen-year-old girl, hardly able to speak English. You've seen King Henry. He barely recognised me last time we met, so Queen Margaret needs to show the people her son will become a strong, decisive king.' He frowned. 'Where will this end?' Jasper's question required no answer. He was thinking of his father and knew Sir John would be remembering his son.

They sat in silence, then a thought occurred to Jasper. 'Will the king and queen return to London?'

'I fear we've lost too many men. I suspect the mood in London has changed since the general pardon.'

'York is persuading our followers to turn their coats?'

'An order has been issued. All who are prepared to swear allegiance to York are to be pardoned.' He looked sharply at Jasper. 'You and I are, of course, excluded.'

'I will never swear allegiance to York. There was a time...'

The sense of loss overwhelmed him. First his mother and sister, then Edmund, now his father, all gone. He tried to live a good life, say his prayers, look for the best in people, yet everyone he loved had been taken from him. Deep grief welled up in his chest. The slow-burning yew log crackled as flames reached fresh sap, snapping him out of his self-pity.

He studied his old friend John Scudamore, a good loyal man, once the heart and soul of any banquet with his jokes and often bawdy songs, his spirit now crushed by the cruel murder of his son. As they sat together in silence, each lost in thoughts of what might have been, Jasper sensed a new purpose.

Lady Margaret said he'd been spared for a reason. He would dedicate his life to bringing peace to his troubled country and do whatever it took to protect the few who remained dear to him. His half-brother, little David Owen, his sister-in-law, Lady Margaret, and most important of all, her son Henry Tudor.

Flakes of late snow drifted from a dove-grey sky as Jasper took a fresh sheet of parchment and wrote a new letter to his loyal friends holding Denbigh Castle for Lancaster in North Wales. Before Sir John's visit his shame at defeat made it impossible to find the words yet now his quill flew across the page:

*To the right trusty Roger Puleston, we greet you well and suppose you have well in you remembrance of the great dishonour we now have by traitors March, Herbert, the Dunns and their affinities, as well as letting us of our journey to the king, as in putting my father your kinsman to the death...*

Jasper's chair creaked as he sat back heavily, staring at the truth of the stark words he'd written. William Herbert, the Dunns and their kinsmen, good Welshmen, from old families, conspired with York and murdered his father. His anger flared, Lady Margaret's words forgotten, as he wondered who he could now rely on to support his cause.

The clanging bell of St Mary's church sounded across the otherwise silent town, marking the hour. He had woken early, his head full of plans for the future. His father had known great loss and would have understood his need to hide from the world in his grief, yet now he felt a new sense of urgency. He took his sharpest knife and trimmed the point of his quill before continuing: *...we purpose with the might of the Lord, and assistance of you and other our kinsmen and friends, within short time to avenge.*

He read the letter several times as the black ink dried then signed it. *Written at our town of Tenby the twenty-fifth day of February. Pembroke.* As he did so, he knew it would be better to risk the journey to North Wales in person. The letter would be exactly the sort of evidence York would use to condemn him as a traitor.

The thought made Jasper curse Edward of York. The young boy he'd once thought of as a friend put at risk everything he cared about. Sir John warned him about York's patrols, pressing deeper into Wales in a determined search for those who escaped their deadly trap. It could only be a matter of time before they reached Pembroke Castle and threatened the safety of Lady Margaret and little Henry.

A plan began to form in his mind of a way to throw them off the scent. He took a fresh sheet of parchment and began to compose a letter to Henry Holland. He could no longer afford the luxury of liking those he must rely upon. In such dangerous times, who better to appeal to than the most dangerous man still loyal to the king?

## 3

## APRIL 1461

The Wheel of Fortune turned yet again when Sir Henry Stafford arrived with news of the crushing defeat of Queen Margaret's army. The son of the influential Duke of Buckingham, Henry Stafford was Jasper's choice of husband for Lady Margaret. Eighteen years older than her, he had no fortune, although hers would be more than enough for them both. They married shortly before Margaret's fifteenth birthday, and she remained at Pembroke with her son when Henry Stafford left to fight for the king.

Sir Henry sent a herald ahead to give notice of his arrival, so Lady Margaret waited with Jasper at the castle gate as he arrived. Her well-fitting emerald green dress made her look older and, Jasper thought, not unattractive. Sir Henry's right arm was bound in a bloodstained sling and he needed two men to help him dismount. Several of his retinue had bandaged wounds and one man seemed as if he needed urgent attention.

Lady Margaret greeted her husband cordially, offering him her hand to kiss. 'We give grateful thanks to God to see you safe, Henry, after so long with no news.'

'I regret I bring the worst news, Margaret.' He could not manage a smile for her. 'Let us find somewhere private.'

Jasper noted the dark shadows under Sir Henry's red-rimmed eyes, and how the fur of his fine bearskin cape was soaked and matted with mud. 'I shall arrange for your men to be served hot soup in the kitchens, Sir Henry. Will you join me after in the great hall and tell me your news?'

'I must caution you, my lord, what I need to tell you is not good, for Lancaster, at least.'

Jasper sensed the shadow of a sense of foreboding. 'Then the sooner I hear it the better, Henry.'

He watched with unexpected jealousy as Margaret took her husband's good arm and led him towards her rooms. Although Henry Stafford was only a little older than him, he walked stiffly, like a much older man. Jasper thought they seemed more like a father with his daughter than husband and wife. If the news was not good for Lancaster it could mean York had taken King Henry again, or worse.

Rebuilt at considerable expense, the great hall of Pembroke Castle had a splendid new hammer-beam roof and windows of precious leaded glass. Striking Flemish tapestries of hunting scenes decorated the walls, one of the few clues to Jasper's great wealth. The antlers of a large stag proudly decorated the wall above the impressive stone hearth, where a fire of blazing logs roared.

Platters of roast beef and trenchers, hot from the kitchens with the appetising aroma of freshly baked bread, sat on the scrubbed oak table. Jasper waited while his serving girl filled a silver tankard with ale for Sir Henry, who drank from it appreciatively.

'We met York's army on the old London road near a village called Towton in Yorkshire. Outnumbered them, we did, but their archers had the wind in their favour, while ours fell short. York's men started using our own arrows against us.' He nursed his bandaged arm as he took a trencher of bread and beef and ate hungrily.

'Is Baron Welles dead?' Jasper guessed Sir Henry's bad news for Margaret concerned her stepfather, who'd fought in the north with Sir Henry.

'He is. Margaret was fond of him, a good man and a great loss.'

'What of the king?' Jasper held his breath.

'Escaped to Scotland, by all accounts.' Sir Henry watched as the serving-maid refilled his tankard of beer, then drank deeply before continuing. 'It started snowing and our men lost heart.' He shook his head at the memory. 'They turned and ran like a herd of frightened deer. It wasn't a battle, Jasper, it was a bloody massacre.'

Jasper regarded Henry Stafford with new respect. He had never been in good health and as the second son carved out his own place in the world. He could have found reasons to stay with Margaret at her manor house in Bourne, which they made their home. Instead, he rode to fight for the king and now must turn his coat or be outlawed by York with a price on his head.

'How is your arm, Henry?' Jasper glanced at the fresh bandage of white linen Margaret insisted on.

'Broke it when my horse fell on top of me. Lost his footing on the ice and I thought it was the end of me. In truth he probably saved my life, as York's army passed me by.'

'Has the break been set and splinted?'

'They did the best they could—and I shall count myself fortunate not to lose it.'

Jasper stared at the tankard of ale sitting untouched before him. 'What are your plans now, Henry?'

'I must tell you, Jasper, that the cause of Lancaster is lost. I shall take Lady Margaret back to Lincolnshire and rest a while.'

'You intend to take York's offer of a pardon?' Jasper's words echoed in the great hall, the question that had rattled in his mind from the moment Sir Henry returned.

'If he will, but I've no wish to become your enemy, Jasper.'

'It will never come to that.'

Sir Henry raised his tankard. 'Here's to lasting peace in England.'

'And in Wales.' Jasper raised his tankard and drank the bitter tasting ale.


He doubled the guards and gave orders to be alerted at the first sign of York patrols, day or night. The small band of recruits shivered in the cold as they practised weapon drills within the castle's outer ward. Some seemed too young to grow a beard. Others, their best years behind them, knew their best hope was to stay within the impregnable walls of the great fortress.

Sir John Scudamore, now appointed Constable of Pembroke, limped over to where Jasper watched. He was followed by a well-built man with a grin on his face, wide enough to make Jasper call out in welcome.

'Gabriel! By God it's good to see you again.' He clasped the Irishman's hand. 'I see you have your sword back?'

Gabriel dropped his hand to the pommel. 'I didn't doubt you for a moment, my lord.'

'Your shoulder is healed?'

'The wound was deep, but I'm pleased with how well I've recovered.' He sounded serious. 'I'm grateful for what you did for me, my lord, and am in your debt.'

Jasper smiled. 'Well, now I've important work for you. Sir John will show you round. I expect you are hungry after your long ride?'

'I am, sir.'

'You will find me in my study after you've had something to eat. We've much to discuss.'

He watched the Irishman follow Sir John to the castle kitchens, relieved to see Gabriel arrive, and glad he had recovered well from his wound, as there was more to it now. Jasper's ambitious plans for the future could depend on what the Irishman knew.

Jasper's study overlooked the muddy, meandering River Cleddau. Small and sparsely furnished, with no rushes on the bare stone floor, it seemed more like a servant's room than the office of one of the wealthiest men in Wales. As he entered he caught a breath of woodsmoke from the fire in the hearth and reminded himself to tell his servants to check the chimney, a favourite nesting place for rooks.

He tidied his dark oak table, sorting papers and letters to be answered, then crossed to the window and stared down at a boat bringing much needed supplies. The tide fell quickly on the river, so the crew hurried as they moored at the castle wharf. He watched them throw ropes and call out to the men waiting on the quayside. Sometimes he wished he could live a simpler life, with only the tides to worry about. A confident knock sounded at his door and he opened it to see Gabriel.

'Come in. I'd like your help on a plan I've been thinking about, but first, have you seen anything of York's patrols?'

Gabriel sat in one of Jasper's comfortable chairs. 'That's why it took so long to reach here, my lord.' He glanced at the parchment map of Wales on the wall, the main castles featured as prominent, larger-than-life landmarks. 'York's men are in Carmarthen, so it won't be long before they are at our door.'

'That's what I wanted to talk to you about.' Jasper lowered his voice, although they couldn't be overheard. 'They know I'm here. We're preparing the castle for a siege, but I lost my best men at Mortimer's Cross.'

'I'm sorry to hear about your father, sir.'

Jasper nodded in acknowledgement. He still found it difficult to think about his father's fate, yet he brightened at a memory. 'He used to sit in that chair you're in now and tell me I should marry.'

'He was a good man, my lord.'

'You met him?'

'The first night we camped on the march, he came to talk to us, thanked us for our support for King Henry.' Gabriel smiled. 'He knew we were mercenaries, but his words meant a lot.'

'I had no idea.' Jasper recalled how he'd been so preoccupied during the march he had hardly spared any time for his father, squandering their precious last days together, something he would regret for the rest of his life.

'This plan, sir. How can I be of help?'

'It's me they're looking for, Gabriel, so I must draw York's men away from Pembroke. I intend to leave Sir John in charge here and take the fight to North Wales.'

'You want me to stay here, help defend the castle?'

'No. I need you to come with me—but there's an important job I must ask you to do before we leave.'

'I'm at your service, sir.'

'Good. I need you to ride to Tenby this evening and visit as many taverns as you can. York has spies in the town, so I need them to hear that I'm off to North Wales at dawn to rebuild my army there.'

'So they divert their patrols north?'

'Exactly. The thing is...' He studied the Irishman for a moment, making a judgement, 'I've no intention of riding into another of York's traps.'

'You'll travel by sea?'

'I will, but not directly to North Wales. I've asked the Duke of Exeter to cause York sympathisers there as much distress as he is able, and let it be known I'm behind it.'

'Where are we sailing to, my lord?'

'Ireland, Gabriel.' Jasper smiled. 'I'm taking you home— and I'll be needing your help to raise an army.'

Their little fat-bellied ship rolled in the relentless waves of the Atlantic, challenging the crew to hold a steady course as the dark coast of Wales slipped into the distance. An ageing hulk, she was clinker built all the way to the keel. Her wedge shaped hull made the ship more seaworthy than the flat-bottomed cogs, and helped prevent her from making as much leeway.

Her captain and crew seemed unaware of their passenger's true purpose or identity. Jasper allowed his dark beard to grow thicker and a rakish cap with a black hunting cloak completed the disguise. He could easily be mistaken for a merchant and told Gabriel to call him sir in public. He leaned on the taffrail, watching graceful gulls dipping in their wake.

Word of Edward's coronation had spread through Wales like fleas on a dog, passed by word of mouth in markets and taverns faster than a man could ride. Jasper knew the reason. The people tired of the civil war and Edward promised peace and prosperity. They had seen their menfolk march off in King Henry's name and not return. The price of loyalty to the cause of Lancaster was too great.

Jasper recalled his farewell meeting with Lady Margaret, the only person other than Thomas White and Gabriel to know the truth of his plan. She had needed to leave Pembroke for the long journey to her home in Lincolnshire and urged him to be on his guard.

'I wonder if anywhere is safe from the reach of York, now he has made himself king.'

Jasper heard a rare note of bitterness in her voice. 'Your husband will be pardoned by Edward, and your son will be safe here.' He tried to sound more confident than he felt. 'My plan will mean Pembroke Castle will be left in peace, for now at least.'

'You must be careful who you choose to trust.' Her sharp eyes had fixed on his. 'Edward will be granting favours to those who helped put him on the throne, making outlaws of those who support the rightful king—even those once loyal to us will be putting their own interests first.'

'There are still enough loyal to the cause, if I can rally them in time.'

For a moment he thought Margaret would embrace him. Instead, she regarded him with sadness in her eyes, then her impassive mask returned.

'I shall remember you in my prayers, Jasper Tudor. God go with you.' She left, without once looking back.

Now, as the last of Wales began to slip below the horizon, he recalled that final moment and said a prayer for her safety. They had sailed in secret before dawn, so there should be no reason for York to even think he had left for Ireland. Henry Holland would enjoy raising merry hell in North Wales in his name, yet Jasper worried about the castles at Harlech and Denbigh, held for the true king, as well as Pembroke.

Before they left Thomas White gave him the name of a merchant in Cork who could be relied on to pass a message. Other than that he must rely on visiting ships for news. The uncertainty troubled him, for all his life he had been at the centre of events, the king's agent and the queen's right-hand man in the Palace of Westminster. Lady Margaret had been right. York had made him an outlaw, and crowned himself king.

He heard boots clomping on the deck behind him and turned to see Gabriel looking a little worse for wear and without his cap. Gabriel gripped the rail with both hands and leaned out over the sea, heaving, before hauling himself upright and wavering unsteadily on his feet as he wiped his mouth on his sleeve.

Jasper smiled at the sight. 'I thought you always wanted to be a sailor?'

'I did, sir, but there are plenty of taverns in Tenby and it turned into a long night.'

'You managed to spread the word?'

'It was easy, sir. When they found out I was from the castle, they all wanted to know what you are doing about Herbert.'

'Well, let's hope William Herbert takes the bait like the greedy codfish he is.' Jasper peered back towards Wales, already out of sight.

'The crew told me we're bound for Cork. What's our plan once we reach there, sir?'

Jasper glanced across the deck to see they would not be overheard, then pulled a purse from inside his doublet. It felt heavy in his hand and he opened it to show Gabriel a fortune in gold nobles. 'I need your help to find men we can trust.'

Gabriel took a step back. 'There's enough there to pay for an army.'

'An army is what we need,' Jasper pocketed his purse, 'a good ship, horses and men who will fight for the king.'

'They'll be loyal to the king's coin.'

Jasper nodded. The Irish would find no other reason to favour the true king over the usurper Edward. 'I've been thinking about York's ambush. We didn't stand a chance, as my horse fell from under me before I even saw their archers.'

'I wish you luck, sir,' Gabriel sounded dubious, 'I may be wrong, but it's not going to be easy to find skilled archers in Ireland.'

'Not archers, crossbowmen. No more marching into traps,

Gabriel. We will travel light and hit them hard, then be off before they know what's happened.'

'Skirmishers?'

'That's right. I want to put the fear of God into any men of York who think Wales is an easy target.'


Cork harbour bustled with activity despite the late hour as their little ship moored alongside the old stone quay. Shouting men loaded baskets of fish onto wagons, and gulls squabbled noisily for scraps as fishermen sorted their catch. The salty reek of fish fought with the stink of open sewers, which ran down shallow channels into the River Lee and on into the sea.

'Enjoying the fresh air of Ireland, Gabriel?' Jasper grinned, recalling their time at Llanthony Priory when his friend talked of the great beauty of his homeland.

'It sure is good to be home again.' His Irish accent already sounded richer. 'One day we'll ride to Waterford, and then you'll see.'

'First, we must find somewhere to stay, for the night, at least.' Jasper stared up at the high city walls and made a mental note to build them higher at Tenby. The thought reminded him of those he had left behind. He said another silent prayer for the safety of Lady Margaret, now travelling to Lincolnshire, and her young son Henry, in Pembroke Castle.

Three entrances led into the prosperous walled city of Cork, the bridges at the north and south gates and the central Marine Gate at the east end of Castle Street. They slipped through this into the crowds and passed unchallenged down the cobbled main street, with its herringbone pattern of narrow side-alleys. Jasper was glad to use the raised wooden trackways to keep out of the foul-smelling slurry from over-flowing drains.

After asking directions they found the two storey timber-framed house where Thomas White's merchant friend lived. An elderly maidservant answered their knock and pulled her black woollen shawl around her shoulders, eyeing them suspiciously when they asked to see Master Conley. Jasper saw her hesitation and handed her Thomas White's letter of introduction.

'Would you kindly tell your master we wish to discuss his business interests in Wales?'

The woman invited them to wait in the dark hallway and shuffled off, muttering to herself. When she eventually returned she led them to Master Conley's study. A large man with thick, greying hair, he gestured for them to take a seat, studying them both with interest before speaking with a strong Irish accent.

'I am intrigued. Thomas White asked me to offer you every assistance, yet he neglects to say what brings you to this fair city.' His voice carried a hint of irony.

'We are here to recruit men to fight for the true king.' Jasper saw how Master Conley's eyebrow raised at the words.

'Ah, yes. In England there is a new king, yet the old one is still alive and well in Scotland.' He smiled with the easy good humour of one who can afford to. 'Quite a predicament for those who live in Wales.'

'More than a predicament, Master Conley.' Jasper's voice now had an edge. 'Unless we act decisively, the country will be ravaged by a civil war.'

Conley studied Jasper with renewed interest. 'I can help you find men, and I own a little property on the outskirts of the city where you are welcome to stay.' His voice became conciliatory. 'But may I offer you some advice?'

'Of course.'

'I think, sir, this particular ship has sailed. The new King Edward has pardoned most of those who would oppose him. He has promised a better future for the people than they enjoyed under King Henry's rule.'

The housekeeper returned, carrying a jug of wine. Conley took a sip from the goblet she offered him, then nodded in approval, waiting while she served Jasper and Gabriel. 'If you choose to fight him now I think,' he took another sip, 'you will find it a somewhat lonely and unrewarding venture.'

Jasper sipped his wine before replying. It tasted sweet and aromatic, with a rich earthy flavour. He glanced across at Gabriel, who had already drained his goblet. 'Queen Margaret has an army in Scotland, and I'm sworn to support her.'

'In that case, take care, my friend. While King Edward lives, he will remove the heads of those who threaten him.'

Jasper would never call himself a superstitious man yet Conley's words rang out like a grim vision of the future. Again he recalled the vengeful knight in burnished armour, scything his way through the Lancastrian ranks. He had sworn to support Queen Margaret but he would not underestimate the challenge ahead of them while Edward of York lived.

## 4

## AUGUST 1461

The man-shaped target appeared from its hiding place as if by some magical force as Gabriel tugged at the end of a long rope. In a flash it bristled with crossbow bolts and fell to the ground as a cheer rang out from the men hidden in the bushes. Jasper watched, pleased with the progress they had made recruiting and training the fifty mercenaries he had chosen.

His skirmishers practised with their crossbows every day and soon learned how to shoot with accuracy. They would take years to build the muscle strength necessary to use the powerful longbow—years he couldn't spare with York's power and influence increasing each day.

Master Conley showed considerable modesty when he called this his little place on the outskirts of the city. Any English noble would be proud to own such a fine house, with woodlands well stocked with game. Most importantly for Jasper, Conley's property offered privacy while he trained his men, despite its proximity to Cork.

So far the men took no interest in his true identity and even the curious merchants of Cork seemed easily satisfied by their cover story. The long history of the English recruiting Irishmen to fight their wars meant large numbers sailed to France and Normandy. Now they fought in England's civil war, for whichever side paid the best.

Each week Jasper called at the house of Master Conley to see if visiting ships brought any messages from Wales. There were none so far, although he did learn of a merchant trader bound for Waterford. Gabriel had become restless and asked if he could sail on the voyage.

'I would like to see Waterford again, track down my family there.'

'You've worked hard and served me well, Gabriel. I think we both deserve a break from the delights of Cork.'

'You won't regret it, sir.' Gabriel smiled in appreciation of the irony. 'There's no prettier place than County Waterford.'

The *St Helene*, a strongly built carrack, was well suited to regular crossings of the channel between Ireland and Wales. Jasper smelt fresh tar as he crossed the gangplank and noted the scrubbed deck and neatly stowed ropes, an encouraging sign. Master Conley had bought half her cargo of bales of Welsh fleeces, and the remainder were destined for the wool-merchants of Dublin. Her captain, a stocky, long-bearded Welshmen, wore a fisherman's cap and peered curiously at Jasper when they met.

'Do I know you, sir?' The challenge in his voice echoed his abrupt manner.

Jasper preferred to tell a half-truth to a lie. 'I'm often in Tenby on business, you might have seen me there?'

'Quite possibly.' The captain's eyes brightened at the sight of Jasper's silver coins, payment for their passage north, which he slipped into a pocket. 'There's a fair wind, sir. If it turns we'll rest awhile in the bay at Tramore, but I hope to make landfall before midnight.'

'Thank you, Captain.' Jasper led Gabriel to the bows, out of the way of the men loading the ship, before the captain could ask more questions. The longer he could divert York's search for him to North Wales the better.

They watched as the men on the quay cast off the heavy mooring warps. Jasper turned at the sound of a loud splash, and saw men in the longboat had carried the anchor as far from the ship as possible and dropped it to the seabed. The master bellowed to men on the capstan to warp the ship out to it and the deck shuddered under their feet as the ship pulled away from the quay.

Once the anchor was hauled aboard they cleared the busy harbour and sailors began unfurling the sails and heaving on halyards. A light breeze soon billowed in the mainsail, and the ship lurched forward with the power of the wind. Sailing had always fascinated Jasper and he promised himself one day he would own a ship.

The dark, tranquil waters within the sheltered bay of Cork's Lough Mahon gave little clue to conditions out at sea, although a cloudless, pastel sky offered the promise of good sailing as they picked their way down the River Lee. When they passed the outer islands Jasper saw the first white-crested waves and tasted the tang of salt in the air as the wind freshened.

'What do you suggest we do in Waterford, Gabriel?'

'We could buy some fine horses and ride back?' His face lit up at the thought. 'My father used to talk of the hobelars, the Irish cavalry.' He saw Jasper's puzzled look. 'They called themselves the skirmishers, sir. Rode Irish hobbies, swift and light of foot and good in the bogs and woodlands of these parts.'

'We can find them in Waterford?'

'There's a horse fair every month.' Gabriel looked thoughtful. 'They don't breed true hobbies now, though, no call for it, but we might find a few crossbreeds if we're lucky.'

Jasper agreed. 'I still miss my old horse.' A sharp memory of their defeat at Mortimer's Cross caused his bitter anger against Edward of York to rise in his blood, darkening his thoughts. Jasper stared out to sea, east towards Wales, and wondered how Henry was in Pembroke. He'd heard no news of York's men invading West Wales and said another silent prayer that his plan would work.

Waterford horse fair, a noisy celebration, seemed to involve most of the population of Ireland's second city. Swearing Irishmen argued over horses and ponies of every size and temperament. Most of the men seemed drunk from the strong local beer, dispensed from wooden barrels at street corners. Ragged, bare-footed urchins squealed with delight as a juggler brandished brightly blazing torches, deftly throwing them high in the air and catching them.

Groups of musicians with drums and fiddles sang and played reels and jigs outside the taverns. People danced to the lively music and others clapped and cheered to encourage them. Gabriel stared at the women in colourful dresses, their long dark hair tied back and woven with silk ribbons. One called out to him and pulled her long dress provocatively up to her thigh to reveal a bare leg.

Jasper smiled at the sight. 'Would she be one of your sisters, Gabriel?'

'Fortunately not.' Gabriel replied, without looking away from the women. 'I told you there's no prettier place than this, sir.'

The aroma of roasting meat drifted over to them and they followed it to the market square, where street vendors sold them trenchers of bread with thick slices of salty tasting pork. They washed it down with tankards of strong ale and began examining the horses for sale. Gabriel seemed to know exactly what he wanted and soon found a lively young stallion with large dark eyes.

'This one has more than a bit of hobby in him.' Gabriel patted the horse on the neck, running an expert hand over its flanks and back. 'Good muscle, that's what we're looking for.' He pulled open the horse's mouth and nodded in approval as he checked its teeth. After some haggling with the owner they bought the horse and a lively black mare from the same breeder, together with saddles and bridles.

As they led the horses away the street began to be cleared by men shouting and ushering the crowds back. Jasper sensed the buzz of excitement, but couldn't understand what they were saying.

'What's going on?'

'They're getting ready for the race, sir. Waterford fair is famous for its horse-racing.'

Now Jasper could see they were calling out for riders. 'Do you think we would stand a chance against these local men?'

Gabriel grinned. 'I am a local man, sir, and ready to prove the worth of this fine horse.'

They soon mounted up and joined the throng of riders already gathering at the start line. Some rode bareback, with simple rope bridles, others already pushing forward and jostling for the best position. One rider swayed unsteadily in his saddle, almost too drunk to ride. There seemed to be no rules and it seemed to Jasper as if too many riders hoped to compete in such a crowded place.

Gabriel reined in his lively horse and glanced across at him. 'Take care on these cobbles, sir, and watch for the other riders, they don't always play fair.'

'What's the prize for winning?'

'A flagon of ale.'

Jasper glanced at the determined faces of the men around him and realised more was at stake than a flagon of ale. Reputations could be made or lost at these races, both for the horses and the tough Irishmen who rode them. An eager, shouting crowd jostled for a better view on either side of the cleared course. Men called out for bets to be placed and a scuffle broke out but was stopped before it could become a fight. An attractive young woman appeared from nowhere and reached up to tie a red silk ribbon around Jasper's arm.

'For good luck, sir.' Her eyes shone with amusement as she spoke.

Gabriel called across to him. 'She favours you, sir!'

Jasper raised a hand in thanks and saw her smile in acknowledgement. She reminded him a little of a woman he had known in North Wales so long ago. He had been so preoccupied with recruiting and training his skirmishers, he had almost forgotten about Mevanvy and the little dark-haired daughter Ellen, she claimed was his.

Myfanwy's eyes sparkled with the same seductive sense of fun whenever she looked at him. He had no way of knowing if the child could be his but in his heart he knew it might be, so he provided her with a good house and enough money to live comfortably.

He smiled to himself as he recalled his father's reaction when he learned he had a granddaughter. His father could hardly disapprove, as he had fathered a child with his maidservant Bethan. The boy, Jasper's half-brother David Owen, now lived with Bethan at his father's old house in Beaumaris. He wondered when he would next be able to see them and resolved to also visit Mevanvy and Ellen.

The crowd fell into a tense silence as a steward raised a flag high in the air. Jasper glanced across at Gabriel and saw the grim look of determination on his face. The man with the flag dropped it with a flourish and they raced from the line. Jasper soon found himself a good length behind the closest horse. Gabriel hadn't made the same mistake and rode dangerously close to the horse in the front.

Hooves thundered on hard stone as they raced for the first corner, a sharp right-hand bend in the road. The crowd urged them on with cheers and shouts for favourites and Jasper started gaining ground, pulling ahead of several horses. Jasper knew they must complete two circuits of the course, and he could see the leading riders, so was still in with a chance.

As they crossed the start line for the second time he found himself scanning the crowd for the woman who'd given him the ribbon. She waved as he passed, and his neck tingled with an unexpected flush of pride that she had chosen him from all the riders. They reached the right-hand corner again, galloping as hard as they could. Another rider slammed into Jasper's flank and his horse stumbled, pitching him into the air. The last thing he heard was a woman's high-pitched scream.


Jasper woke in a strange room that smelt of woodsmoke and the sweet scent of lavender. He was lying in a comfortable wooden bed, covered with a thick woollen blanket. Bright sunlight streamed through the open shutters of a small window. He rubbed his eyes and tried to remember what happened. Then he realised he was naked.

The sound of a woman singing as she worked drifted through the half-open door. Jasper studied his surroundings. Fresh rushes covered the floor and neatly tied bunches of lavender hung from thick wooden beams but he couldn't see his clothes. Close to the side of his bed sat an old rocking-chair, draped with a woollen shawl which suggested someone slept there the previous night.

He remembered falling from his horse and being carried

through the crowd by shouting men. He had brought a small fortune in gold and silver coins to Waterford, enough to buy two dozen horses, and now it was all gone.

'Hello?' He called out.

The singing stopped and a young woman appeared in the doorway, drying her hands on her cotton apron. He recognised the girl who gave him the ribbon. She seemed different with her dark hair loose over her shoulders, but he saw the mischief in her eyes as she stood looking at him.

'How are you feeling?' Her soft Irish accent had a note of concern.

'I was knocked out?'

'We thought you might be dead.' She stepped closer. 'I am glad you're not, sir.'

'How did I get here?' Jasper felt confused but relieved to find he was otherwise uninjured.

'They carried you here, sir. I said I would look after you.'

'It seems you have,' Jasper smiled, 'where are my clothes?'

'You fell in the dirt. I cleaned them for you and now they're drying in the sun.'

'How is my horse?' He liked the fine Irish horse and hoped it wasn't lame.

'Your horse is fine, and your money is safe.' She sat in the chair at the side of his bed. 'Although I can't imagine how a fellow such as yourself comes to be carrying such a fortune?'

He stared at her, trying to decide how much to tell. 'I must thank you, but I don't even know your name.'

'Máiréad.' She leaned forward. 'And what would your name be now, sir?'

'Jasper.'

She smiled. 'I've not heard it before, but I've not travelled far. Your friend told me you sailed here from Cork, but I can tell from the way you talk that's not where you're from.'

'I'm from Wales.' He saw her quizzical look. 'Although my

mother was French. When I was a boy she told me Jasper was the name of one of the three wise men, and she had always liked it.' He blurted it out, a half-forgotten memory he had never mentioned to anyone.

Máiréad reached out and caressed his bare chest with her hand. 'I like it. I knew there was something... different about you, as soon as I saw you.' Her voice sounded softer now and her eyes flashed with desire. He pulled her closer and kissed her, feeling her respond to his touch. Many years had passed since he'd held a woman in his arms. It felt good to forget his worries and surrender himself to this beautiful woman from Waterford.

Jasper lay back on the bed, watching as Máiréad dressed and combed her long dark hair in the early morning sunlight. As she fastened it with a ribbon he recalled how she tied a ribbon around his arm at the horse fair. Supposed to bring good luck, in a way it had, although not at all as he expected. It seemed as if he'd always known her, no awkwardness, no holding back. He had a sudden memory of her, naked on top of him, a look of rapture on her face.

She seemed to sense his eyes on her and smiled. 'Your friend asked me to tell you he's travelled to Kilkenny to see a horse-trader. He persuaded me to let him take your money. Was I right to do so?'

'Yes,' Jasper smiled, 'he's a good man. Did he say when he would be back?'

'Tomorrow.' She leaned over and kissed him. 'That means we can spend the day together?'

'I would like that.'

'I could show you one of my favourite places, by the river, not far from here.'

He replied by kissing her, softly at first, then with a deep longing and urgency that revealed his true intentions.

Máiréad laughed and began unfastening her dress.

A skylark sang in a cerulean sky as she led him down the narrow track to a secluded grassy clearing overlooking the river. The path was already covered with fallen leaves, and Jasper knew he must soon return to Wales, ready or not, but for now the spectre of York seemed a distant memory.

Máiréad carried a wicker basket from which she produced a blanket for them to sit on, as well as a platter of rye bread and cheese with slices of cured ham and two small cups, which she filled with a rich red wine.

'I've been saving this, for a special occasion.'

Jasper raised his cup in acknowledgement. 'I am honoured, and grateful.'

'Sláinte mhaith.' She laughed at his questioning look. 'Good health in Irish.'

'Sláinte mhaith.' He raised his glass again and tasted the wine, impressed at the quality. She had a talent for surprising him but he knew nothing about her. 'Tell me, Máiréad, is there someone in your life?'

She hesitated for a moment, staring at the steadily flowing river before answering. 'There was someone, once.' A flicker of sadness showed in her eyes. 'He drowned.' Her voice sounded cold at the memory. 'His boat was lost in a storm, two weeks before our wedding day.'

'I'm sorry to hear that.'

'Do you have someone? A wife?' Her question hung in the air and he could see she was bracing herself for his answer.

'No,' he smiled at a memory of his father, 'although there are plenty who tell me it's time I did.'

'What brought you here, Jasper?'

'I sailed here, on a merchant ship.'

She smiled at his joke. 'You don't seem like a merchant.' Her words sounded like an accusation.

He took another sip of wine before responding, already feeling it going to his head. 'Why not?'

'Merchants don't race horses through the streets, for a start. Your sword looks well used, and all the merchants I've met are only concerned about money.'

'And I am not?'

'You didn't even ask how much money your friend took.'

'I trust him, and I know I can trust you, Máiréad.'

She blushed at his compliment. 'But you'll forget me soon enough when your friend returns.'

He was thrown by her unexpected challenge. 'I must ride back to Cork and then...'

'Take me with you.'

She deserved to know the truth. 'You are right. I am no merchant. I came to Ireland to find men to help defend King Henry.' He watched the river, busily making its way to the sea, the water sparkling in the late-summer sunshine. The idyllic surroundings had allowed him to forget his purpose in coming to Waterford.

For the first time, he was struck by the futility of his situation. The best he could hope for was to keep the king safe until the people tired of York's promises. Queen Margaret would do whatever it took to restore her husband to the throne, but Jasper knew she was doing it for the sake of her son. The rot had set in too deeply and whatever the outcome of this civil war, his life would never be the same.

As a young man he had always known he must marry well, as his brother Edmund had done, an heiress from the royal line. Now he'd been made an outlaw he could marry for love, if he wished. He realised Máiréad was waiting patiently for his answer, hope in her bright eyes.

'I would like to take you with me, but I cannot.'

She placed her hand on his arm. 'I could ride with you to Cork. It would be an adventure.'

The pleading in her voice won him over. 'If that's what you would like.' He placed his hand over hers. 'When the time comes for me to return to Wales you must stay behind for your own safety, but for now...'

He was happy to live for the moment. She beamed with delight at his words, then leaned forward and kissed him. He let her push him back into the soft grass and they lay in each other's arms, enjoying the peaceful sounds of the birds singing and the river rippling musically. For the first time since he could remember, he didn't have a care in the world.

Gabriel appeared early next morning looking even more pleased with himself than usual. 'I've found us a dozen good strong horses, sir, and a drover who'll take them to Cork.'

'That is good news.' They needed twice that number but it was a start. 'You've met Máiréad? She'll be joining us on the ride back to Cork.'

Gabriel gave him a knowing look and smiled at Máiréad. 'I'm grateful to you, for taking such good care of him.'

'It was no trouble.' Her eyes widened with anticipation. 'I'm looking forward to seeing more of the country. I've never been far from Waterford.'

Jasper began fastening the silver buckle on his sword belt. 'It's a long ride, so we must leave soon.'

Gabriel understood. 'I will ready the horses.'

When he'd gone Jasper took Máiréad in his arms and kissed her. 'Thank you.'

'I must thank you, for taking me with you.' She pulled him close and kissed him again. 'Because I think I'm falling in love with you, Sir Jasper.' Her eyes shone with happiness and she sang as she fastened the shutters at the windows.

The ride took two days, travelling down the winding drover's roads through sleepy villages and wild estuaries. They rested overnight at a tavern in the coastal town of Dungarvan, at the mouth of the Colligan River. By the time they reached Cork the setting, late-summer sun cast long shadows and washed the evening sky with a brilliant amber, streaked with gold.

Jasper's servant looked relieved when he heard the horses and came out to greet them. 'You had a visitor, sir. He left a message for you to call on him as soon as you return. He is staying at the house of Master Conley.'

'Did he tell you his name?' Jasper's sense of foreboding returned. 'When did he call here?'

'His name is Thomas White, sir. He sailed from Tenby last week.'

Jasper told the others to find something to eat in the kitchens and rode into Cork alone and troubled. His friend was too busy a man to wait for his return without good reason. Thomas White met him in one of Master Conley's private rooms and closed the door. Jasper sat in one of the chairs but Thomas remained standing at the window, the last of the sunset silhouetting him and making it hard for Jasper to see his eyes.

Always clean-shaven in a fine velvet tunic with a long surcoat, Thomas White could easily pass for a nobleman. Jasper knew he had started with next to nothing and worked his way up through his integrity and skill in business to become a wealthy man, as well as one of his most trusted friends. He spoke with the soft accent of West Wales and now he cleared his throat, as if unwilling to share his news.

'There's no easy way to tell you this, my lord, which is why

I've come in person. William Herbert has taken Pembroke Castle.'

'My God! Was Henry able to escape?'

'I regret to say he was not. Herbert has him.'

Jasper sat back in shock. He had left more than enough men behind in Pembroke Castle to stand up to York's entire army, at least until he was able to return with his Irishmen. It was too much to comprehend.

'What of Sir John Scudamore?'

Thomas White shook his head. 'I understand he surrendered the castle to Herbert's men without a fight.'

Jasper cursed. He'd been a fool to trust Henry's safety to Sir John, a broken man with nothing to lose. At the same time, if he had remained in Pembroke he would now be besieged by William Herbert, who had everything to gain by holding the siege for as long as it took.

'What about Tenby?'

'A fleet of York's ships blockaded the harbour.' Thomas White sounded apologetic. 'It was hopeless, my lord. There was nothing anyone could do.'

'Tenby is lost?'

Thomas White nodded grimly. 'There is more, I'm afraid. It's said that all your estates and titles are forfeit to the king.'

'A false king!' Jasper spat the words out in his anger.

Thomas White continued, ignoring the outburst. 'York's men wait at all the ports and harbours in South Wales to arrest you, my lord. There's a price on your head, so it's no longer safe for you to return.'

Jasper saw Thomas White had more to say, something so bad he could hardly bring himself to speak the words. 'Go on. I need to know.'

'I'm sorry to report that William Herbert claims you ran from his men at Mortimer's Cross, and that it was he who captured your father.'

## 5

## OCTOBER 1461

J asper raised the heavy axe above his head and brought it down, cleaving the thick yew log in two and embedding the blade deep into the block. He'd been working at the woodpile since dawn after a sleepless night, worrying about the future. He worried for the safety of Henry, and the promise he had made to Lady Margaret to protect her son.

He also worried about the loss of his fortune from his estates in Wales. The income from them once made him wealthy, but now his concern was how he could fund an army to support the Lancastrian cause. It could only be a matter of time before he would be formally attainted by York and lose everything.

Jasper's muscles tensed in a surge of anger at the harm William Herbert could do to his reputation. Herbert would brand him a coward, fleeing from Mortimer's Cross and now running from West Wales at the sight of York's soldiers. There would be no way to defend his good name and few would care to listen to the truth.

He swore loudly as he swung the axe, cursing York and all

he stood for. At first, he imagined William Herbert's neck on the block, then it was the turn of Edward of York to feel the blade of his axe. His anger and frustration eased, he could think clearly for the first time since his meeting with Thomas White.

He had never blamed William Herbert for his part in his brother's death in Carmarthen but the thought always nagged at him. Now it seemed Herbert openly claimed responsibility for his father's capture, if not his execution. Jasper tugged the axe free of the block and set up another heavy log. Again, he swung the axe and brought it down with such force the two halves of the log sprang into the air.

He stopped to gather his breath and wiped the sweat of his exertion from his brow. Gabriel and Máiréad had listened in silence as he told them the news from Wales. He kept nothing back, as they deserved to know and would find out soon enough. In a way it helped to say the words out loud, to share the bitter thoughts that buzzed in his head like angry hornets.

A plan began to form in his mind. It would not be easy, but circumstance had changed him into a man with nothing to lose. He must take risks to stand any chance of defeating York. He comforted himself with the knowledge that York had not won everything. Thomas White told him the great fortress castles of Harlech and Denbigh still held for Lancaster. King Henry and Queen Margaret were now safe in Scotland, rebuilding their Lancastrian army, and he had his Irish mercenaries, not enough in number, yet keen to fight.

Jasper left the axe buried in the chopping-block and went in search of Gabriel. He found him in the kitchens with Máiréad and sensed they had been talking about him.

'We're going to Scotland.' He announced, gratefully taking the tankard of bitter tasting ale Máiréad poured for him, enjoying its refreshing coolness after his hot work.

Gabriel seemed pleased at the news. 'We'll need a ship, sir, big enough to take all the men and horses?'

'Master Conley has offered me a ship, at a price.'

'When do we sail?'

'Ready the men, Gabriel. I shall ride to Cork to arrange our passage.' He turned to Máiréad. 'Will you come with me? We'll need provisions and I'll bet you can strike a fair price?'

'I will, my lord,' she gave Gabriel a brief look of triumph and smiled at Jasper, 'I must change into my riding clothes.'

Gabriel waited until Máiréad was out of earshot. 'Will you be thinking of taking her to Scotland, sir?'

Jasper drained his tankard of ale. 'If she wishes. Scotland is no more dangerous for her than here.'

Autumn mists wreathed Linlithgow Palace, rising from the loch like ancient ghosts and making the rooms damp and musty, despite fires kept blazing in the hearths. Jasper pulled his heavy cloak around his shoulders and wished he could return home to Wales. He rode around the tranquil loch each morning, despite the uneven, muddy path, to gather his thoughts for the future.

The king had remembered him, but appeared older than his forty years, his hair and beard already turning grey. He had a distant look in his eyes and dressed in simple clothes, more like a priest than the King of England. Queen Margaret also seemed tired, but far from defeated. Still an attractive woman, she seemed pleased to see him and ordered a banquet to celebrate his safe arrival from Ireland.

Privately, she confided to Jasper she struggled to pay her soldiers and many were deserting to York. 'King Louis will lend me the money.' Her voice sounded defiant, her French accent returned now there was no need for her to pretend to be English.

Jasper reined in his horse and turned to look back at the rambling palace, reflected in the untroubled waters of the loch. Queen Margaret wished for him to negotiate with the devious King Louis of France on her behalf, and he could see why. It was not for her bewildered husband or even for herself.

Her only interest was in the future of her son, Prince Edward of Westminster. His horse snorted with impatience and stamped a hoof on the hard ground, snapping him out of his reverie. He spurred it on and cantered back around the loch to the palace, his mind still full of concerns. The mists were already lifting in the autumn sunshine and there was much to be done.

The banquet proved a modest affair compared with the extravagance Jasper once witnessed at Westminster Palace. The guests were Scottish nobles, few of whom he could recall meeting before. Several of their whispering ladies openly cast admiring glances at Jasper, who dressed in a fine black velvet doublet and hose and wore his gold chain of the Order of the Garter with his badge of St George.

The great hall of Linlithgow Palace, rebuilt regardless of expense by King James II, seemed wasted on his successor, the ten-year-old James III, who had little use for it. He remained with his mother, Queen Mary, still in mourning at Ravenscraig Castle after her husband was killed by his own cannon, which exploded and shattered his legs at the siege of Roxburgh the previous year.

Jasper recognised several of King Henry's Flemish tapestries, brightly coloured religious themes, fixed to the walls of the great hall with hooks and cord. The priceless hangings were creased from being folded for their journey to Scotland, a sign of the hasty retreat of the royal family from England after the bloody defeat at Towton.

An usher called all present to stand as Queen Margaret made her grand entrance, followed by young Prince Edward. She wore a gold coronet over a gossamer veil, with a gown of burgundy silk brocade. Diamonds and rubies sparkled at her white powdered neck, and Jasper understood she could not miss this opportunity to remind the Scottish nobility she was still the Queen of England.

A group of minstrels began to sing muted French ballads of courtly love to the accompaniment of a lute and flageolet. Once the guests were seated liveried servants brought wine in silver cups and gilded platters of salted venison and loin of veal. King Henry's high-backed chair at the side of the queen stood empty and she invited Jasper to take it.

'The king chooses to spend long hours praying on his knees in that cold chapel,' she explained. 'It's not unknown for him to miss his meals or forget even a banquet in honour of his half-brother.'

'How frequent are his lapses, Your Highness?'

The queen's forehead furrowed in a look of concern. 'He retreats into his own private world. It has been worse since that murderous son of York held him like a commoner.' The bitterness in her words caused several heads to turn in their direction.

She waved a gold-ringed hand to summon a servant to bring wine and studied Jasper's face for a moment before speaking. 'I was sorry to learn of the death of your father.'

Jasper watched as the servant poured a generous measure of the rich red wine into his cup. 'He wanted me to head north, to meet you, my lady. If I had listened to him we might have escaped York's trap.'

Queen Margaret put her hand on his arm. 'You must not blame yourself for York's treachery. Your father came to

Normandy to escort me when I first travelled to England. I remember being intrigued to meet the servant who married a queen.' She smiled at the memory. 'I was young, barely fifteen years old, and he showed me great kindness.'

'My father was always most loyal to you, my lady, as am I.' Jasper tasted his wine, noting the flicker of pleasure in the queen's eyes at his words. Even now, the thought of how he abandoned his father made him descend into a dark place, but the intense flavour of the wine helped brighten his mood a little.

Prince Edward, seated on the other side of the queen, clapped his hands and called in his reedy voice for sugared plums. Again, Jasper wondered if the boy had the makings of a king, and if it was too late for him to learn his manners.

The queen's expression hardened at Jasper's momentary look of disapproval. 'Edward, tell the Earl of Pembroke how well you are doing with your archery.'

'I shot a deer. Killed it dead with my arrow!' He acted out the scene, reminding Jasper a little of himself at the same age.

'We will make a warrior of you yet,' Jasper smiled, 'my father taught me to use a bow when I was a boy, but we only used targets of straw.' A thought occurred to him. 'Would you like to watch my Irishmen practice with crossbows tomorrow, Prince Edward?'

'I would, sir.' Edward tugged at his mother's sleeve. 'I should like a crossbow of my own.'

Queen Margaret smiled adoringly at her son. 'So you shall. Sir Jasper will choose one for you.' She smiled at Jasper, her eyes twinkling with amusement. 'And I will also see your Irish-men. How many do you bring to Scotland?'

'Fifty, Your Highness.'

'I hoped for more,' she shook her head, 'York has an army of thousands.'

'My men are trained as skirmishers.' Jasper realised he

sounded defensive. 'You are right, my lady, York has thousands to fight for him, yet that brings its own problems.'

Queen Margaret waited while her servant refilled her cup. 'Indeed it does. Our army lost the support of the people after our victory at St Albans. They looted every village and town we passed through, and at one point I feared for my own safety.'

'Rest assured we will move fast, my lady. Strike hard when York least expects it and be gone like ghosts, to fight another day.' Jasper leaned towards her and lowered his voice. 'Can we rely on these Scots to ensure the safety of the king?'

Queen Margaret glanced at her guests, who seemed more interested in their drink than anything she said. 'Queen Mary has been good to us, offering her Scottish soldiers, giving us sanctuary in this fine palace, but I understand from a trusted source she would consider marriage to York, if the opportunity presents itself.'

Jasper sat back in his chair, realising their situation in Scotland could be more precarious than he had thought. 'May I ask, who is your source, my lady?'

'The good Bishop of St Andrews, John Kennedy. He is a trusted advisor to Queen Mary and loyal to our cause,' she moved closer to Jasper, 'and has proposed a solution to our problem.'

'What is he suggesting?'

'Queen Mary wants the town and castle of Berwick, which I am willing to concede, and we hope to arrange the betrothal of my son to her eldest daughter Margaret.'

Jasper glanced at Prince Edward, happily gorging himself on a dish of sugared plums. 'Then she would do all in her power to see him one day inherit the throne.'

'It is a high price, but her daughter is only six years old, and what is marriage if not a means to achieve an end?'

Again, he heard the bitterness in her voice and Jasper

realised how difficult it must have been for her, to come to England as a girl and cope with Henry's frequent lapses. Once the most powerful woman in the land, it must now take all her resolve to make such concessions to Queen Mary, a dowager regent from a lesser noble family. He recalled that Margaret's father was the proud King René of Anjou, and saw more than a little of his renegade spirit in her.

'We cannot allow York to take control of Scotland, my lady, so perhaps the price is a fair one.'

The queen lowered her voice. 'You think we can win this war?'

'I do, my lady.' He drank deeply from the intoxicating wine, already feeling less reserved, and looked into Margaret's sapphire-blue eyes. A year older than him at thirty-one, he admired her strength and courage. 'Together.'

'It's good to know there is at least one man I can rely on in these troubled times.' The suggestive note in her voice was not lost on Jasper.

He smiled at her flirtatiousness. 'At your service, my lady.' Once her words would surprise him in such a public place, but now everything had changed, thanks to York and his followers.

This time he could not mistake the look which passed between them. It might be the consequences of too much good wine, but Jasper found himself wondering about new possibilities. Her high-necked gown revealed little, but she had a shapely figure and he had a good imagination.

'We must discuss this further.' Her hand returned to his arm, and remained there, a sign of her regard for him.

His reply was interrupted by servants bringing the silver dishes of the next course yet he had seen acknowledgement in her eyes. The minstrels began playing a lively tune and Jasper's spirits began to improve for the first time since arriving in Scotland.

He picked at a plate of sturgeon, ruined with the spicy

sweetness of too much powdered ginger, his mind on other things than food. Jasper pushed the plate to one side and pulled morsels of breast meat from small wild birds, also sprinkled with exotic spices.

Some of the younger guests joined in a boisterous dance in the open area of the hall, forming pairs, calling out and clapping in time to the music. He saw Queen Margaret laugh at their antics and realised the banquet must be a welcome respite from the strain of life in exile. Her alliance with the Scots could only be described as fragile and, for all they knew, York already plotted to surround Linlithgow Palace with his army of thousands.

A trumpeter sounded a fanfare, and servants bore the centrepiece of the banquet in amidst cheering, unruly guests. A whole wild boar, glazed with sugar, lay prostrated upon a bed of bright marigolds, the queen's personal emblem. The enormous platter thudded down before Jasper. He glanced at the happy Queen Margaret, becoming ever more conscious of occupying the king's chair.

Later that night Jasper lay awake, recalling his conversation with the queen. His door creaked as a shadowy figure slipped in and dropped her gown to the floor. He had the briefest glimpse of naked breasts before she climbed into his bed and embraced him. Jasper held her in his arms and wondered how she would take his news.

'I've missed you.' She kissed him with renewed passion, pulling him closer.

He returned her kiss and stroked her silken hair. The scent of lavender reminded him of their first time together in Ireland. 'I've secured you a position as a handmaiden in the queen's household.'

Máiréad sat up. 'She has more than enough servants?' There was an edge to her voice, although she didn't sound displeased.

'A queen can never have too many beautiful ladies to wait upon her.'

'Or too many gallant knights?'

Jasper pulled her back down and held her close, choosing to ignore her remark.

'I saw you, at the banquet.' Máiréad persisted. 'You didn't notice me, as you had more important company.'

'You're not jealous?'

'Perhaps I am. I know you well, Sir Jasper Tudor. I know that look in your eyes.'

He gave her a kiss to silence her, then decided his news could wait no longer. 'I need to travel to Normandy, to raise money for our cause.'

'And you wish me to remain here, with these Scotsmen?'

'For now, although the queen will also make the journey, once I let her know it's safe.'

'Is France not safe? She is a Frenchwoman?'

'They call King Louis of France Le Rusé, the cunning king —the spider. He is not beyond siding with York, if he sees advantage in it.'

'Do you think the King of France will listen to you?' Máiréad sounded doubtful.

Jasper smiled at her. 'The King of France is my uncle, on my mother's side. I may no longer own a fortune to bribe him with, but I am a son of the House of Valois, which should count for something.'

She remained silent for a moment as the information sank in. 'The queen, she will travel with her household?'

'Of course.'

Máiréad lay back in his bed. 'I should like to see Normandy. Will you teach me to speak French?'

He looked into her eyes. 'Je t'aime.'

'What does that mean?'

'It means I love you.'

Freezing rain lashed the deck and the dark North Sea churned in a turbulent mood as they set sail from Edinburgh, waves slapping the hull and splashing salty spray high into the air. Jasper sheltered in the damp cabin and braced his boot against a wooden post as the ship heeled heavily to starboard. They had brought four of the best Irish skirmishers, which meant persuading their lively horses to board the ship.

Despite blinkers and their recent passage from Ireland by sea, the precious horses became a concern as they whinnied and kicked in the confines of the rat-infested hold. Jasper ordered his skirmishers to take turns to act as groom and keep watch over the horses day and night. Gabriel kept himself busy checking on them every hour and returned dripping wet, clutching a steaming bowl.

'Pottage for you, my lord.' He grinned as he handed it to Jasper. 'I spilt some on the way from the galley, but it's wet and warm—and tastes better than it looks, sir.'

'I'm grateful to you, Gabriel. We've a long trip ahead and I fear the seas are worsening.'

Gabriel pulled off his wet cloak and twisted it to wring out the rain and seawater. 'The horses seem to be settling down a little, sir.' He grinned. 'Tough breed, you see. Good Irish stock.'

Jasper tasted the pottage, a greasy soup thickened with crushed oats yet oddly satisfying after the over-spiced food at Linlithgow Palace. As he ate he recalled his farewells. Queen Margaret seemed grateful for his offer to pave the way for her visit, although she confessed concern for the king, who had succumbed to the cold and taken to his bed. Jasper visited him before he left, and found the king in a sombre mood.

'I will pray for your return with good news.' The king's voice rasped and he shivered with his cold despite thick furs and a good log fire. 'I would like to travel with you,' his eyes fixed on Jasper, 'I've never been to France, although Margaret speaks of it with great fondness.'

Jasper knelt at the king's bedside and studied the king's pale features, remembering their first meeting, on his return from the care of the nuns at Barking Abbey. He'd been in awe of King Henry then, the richest and most powerful man in the land, chosen by God to rule, yet now the king seemed a mere shadow of his younger self.

'I remember you in my prayers, Your Highness, and wish you soon recover good health.'

'Take care, my brother, and God go with you, for you are the last of my family.'

'You have Prince Edward, a good strong son, Your Highness.'

Henry shook his head in bewilderment and for a moment Jasper thought he'd forgotten he even had a son, then he brightened and gave him a rare smile. 'Yes, my son, heir to the House of Lancaster.'

'And, of course, Queen Margaret.'

'She is a pillar of strength to me,' the king interrupted, as if remembering he had family after all. 'I give thanks in my prayers for her love and support.'

'The queen needs you at her side in these troubled times, Your Highness.'

King Henry crossed himself. 'God help us all.'

At last Jasper heard the cry he'd been waiting for, 'Land Ho!'

The plunging and heaving of their ship had prevented him from sleeping for three long nights since they left Scotland and he rubbed his tired eyes to study the horizon. The flat, feature-less outline of the Flanders coastline emerged from the relent-less expanse of water like a dark sea-monster, rising from the depths.

He hoped to avoid encountering Philip, Duke of Burgundy, and chief rival to the King of France. To do so could waste precious time and compromise his delicate negotiations with King Louis, although as part of the Valois family he provided an option of last resort. Gabriel joined him at the rail, also looking tired from their long voyage yet relieved at having arrived safely.

'The horses made the voyage in good shape, sir, although they will be glad to be back on dry land, as will I, by God.'

'Good.' Jasper peered out at the still ominous share of the land growing ever closer and felt a new sense of purpose. 'Tell the men we will find somewhere in Flanders to rest—we have a long ride ahead to Normandy.'

## 6

## JUNE 1462

The countryside of Flanders offered Jasper and his men little cover as they rode south, travelling fast and tracking close to the coast. It would have been an easy enough journey were it not for the westerly wind from the sea and the rain that saturated their clothes and turned the narrow roads to slippery mud. Gabriel rode in the lead as he claimed to have some knowledge of the area. He seemed to be enjoying his new responsibility and twisted in the saddle, rainwater dripping from the brim of his hat, to see the others were still close behind.

He caught Jasper's eye and grinned. 'I wish we were back in that leaky old ship now, my lord!'

Jasper agreed, as the rain had long since won its battle with his riding boots. It was supposed to be summer, yet the trickle of water soaking through his riding cape into his doublet felt unpleasantly cold.

'You handled the horses well, Gabriel. I thought we would never have them ashore.'

Gabriel chuckled at the compliment. 'Spoke to them in Irish, sir.'

'You must remember to do the same if we meet anyone on the road.'

'Irish mercenaries, riding to try our luck en Bretagne.' He exaggerated his accent, throwing in the French with a flourish of his hand.

Jasper nodded in approval. They stayed away from towns and went out of their way to avoid the main roads, although even in the small villages they passed through he imagined the eyes of the local people were on him. He carried a letter from Queen Margaret but hoped he wouldn't have to use it. Her cousin, the new King of France, would be difficult enough to deal with, without making their negotiations more complicated by involving the Duke of Burgundy.

He recalled his confident words to Máiréad, when he'd told her his lineage of the House of Valois should count for something. He'd wanted to reassure her, yet for all his life he had thought of himself as a Welshman, not French. Since he was a boy his father proudly taught him all about his Welsh ancestry. He also taught him to never take his wealth for granted, which was just as well, now it had been stolen from him.

His mother rarely spoke about her family in France, or if she had he'd been too young to remember. The years distorted his memory of her, yet he could hear her soft accent even now, singing French lullabies to him as a child. He was only five years old the night the soldiers came to their house and took her away, to the Abbey of St Saviour in Bermondsey. He had no idea he would never see her again.

Thinking of that grey dawn brought back long repressed feelings of confusion and worry. He'd been rudely woken with his brother Edmund and hurriedly dressed to the sounds of soldiers shouting orders outside. He remembered seeing the red-faced, anxious servants, running up and down stairs with bundles of clothes and such possessions as they could carry to the waiting wagons.

His father told them it would be a great adventure, and he would come for them as soon as he could. Jasper smiled to himself as he remembered how he tried his best to reassure them, despite their dire situation. He'd handed them five gold nobles each, told them to be brave boys and to always remember they were Tudors.

The soldiers took them on a long journey and placed them in the care of the Abbess of Barking, for religious education. It was no adventure, although the abbess had been kindly and treated them well, allowing them servants and even giving permission for them to practise with their bows as a reward for good behaviour.

As he rode towards Brittany, Jasper realised the nuns at the abbey taught him much that would stand him in good stead now. The strict but well-ordered routine of their devout lives instilled in him a useful self-discipline and he eventually learned to be patient. He remembered the abbess would always tell them *maxima enim, patientia virtus*, patience is the greatest virtue, when they asked how long it would be before their father came for them. The nuns sacrificed everything for their faith, yet still seemed content with their simple lives.

Now he understood his father had no choice in the matter, but at the time it felt they had been forgotten and abandoned. He prayed faithfully with his brother Edmund every day for his parents to return. There was no word, not even a note or a letter. Three long years passed before he saw his father again and learned his mother was dead, as well as a sister he had never seen.

They reached the border with Brittany without challenge, having made the best of daylight and stopping each night to sleep in barns and outhouses. The local farmers and villagers seemed happy to take Jasper's silver to provide food and ale for his men, and knew better than to ask questions of the Irishmen. Jasper guessed they had seen plenty of mercenaries passing through, ready to fight for anyone with money.

Their destination, the Château de Clisson, grand fortress residence of Francis, Duke of Brittany, perched over a tributary of the River Loire, the Sèvre Nantaise. Dominated by a massive keep, the duke's château was defended by a wide, green moat and from the highest tower flew the black and white ermine flag of Brittany.

Jasper led his men across the narrow stone bridge to the high gatehouse and announced himself to the liveried guards in French. After a short wait, the duke appeared in a doublet embroidered with a rampant lion. Well built, handsome and clean-shaven, he studied them appraisingly.

Jasper realised he must look more like the soldier of fortune he pretended to be than an earl and garter knight. Mud from the road spattered his plain clothes and boots and he hadn't washed or slept properly for a week. Only his fine sword with its engraved silver hilt offered any clue to his true identity.

He eyed the armed guards flanking the duke and saw they were ready to act. One word from Duke Frances and he could face long imprisonment for ransom, or worse. He had decided to take risks for Lancaster and now it could be time for him to pay the price.

'Sir Jasper Tudor? Son of Queen Catherine, of the House of Valois?' The duke spoke in French, his voice cultured, with little trace of the accent of the region yet questioning, as if he doubted the truth of Jasper's claim.

'At your service, Duke Francis.'

'Come. I am intrigued to understand what has brought you to Clisson.' He gestured to the guards, who stood aside to let Jasper and his men pass.

They followed him through the gatehouse into a courtyard paved with cobblestones. A magnificent bronze cannon pointed malevolently towards the entrance and Jasper noted it stood ready for use if the château ever came under attack. The heavy iron-studded doors of the gatehouse slammed shut behind them and Gabriel gave him a cautionary glance as he took the reins of his horse.

Jasper followed the duke across the courtyard to one of the towers and up a flight of stone steps into a high-ceilinged room. Swords and shields, some with the patina of great age, decorated the curved stone walls. In a recessed niche stood an old stone sculpture with the unmistakable features of the duke, although Jasper realised it must be one of his ancestors.

Duke Francis waited for his guards to close the door. 'What brings you to Brittany?' There was a challenge in his voice and he stared, unsmiling, as he waited for an answer.

'I come as the ambassador of Queen Margaret of England.'

'The deposed queen?'

'The rightful queen of King Henry, my half-brother.'

'Daughter of the King of Naples, and cousin of Louis, King of France.' The duke scowled in contempt.

Jasper took a deep breath and fought back the tension as he realised it would not be easy to win over the suspicious duke. 'I will be direct with you, my lord. These are difficult times for the House of Lancaster...'

'I cannot help you.' The duke interrupted, shaking his head.

'We could have met the Duke of Burgundy, yet we chose to offer our hand of friendship to Brittany.'

'And what would you have me do?'

'We suspect Burgundy could side with York, and with King Louis, we both know anything is possible, yet Brittany has fought to remain independent.' He watched the duke's reaction. 'We would ask you to provide us with men and ships, but most of all we value your knowledge of King Louis, his strengths—and his weaknesses.'

'King Louis is only interested in himself.'

'Queen Margaret hopes King Louis will fund our cause.'

'I doubt it.'

'In return for Calais?'

'The English will never forgive Queen Margaret if she surrenders Calais,' the duke paced the room as he thought aloud, 'yet you are right. It would be a great coup for Louis, although of course, Calais is not within your gift. Is it not held by men who are loyal to York?'

'With your help, Duke Francis, we shall dangle this carrot in front of the King of France.'

'Don't underestimate King Louis, he's no fool.' The duke's voice echoed in the sparsely furnished room.

'Queen Margaret will sign a treaty, promising Calais once King Henry is restored to the throne.'

'And what does Brittany gain in return for helping you?'

'An alliance between the House of Lancaster and the House of Montfort.'

Jasper recognised the weary messenger who arrived from Scotland as one of the Irishmen left behind as the queen's personal guard. The man's clothes bore the dirt of his long, exhausting journey and he brought news that the queen had sailed from Kircudbright on the western coast of Scotland.

'Her Highness chose to sail through the Irish Sea to avoid York's ships in the English Channel, my lord. She plans to make landfall at Saint-Nazaire.'

'How long ago was this?' Jasper's relief was overtaken by a sense of foreboding.

'Two weeks, my lord.'

'And the king? What of King Henry?'

'For all I know he is well, my lord.'

A thought occurred to Jasper. 'Why is there no letter from the queen?'

'The queen did send a letter to you, my lord. The man carrying it was captured and executed for treason.'

Jasper cursed. He rewarded the messenger with silver and visited the duke's gaudily decorated chapel. The lifelike, blue-robed figure of the Virgin Mary, surrounded by gilded cherubs and angels watched as he knelt before the altar and prayed for the queen's safe passage, then lit votive candles in memory of his mother and father and his brother Edmund, taken before their time.

Duke Francis considered Jasper's offer of an alliance for more than a week without agreeing to a loan, then they found common ground by chance. Jasper watched the duke's men practising archery at the butts in the courtyard and offered to demonstrate the skills of his Irish skirmishers, hand-picked by Gabriel to accompany them to Brittany. A target was set up and, on Jasper's signal, his men galloped into the courtyard, the hooves of their horses clattering on the cobblestones. They fired their crossbows from horseback with deadly effect before turning and riding off in a heartbeat, leaving the château strangely quiet.

The duke crossed to the target and tugged one of the bolts bristling from it, examining the sharply barbed point. 'Skirmishers?' He smiled at Jasper for the first time, holding up the short crossbow bolt. 'Your men are assassins, Sir Jasper.'

'The days of chivalry are over, Duke Francis.' Jasper returned a wry smile, glad to at last find a way to engage the duke. 'I learned to strike and be gone. My men are few in number yet worth ten times as many.'

'They are Irishmen, though? Mercenaries?'

'You are right, but I've found them loyal enough.'

Duke Francis nodded curtly. 'I will agree to your alliance, Sir Jasper, and I will cover Queen Margaret's expenses while she is here, but we must be clear this loan is to be repaid in full.'

'As soon as we've defeated York.'

'Yet it would seem your cause is already lost?'

Jasper refused to acknowledge the truth of the duke's frank words. 'My duty is to restore the rightful king and I will do whatever it takes.'

'I respect your loyalty to the House of Lancaster, Sir Jasper, but let us suppose King Louis agrees to finance your war. How many men will you need to overthrow Edward of York, now he has made himself king?'

The duke's words echoed in Jasper's mind as he waited for the queen to arrive. He found himself recalling the frail, absent-minded King Henry he'd last seen at Linlithgow Palace. Although familiar with the king's lapses, it seemed impossible to imagine he could ever rule the country again. Their best hope now rested with the queen and their arrogant son, Prince Edward.

After sharing the messenger's news with the duke, Jasper took lodgings overlooking the old fishing harbour at Saint-Nazaire, at the mouth of the River Loire. The queen's ship was overdue, although Jasper told himself it was too early to worry. There were many reasons for delay on the long voyage from the west of Scotland.

Each morning he woke at first light and took his walk along the harbour, always keeping a hopeful eye on the horizon. He learned how the rise and fall of the tides ruled the lives of the fishermen of Saint-Nazaire. They would sit on the old granite wall mending their nets and baiting crab pots with foul-smelling fish heads until water filled the harbour, then set off in an assortment of small boats to earn a living from the sea.

Some days they returned with baskets of long-legged spider crabs and aggressive black Breton lobsters. Other times Jasper watched them unload their catches of glittering sardines and anchovies, which spilled over the quayside as a feast for flocks of noisy seagulls. The fishermen seemed suspicious of him at first, but soon began sharing tales of battles with the giant tuna which they caught in the summer season, as well as less welcome stories of sudden and deadly storms.

Gabriel ensured lookouts kept a vigil night and day to alert them of the first sign of the queen, and two weeks passed before they sighted a ship flying the brightly coloured Royal Standard. The early dawn sunrise warmed the air as Jasper waited on the quayside. The ever-present gulls wheeled and shrieked in grey skies and the horses of the carriage he'd ordered whinnied impatiently as they stood ready.

The ship was smaller than he expected, a two-masted merchantman, the sailors already reefing the sails as it approached the shallows of the old fishing harbour. The heavy iron anchor plunged with a splash into the water fifty yards from the shore and the crew waved and called out to the men on the quayside. Gabriel stood by with a longboat and, at a nod from Jasper, set off at a brisk pace towards the ship, his oarsmen straining in unison against the incoming tide.

It seemed an eternity before the boat began its return journey and finally moored to a rusting iron ring at the stone steps, which Gabriel had scraped clear of the slippery green seaweed. Jasper watched as Queen Margaret and her ladies made their way towards him. Although pale and tired, the queen raised a gloved hand in welcome when she saw him, clearly relieved to be safely back on land.

He smiled as he recognised the familiar figure of Máiréad

among the servants accompanying the queen. Her long dark hair was tied back under a linen coif and her once fine dress creased and stained from her long journey. He found himself thinking she should be safe in Ireland, yet felt glad of her company now, as there was no knowing how long they would need to stay.

'Welcome to Brittany, Your Highness.' He bowed and took the queen's arm to lead her to the waiting carriage.

Queen Margaret forced a smile. 'It is good to be back on dry land, Sir Jasper.'

'How was your voyage, Your Highness?'

'We owe our lives to the captain,' Queen Margaret glanced back to the ship, now sitting peacefully at anchor, 'and thank the Lord our prayers are rewarded.'

Jasper helped the queen climb into the carriage. 'First we will visit the Château de Clisson, where Duke Francis has agreed for you to be his guest.'

'He has agreed to an alliance?'

'He has, Your Highness, and also to a loan. The duke is an honourable man, and a valued supporter of our cause in these difficult times.'

Later, as Jasper lay in the darkness with Máiréad he admitted the truth. 'I feared the duke would throw us in his dungeons. He is a deeply suspicious man and didn't take kindly to my request for money.'

She sat up in his bed, a look of concern on her face. 'How did you persuade him to help the queen?'

'Your countrymen won him over, not me. They've been training the duke's men the skirmishing skills they learned in Ireland. They do well, despite their poor command of the language.'

Máiréad lay back beside him. 'I've missed you, Jasper.'

'And I've missed you,' he put his arm around her, enjoying her warmth, 'although I've thought of you every day, and worried when I heard you were sailing the long way round.'

'The voyage was a difficult one, Jasper,' she pulled him closer, 'we were nearly forced to seek refuge in Ireland—I would have been tempted to jump ship!'

'I like the sea, but it can be hard,' he agreed, 'once all we had to eat were old biscuits riddled with worms.'

'Well, we made it here. I had grown tired of Scotland, so now I'm looking forward to seeing Brittany.'

'I forgot to ask after the king,' Jasper stroked her hair, letting it run through his fingers like silk. 'How is he?'

'I must tell you... King Henry is unwell. They found him unconscious in the chapel and thought him dead.'

'Yet he's recovered now?'

'The queen ordered him to be fed by force.'

Jasper pondered the consequences of her news. 'Who watches over the king now?'

'A bishop. His name is John Kennedy,' Máiréad put her arm around Jasper to reassure him, 'a good man, and they say he understands the king's condition.'

Jasper recalled the queen telling him Bishop Kennedy was one of the few men in Scotland she felt she could trust. At the same time, he secretly doubted it. The bishop's first loyalty would always be to Queen Mary, as her advisor and deputy in the regency, not to Queen Margaret or King Henry. Now the king could be in danger, not only from York but also from his hostess, the Queen Regent of Scotland, who had much to gain by betraying his trust.

'I must return to Scotland, to ensure the king's safety.'

'What of the queen's safety?'

'The queen will be safe enough here in Brittany until I return.'

'And me?' She took his hand in hers. 'I travelled all this way to Brittany to be with you, and now you talk of returning to Scotland?'

'It's my duty to safeguard the king. I promise to return as soon as I can, Máiréad, and while I'm away the queen will need you.'

Máiréad ran her finger slowly down his bare chest and pulled him back down onto the bed. 'And I need you, Jasper Tudor.'

## 7

## SEPTEMBER 1462

J asper rubbed grime from the thick leaded glass of the window in Edinburgh Castle and peered down at the maze of narrow streets in the sprawling city below. A few cobwebs needed to be brushed away and the old furniture was past its best, but the room felt warm and comfortable. He suspected he'd arrived at Linlithgow Palace just in time to prevent King Henry being handed over to York. As a precaution, he had moved him to the capital, where a sizeable garrison could be relied on, for now at least.

The king seemed content in Edinburgh with a priest of Jasper's choosing to replace Bishop Kennedy, who was now effectively Regent of Scotland, as Queen Mary had fallen gravely ill. The priest, John Blacman, spent a year as a Carthusian monk and still wore undyed woollen robes, with the pale scapular which earned them the name of the white monks.

Once Jasper's tutor, Blacman was now responsible for the education of Prince Edward. Discreet and loyal, Blacman persuaded the king his Carthusian routine offered a better way to follow his faith than long hours of solitary prayer. He rose at first light for *Angelus*, followed by mass in the chapel and *Lectio*

*Divina*, a meditative reading of the Bible. The rest of his day was spent as if he had become a monk, and although his health seemed to be improving, Jasper worried Henry had become detached from his responsibilities in the real world.

He asked the priest to see him in the young prince's private study, formerly a library. Still lined with shelves of obscure old books, mostly in Latin, it had the advantage of being far enough from the king's room for them to talk without being overheard.

'You've done well, Master Blacman. The king has suffered none of his lapses since you returned to his service?'

The softly spoken priest nodded in acknowledgement. 'He has not, my lord.'

'Thank God! I feared he might not recover but your company seems to rekindle his spirit.'

'I am grateful, my lord, to be in the service of the king once more, and to be appointed tutor to his son.'

'I hope Prince Edward will learn how to conduct himself for the day he must become king?'

'He is a spirited boy.' The priest nodded knowingly, a shrewd look in his eye. 'He reminds me more than a little of yourself at the same age.'

Jasper smiled at the thought. 'We are related, of course, through my mother.' He decided it was time to raise his concern. 'I wonder, Master Blacman, if it's right for the king to live like a monk?'

'King Henry is most devout, with great humility and knowledge of the scriptures.' He sounded like a tutor again, his tone firm, as if he was speaking to a boy. 'He needs the discipline of an ordered life.'

Jasper recalled a time, long ago in Windsor, when John Blacman had shown great patience yet been a hard taskmaster as they struggled with his Latin texts. He and his brother Edmund once lived in awe of him, one of the wisest men they knew. Master Blacman could have become an eminent scholar or turned his hand to politics, yet he had chosen the simple life of faith.

'As the true anointed king, he needs to understand our situation.'

Blacman held up a hand as he had when Jasper was his pupil. '*Nos in diem vivimus*, we live day by day. One step at a time, my lord.'

'It's good he listens to you.' Jasper looked directly at Blacman. 'I wish you to remind him of his duties as king, when you judge the moment to be right.'

Blacman fidgeted with the silver crucifix on a chain around his neck as he replied. 'I must tell you, my lord, the king shows no interest in worldly matters.'

'He must.' Jasper tried to keep the irritation from his voice. 'We all make sacrifices for the House of Lancaster, Master Blacman. Good men gave their lives, others risk everything in King Henry's name.'

Blacman stared at the rushes on the floor, avoiding Jasper's eye. 'He acts more as the servant of me, a poor priest, than the King of England.'

'Well, he is still King of England, and one day I will see him back on the throne.'


Jasper had regretfully advised Queen Margaret of the dangers of sending letters or even trusted messengers who might fall into York's grasping hands. This meant no news came from Brittany and he couldn't reassure the queen that Henry was recovering well. In the absence of any information he hoped the queen would wait for his return and not compromise negotiations with King Louis by taking matters into her own hands.

Their isolation in Edinburgh Castle also meant news from England was slow to arrive, so Jasper sent Gabriel south to learn what he could of York's plans. The Irishman proved to be a good listener, although the news he returned with was not good. Gabriel showed none of his usual humour as he described what he had learned.

'There is no sign yet of York's army, sir, although I heard the Earl of Worcester, Sir John Tiptoft, has been made Lord High Constable of England. His men are hunting down Lancastrians to charge with treason.'

Jasper shook his head. 'I knew Tiptoft when he served the king as Lord Treasurer. He is a devious, ambitious man, Gabriel, a dangerous combination. I never trusted him but can see why York chose him to do his dirty work.'

'They say there are pardons to any who swear allegiance to York. They are executing any who do not, calling them traitors, on Tiptoft's orders, regardless of rank or position.'

'We will avenge those who suffer at Tiptoft's hands one day soon, Gabriel, you can be certain of that.'

'I also heard a rumour there is to be a truce between York and Scotland. Will we soon be taking the king back with us to France, sir?'

'I wish we could but the dangers are too great. He will be able to add little to the negotiations, so it's better for our cause that King Henry is not exiled to France until we have no other choice. This castle is well defended, so for now he is as safe here as anywhere.'

They took the risk of sailing on a merchant ship returning to Harfleur with a cargo of precious sea coal, gathered by women from the seams exposed on beaches and valued for its use in smelting iron. Jasper could easily pass for an Irish adventurer, leaving Gabriel to do most of the talking for them. He had allowed his dark hair and beard to grow unkempt and wore an old leather jerkin with a sailor's cap.

The voyage began well and they made good time with favourable winds and fair weather. One of the French crew, a weather-beaten sailor, his face still blackened from loading coal, pointed to a fast-moving ship on the horizon as they left the vast expanse of the North Sea and entered the English Channel.

'Warwick!'

Jasper squinted towards the distant ship but couldn't make out any flag. 'How do you know that's Warwick's ship?' He spoke in French, trying to conceal his mastery of the language.

The man pointed again. 'See the guns, there on the quarter-deck?' Warwick says he's keeping the Channel safe from piracy.' He gave a rasping laugh. 'But he is the greatest pirate of them all.'

Now they saw the dark barrels of the cannons jutting from the approaching ship. It flew no flag, yet it was likely to belong to the Earl of Warwick, now made Captain of Calais. Ambitious and determined, Warwick knew Jasper from his time at Parliament in Westminster. If he boarded their ship there was a real danger of being recognised.

He turned to the sailor. 'Do the patrols usually board us?'

'There is nothing we can do to stop these thieving English,' the Frenchman spat over the side, 'last time they seized our cargo.'

Warwick's ship continued to sail on a heading that would take it directly into their path. Jasper saw Gabriel's frown of concern and an idea occurred to him. 'We must find the bosun and ask him to put us to work, the dirtier the better.'

They worked busily in the dark, dusty hold, loading canvas sacks with the loose coal, their hands and faces already black from the task. A shouted challenge came from the deck of the patrol ship and the master of the merchantman called back in reply. Warwick's ship drew alongside and they heard ropes being thrown, soon followed by a commotion of boots on the deck above them as Warwick's men boarded, shouting orders at the crew.

Daylight flooded the hold as the top hatch banged open. Jasper stared up to see York's greatest supporter, Sir Richard Neville, looking down at him, armed men to each side. The Earl of Warwick was a flamboyant figure, like a Roman centurion in a flowing, scarlet cape. Jasper felt a shiver of dread as he saw the greed and contempt in Warwick's dark eyes. One word from him and all would be lost.

'Is this all there is?' Warwick spoke in perfect French, an arrogant edge to his voice.

For a moment Jasper thought the question was meant for him, then heard the captain answer.

'Sea coal, my lord, bound for Normandy.'

'Nothing else?'

The captain shook his head. 'I give you my word, my lord.'

'Your word?' Warwick scowled at the captain. 'I will take half for my trouble. Have it loaded to my ship—and don't try to deceive me, or we will find out how well you can swim!'

The captain began shouting orders, calling for men to help. Warwick left as briskly as he'd come and Jasper realised he had been holding his breath. After the cargo hatch banged closed Gabriel joked about their close shave, yet if Warwick had seen through his disguise he would surely have followed the Earl of Oxford to the executioner's block on Tower Hill.

As Jasper feared, Queen Margaret had soon tired of the grudging hospitality of Duke Francis and left to visit her father at Angers, some seventy miles inland. It took them two days to reach Duke René's castle, a magnificent fortified château on the banks of the River Maine, with seventeen high towers, each crowned with distinctive conical tiled roofs.

Duke René greeted them in person when they announced themselves at the buttressed gatehouse. A jovial, portly man, whose sharp eyes missed nothing, Duke René had known both poverty and enormous wealth. As well as Duke of Anjou, he was the Duke of Bar, the Count of Provence and, more controversially, also used the title of King of Jerusalem.

The duke spoke quickly in French, keen to learn of developments in England.

'Tell me, Sir Jasper, how is my son-in-law?'

'King Henry is safe in Edinburgh Castle, and I'm pleased to say he is in good health, Duke René, as is Prince Edward.'

'Ah, a fine boy, do you not think so?'

'Prince Edward certainly shows spirit.' Jasper looked around for the queen. 'I trust your daughter Queen Margaret has arrived safe and well?'

The duke beamed with pride. 'Indeed she has, and her cousin, King Louis, is already on his way to meet with her.'

He led them through his well-kept rose gardens to the great hall, where Queen Margaret sat surrounded by finely dressed French ladies. Jasper couldn't see Máiréad, but his attention was caught by an attractive young woman in a richly embroidered gown and a necklace of glittering diamonds, who smiled as their eyes met.

'Welcome to Angers, Sir Jasper.' Queen Margaret glanced at the young woman to her side. 'May I introduce Duchess Jeanne de Laval, my stepmother?'

Jasper knew the wily old duke remarried after the death of Margaret's mother, although no one told him it was to a woman younger than his own daughter. 'I am charmed to meet you, my lady.' Jasper saw the twinkle of amusement in her eyes and nodded to Queen Margaret. 'I wish to meet in private, Your Highness, as there are important matters to discuss.'

'Of course, Sir Jasper, once you have been able to clean the dust of your journey.'

Jasper realised in his enthusiasm to reach the château he'd not stopped to wash off the traces of black sea coal since arriving in France. His disguise as a mercenary and unkempt beard had become so familiar he had forgotten the strange impression he must make on the duke and his attractive wife.

He was a different man by the time he saw the queen next, having washed off the dirt, trimmed his beard and changed into his best doublet and hose. He also wore his gold livery collar, the royal badge of the House of Lancaster, with his Order of the Garter star, his few remaining possessions of value.

The queen had also changed into a striking gown of a purple satin so dark it appeared black until she moved in the light. A gold coronet on her headdress made her look regal and she seemed happier than Jasper remembered seeing her for a long time.

'My apologies, Your Highness.' Jasper bowed deferentially. 'I overlooked my appearance in my desire to see you again.'

She smiled. 'I thought you made a rather splendid mercenary, Sir Jasper. Now tell me, truly, how is the health of the king, and how is my son?'

'The king is much recovered, and has given me letters of credence for King Louis. He asked me to tell you he prays each day for your safe return.'

'That is good news.' Her voice softened a little and she put her hand on his arm. 'I thought I would never see the day.'

'Prince Edward also has a new tutor, Your Highness, a Master Blacman.'

'I miss my son,' her eyes misted with tears, 'but you are

right, Sir Jasper. He is safer in Scotland. I trust his tutor treats him kindly?'

'Of course, Your Highness, and you may rest assured they are well out of the reach of York's men.'

'What is the news of York?' The tenderness vanished from her voice.

'I heard the Earl of Worcester has been made Lord Constable of England. He persecutes our supporters with contrived charges of treason.'

She made the sign of the cross. 'It grieves me to know good men are dying for our cause.' The queen studied his face, her eyes full of resolve. 'King Louis has agreed to a meeting, and we must agree whatever it takes to return to England with an army.'

'Calais?' Even as he said the word he felt a stab of regret they would be forced to agree the transfer of Calais. There would be consequences when the people of England learned the price paid for freedom from Yorkist rule.

Queen Margaret seemed to be reading his mind. 'Whatever it takes, Sir Jasper. We no longer have any choice.'


Máiréad sat in the window-seat of Jasper's room in the grand château of Chinon, overlooking the peaceful River Vienne, combing her long dark hair in the bright autumn sunshine. The summer residence of King Louis, Chinon was a short journey from Angers and, so far, at least, the meetings had gone well.

Jasper rubbed his eyes and yawned, stretching his arms. The banquet had been a lively if somewhat over long affair, with lengthy speeches and far too many courses. Although he had refrained from drinking too much wine, the hour was late before he'd been able to slip away to his rooms to meet Máiréad.

Their host, King Louis, seemed in a jovial mood, happy to entertain them with his tales of hunting wild boar at his country estate and seemingly unconcerned about the situation in England. Behind the bluster Jasper noted that Duke Francis' warning had been right, he was not a man to be underestimated. King Louis chose not to mention he had declared war on England, soon after taking the throne of France, or that his great rival Duke Philip of Burgundy had prevented his attempt to seize Calais by force.

Máiréad noticed Jasper was awake and smiled at him. 'I was thinking... my little cottage in Waterford seems so far away from here.' She stared out of the window to the tranquil river below. 'When I was young I used to dream of seeing the world, but never imagined being in such a grand palace with kings and queens.'

'And knights,' Jasper added.

'Yes—I did wish for a handsome knight to sweep me off my feet and save me,' she laughed, 'although I think I saved *you.*'

'For which I am most grateful, my lady.'

'At your service, sir, as ever.'

She finished combing her lustrous hair then crossed the room to sit on the side of his bed. As he watched her, Jasper realised Máiréad had learned much from Queen Margaret's ladies. Although her pale lilac dress was simply made, she had altered the waist with silk ribbons so it fitted her well, giving her an elegance she lacked when he first met her. She could easily pass for a lady-in-waiting now, rather than a maidservant.

'You look beautiful, Máiréad.'

She smiled at his compliment and took his hand in hers. 'And what did you dream of, as a boy?'

'I used to dream of being a lord, with a castle of my own,

in Wales, where I could live with my family, my father and brother, away from the noise and dirt of London.'

'Which is what you did?'

'I was able to escape the politics of the court and Parliament, for a while, at least,' he smiled at the memory, 'they were happy times in Pembroke and in Tenby, where I have a house overlooking the sea.'

'Was there a woman in your life then?' The faintest trace of jealousy added an edge to her question.

With a jolt Jasper realised he had been so preoccupied with supporting Queen Margaret he'd hardly given a thought to Lady Margaret or her young son Henry, and hadn't been able to write to her without putting her in danger. Máiréad stared at him, waiting for his answer.

'There was a woman once... but when my brother Edmund died I promised to care for his widow and her infant son.'

'Where are they now?'

'She lives with her new husband, Sir Henry Stafford, in Lincolnshire.' He frowned as painful memories rose to the surface. 'Her son Henry was taken by York's men after I escaped to Ireland—I couldn't stay to protect him.'

'Do not blame yourself.' He felt her squeeze his hand. 'We have a saying in Ireland. No matter how long the day, the evening will come.'

He sat up, his darkening mood overtaken by a new sense of purpose. 'It will, Máiréad. I promised his mother I would take care of him and I will find him, when we regain control of England.'

'How long do you think we'll be here for?'

It was a good question. 'King Louis has agreed to a loan. Not as much as we wished for but twenty-thousand pounds is enough to pay for a fleet of ships and an army, so all that remains is for the queen to sign a treaty.'

'Then we will return to Scotland, to Edinburgh?'

'It will take time to recruit and train enough men, but every day we delay could tip the balance in York's favour.'

'I see that worries you.' Máiréad leaned across and kissed him. 'You know the queen has great faith in you. When all this is over you will be well rewarded, and then you will forget me?'

He playfully pulled her onto the bed as his answer, his concern for Henry, the tension of the negotiations and even his worries about Calais forgotten.

# 8

## NOVEMBER 1462

J asper galloped across the deserted beach, his heart pounding and his horse's hooves leaving a deep, pock-marked trail across the hard-packed sand. He rode dangerously fast, partly to vent his frustration with his situation, yet also for the sheer, reckless thrill of it. He reined in his horse and raised his hand to shield his eyes from the dazzling late autumn sunrise.

In front of him the distinctive, silhouetted shape of the Holy Island of Lindisfarne rose like a leviathan from stormy, white-crested breakers. The old priory on the island was acces-sible to pilgrims at low tide by a stone causeway, now deep under the cold grey waters of the North Sea. He worried about Queen Margaret and her invasion fleet, which would be making the risky voyage to Scotland, despite the dangerous conditions.

Jasper had seen the king safely aboard the queen's flagship then sailed ahead of the fleet with his Irishmen to secure the Northumberland castle at Bamburgh. One of the last Lancas-trian strongholds in England, Bamburgh's garrison of three hundred men served under Sir William Tunstall, who readily handed them over to Jasper once he learned of the approaching fleet. The high fortress, overlooking the sea and a natural, drying harbour, meant plenty of warning if York decided to attack. The ten-foot thick walls of the keep also hid a secret well, dug deep into the rock.

Loyal Lancastrians, including Lady Margaret's nephew, Sir Henry Beaufort, soon rallied to the queen's call for support. They met the queen's fleet of more than forty ships, which left France carrying up to eight hundred men, under the command of the queen's supporter in France, Captain Pierre de Brézé. They had embarked as many soldiers as Scotland could muster, before sailing back down the coast to Bamburgh.

The new Lancastrian army had risen again from their cruel defeat at Mortimer's Cross, and the massacre of loyal men at Towton. Jasper allowed himself a wry smile as he imagined how surprised York would be. He watched the violent waves growing ever larger in a freshening wind, and prayed for the safe arrival of the overdue fleet. He had achieved what he'd set out to do. Bamburgh Castle was secure, and once they gained control of the castles at Alnwick and Dunstanburgh it would be time to confront Edward of York, the self-appointed king, and hold him to account.

The forest of masts appeared through the mists a week later than expected, to a cheer from the men waiting in Bamburgh. The fleet took time to set anchor and Jasper counted forty-three ships of assorted age and size. He recognised the flagship, a high-masted French caravel, rigged as a man-of-war, belonging to Captain Pierre de Brézé. The rest of the invasion fleet included round-bellied carracks, able to carry troops and horses in their cavernous holds, several old high-sided cogs and even a few tan-sailed fishing boats.

Voices carried well across the water as sailors called out to each other and lowered longboats for those going ashore. Soldiers crowded the decks, some wearing armour, others carrying bows, long halberds and pikes. French and Flemish voices and the distinctive curses of Scotsmen rang out as they jostled for a view of the shore.

For the first time, Jasper realised this was in truth a foreign invasion of England, as the Frenchmen on the ships far outnumbered the English troops and even his own skirmishers came from Ireland. He wished the loyal Lancastrians in Wales could join them but they needed to hold Harlech Castle for the king. One day soon, he hoped, the Welsh would be able to join forces with the queen's new army.

Sir Henry Beaufort, in the first boat to arrive, sat next to a hunched figure, his head hidden under a large black hat. The man raised a hand in greeting and Jasper recognised him as King Henry, returned to England at last. Queen Margaret sat behind the king, huddled in a woollen shawl and accompanied by a tall, athletic man with a fine sword, who Jasper guessed must be the French captain, Pierre de Brézé.

'Welcome to Bamburgh!' Jasper called out.

Henry Beaufort recognised him, and raised a hand in greeting. 'Jasper Tudor!'

Jasper watched as Henry Beaufort helped the king ashore and Captain de Brézé assisted the queen from the longboat. It was impossible to step ashore without getting their feet wet so the captain lifted the queen in his arms before setting her down on the dry sand. Jasper saw the queen beaming with relief after what must have been a long and difficult sea voyage.

He bowed. 'It's good to see you safe in England, Your Highnesses.'

'And you, Sir Jasper.' Queen Margaret glanced at the Frenchman. 'My loyal friend Captain Pierre de Brézé.'

Although they had never met, Jasper knew de Brézé by reputation. An experienced soldier, he led the fight against the

English in Normandy and his son was married to the illegitimate half-sister of King Louis, Charlotte de Valois. Jasper appreciated the importance of his involvement and had already noted the familiarity with which the Frenchmen treated the queen. The captain's grey eyes belied his smile of welcome, and Jasper's instinct told him he was being judged.

'It is my pleasure to meet you at last, sir.' He spoke in French.

Captain de Brézé replied in perfect English. 'I am honoured to meet you, my lord.' He bowed briefly.

'I've posted scouts to warn us if York's army is sighted,' Jasper studied the fleet, visible for several miles along the exposed coast. 'There isn't a moment to lose if we are to take advantage of our surprise.'

Captain de Brézé glanced at the longboat with its waiting oarsmen. 'I shall return to the ship and ensure the men disembark without delay.'

As they watched the longboat return, the men rowing hard against the waves of the incoming tide, Jasper spotted Máiréad in one of the approaching boats, sitting with the queen's servants. She smiled happily when their eyes met. He raised a hand and waved, relieved to see her again.

When at last he could speak to her in private he sensed she was excited about something. He led her up narrow, spiral steps to the small room in a high tower he had chosen for himself, away from the royal apartments, with their watchful guards, then closed the door and took her in his arms.

'What is it, Máiréad, what's happened?'

'Nothing's wrong, or at least I hope you don't think so.' She embraced him and lay her head against his chest. 'I am with child, Jasper.'

.  .  .

Ominous clouds filled a dark sky as they marched down the coast to the great castle at Dunstanburgh, the largest of the northern fortresses, less than ten miles south of Bamburgh. Jasper was deep in thought about the news Máiréad shared with him the previous night. He remembered Mevanvy in North Wales and her pretty, dark-haired daughter Ellen. He had been attracted by her wild spirit yet found it hard to believe he could truly be the only man in her life.

It felt different with Máiréad. He loved her, and was certain the baby must be his, but in such dangerous times the prospect of fatherhood became one more thing to worry about. York would send his army as soon as he learned of the invasion and a battlefield was no place for a woman carrying a child. Jasper decided he must find a way to send her back to the safety of Waterford, at least until the civil war in England was over.

He rode at the side of Captain Pierre de Brézé, followed by a division of Irish, French and English soldiers, while Sir Henry Beaufort headed for Alnwick Castle with his Scottish troops. Jasper thought the Scots an ill-disciplined bunch, recruited in haste with no time for training, yet Henry Beaufort laughed when he shared his concern and seemed confident he could make an army of them.

The French captain pulled his fur-lined cape around his shoulders as it started to spit with rain and cursed the English weather. He glanced back at the straggling line of men marching behind them, then turned to Jasper.

'This castle, it has a garrison, Sir Jasper?'

'Enough to hold it in a siege, and the constable of Dunstanburgh is Sir Ralph Percy, a good man, loyal to the king.' He decided the captain needed to know the rest. 'I should tell you he surrendered the castle once to York, and many of his men deserted or turned their coats.'

'So, can we trust him?' The Frenchman sounded doubtful.

'Sir Ralph comes from one of the oldest Lancastrian families in the north. We have to trust him, and I've sent a man ahead to warn him of our arrival.'

The rain eased and unexpected sunshine warmed them as the jagged outline of Dunstanburgh Castle appeared on the skyline. Jasper called the men to a halt as they approached the massive three-storey gatehouse, and rode up to the gate alone to announce himself. Although he didn't know Sir Ralph Percy well, he recognised the stocky, grey-haired knight who greeted him like a long lost friend in a loud northern accent.

'Tudor!' Sir Ralph examined the waiting men with the eye of an experienced campaigner. 'The king has returned with an army of Frenchmen and mercenaries?'

Jasper smiled at Sir Ralph's bluff manner. 'More Englishmen are on the way, as well as the Scots—and I've enough men to reinforce your garrison.'

'You are most welcome, Tudor, as I'll wager we'll be needing them, whatever country they come from!'

Jasper gestured towards the captain, who rode forward and dismounted. 'This is Captain Pierre de Brézé, commander of the queen's fleet.'

Sir Ralph nodded. 'I've heard of you, Captain. You saw us out of Normandy?' There was a challenge in his voice.

'Only doing my duty, Sir Ralph.'

'Well, if you've brought the king back to England, you are welcome here, Captain.' Sir Ralph gestured for them to enter. 'Your men must be wanting a jug of ale!'

Despite feeling a little worse for wear after a late night as Sir Ralph's guest, Jasper left Pierre de Brézé to organise the reinforced garrison and set out on the eight mile ride south-west to the siege of Alnwick Castle the next day. Riding with Gabriel and a dozen of his Irish skirmishers for company, he had an important message for Henry Beaufort, who was leading the siege.

Behind Sir Ralph's bluff exterior was a well-informed and shrewd campaigner of many years. He'd heard from a good source that Edward of York was ill and had taken to his sickbed in Durham. Jasper smiled to himself as he recalled the colourful language as Sir Ralph cursed York and all he stood for. More serious was the news that Warwick had already returned from Calais to personally take command of York's army.

Jasper remembered what he'd seen when he stared into Warwick's eyes that day in the Channel. The people called Warwick 'the Kingmaker' for a reason. As Edward's right-hand man, he had swayed the loyalties of many English nobles in York's favour. He was also one of the richest men in the country, yet despite his fortune and success, still ruthlessly ambitious.

They had been riding for an hour when Gabriel pointed to the horizon.

'Something burning, my lord.'

Jasper found it hard at first to see the smoke against the late autumn clouds, then spotted the grey smudge rising into the sky.

'It could be a bonfire, or farmers burning stubble, but have the men keep on their guard.'

They travelled warily, keeping from the main roads and always watching the sky. As they drew closer they saw the smoke must be from a sizeable fire and the familiar tang of burning wood drifted on the damp air.

'Should we return to Dunstanburgh, sir?' Gabriel glanced back the way they had come. 'We could warn them and return tomorrow with more men?'

'There is no urgency to reach Alnwick, Gabriel, but we must find out first if this is York's army.'

'Let me ride ahead, sir? I'll keep my head down.'

'We'll stay together,' he smiled, 'we are skirmishers, after all.' Jasper faced the men listening behind him. 'Keep your wits about you. York's army could be as many as ten thousand men, so even if we did go back for reinforcements we could still find ourselves outnumbered.'

As they cleared the brow of a hill they saw the burned cottages ahead, the thatched roof of one still billowing smoke. Jasper approached the man trying to salvage what he could from his ruined home.

'What happened here?'

'Scots, sir.' The man wiped his brow with a blackened rag. 'The Scottish rebels came looting whatever they could carry.'

'Have you seen York's men?'

The man shook his head. 'Only those thieving heathens, sir.'

Jasper gave the man one of the last of his silver coins and led his Irishmen towards the castle. Gabriel rode at his side and glanced back at the ruined cottage.

'It seems Sir Henry lost control of his Scottish army.'

'I feared as much—we have enemies enough, without turning the local people against us.'

Once in sight of the castle they could see the drawbridge raised high over the wide moat, and the entrance sealed with a heavy iron portcullis. There was no sign of activity in the castle but a group of French mercenaries blocked the road and stopped a wagon. Jasper spotted Henry Beaufort, who grinned in welcome.

'Trouble with your Scotsmen, Henry?' Jasper rode up to him and dismounted.

'They went foraging for supplies.' Henry Beaufort glanced back to where a thickening trail of smoke continued to rise into the air, like a pointing, accusing finger. 'I think the Scots have deserted, and we've hardly begun the siege.'

'At least we still have the French. What's the strength of the garrison?'

'We think there's a token force but when we arrived they were already barricaded in, so it might take some time.'

'We may not have long. Sir Ralph Percy told me Warwick has already mustered an army. I fear he'll soon be sending reinforcements for the garrison.'

Henry Beaufort swore an oath as he studied the raised drawbridge. 'I will follow York's example and offer any who side with us a pardon, then execute the rest.'

Jasper agreed, although he found Beaufort's joke too close to the truth. 'I'll take my skirmishers and scout ahead for Warwick's army. I wish you luck, Henry.'

They rode for a further two days before tell-tale noises carried in the still morning air, alerting them to the presence of men preparing for battle. The sharp clink of hammers on metal, raised voices as commanders barked orders and the ominous thud of axes on wood. Jasper gave the signal and his men left the track and found cover in the trees, crossbows at the ready. He gestured for Gabriel to come forward.

'Tell the men to lie low while we take a look.'

They moved silently, making use of the trees and undergrowth for cover, before the enemy camp came into view. Canvas tents laid out in ragged rows covered several meadows. Warwick had brought an army of thousands to the north. Gabriel whispered a curse and pointed to a row of wheeled artillery, several of which were larger than any Jasper had ever seen.

'We'll be no match for them, sir.'

'We must return to Bamburgh and warn the queen. Send riders to tell Sir Henry and Sir Ralph what we've seen. It only took days for us to reach here and they look ready to move at any time.' Jasper studied the fields of men in front of them. 'We'll need more experienced men from Scotland. In the meantime our only hope is to hold the castles until they arrive.'

Queen Margaret listened in silence to Jasper's account of Warwick's army. The only good news he could bring her was that the garrison at Alnwick surrendered without a fight. More men had marched to support Sir Henry Beaufort, with heavy cannons, laboriously hauled by oxen all the way to the castle.

The queen crossed to the window and stared out to sea, where her fleet waited at anchor, then turned to Jasper. 'I must return to Scotland.'

'I will go, Your Highness. If I take your fastest ship and the best crew I'll make good time.'

The queen shook her head. 'They will never send more men unless I ask for them in person.'

'What about the king?'

'He will return with me to Scotland.' She lowered her voice. 'His lapses have returned and although I pray for his recovery...' Her eyes revealed her doubts.

'The king will be safer back in Scotland, Your Highness, and if Warwick realises there is no longer a great prize for him here, he might decide to hold back until the spring. There's no more miserable work for a soldier than a winter siege, and he knows how harsh the winters can be in Northumberland.'

'I must tell my ladies to prepare for the voyage right away, Sir Jasper, as the risk increases with every passing moment.'

That night Jasper held Máiréad tightly in his arms and caressed the barely discernible bulge of the next generation of Tudors, his little son or daughter. Although only a week, so much had happened it felt longer since they had been able to spend time together.

'I've missed you, Máiréad.'

'I've missed you too, Jasper. It seems I make these great voyages to be with you yet each time you slip through my fingers in the name of duty.' She took his hand in hers and held it tight, as if she thought he might escape.

'My duties keep me too busy of late.' He pulled her closer and kissed her on the lips. 'I wish...'

She stroked his dark beard, now neatly trimmed. 'What do you wish for?'

'I wish we lived in simpler times, Máiréad, with none of these endless wars.' He ran his fingers through her hair, enjoying the silky feel of it. 'I wish you could have met my father.'

'Tell me about him.'

'I've told you.'

'Tell me again, I like to hear.'

'He was an adventurer who risked everything for the woman he loved, my mother. He was a proud Welshman and spent all his life wishing he was back in Wales.'

'Like you?'

Jasper smiled and gave her a playful pat. 'Yes, like me.'

'You told me once he was proud to be a grandfather.'

'He was. Little Henry meant the world to him.'

'So he would be just as proud of your son.' She kissed him.

'Or daughter. We could be bringing another Irishwoman into the world.'

'Half Irish.' She furrowed her brow as she tried to work it out. 'One quarter French and one quarter Welsh.'

'It's a sign of these strange times we live in,' Jasper smiled. 'We are all mongrels at heart, yet still we fight.'

'I worry for you, Jasper, when you ride off like you do. I always fear you won't return.'

'I've learned how to keep safe, even if it means people accuse me of running from a fight. There are plenty of dead heroes but you give me a good reason to return safe.' He patted the tiny figure inside her. 'Now there are two reasons.'

'Do you want me to return to Scotland with the queen?'

He looked into her sad eyes, deep with mystery, and sensed she could divine his thoughts. 'I want you here with me, but it will be too dangerous when Warwick's army arrives.'

'I want to stay here with you.' She hugged him with both arms. 'Surely this castle can keep us safe?'

'Have you ever seen what happens in a siege?'

'No, but I can imagine.'

'Can you imagine what it's like to be surrounded by ten thousand men firing great cannons day and night? Can you imagine men having to eat their own horses because they're starving? Can you imagine—'

She gave him a kiss to silence him. 'I will sail with the queen. Not for you but for the sake of our baby.'

Jasper replayed their last conversation in his head many times, his way of escaping the nightmare his confined world had become. At first, it offered hope, a reminder there was much to live for, a reason for all the suffering and sleepless nights. Now it pained him to remember their special times together.

He remembered the sadness in her eyes as her boat rowed steadily from the shore to the waiting fleet, how she had raised a hand and waved farewell. They made the pretence this was a temporary setback. Queen Margaret discussed with him what they would do when she returned with her new Scottish army. Even the king refused to pack his few possessions, on the grounds he would soon return.

At least he was no longer responsible for the men of the garrison at Bamburgh, as before she left, the queen appointed

Sir Henry Beaufort commander. As his second-in-command, Jasper busied himself with overseeing the strengthening of the defences. Men worked all the daylight hours, robbing stone from wherever they could find it to reinforce the weakest points. He was painfully aware he had done the same at Pembroke and even in the town of Tenby, to so little effect, but the work kept his mind off the true danger of their situation.

Gabriel knocked on the door of Jasper's room one evening, carrying a jug of ale.

'I thought you could do with a drink, sir.'

'Come in, Gabriel.' Jasper gestured to the empty chair by the fire. 'Warm yourself a little, we've much to discuss.'

He took two pewter cups from a shelf and watched as Gabriel filled them. He'd been so preoccupied with Queen Margaret and King Henry's departure he had hardly spoken a word to his right-hand man, at his side since the horrors of Mortimer's Cross. Gabriel drank deeply from his ale and stared into the flames of the fire, as if there was something he wanted to say.

'Some of the men are... concerned, sir.' He took another drink from his cup. 'I fear they have no confidence in Sir Henry Beaufort and many could desert if they see their chance.'

Jasper nodded. 'I understand why—we've seen what's on the way.' He took a sip of the cold, bitter tasting ale. 'I fear only the harshest of winters could save us now, Gabriel.'

'You've seen how much there is in the stores, sir. Do you think we can last until the spring?'

He took a deep breath. 'In truth, I doubt it. It's my duty to try, though. I've promised the queen I'll help Sir Henry hold this castle until she can send reinforcements.'

Gabriel sat in silence for a moment. 'I think we should let the skirmishers leave, sir. They've served you loyally, but we have too many men to feed, and they should go now, get out while they can.'

He spoke quickly, and Jasper could see Gabriel felt unhappy to be suggesting such a thing, after all they had been through together, yet he had a point. They had more men than necessary to hold the castle, a luxury they could no longer afford.

'You are right, as ever.' Jasper drained his cup and made his decision. 'I will speak to the men in the morning,' he looked across at Gabriel, 'and you? Do you wish to go with them, while you can?'

'I'll stay with you, sir, until the Scottish army arrives.' He refilled their empty cups.'

'I'll drink to that. If anyone can persuade the Scots to send an army, Queen Margaret can. In the meantime, we must plan for how we can stretch out the remaining supplies.'

After Gabriel left Jasper walked up to the battlements and faced the bitter easterly wind that whipped the waves into towering breakers. The freezing air drained the warmth from his bones and he shivered as he recalled saying they needed a hard winter. It seemed his wish would be granted.

He was about to return to his room when a flicker of light below the horizon caught his eye, coming from Holy Island, a mile offshore. For a second he thought it might be Warwick's army, using the sacred island as a base. He watched and saw the light flicker again and grow brighter, then vanish. It could be pilgrims or the monks who spent their lives there but something about the loneliness of the tiny light bothered him.

## 9

# DECEMBER 1462

J asper woke with someone roughly shaking him, dazzling him with a lantern so bright he couldn't see their face. The man talked excitedly, his words not making sense. The light stung Jasper's eyes and he rubbed them, trying to gather his wits, still drowsy from lack of sleep.

'What is it? What's going on?' He heard the annoyance in his raised voice.

'They're here, sir.' The man pointed a grubby finger towards the door. 'I've been sent to tell you, sir, told to wake you like you ordered.'

He studied the thin-faced man holding the swinging lantern and recognised him as one of the guards keeping watch. Alert in an instant, he understood the waiting was over. Warwick's army had arrived at last and their battle for survival would begin.

'How many? Where are they?' He reached for his boots and pulled them on, knowing all their lives depended on the answer.

The guard's wide eyes revealed the panic of a man who has

seen a vision of his own death and knows nothing he does can prevent it. Jasper recalled the same look in the eyes of men as he tried to defend the king in the carnage of St Albans and later at the massacre of his army at Mortimer's Cross.

'There's hundreds of them, sir.' He shook his head. 'No, thousands, too many...' He took a step back, towards the open door and beckoned with his free hand. 'Come and see, my lord,' his voice sounded urgent, 'they have us surrounded!'

Jasper pulled on the padded jack he wore for protection against arrows and strapped on his sword out of habit. Although of little use to him in a siege, the familiar weight of the sword at his belt gave him confidence he didn't feel in his heart. He glanced at his armour, neatly piled in the corner of his room, and chose only his open-faced sallet helmet, which he put on without fastening the leather chin strap.

He heard the noise made by Warwick's army even as he climbed the stone steps to the high battlement and looked out. The rising sun cast long shadows in the early dawn and light sparkled on a heavy frost, making the scene in front of him look surreal. The guard had not exaggerated. Thousands of men filled the familiar open fields in front of the castle, swarming over every patch of ground like busy wood ants, already digging defences, shouting orders and hammering wooden stakes with mallets.

He had taken the precaution of ordering men to cut down the trees and demolish the outbuildings that might offer their enemy cover, but it made no difference. The sheer scale of Warwick's forces seemed overwhelming. They were also closer than he'd expected. Even as he watched he saw his cross-bowmen had them within range, already picking their targets.

A sharp yell of pain rang out as a lucky shot from a crossbow struck one of Warwick's men in the back. Jasper watched as they withdrew, dragging the wounded soldier with them, to a cheer and shouted insults from the men high on the battlements. A small victory in what would become a one-sided battle. He had imagined this moment many times over the previous weeks, yet now they seemed woefully unprepared.

He sent men to rouse Henry Beaufort with a message to meet him in the great hall without delay. Their commander soon arrived and ordered his servant to begin fastening his armour while he listened to Jasper's assessment. A deafening boom sounded as the first of the cannons began pounding the castle walls. Sir Henry flinched as heavy chunks of plaster fell from the ceiling of the grand hall, crashing to the tiled floor.

'By God! Warwick should have sent a herald before opening fire, I would expect him to at least offer us the chance of an honourable surrender.'

Jasper glowered at him. 'You forget your duty to the king, Sir Henry.' His stern voice echoed from the roof of the great hall and his hand fell to the hilt of his sword. 'We will not surrender. Not yet, at least.'

Henry Beaufort put a calming hand on Jasper's shoulder. 'I promise you it sticks in my gullet to pretend allegiance to York —but it could buy us time until the queen returns with a new army.' He adjusted a buckle on his breastplate. 'What do we have to lose by talking?'

A second cannon thundered in reply, then a third, making the ground vibrate under their feet. Jasper cursed Beaufort for his disloyalty as he tried to decide what to say. He couldn't believe the siege had hardly begun yet already Henry Beaufort talked of surrender.

'I fear this is more than a siege, Henry. Warwick must know he's been robbed of his prize now the king and queen have sailed to safety.' He flinched as yet another cannon boomed. 'It's Edward of York that army outside follows, not his dog. If York is ill, we may not need to wait until the spring. Warwick might be skilled at turning people's heads from their duty to King Henry but he is a poor commander. He should have won the day in St Albans last year, yet we outflanked him and drove his army from the field.'

'What are you thinking—that Edward might die?' Henry Beaufort appeared unconvinced. 'What can we do? Fire a few arrows?' He began to sound exasperated. 'Even if we kill a hundred of Warwick's men, he has thousands ready to take their place.'

'Don't you see Warwick's plan? He intends to prove himself worthy by wiping out the last Lancastrians in the north—and taking our castles for himself.'

Henry Beaufort buckled his sword belt. 'We will hold this castle for as long as we can—'

Another deep, thunderous boom interrupted his words, followed immediately by the crash of a cannonball and shouts of alarm. From the direction of the noises the target must be the massive wooden doors of the castle gatehouse, constructed long before the use of heavy cannons. It seemed as if Warwick had been listening and this was his reply.


They endured weeks of relentless bombardment, which shook even the thick walls of Bamburgh Castle and sent deadly frag-ments of stone and wooden splinters into the air. Even when the cannon fire ceased, Warwick's archers launched a hail of arrows, fired high over the walls. Jasper inspected one of the fallen arrows and noted how the tip was soiled, an old trick to ensure the wound became infected.

With no apothecary or herbs to treat the wounded, the burial parties kept busy digging makeshift graves within the castle ward, eventually resorting to a communal pit where the dead were thrown. Without lime to cover the bodies the unmis-takable stink of death soon drifted in the air despite the winter chill, an unhealthy reminder of their fallen comrades

Their attackers seemed unconcerned about their encampment being within range of his bowmen, so at midnight Jasper's archers lining the battlements lit their pitch covered arrowheads from braziers and fired into the darkness. Some tied parchment from the castle records to the shafts, filled with precious gunpowder. Jasper watched as the burning arrows curved in a great arc through the night sky, falling well inside the sleeping enemy camp.

The effect was like thrusting a stick into a nest of hornets. Shouts of alarm were followed by explosions as flames reached the gunpowder. A screaming man ran from a burning tent and a panicking horse bolted, trampling men under its hooves. Poorly aimed arrows fired back fell short, as for once the cruelly freezing winter winds blew in Jasper's favour. He wondered if Warwick would be somewhere in the chaos he'd created but doubted it. Henry Beaufort had been right, for his archers and crossbowmen barely made an impression on the well-equipped and provisioned enemy force.

All the same Jasper understood the value of another small victory for the morale of his men. He allowed them to celebrate by slaughtering the last two horses, although the rich meat was soon gone before all his men had their share and Jasper saw none of it. Instead he set an example by insisting he had only the same strict rations as his men and felt the same pangs of hunger from his meagre diet.

Gabriel looked concerned as Jasper entered the storeroom, once piled high with supplies but now cavernous and empty, their voices echoing. Even allowing for the deserters they still had more than three hundred hungry men to feed. Jasper counted the remaining sacks of grain used to thicken their greasy pottage and shook his head.

'How long will it last?'

'A week, sir, two if we reduce the rations even further.'

It was even worse than Jasper feared. 'We must, Gabriel, right away.' He saw the strain of the siege was starting to tell on even the tough Irishman. 'I don't want the men to learn we're out of food, at least until they have to.'

'The well is still good, sir,' Gabriel forced a weak smile, 'at least we won't go thirsty.'

'Thank God. I've heard a man can last for three weeks without food but only three days without water.' Jasper tried to smile back but the truth of his words prevented it.

He left Gabriel and continued on his circuit of the castle, checking on the guards and offering them such encouragement as he could, despite the biting December North Sea winds and freezing rain, which sapped a man's spirit and made the castle feel bleak and damp. Jasper shivered as he stopped to survey the damage done to the gatehouse by Warwick's artillery. The portcullis remained intact but the doors had been shattered and he guessed they could be breached in the next all-out attack.

The helplessness of their situation weighed heavily on his conscience. He could only guess how many men already died as a consequence of him persuading Henry Beaufort to hold on until the queen's reinforcements arrived. He also found himself wondering if the loss of Bamburgh Castle would make any real difference to their cause. At the same time he could never swear allegiance to Edward of York and would rather die fighting than face the executioner's axe.

It seemed improbable Queen Margaret could raise enough Scotsmen to match Warwick's army, let alone outnumber them. Too late, Japer realised they should have pressed King Louis for twice as many men, and sought an alliance with the Duke of Burgundy. Even the surly Duke Francis might have seen advantage in providing a thousand men to support the queen's invasion of England. Instead, they risked everything with barely one tenth of the army arrayed before him.

∾

Jasper climbed the steps to the battlements and watched with a heavy heart as Henry Beaufort stepped from the postern gate carrying a white flag of truce, the pathetic symbol of their lost hope, and disappeared into the ranks of their enemy. He immediately regretted agreeing to let him go, yet they had run out of options. Warwick's army, by far the biggest he had ever seen, stretched to the far horizon.

The first of the winter snows dusted the ground and the year coming to an end before Henry Beaufort returned, alone and again carrying a flag of truce as he approached, to avoid being mistaken for the enemy. He insisted on meeting in private, so Jasper led him up the spiral steps to his room in the tower, feeling a familiar sense of foreboding in his chest. Whatever Henry Beaufort had to tell him was not going to be good news. He gestured for Beaufort to take a seat.

'Tell me as it is, Henry.'

Henry Beaufort sat grim-faced for a moment, then nodded. 'The queen's fleet was caught in a terrible storm, Jasper. Many of her ships foundered on the rocks.'

'The king? Does he still live?' He hardly wanted to hear the answer.

'I heard the king and queen, as well as her French captain, made it safely to Berwick in a longboat, but after that there is no news.'

'All the fleet is lost?' It seemed impossible that more than forty ships, over four hundred men, could have been lost, even in the worst storm.

'It was a disaster, Jasper. Many turned back and tried to land on Lindisfarne Island but...' He shied away from Jasper's questioning eyes.

'What happened?'

'The men were stranded and couldn't make it back, even at low tide, as Warwick's troops occupy the beaches. John Manners, one of Warwick's captains, crossed to the island and ordered his men to massacre anyone still alive. No one survived.'

'My God! Are you certain of this?'

Beaufort looked at Jasper warily, as if he expected Jasper to blame him. 'Manners bragged of it. He showed no remorse.'

Jasper found it hard to concentrate on Henry Beaufort's words. Such loss of life was too great a blow to comprehend. He should have tried to talk them out of sailing so late in the year but if anyone must take the blame, Pierre de Brézé, an experienced captain, should have known better.

'What of York? Is he dying?'

Beaufort shrugged. 'He suffered from fever, by all accounts some form of pox.'

'And Warwick, does he offer a pardon?'

Henry Beaufort shifted uncomfortably in his chair and avoided Jasper's eye. 'For the men who swear allegiance to York.'

'What about the commanders?'

'He will pardon me, in return for payment, and Sir Ralph.'

'And me?' He already guessed the answer.

'He swears he'll have you executed for treason.'

Jasper felt a shadow pass over his future, each of Henry Beaufort's words ringing like iron nails being hammered into his coffin. Warwick had won and Jasper fought the sense of helplessness that threatened to overwhelm him.

After Beaufort left Jasper knelt at the side of his bed, as he had every night since he arrived, and prayed for King Henry and Queen Margaret. It seemed his prayers had been answered and he thanked God they were delivered safely from the storm that brought death to so many.

He said a prayer for the men who put their faith in his leadership, that they would be treated justly by Warwick, to whom they must now surrender. There wasn't enough food to last so many men until the spring, and to even try would be futile.

Jasper asked God to forgive his sins, for his own fate seemed certain. As he prayed, he felt a stab of regret that he would never rescue his young nephew from marriage to the daughter of his old enemy, William Herbert, who stole his birthright and even his title of Earl of Pembroke.

He cried out, his despair echoing in the empty room. 'No!'

Tears of grief flowed down his face as he prayed for the soul of his beautiful Irish lover, Máiréad. Henry Beaufort was certain there were no other survivors of the shipwreck, so he could only pray she didn't suffer at the end. He wept for the soul of the unborn baby she carried, the son or daughter he would never know.

The garrison of Bamburgh Castle surrendered on a cheerless Christmas Eve. Many were too weakened and ill from lack of food and the relentless cold and rains of a harsh Northumbrian winter to march out through the gates. Jasper collapsed from hunger the day before. He suspected Gabriel gave him his own rations, yet he still felt unsteady on his feet.

He pretended to be an Irish mercenary of no consequence and surrendered with his men but was recognised and promptly arrested. Beaten senseless by his captors and chained from wrist to ankle, he waited under close guard for the arrival of the victorious Earl of Warwick, commander of York's forces in the north.

Jasper descended into a dark, numb void of despair, not for himself but the men who'd followed him so loyally and could be executed if they refused to swear allegiance to the usurper king. He refused the offer of a priest to hear his confession, having finally lost his faith in an unjust God. Instead he tried his best to surrender to the cold, seeping into his bones from the frozen ground, just as they had surrendered the castle, without a fight. It would be a merciful release.

The toe of a soldier's boot kicked hard into his ribs and announced his time had come. Cold winter air froze his breath as men dragged Jasper out to face his enemy. He looked up, not into the sharp, cruel eyes of Warwick but a younger, less ambitious version, Sir John Neville, Lord Montague.

'My brother would have your head today, Tudor.' His voice had a mocking tone.

Jasper studied John Neville, without seeing any need to answer. He remembered him from his time in the Palace of Westminster so long ago. He had always thought Neville a fair and decent man, unluckily born into the wrong family. A glimmer of hope rippled on the surface of his despair. One last act of redemption could be within his reach.

'I wish to beg a great favour from you, sir.' His voice sounded weak from his captivity and he found it hard to stand. All he'd eaten for several days was the foul-tasting gruel served to prisoners.

A flicker of interest crossed John Neville's face. 'And what would that be?'

'My men, they are mercenaries, not Lancastrians. They have no loyalty to King Henry.' He looked John Neville directly in the eye. 'I ask you to please spare them, sir.' He held his breath, the lives of those who had become his friends depending on the answer.

Neville returned his gaze. A dog barked somewhere in the distance, breaking the painful silence. 'You are fortunate, Tudor. King Edward has shown great compassion. His orders are that you and your men are to be escorted from England and released.'

It took a moment for his words to register in Jasper's tired mind. Tears formed in his eyes as he knew they would all be spared. 'Thank you.'

## 10

## JANUARY 1463

The straggling line of soldiers marched north to the border through a fresh fall of snow, deep enough to obscure the path, if not for the footprints of the man in front. Jasper began to lose the feeling in his fingers, yet felt grateful to be alive, to survive almost certain death yet again, against the odds.

Behind him marched Gabriel, his sense of humour tested by recent events yet still Jasper's most loyal supporter. Wearing a pair of sturdy boots won in a game of dice, he passed the time by asking questions, not all of which had easy answers.

'What will we do when we reach Scotland, sir?'

'Find Queen Margaret and explain our plan.' Jasper allowed himself a smile as he waited for the inevitable reply from behind him.

'We have a plan, my lord?' He sounded doubtful.

'Indeed we do, Gabriel. Did I not discuss it with you?'

'You did not, sir.'

'You think we surrendered Bamburgh without a plan?'

'I did, sir. I thought we had run clean out of Irish luck this time.'

Jasper glanced ahead to see the men escorting them were out of earshot. 'We make our own luck, Gabriel.' He lowered his voice. 'Sir Ralph Percy has been made Constable of Bamburgh by Lord Montague. Did that not strike you as an odd choice?'

For the first time in many hours of marching, other than the steady crunch of boots on snow, there was silence behind him while Gabriel considered this piece of news.

'He intends to turn his coat again and surrender it back to Lancaster?'

'When he can. The success of the plan demands absolute secrecy. Sir Ralph's life depends on it, as well as his ability to convince Sir John Neville.'

'We were fortunate it was the younger brother who accepted our surrender and not the one they call the Kingmaker.'

'Indeed we were fortunate.'

Jasper peered into the distance and saw the town walls and castle of Berwick on the horizon at last. It had taken them since first light to march twenty miles through the freezing white landscape. He rubbed his numb hands together to restore the circulation. Fortune's Wheel had turned again and he sensed new opportunities ahead. He'd lost everything except the ragged clothes he stood up in, yet been given the chance to learn from his mistakes and to live to fight another day, for which he would always be grateful.


Good meals, a shave and a smart doublet transformed Jasper by the time he was granted an audience with Queen Margaret. She wore a sombre black gown with a necklace of dazzling white pearls and a French coif, and studied him with questioning eyes. The events since their parting had almost been too much for them both yet, like him, she seemed to have lost none of her spirit.

'You look well, Sir Jasper, for a man who has survived a siege.'

'We held Bamburgh for as long as we could, Your Highness.' He gave a bow and glanced at her ladies-in-waiting, who he guessed were Scottish noblewomen. 'May we speak in private, my lady?'

Queen Margaret dismissed her ladies and they left in a rustle of silk skirts, some casting curious glances at Jasper. As the door closed behind them she gestured for him to sit close to her. Now he could look at her, he noticed the darkness under her eyes and the deepening frown lines. The queen was still an attractive woman yet the past months had left their mark. She reached out and touched his hand, a small but significant gesture of tenderness.

'I prayed for you, Jasper Tudor.' Her eyes misted with tears. 'I feared I would never see you again.'

Jasper fought back the rush of emotion. He wasn't yet recovered from the loss of Máiréad and his own brush with death. He had often wondered how it must have been for his father as he waited for his execution. He knew now how men cling to the slenderest thread of hope and how they can even question their faith in God.

He took her hand in his and touched it briefly to his lips. Close enough for the heady scent of her perfume to reach him, the aroma of exotic roses, like in her proud father's garden at his château at Angers.

'You were always in my prayers, my lady.'

'You heard what happened with my fleet?'

'I was told you were shipwrecked and barely escaped with your life.'

'Four of our ships were lost, including mine. I thought it was the end for us all. I've seen what the sea can do but never known anything like that night. It's only thanks to Captain de Brézé that King Henry and I are here now.'

'The captain? He survived?'

She nodded. 'He is on his way with the Earl of Angus, at the head of a Scottish army to relieve our northern castles.'

Jasper could hardly believe it. If only they had known help would be coming so soon he might have persuaded the men to hold on. He felt again the bitter shame at having let her down and failing to believe in her.

'You wish me to return to Northumberland?' The prospect did not appeal to him. He doubted York would be so lenient if he was captured a second time.

'No. I wish you to return to France. King Louis likes you.'

'I would be honoured, Your Highness. I think we should build our alliances there, not only with King Louis but also with the Duke of Burgundy and his son, the Count of Charolais.'

'That would be prudent, as I fear York will soon be testing our allegiance with the Scots.'

He hardly dared ask her his next question and took a deep breath to steady his fast-beating heart. The question had gnawed in his head like a dog with a bone all the way on his long march from Bamburgh Castle, yet part of him didn't wish to know her answer.

'There was an Irishwoman, one of your maidservants, named Máiréad.'

'Yes, I remember her. I know you were close.'

'She was with you—when you were shipwrecked?'

'I am sorry, Jasper.' She would not meet his eyes.

'She was lost?' His voice became little more than a whisper and his heart hardened as he finally accepted the truth.

'We barely managed to get the king into the boat before our ship went down.' She lightly squeezed his hand, just as Máiréad had done to comfort him.

Jasper waited for more than an hour before a liveried servant came to lead him through seemingly endless grand corridors to the court of Philip, Duke of Burgundy. He guessed the wait was deliberate, a sign of how little importance the duke placed on him and the weakened House of Lancaster. All the same, he had been granted an audience, which was all he had asked for.

Ten-foot high ornate gilded doors opened and he had his first glimpse of the duke's legendary inner sanctum. The stories he had heard were true. It was grander even than that of the king. From the magnificent wall hangings to the polished floor of Italian marble, the sheer scale and extravagance of the room was contrived to impress. Jasper had never seen Duke Philip, known by his people as Philip the Good, and expected him to be seated on a throne, surrounded by a small army of courtiers and advisors.

The pale, thin-faced man standing alone by the window was a complete surprise. His large black hat and dark tunic with a collar and cuffs of dark fur emphasised his sallow complexion. His long, thin nose and receding chin would suggest weakness, if not for the confident superiority in his sharp eyes.

'I've heard a great deal about you, Jasper Tudor.' His voice sounded cultured, with a Flemish accent but he spoke in French.

'It is my pleasure to meet you at last, Your Grace.' Jasper replied in French and briefly bowed. 'I bring letters from King Henry, the true King of England, and Queen Margaret, who asked me to convey their good wishes, Your Grace.'

The duke studied him impassively. 'You know I was once married to your mother's sister, Countess Michelle of Valois?'

'I heard she was greatly loved by the people.' Jasper recalled a rumour her food had been poisoned.

'A sad loss.' The duke crossed himself. 'I still remember her in my prayers.' He seemed lost in thought for a moment, 'Your mother was a good woman, quite beautiful, yet your father worked as a servant?' He sounded intrigued.

'My father was descended from a long line of Welsh princes, Your Grace.'

'And now you come on behalf of King Henry, asking for my support?'

'I do, Your Grace. King Henry wishes an alliance with Burgundy.'

'You put me in a difficult position, for as they say, that bird has flown. You no doubt are aware of this, yet still you ask?'

'I know Edward of York has you under an obligation, and threatens consequences for your trade with England if you support the House of Lancaster.'

The duke raised an eyebrow at Jasper's directness. 'I think I can save you a great deal of time. I suspect you plan to seek support from King Louis and your cousin Duke Francis?'

Jasper hesitated, unsure how to answer.

The duke stared at him, unsmiling yet with a shrewd glint in his eye. 'We have all agreed with King Edward not to help each other's enemies, but you, Sir Jasper, are family, of the House of Valois, as is King Henry. I must therefore grant you safe conduct. You may inform Queen Margaret I will show her courtesy, even if I cannot support her cause.'

Queen Margaret would be devastated to learn King Louis had already reached agreement with York, after she had worked so hard to win him over. Anything the French king signed could be torn up just as quickly. Louis was no gentleman and his word counted for little. At the same time he heard the sound of another door closing on financial support for their cause and now it seemed the hands of Duke Francis had also been tied.

. . .

Jasper recalled Duke Philip's words as he stood on the quayside at St Malo, admiring the results of more than a year of negotiation. In a stroke of good fortune, he found a kindred spirit in the duke's son, Charles, Count of Charolais. Handsome and well educated, Charles descended from the House of Lancaster on his mother's side and openly admitted to Jasper that he had been told to keep an eye on him. Charles would one day become Duke of Burgundy and, as well as covering Jasper's expenses, saw advantage in keeping his options open.

Then came the not unexpected news that Queen Mary of Scotland had also signed a peace treaty with York and the last hopes of a Lancastrian alliance were dashed. At least King Henry was now safely back in Bamburgh, under the protection of both Sir Henry and Sir Ralph, both of whom reneged on their oaths of loyalty to York and returned to the castle with their men, as promised, at great personal risk. Both would surely face execution if they were ever captured.

Queen Margaret and Prince Edward were forced into exile at the Castle St Michel, in Barrois, belonging to Margaret's brother John of Anjou, the Duke of Calabria. She gathered around her several loyal Lancastrian lords, as well as ladies-in-waiting, to create her royal court in exile. Jasper persuaded Sir John Fortescue, the Lancastrian Chancellor in exile, to undertake the challenging responsibility of preparing the young prince for his future role as king.

Jasper visited Castle St Michel regularly with news of his progress, and acted as the queen's intermediary, travelling north to Burgundy and south to Brittany to negotiate support for the House of Lancaster. At his last visit they agreed it was time for him to return to Wales, to see if he could rebuild a Welsh army.

King Louis had tired of Jasper's requests for support and grudgingly paid for three ships, now being loaded with supplies for the voyage to Wales. They would never be enough to mount an invasion but even if he could not raise an army of Welshmen, he would do everything in his power to make sure the great castle at Harlech stayed out of the hands of his old enemy, William Herbert.

Gabriel had finally achieved his boyhood ambition and been given charge of their little fleet, a role he had taken to with great enthusiasm. On Jasper's instruction he had overseen the conversion of the duke's tired old merchantmen into makeshift warships, which still had the outward appearance of merchant traders yet were stripped for speed. Each also carried new swivel guns, hidden below decks, which could be mounted on pivots fitted to the rails and could fire buckshot as well as four-pound cannon balls.

With luck, they should not attract the attention of English patrols until safely around Land's End but if they did, the plan was not to give up without a fight. The Breton crews were strengthened with more than fifty French mercenaries and the last remaining Irishmen, who acted as Jasper's personal guard and followed him with such loyalty he thought of them as brothers. They still practised their skirmishing skills and carried crossbows slung over their shoulders, with their deadly roundel daggers at their belts.

Much to the relief of the men, Jasper decided they would not carry horses on such a long voyage but try to purchase some once they made landfall in Wales. He had kept back some of the meagre allowance provided by Duke Francis, although he hoped loyal Lancastrians would help cover such expenses. At one time he would never consider asking for money in the name of the king but now he had no choice.

Gabriel appeared at Jasper's side. 'Ready to set sail when you wish, sir.'

Jasper nodded in acknowledgement. 'Well done, Gabriel. I'm looking forward to seeing Wales again after so long.'

Gabriel studied the fluttering pennant at the mast top. 'I can't tell how long for, sir, but the winds are in our favour now.'

Jasper pointed to the horizon. 'Our escort, Admiral Alain de la Motte.' He gave a wry smile. 'He wants to be certain I leave this place. King Louis has accused the duke of breaching the treaty by helping us.'

'Did King Louis not fund our voyage, sir?'

'He did, although the price of five hundred pounds was to see the back of us, so we had better oblige him. Have your men hoist flags of Brittany, Gabriel, at least until we are safely out of the range of York's patrols.'

A freshening breeze filled their sails and the rigging of Jasper's ship creaked with the strain as it heeled. As they waved off their escort past Land's End Jasper felt in control of his own destiny for the first time since he left Ireland. He had been glad to serve their cause as envoy to the queen, and achieved more than could have been expected. Now at last he could make decisions for himself and was answerable only to his conscience.

They headed up the Irish Sea and Jasper regretfully decided they should give the south of Wales a wide berth. Instead they would make landfall under the cover of darkness in the sheltered waters of the Mawddach estuary off Barmouth. Harlech Castle stood on high cliffs overlooking the coast but Jasper worried that Herbert might have sentries watching the approaches, so he left enough men to protect his ships and had the rest ferried ashore in rowing boats.

He warned his men to be vigilant and ready for a fight as they marched north in the darkness, and felt relief when they finally sighted the lights of Harlech ahead, the castle a dark shape high on a rocky hilltop, dominating the skyline. Taking cover behind the crest of a hill, they watched for any sign of movement by York's forces.

Jasper nodded to Gabriel. 'Take a couple of men, and good luck, Gabriel.'

They had discussed the possibility that the castle had already been taken by Herbert, in which case it could be disastrous to march up to the gatehouse. They also risked being mistaken for the enemy if they approached unannounced, so Gabriel came up with a plan to pretend to be a passing Irish trader wishing to supply the castle.

Jasper said a silent prayer as he waited. Harlech remained their last remaining stronghold in Wales but he remembered how easily Herbert took Pembroke Castle once the men holding it lost heart. He heard a cough and the scrape of a boot on gravel in the darkness and breathed again with relief to see Gabriel return with a reassuring grin on his face.

'The castle held, sir.' He sounded breathless from his brisk climb up to the gatehouse and back. 'The garrison commander welcomes you, and asks that you join him for a jug of ale to celebrate your return to Wales.'

Captain David ap Einion, the commander of Harlech garrison was a portly, bald-headed veteran of the wars in France with a voice that boomed in a strong Welsh accent. He embraced Jasper warmly once his men were safely inside the castle walls.

'It is truly good to see you, my lord. We've heard all manner of rumours yet not had much news since Sir Richard Tunstall left.'

'A good man,' Jasper recalled a tall figure who fought so bravely for the king at his side in St Albans. 'He has returned to Bamburgh?'

'He has, sir.' The captain smiled. 'I think he found Harlech too cut off from the world.'

'He will find Bamburgh little better, Captain. Give me Wales any day over Northumberland.'

Jasper slept through until noon the next day, his long sea voyage and the captain's hospitality having taken its toll. Now he was finally in a position to strike a blow against William Herbert, if only he could find him. Rumours he'd heard as far away as Brittany about the siege of Harlech Castle proved to be false, as in truth attacks were rare and the high vantage-point meant it was impossible for Herbert's men to take them by surprise.

He took a tour of the castle and climbed the steps to the top of the battlements. He could see across to Ireland and as far as the mountains of the Welsh heartlands. The height from the top of the battlements to the ground made him feel dizzy as he looked down. If an attack came, it would be the well-chosen location and solid stone mass of the castle that saved them, rather than the number of men defending it.

He found Captain ap Einion checking the records of supplies in his office. A small, dimly-lit room near the gate-house, there seemed barely enough room for his large oak desk, covered with papers. An old cannon ball served as a paper-weight, and an impressive iron stand held his inkpot and quill.

'My father used to tell me stories of the great Welsh rebellion led from here by Owain Glyndŵr.' Jasper picked up the iron ball, impressed by its solid weight.

The captain nodded proudly. 'This castle was Glyndŵr's base, after he starved the English out.'

'What do you do for supplies?' Mention of being starved out reminded Jasper of the nightmare of Bamburgh and had no wish to repeat the experience.

'You'd be surprised how much support there is for our cause, my lord,' the captain smiled, 'despite what York would have you believe. Some bring us money, others food and casks of ale, whatever they can spare.'

'And your men?'

'We've had a few deserters but that's to be expected—and I don't think they've gone running to William Herbert. Back to their womenfolk, more likely.' He laughed at his own joke.

'Do you know where Herbert can be found?'

'You're in luck, my lord. We've been informed Lord Herbert has been granted two thousand pounds and appointed Constable of Harlech. He is bound to show his face here soon enough.'

'I trust you are right, Captain, as I have a score to settle with Lord Herbert.'

'I almost forgot. There is something I must show you, my lord.'

The captain searched through his papers, muttering as he did so, then found a folded parchment bearing the Great Seal of Parliament. He handed it to Jasper, who took it to the light of the small window to read. It was an order to surrender Harlech Castle, or all the entire garrison would be charged with treason and any lords within attainted.

'Well, Captain, one service Lord Herbert has done me is that I no longer have any lands for York to confiscate.' He handed the parchment back to the captain who threw it in his pile. 'Let's show them why we will never surrender.'

## 11

### JUNE 1468

The horses seemed to sense something was about to happen. They grazed the lush grass of the hillside but now several stopped, heads raised with their ears flicking forward, while others cantered further away. They would have been taken from farms and villages all over North Wales for use by York's army. Jasper watched from the cover of a ridgeway. There were more than he could easily count and they looked to be in good condition.

Gabriel smiled as he studied them. 'They look like ponies to me, sir.' He kept his voice to a whisper.

'Welsh cobs, bred from mountain ponies, Gabriel.' Jasper felt strangely defensive. 'They are tough and intelligent. Not as fast as your Irish horses, but quick enough, and if we run out of feed they can fend for themselves.'

'There don't seem to be any men guarding them.' Gabriel scanned the perimeter as far as he could see.

Jasper glanced at the last sliver of moon still visible in the grey velvet dawn. 'It's early, but it looks as if Herbert's men have grown complacent.'

He glanced along the ridge to ensure his men were all in

place and realised what had troubled him since they discovered Herbert's camp. He had never in his life ordered a man to be killed in cold blood. In every battle of this dreadful civil war he had been defending the king, the Lancastrian cause, or fighting for his life.

'If you come across any guards I want them taken alive. Unharmed, unless we have no choice.'

Gabriel understood. 'I'll pass word to the men, sir.' He slipped away without a sound, leaving Jasper to keep watch.

Captain ap Einion had provided him with an open-faced steel helmet and a battered breastplate of uncertain age. He loosened the strap on his helmet and adjusted the wool padding inside to prevent it rubbing against the back of his neck. He missed his suit of armour, made by craftsmen and now long gone, together with his fine sword and many of his most prized possessions. It irked him to know they were now being used by York's men.

He would have liked to surround the entire camp and capture every man inside, including Lord William Herbert, the man who stole his birthright and kidnapped his nephew, Henry. The stakes were higher now than ever before, as if he was captured it would mean certain death. He had no wish to put the extent of York's compassion to the test. Instead he must live within his means, strike this blow and escape while he could.

Gabriel raised a hand high in the air, the sign that all the men were ready. They had been longing for some real action, and now was their chance at last to show what they could do. He raised his hand and dropped it, the signal meant there would be no going back.

His men were in two divisions. Jasper lead the diversionary attack, planned to cause as much chaos as they could to draw the guards away. The second, smaller division under Gabriel's command had the challenging task of capturing as many horses as possible and driving them down the valley, all the way back to Harlech.

Their plan depended on taking William Herbert's men by surprise. Captain ap Einion looked apologetic when he explained his guards were only trained to defend the castle. They never risked leaving the safety of the fortress to attack Herbert's patrols, let alone raid one of his camps. Jasper knew how soldiers could fall into easy habits and forget the dangers they faced. It would be a gamble, but it was time to take risks and the sun had yet to rise, so he also expected most of Herbert's men to be sleeping.

Their main weapon was one of the oldest known to man. His skirmishers had practised the skill of preserving a flame, carried in a blacked-out lantern, to light the torches they carried made from cotton rags soaked with tar, then throwing them onto anything that would burn well and making good their escape. They had learned the keys to success were timing and stealth, as many fires had to be lit at the same time, and they must all escape before the alarm was raised.

A barking cough sounded from somewhere within as they entered the camp, but it seemed they had neglected to post guards. It looked as if the scouts Jasper sent out to spy on the camp were right. They drew him a rough sketch of the layout, a circle of tents around a group of farm buildings, including the old barn, chosen as their main target. Roofed with slate, they had no idea what the barn contained but hoped the timbers would be dry enough to burn.

The men spread out, keeping low and using such cover as they could find. Jasper drew his sword and watched as they gave him the thumbs up signal, then returned it. One by one they crouched to the ground and lit their torches. The first flames hardly began burning when a half-dressed man emerged from one of the tents with a loud curse, buckling on his sword.

'Stand to!' He bellowed. 'Stand to! We are under attack!'

A well-aimed crossbow bolt struck him in the chest and he collapsed like a falling tree but he had done his job, as a dozen more of Herbert's soldiers came running from the barn. Some lashed out at Jasper's skirmishers, swinging long halberds with pointed axe-heads that could pierce armour.

Others had swords and were better prepared, reacting swiftly to the invasion of their camp. One of their commanders, a tall, thick-set man with a sallet helmet and an engraved breastplate over his doublet, called for water to douse the flames while another yelled for the guards.

The Irishmen were hopelessly outnumbered and began to be surrounded by Herbert's men. Jasper heard one of his skirmishers cry out in pain as he was cut down by a savage slash from a sword. Others ran, throwing their burning torches into the tented camp as they left.

Fires blazed brightly in all directions, the acrid smell of burning adding to the sense of panic and danger. The wall of the old barn finally caught light with leaping orange flames that crackled loudly as they rose into the sky. Thick, choking smoke billowed into the early morning air, creating more confusion among the men in the camp.

'For the king and Lancaster!' Jasper drew his sword and held it high, the signal to the small army of French and Breton mercenaries he'd ordered to wait at the edge of the camp. He had hoped it wouldn't come to this but had no choice if he was going to save the lives of the Irishmen who served him so loyally.

The Bretons swept into the camp, yelling at the tops of their voices, and cut a swathe through Herbert's soldiers, some of whom threw down their weapons and ran, rather than face this new wave of attackers. Jasper found himself caught up in the thrill and danger of the battle, his wish to only take prisoners forgotten in a surge of anger.

The battle brought back painful memories of the ambush at Mortimer's Cross and his father's cruel execution at the hands of York's men. He narrowly dodged a swinging pole-axe and thrust with the sharp tip of his sword, wounding the soldier before turning to fend off another. Too late, he felt searing pain as a blade slashed at his right arm. Only his padded jack saved a deeper wound, as the violence of the blow numbed his hand, causing his sword to clatter to the ground.

Ignoring the blood flowing from the cut he reached for his dagger and plunged it into the body of his attacker, who stared at him with a look of horror and surprise then fell backwards. No longer able to fight, Jasper picked up his fallen sword and glanced around him. The men he brought with him all the way from Brittany had clearly won the day. Dead and dying soldiers lay among the still burning tents and the air filled with the acrid tang of smoke made his eyes water.

He raised his sword high again with his left hand and roared the order to cease fighting. Herbert's remaining men began throwing down their weapons and surrendering. Jasper searched their soot-blackened faces until he found their commander. The man removed his fine helmet to reveal short-cropped hair turned grey with age and stared back at Jasper with a mixture of anger and curiosity on his weather-beaten face.

'Captain Gwynfor Philips, of Lord Herbert's guard,' he gruffly introduced himself. 'I ask that you spare my men, sir.' He glanced at his surviving comrades and scowled when he saw how many lay dead. 'They are all good loyal Welshmen.'

'Sir Jasper Tudor, servant of the true king and rightful Earl of Pembroke.' He saw the man's eyes widen with surprise at his name and the title, taken by Lord Herbert as his own. 'You are fortunate, Captain. In King Henry's name I pardon your men, and any who wish to join us are most welcome.'

'We can go free, my lord?' The captain sounded puzzled, yet there was new respect in his tone.

Jasper nodded. 'Give Lord Herbert my regards when you see him next.'

The celebrations at Harlech Castle were muted out of respect for the good men who died that day, including four of Jasper's Irishmen. The bandaged cut on Jasper's arm needed to be sewn closed, an experience which proved more painful than the original injury. The soldier who acted as the garrison physician was also the cook, and cautioned him to be vigilant for any sign of fever, which could lose him his arm, or his life, if he was unlucky.

Jasper thanked the man for his comforting words and made his way to the castle's small chapel, built against the north wall. At the altar where Owain Glyndŵr might have prayed, he said a prayer for the souls of the loyal men lost in the battle. As he knelt in silent contemplation, he recalled the thrill of their unexpected victory. It seemed his luck had returned at last, as had his faith in God.

Jasper sent men out into the local towns and villages to spread the word. The House of Lancaster had returned to Wales and any men who wished to help restore the king were welcome. News of Lord William Herbert's defeat travelled swiftly, for within a week more volunteers arrived at the castle than could be comfortably billeted within its towering walls.

Captain ap Einion did his best yet admitted his concerns. 'If many more come, my lord, we'll not be able to feed them all. I've never seen the like of it.'

Jasper could tell such numbers of men would soon overwhelm his supplies. 'I can't turn them away. What about the townspeople? Can we rely on them to provide for our men?'

'I will see what I can do, my lord, but as you know, every space in the castle is full.'

'We have the horses we recovered from the enemy camp and we also have plenty of weapons, thanks to Lord Herbert.' He peered out from the captain's window at the crowds of men gathering outside, some wearing armour, others carrying pitchforks and billhooks. 'There must be more than a thousand. We can't take on York's army but we've enough to send a message to his Parliament in London that Wales supports the true king.'

'Do you plan to go after Lord Herbert in South Wales?'

'I could march these men to Pembroke but the castle there will never be taken by siege.' He shook his head. 'I personally made sure of it. No, Captain, we will go instead to Denbigh. I took the garrison there before with my father, and with God's grace we shall do it again.'

They set out at first light under an overcast sky, Gabriel riding at Jasper's side at the head of a hundred mounted soldiers, with over a thousand marching behind to the beat of drums. Behind them followed wagons loaded with supplies, and an itinerant blacksmith, his tools clanging as his cart negotiated the rough track. Jasper had spent the last of his money on supplies for this Welsh army, so there would be no going back.

Gabriel looked ahead at the mist covered mountains in their path. 'How far is it to Denbigh, my lord?'

'Some fifty miles, if we follow the drovers' trail through the hills, but we need to stay on the roads and visit as many villages as we can.' Jasper turned to look at the line of horses and men, extending behind them for as far as he could see. 'Captain ap Einion warned me North Wales has its share of York's spies and informers, so there's little chance of us being able to take the garrison at Denbigh by surprise.'

'We can be sure of a warm welcome then, sir?'

'We can, Gabriel. It's impossible to take so many men across the country without being seen, so instead of trying to hide we will openly recruit as many as we can on the way.'

'You think more men will join us?'

Jasper nodded. 'These hills are where my grandfather fought at the side of Owain Glyndŵr in the last Welsh rebellion and now we follow in his footsteps. He led the attack on Denbigh the year my father was born.' He smiled to himself as he remembered his father's stories. 'I think we can expect many more Welshmen to rally to our cause, Gabriel. They have waited long enough.'

They stopped overnight at a deserted farm, where it seemed the occupants had fled at their approach. Although they found a spacious barn and several outbuildings, many of the men slept under the stars. Fortunately it was a mild night and the cook from Harlech Castle, who'd volunteered to march with them, supervised the rations. In no time he was preparing vast cauldrons of hot stew and roasting a fine bullock and several pigs that the men captured and slaughtered.

Jasper hadn't forgotten how the Scots made themselves unpopular with the local people through their looting and pillaging in Northumberland, but this was different. Most of his men were local, turning out to defend their lands and what they believed in. As if to prove him right, nearly two thousand men followed Jasper into Denbigh, a town which supported York for the past five years.

The townspeople hid behind bolted doors and shuttered windows, frightened by exaggerated tales of the new Lancastrian army. The sight of the castle brought back memories for Jasper of the last time he was there. His father thought him reckless and did his best to stop him storming the postern gate, which could have been a death trap for him and his men. He was younger then, and perhaps his father was right, his actions had been a little reckless.

Now he preferred to at least try to achieve a negotiated surrender, if it meant no more of his men would die for their cause. He established his command post in a house on the edge of the town and wrote a letter, offering a full pardon in the name of King Henry for any men who surrendered. He sealed the letter and entrusted it to one of his commanders, who delivered it to the castle gatehouse under a flag of truce.

Their reply was defiant and Jasper cursed, his face grave. 'It seems the garrison learned of our approach and are well provisioned for a siege.'

'There's no time to wait and starve them out, sir?'

'Every day we delay allows York's army to draw closer.' He shook his head at the scrawled letter of reply from the garrison commander. 'They play for time. I expect they can see we have no artillery or the great siege engines Roger Puleston used to such good effect the last time we stormed the castle.'

'We could build scaling-ladders, sir?' Gabriel was undeterred. 'An attack in the small hours of the morning could catch them unawares?'

'The walls are too high.' Jasper considered the idea for a moment and dismissed it as too great a risk for his men. 'You remember the siege in Bamburgh—would they have stood any chance of breaching our defences with ladders? I'm certain they're watching us, trying to guess our next move, and will be ready, even in the small hours.'

'What can we do then, sir? We can't send all these men back home.'

'People thought the House of Lancaster was dead and buried, and I can understand why. You saw William Herbert's camp. They hardly bothered guarding it.'

'They will now, my lord, we taught them a hard lesson?'

'Exactly, and you've seen how many men followed us since. More than we can properly feed and arm, Gabriel, and that could be just the start.'

'What do you have in mind, sir?'

'The men holding the castle don't take us seriously. They know they only have to wait and York's army will be here soon enough. I don't like it, but we must burn the town.'

'What about the people, sir?'

'We'll give them until nightfall to leave. Send your men door to door, and make sure they understand, Gabriel. I don't wish innocent lives on my conscience.'

'I don't think the men will like it, sir.'

'We have no choice, Gabriel. If we march back to Harlech no one will ever take us seriously. I want to force William Herbert to show his face, and this is the only way to do it.' His voice was firm now.

Gabriel left without a further word, leaving Jasper wondering if he was right. They arrived at Harlech without a proper plan, other than to harass the Yorkists where they could. Their early success was partly down to luck, rather than the result of a planned campaign. He remembered telling Gabriel once that you make your own luck, and he still believed that to be true. Only those who rolled the dice could ever hope to win.

These were violent, dangerous times. If he wanted Edward of York's attention, he knew what he needed to do. He wrote a second letter, addressed to William Herbert as Constable of Denbigh Castle, giving the garrison until sunset to surrender, or the town would be burned to the ground. Jasper watched as his messenger left to deliver it, and prayed he had done the right thing.

Bright orange flames lit up the sky for many miles. As soon as the sun dropped below the horizon, his men followed Jasper's orders, after allowing the residents of Denbigh to salvage what they could. Many of the houses were old and built so closely together the burning embers drifted easily across the narrow streets, starting new fires where they fell.

As Gabriel predicted, some of their soldiers deserted, rather than take part in the burning, but most understood the reason for their orders and did their work with ruthless efficiency. Any food and drink they found was loaded onto wagons to feed Jasper's new Welsh army. He could have stopped the looting, but the people of Denbigh supported York, so these were the spoils of war.

Small children cried and women screamed as they watched their homes destroyed by the fires. Old men bravely cursed King Henry and all who stood for him. Some even tried to fight Jasper's soldiers, but before long the firestorm took on a life of its own, burning out of control. They all retreated from the blazing inferno that had once been the thriving, Yorkist town of Denbigh.

## 12

### JULY 1468

The elderly wool-merchant seemed sure of his facts, yet Jasper questioned him again, as lives could depend on what he decided to do next. He had mixed feelings as they marched from the burning town, laden with booty in the name of King Henry. It was not what the king would ever wish to be done in his name, for families to be evicted from their homes to watch their town raved by the fires.

Keen to win back the good will of the people of North Wales, he prevented his men from looting any more villages and set up court in the name of the true king in the town of Flint, where they had a cautious welcome from the inhabitants. More men deserted, yet more still arrived to volunteer for the true king, and he kept them busy practising their drills under newly appointed commanders.

Now this man had sought him out to warn of the approach of Lord Herbert's army, sent by York to end the Lancastrian revolt. It was what Jasper always wanted, to face his old enemy on equal terms in Wales and have the chance to bring him to account. The problem was he must rely on the word of the man in front of him—a wool- merchant he had never met, who could be a Yorkist agent.

The merchant wore a pleated tunic and leather boots of good quality, yet lank grey hair showed under his faded felt cap and his darting eyes put Jasper on guard. It would be easy enough for William Herbert to buy the loyalty of such a man and have him lead them into a trap. All the same, the man spoke earnestly and deserved to be heard.

'Tell me, how many men does Lord Herbert have?' Jasper tried to keep his tone conciliatory but there was an urgency to be certain of the truth.

'Lord Herbert has commissions of array from Parliament, sir, to raise an army in the Welsh Marches. They say he has eight or nine thousand foot soldiers, as well as his cavalry and artillery men.'

'Where did you see them, how long ago?'

'I've not seen them with my own eyes, sir, but I heard from my cousin that Lord Herbert has orders to take Harlech and is already on his way to punish those disloyal to York.'

'Are you sure he heads for Harlech Castle, not to Denbigh?'

'I am, sir.' The wool-merchant eyed Jasper uncertainly. 'I heard his brother, Sir Richard Herbert, is riding north with a division of their army, while Lord Herbert rides from the south.'

Again, Jasper wondered if the answer had been too quick, too well rehearsed, too good to be true. He would be able to surprise one half of Herbert's army as they made their way through the mountains, then reach Harlech in time to prevent its capture. He must send a rider to warn Captain ap Einion, as true or not, the garrison at Harlech needed time to prepare.

Sir Richard Herbert, William Herbert's arrogant younger brother, was one of the men who arrested his father at Mortimer's Cross. If Sir Richard had chosen to speak up for him on that fateful day his father might still be alive, yet he had not, and would pay the price for that failure. Jasper felt his anger rising again at the painful memories rekindled in his heart.

He studied the man who brought such important news. He claimed to be a loyal supporter of King Henry, wishing to play his part in ending what he called the decadent Yorkist rule. If he was William Herbert's spy, he was a brave one, and a convincing liar. Jasper wanted to believe him and allowed himself a moment of reflection. If he was successful, this would be the greatest victory for the House of Lancaster ever seen in Wales.

'You will ride with us. If what you've told me is true, you will be well rewarded for your loyalty to the true king.' He scowled as another possibility occurred to him. 'If your words lead us into a trap—'

'I swear, my lord,' the man's face revealed his concern to be believed, 'it is the truth.'

A skylark warbled its tuneful song overhead as Jasper's men took the narrow track through the long valley, carved from the bedrock over countless centuries by the River Conwy. He looked up into the clear blue sky to see what was making such a noise. Like him, it could be dismissed by some as insignificant, of no consequence, yet the small brown bird caught his attention. Now he hoped to win the attention of the people of Wales, if not all England and particularly those in Westminster.

The path they followed took them through the wooded valley towards the foothills and mountains. Much of the countryside they passed through was wooded, with ancient groves of twisted oaks, although the higher ground ahead had been cleared for grazing sheep. The ever-narrowing river ran to their right, with the mountains dominating the skyline to the west. This was where they hoped to intercept Sir Richard

Herbert's army, and prevent them ever reaching the coast and Harlech Castle.

Gabriel seemed unusually quiet, his eyes restlessly scanning the hills and checking on the men following behind. Jasper understood the reason for Gabriel's sullen mood. He never voiced his disapproval yet left Jasper in no doubt he opposed their ruination of Denbigh. Jasper's wish to send a message to those hiding behind the safety of the towering castle walls was too effective, leaving barely a single home untouched, yet he would do it again, if necessary.

'We should send scouts ahead, sir.'

Jasper turned in his saddle. 'You're right, Gabriel. I will not be ambushed a second time.'

'I'll take the skirmishers?'

'Take care. I want you back as soon as you sight the enemy.'

Gabriel nodded and turned back to find his men, leaving Jasper to ride alone and reflect on recent events. Despite his attempts at peace in Flint he had played into York's hands as a dangerous rebel, commanding men who terrorised communities and needed to be stopped at all costs. At least now his men would face a worthy opponent on equal terms.

For the first time in months he thought of Lady Margaret Beaufort and wondered what she would say if she knew her son was being taken into battle. The wool-merchant told him young Henry Tudor rode with Lord Herbert for Harlech. It made no sense to Jasper, except as a deterrent. Perhaps Herbert hoped they would hesitate to attack and risk harming the boy. Henry would be about ten years old now and may not even remember his uncle. With a jolt, Jasper realised that he might not recognise his nephew, so many years had passed.

They marched for half a day before Gabriel returned, flanked by two mounted Irishmen.

'The enemy is coming, sir. We don't have much time.'

'Did you see how many?'

'It's hard to be sure, sir, but my guess is they have nearly twice our number.' He sounded breathless.

'They are headed this way?' It was not what Jasper expected. The wool-merchant was certain they would cross the mountains to attack Harlech from the north.

'They are riding west, sir, towards the hills.'

Jasper studied the land around him. The rising hills offered little cover other than the thick, waist-high bracken and a few trees. The closest ridge was some distance above them, too high and far away to be of any use. There would be no chance of taking the enemy by surprise, but at least they knew the wool-merchant spoke the truth.

'We need the men to spread out, form as wide a front as they can.' He glanced back down the trail. 'The French and Breton riders should hold the centre, with the local men behind them. We will take the left flank, Gabriel, with crossbowmen and archers.'

They were barely in place and starting their advance when a dark line of marching men appeared on the skyline. Gabriel was right, it was difficult to assess their strength but the line stretched as far as he could see. Jasper pushed the nagging doubt at the sight of them to the back of his mind and turned to face his men.

He drew his sword and raised it in the air. 'For King Henry, for Lancaster, and for Wales!'

His men surged forward, eager for a fight. His archers had trained since Denbigh and were competent, if not well disci-plined. He led them up the sloping bank and called for them to ready their yew bows. Each man took an arrow from the quivers they carried. The crossbowmen fitted bolts and cocked their weapons, ready for Jasper's command.

The ground vibrated under his feet as Sir Richard Herbert's cavalry charged, swords drawn and lances at the ready, closing the gap between them in a moment. Jasper felt the cold shock of fear as he saw the numbers of them, filling the road far into the distance. If this was only half Lord Herbert's army, they would not stand a chance.

'Choose your targets and fire at will!' He yelled to his archers.

They had been waiting for his order and their arrows loosed into the sky like a hailstorm of death on a silently curving arc. Some fell short but others struck home, toppling riders, who fell under the hooves of those following. Still they came, not even slowing their pace as a crossbow bolt hit one and he fell from his horse, sending it into a panic.

'Keep firing, men!' He encouraged his archers, already running out of arrows.

Jasper glanced down the gentle slope into the track where the mercenaries were already being driven back by Herbert's cavalry. One of the men called out something in French then turned his horse down the bank towards the river. Jasper couldn't understand why, and watched as the rider galloped back the way they had come. Another followed close behind, then another, leaving the foot soldiers unprotected. In an instant the solid wall of men became a scramble as they struggled to run out of the path of the charging horses.

'Stand firm!'

Jasper yelled as the first wave of horses clashed with the men who had obeyed him. Carried forward by the momentum of the charge, the riders slashed down with swords on heads and shoulders with savage force. One was pulled to the ground but his horse continued, galloping over the bodies littering the road like abandoned scarecrows.

He charged back down the slope and swung his sword at the closest enemy rider, who parried the blow and fought back, his blade striking Jasper's helmet with a dizzying clang. Jasper thrust forward, inflicting a mortal wound. The man fell from his horse, only to be replaced by more riders, one swinging a poleaxe that smashed Jasper's sword from his grip, sending a sharp pain up his arm as at least one of his fingers broke with the savage force of the blow.

Without his sword there was little he could do but ride back up the slope to where his archers had run out of arrows and waited with their daggers drawn. They looked to him for leadership but he had no idea what they could do. Gabriel spoke the words already echoing in Jasper's head.

'We are lost, sir. We must escape while we can.' He turned his horse and stared at the battle below them, then turned to Jasper. 'We have no choice,' he cursed, 'they outnumber us—our men are deserting.'

Jasper could see for himself. His broken fingers throbbed and although it grieved him to agree they would have to leave his men to fend for themselves, either to surrender or to run, as he would have to now. His men could expect mercy from Sir Richard but there would be no merciful reprieve for himself if he was caught. Sadness gripped his heart as he looked into the faces of the remaining men around him. Foot soldiers, they would never be able to keep up with him and Gabriel.

'You fought well, but it's time to lay down your weapons and make your way back to your homes as best you can.'

Their fight was over. With one last glance at the one-sided battle still raging on the road below, Jasper rode up and over the ridge, followed by Gabriel. He cursed at how he had failed in battle yet again and forced to abandon the last of his Irish skirmishers who'd followed him so loyally.

Jasper woke with a start and sat up, his heart thumping in his chest. He had been dreaming again of being forced to kneel at the executioner's block, a dream he'd had many times, each more real than the last. This time it was Richard Herbert who wielded the axe, shouting at him, calling him a traitor and coward for running off again and leaving his men to suffer their fate.

After escaping the battle they had not stopped or looked back once, riding hard through the night until they reached the North Wales coast. Claiming they were Irish sailors looking for a ship home, Gabriel sold their horses to pay for food and lodgings at a tavern close to the Flintshire harbour of Mostyn, on the estuary of the River Dee.

Jasper bound his two broken fingers together with a cotton bandage, torn from his shirt. He'd lost his sword in the battle but was otherwise unharmed. Still shocked by their traumatic, crushing defeat, Jasper felt deep regret at his decision to take on Herbert's army. He thanked God they managed to escape, but the thought of the good men who died for their cause troubled him deeply.

He crossed to the small window of the room they shared and stared out. The tide was on its way in and an early sunrise shimmered across the estuary, an impossibly tranquil scene after the horrors of their recent battle. He pulled on his boots and left Gabriel sleeping while he strolled to the water's edge where cormorants stretched their wings like black ghosts. Some might see them as a bad omen but Jasper scorned such superstition.

Instead he scanned the fishing boats moored in the shallow bay, looking for one capable of the long voyage around the coast back to Barmouth, where he prayed their ships would still be waiting. They had no choice but to take a low price for their horses and their remaining money was dwindling fast, so now they must work their passage or take their chances in a less seaworthy boat.

The problem was that all the boats stayed in the estuary, so they would have to risk moving on to Conwy, some thirty miles to the west, despite the danger of being spotted by Yorkist sympathisers. Jasper guessed Herbert's men would have already discovered he wasn't among the dead or captured, and by now would have offered a generous reward for his capture.

He examined his right hand with its already discoloured bandage and saw the sun glint on the ring on his little finger. A gift from King Henry when he was a boy, the solid gold ring once belonged to their mother. In his youth his fingers were as slender as hers, but as he grew he had moved it to his smallest finger, where it remained, even when he was arrested after the surrender of Bamburgh.

Now he pulled it off and studied it closely for the first time in years. Any jeweller could tell it was made from fine gold, perhaps even enough to pay for a boat, if not a ship. He returned to their lodgings with new purpose. The ring was the only thing of value he now possessed, and all he owned to remind him of his mother, but with luck it could change his future.

The old sailboat was small, its lateen sail torn and inexpertly patched, and the price too high, yet Jasper felt his black mood lift for the first time as they cast off into the seaweed littered estuary of the River Dee and headed west along the Welsh coast. His mother's ring paid for a cured ham, two flagons of ale and a loaf of bread, as well as their elderly craft. There was no money for a crew, although they had all made plenty of sea crossings, often in challenging conditions.

'How hard can it be?' Gabriel asked, as he took the helm

and chose a course that took them far enough from the rocky coast but not out of sight of the shore.

'You shall have your answer soon enough.' Jasper pulled on the halyard to improve the set of the sail and tied it off securely. 'At least the weather seems in our favour.'

'How long do you think it will take us?'

'Barmouth is only seventy miles as the crow flies but much further by sea.' He scanned the huge expanse of ocean ahead of them. 'We need to go through the Menai Strait and around Llŷn Peninsula before we might have sight of our ships.'

'Do you think they will have waited for us?' Gabriel frowned. 'It seems a long time has passed since we left them, and I can't see this little boat making it across the Irish Sea if they're not there.'

'Have faith, Gabriel, with God's grace our ships will be there.'


The weather changed for the worse as they sailed around the limestone Great Orme headland into a headwind that whipped the waves into foaming crests. Gabriel battled to keep them on course while Jasper watched the sail. A wave crashed over the bows, swamping them both and sluicing across the deck, soaking their supplies and washing a keg of ale overboard. Gabriel swore as it vanished.

'Can you swim?'

'Like a fish, sir.' Gabriel laughed as another wave hit them hard, almost stopping the little boat. 'I'm from Waterford, remember?' He looked wistful. 'As a boy I spent as much time in the water as out of it.'

'I never learned to swim,' Jasper admitted, 'and now I wish I had.'

Each new wave seemed to take longer to drain from the deck, flooded to the depth of their ankles. As a precaution he took a length of mooring rope and fastened it around his middle, tying the other end tightly around the mast.

'You must be quick with your knife if this tub goes down, sir.' Gabriel seemed to be enjoying the challenge of helming through such rough waters.

At last the shape of Ynys Mon appeared on the horizon. More by luck than skill they had sailed the length of the coast of North Wales without capsizing their old boat. Exhausted and soaked to the skin, they gladly found a sheltered bay in the lee of the island and headed inshore to take a well-earned rest and recover their strength.


Jasper woke to the raucous calling of seagulls overhead and felt the boat rocking gently in the swell. His hair and clothes felt damp and stiff with salt and there was no sign of Gabriel. Looking over the side he saw their boat was still anchored and afloat in less than a foot of water. He heard splashing and looked across to the beach to see Gabriel wading back, his boots tied around his shoulders, carrying a muslin sack.

'Permission to come aboard, sir?'

'I knew you'd jump ship as soon as you had the chance.' Jasper helped him clamber back and watched as he produced a freshly baked loaf from the bag, two apples and a round of cheese.

'There's a farm a short way from the beach, so I've spent the last of our money.'

'We must go before they tell anyone they've seen you. Beaumaris Castle is close by and could be full of York's soldiers. My father lived here once. He used to say news travels faster on this little island than a cutpurse on market day.'

Gabriel heaved their anchor from the sea while Jasper raised the tattered sail to the top of the mast. There was little enough breeze but he was relieved to see they drifted with the current towards the fast-flowing waters of the Menai Strait. Jasper studied the troubled water ahead and recalled his father telling him how he saw several shipwrecks during his time at Beaumaris.

He tore a chunk of bread from the loaf, then cut the thick rind from the cheese with his dagger. It tasted good and was the first thing he'd eaten other than ham since they set out from Mostyn, as their other loaf had been ruined by seawater. He cut another slice and handed it to Gabriel on the tiller.

'We need to watch out for dangerous shoals and rocks, and strange tides from the Irish Sea.'

'I will keep a look out,' Gabriel nodded as he ate, 'but it's too late to turn back now, sir.'

Jasper pulled the bung from their one remaining cask of ale and drank deeply, then took a turn at the helm so Gabriel could drink. The sun burst over the high mountains to their left, reminding him of even greater dangers on the land. He imagined Lord Herbert would have reached Harlech by now, and said a prayer for the men there. Fewer than fifty remained to defend the castle, and although the massive stone walls would withstand even the most modern artillery, the men inside must fear for their lives. His reverie was interrupted by a shout from Gabriel.

'Rocks,' he pointed, 'over there, sticking out of the water!'

Jasper leaned on the tiller and their boat lurched to star-board. The black, seaweed-covered rocks were directly in their path, emerging from the shallow waters like dragons teeth with each new wave. He braced himself as they scraped down the side with an ominous scraping as they gouged their old wooden hull.

Too late, he realised they should have waited for the ebb tide, as the current rushed through the narrow strait in a flood, creating eddies and emerald green whirlpools. Although there was still only a light breeze to fill the sail they were racing along and he strained on the tiller to keep them out of the shallows.

The boat shuddered as he failed and the keel scraped hard as they ran aground then lifted again with the next three-foot wave, surging against the stern and thrusting them into the deeper channel. Gabriel grabbed their last keg, which was about to be washed away, and toppled backwards with a yell over the low gunwale, swiftly carried off in the fast-flowing current. Jasper saw the Irishman's head disappear under the waves, then bob up again some distance away, spluttering and cursing but still holding onto the wooden cask as if his life depended on it.

'I'm coming for you!' Jasper tried to turn the boat but another wave hit and he lost sight of Gabriel.

He scanned the churning water and spotted Gabriel's head as he tried to swim towards the boat. Jasper threw the anchor over the side and took the coiled mooring rope. Although the distance between them was closing he saw Gabriel was tiring.

Keeping a firm grip on one end, he flung the rope as far as he could. It fell well short but Gabriel saw it and made a last determined effort to reach the end before it sank below the waves. Jasper felt the rope go taut and it nearly pulled through his hands as he took the strain. He managed to take a turn of rope around his good hand and then used the thick wooden mast to take the weight as Gabriel struggled to pull himself closer.

At last a hand gripped the rail and Gabriel pulled himself aboard, needing every ounce of his strength, and collapsed exhausted on the deck, soaked through. Jasper helped him sit upright.

'I thought you were lost.'

Gabriel grinned. 'Not this time, but we've lost our ale.' Although he tried to sound cheerful, he was lucky to be alive.

Jasper pulled up the anchor and took the helm again,

trying his best to follow the darker water of the deep channel. His arm ached where he'd strained it saving Gabriel but it was a small price to pay, when men had given their lives. He couldn't help asking himself if it had all been worth it. He had turned the people of Denbigh against the true king and left the last Lancastrian Castle in Wales dangerously vulnerable.

They sailed through the Menai Strait in little more than an hour but light winds meant it was well past noon before they rounded the jutting promontory of the Llŷn Peninsula. They both scanned the horizon for any sign of their ships and Jasper felt a deep foreboding. If their ships were gone, they faced an impossible choice between landfall on the Welsh coast, right under the nose of Lord Herbert's army or risking the crossing to Ireland, which would be perilous in their small sailboat.

'Our ships, sir.' Gabriel pointed, his voice filled with relief.

Jasper looked out to sea and recognised the ships that brought them to Wales. They had waited, and he mumbled a prayer of thanks to God as he steered a course towards them. His mission might have been a failure but he had learned some hard lessons he would never forget.

## 13

## SEPTEMBER 1468

J asper returned from his long and dangerous sea voyage to discover accounts of his exploits in Wales had preceded him, with more than a little elaboration. As the leader of their only active resistance, however futile, he had become the talk of the exiled Lancastrian court. The queen even unsuccessfully petitioned King Louis to send him money. Troubled by the misrepresentations of his adventures, he wished the queen to understand York's hold on the country was so entrenched it would take more than recruiting more men.

Queen Margaret's court had become the last refuge for Lancastrian nobles escaping the hazards of life under York's regime, and each new arrival fed the court's insatiable appetite for news. Jasper was intrigued to be invited to a meeting with the latest refugee from England, none other than Sir Henry Holland, Duke of Exeter, who wished to reveal matters of the greatest importance for their cause.

Although Holland helped him escape to Ireland, Jasper had found it troubling that he was married to Edward of York's eldest sister. Such doubts were all forgotten now as, like Jasper,

Henry Holland had been attainted by York as a traitor, his lands all confiscated for his disloyal wife. He wore a gold Lancastrian chain around his neck and pheasant's tail feathers in his cap, which he removed with a flamboyant gesture as he bowed before the queen. Holland seemed less arrogant than Jasper remembered although there was still the glint of ambition in his eye as he addressed them both.

'I regret to report, Your Highness, King Henry has been captured by York's men and is again held prisoner in the Tower of London.' The duke seemed disappointed at the queen's reaction. 'It was not unexpected?'

Queen Margaret shook her head. 'Do you know if the king is treated well?' The coldness in her voice raised the hairs on Jasper's neck.

Holland seemed not to notice. 'I understand he is content enough with his prayer books and devotions, Your Highness. I've not seen him, although I understand he has been allowed a priest for company.'

He glanced at Jasper. 'Warwick made him ride to London wearing a straw hat, his legs tied to the stirrups, but his foolishness earned him the anger of the people.' Henry Holland smiled. 'King Henry still has more support from the people than I dared to hope.'

'Warwick will pay for his insolence.' The queen spoke in French, the anger in her voice causing Sir Henry to raise an eyebrow.

'If the rumours I hear are true, Your Highness, York has already begun to curb the power of the Nevilles.'

'I've heard the rumours.' The queen sounded dismissive. 'People tell me Warwick was insulted over the secret marriage of York to the Woodville woman.' She shook her head, dismissing the idea. 'I suspect he is more concerned about the appointments of her family members because it erodes his power in England.'

Jasper recalled his last meeting with Warwick, and his close escape at the hands of his younger brother, Sir John Neville. 'I wonder, Your Highness, if this cannot be turned to our advantage?'

The queen nodded. 'King Louis meets regularly with Warwick, which would surely make York uncomfortable?' She put her hand on Jasper's arm. 'It is time for you to see what can be made of Warwick's disloyalty.'

'What did you have in mind, Your Highness?'

'Warwick is a hothead, a vengeful man. They say he made Edward king. If anyone will unmake him, it's the Earl of Warwick, and if anyone can outwit Warwick, it's my cousin, King Louis.'

'I shall leave tomorrow, my lady, and see what can be done.'

Jasper had grown bored of the gossip of the court in exile and welcomed the chance to travel again. This time it would be as the queen's ambassador, rather than as a soldier. As he left the royal apartments to make the arrangements he reflected on the queen's words. It seemed he must welcome an alliance with the man who mocked King Henry so publicly.

He declined Henry Holland's offer to accompany him, suggesting instead that Sir Henry should spend time at the court of his distant cousin, Charles, made Duke of Burgundy following the death of his father. Although Charles had recently married Edward's sister Margaret of York, he claimed to favour neither side, and Sir Henry's task was to make sure this was how it stayed.

For his part Jasper planned to recall his Valois inheritance with King Louis. The King of France had a reputation for mischief making yet also loved nothing better than to outwit his enemies, a game Jasper now knew was far better than risking the lives of two thousand men.

Henry Holland also told him privately that Harlech Castle

was lost, the rebel leaders dragged to London in chains and executed. It had not ended there, for Lord Herbert took his revenge for what happened at Denbigh by burning towns and villages across the north of Wales that supported the Lancastrian cause. The word was that some might never recover and William Herbert now ruled Wales unopposed.

Château d'Amboise, the favourite country residence of King Louis, in the wooded valley of the Loire, had once been a great palace. Now neglected, the gardens were an overgrown wilderness, with weeds and young self-seeded trees growing through the marbled paving. Many of the rooms were locked and barred, their furniture covered with linen sheets and the windows barred and shuttered.

Jasper waited for several days and still saw no sign of the king, although after frequent enquiries Queen Charlotte eventually agreed to an audience. Curious to meet the French queen, after hearing so many conflicting accounts, he hoped to learn when she expected the king to return.

Surrounded by her coterie of noble ladies, Queen Charlotte was half the age of her husband. Although Henry Holland told him she was unlikely to excite a man, Jasper was struck by how she radiated the special beauty shared by women close to giving birth. The queen's shimmering blue satin gown drew attention to her swollen middle and her fashionably tall pointed hat was draped with gossamer so light it floated in the air as she moved. She spoke in French and smiled as she stroked a small lap-dog.

'Sir Jasper Tudor. We are honoured to welcome you to our court.'

Jasper removed his cap and bowed. 'Thank you, Your Highness. I am grateful for your kind hospitality.'

The queen regarded him with expressive pale blue eyes, as if not certain if he was joking. 'The king is hunting,' she looked out of the high, arched window to the castle grounds, towards the distant wooded hills, 'sometimes he goes hunting for days, forgetting me and his duties.' There was a hint of humour in her soft voice.

'I've learned to be patient, Your Highness, particularly with regard to the king.'

She laughed and gestured for Jasper to be seated. 'As have we all.' She fed her dog a morsel of food from a silver dish. 'You are not married, Sir Jasper?'

Jasper smiled at her unexpected question. 'I shall find a bride one day, Your Highness, once my lands are restored.' He noticed her glance at her ladies-in-waiting and suspected they might have been discussing him.

'I was only one year old when I was betrothed to Frederick of Saxony,' she smiled absent-mindedly at the thought, 'I never married him. It was my destiny, you see, to become Queen of France, and I was nine when I married Louis. He was the dauphin then, but I always knew he would be king.'

'*Amor fati*. Sometimes we must be guided by our destiny, Your Highness.'

'Whatever happens to you has been waiting to happen since the beginning of time.' She seemed to be addressing her little dog rather than Jasper.

He recalled the quotation. 'Twining strands of fate weave together our existence and the things that happen to us.' He had heard Queen Charlotte owned one of the finest libraries in France, yet her knowledge of Marcus Aurelius impressed him.

Her eyes met his and a rare connection flashed between them, unnoticed by her watching ladies, the bond of kindred spirits.

Queen Charlotte continued as if nothing had happened. 'And you, Sir Jasper. What is your destiny?'

Again her question surprised him. 'My mother was Queen Catherine of Valois, so it may be destiny that brought me here to know more of my family in France.'

'King Louis has need of men like you, Sir Jasper.' She picked up her little dog and seemed to be addressing it. 'He despairs of his self-serving advisors, who tell him what they think he wants to hear.' He saw an unexpected pleading in her eyes. 'You would also be doing a great service to me if you help him find an agreement with Duke Charles. I am sure he will be most appreciative to have you at his side.'

'I am honoured to serve the king, my lady.'

She let her lap-dog jump to the floor. It ran up to Jasper and he went down on one knee to stroke it. The little dog seemed to like it and looked up at him with bright eyes, then gave him a friendly lick, wagging its tail.

'I can see you are a good man, Sir Jasper. You are most welcome in our household.'

'Thank you, Your Highness.'


King Louis' soiled hunting clothes meant he could easily be mistaken for a farm worker were it not for his ebullient presence the moment he entered the room.

'Tudor.' He embraced Jasper. 'You find me in good spirits, and I hear you have been entertaining my wife?'

'Queen Charlotte has been a perfect hostess, Your Highness.'

'You seem to have made a good impression on her.' There was no hint of disapproval in his voice. King Louis clapped his hands to summon servants. 'Bring wine—no, bring us ale.' he grinned at Jasper. 'You are a soldier, you prefer a jug of ale?'

'I would, Your Highness.'

'Take a seat, we have much to discuss. How is my cousin, Queen Margaret?'

'She is well, with the grace of God, and sends her warmest regards.'

A boy brought ale and pewter tankards and they waited while he filled and offered one to the king, then the other to Jasper.

King Louis drained nearly half his tankard and held it out for his servant to refill.

'I heard King Henry is imprisoned in London. Is it true?'

'He is, Your Highness.' Jasper nodded. 'I fear for his health and pray for him every day.'

'We must see what can be done, Tudor. I will speak to the Earl of Warwick when I see him next.'

'My understanding, Your Highness, is that Warwick's men captured King Henry and placed him in the Tower of London.'

'Let me tell you something of the Earl of Warwick, Tudor. He looks at Queen Charlotte and sees a brood mare, nothing more.' King Louis took another drink and gave a satisfied belch. 'He looks at Edward of York, tall and handsome, and thinks he makes a good king.' He stabbed a finger at his own chest. 'I am not tall, and have never been described as handsome, and I know the Earl of Warwick takes me for a fool because of it. You are different, Tudor. You are family, and I can count on your loyalty?'

'Indeed you can, Your Highness.' Jasper judged the moment to be right. 'I wish to spend time in your service, if you will allow me?'

'Of course.' He gave Jasper a knowing look. 'Between us, we will be more than a match for the Duke of Burgundy, and then we will deal with England.' He cursed in French. 'Edward of York thinks he can deceive me?' His voice was raised.

Jasper took another drink of ale. He'd not forgotten how Queen Margaret tried to deceive King Louis with her promise of Calais. 'Warwick is his weakness, Your Highness.'

King Louis narrowed his eyes. 'And the Earl of Warwick knows where York is at his weakest.'

'You think Warwick would turn against York?'

'He has as good as told me so, Tudor.'

'Let us first find a settlement with Duke Charles of Burgundy, Your Highness, then perhaps we shall put Warwick's ambition to the test.'


Late that night Jasper lay awake, recalling the words of Queen Charlotte. She thought it odd he was unmarried, as well she might. In another life he could have married Lady Eleanor Beaufort. She had been a perfect match, from one of the best families, charming, clever and beautiful, yet destiny intervened. He had been obliged to care for Eleanor's cousin, his brother's widow, although he would never have married Lady Margaret as, in truth, he always thought of her like a sister.

He thought again of Máiréad, who could have been at his side, if not for his selfishness. He had wanted her with him, even when it put her life in peril. He had truly loved her and still felt the pain of grief when he thought of her. He consoled himself with the thought that somewhere there was the woman he was destined to marry, who would combine the best qualities of them all.

He felt a new conviction that it was his destiny to play a part in brokering peace between France and Burgundy, and then, God willing, to reconcile the Houses of Lancaster and York. He had faced death many times, yet God chose to spare him for some purpose and he could think of none more worthy.

The Wheel of Fortune had turned again, and now he found allies in the most unexpected places. He wondered if he could ever find it within himself to forgive Edward of York, yet unless he did so there could never be lasting peace. It was beginning to look as if Sir Richard Neville, Earl of Warwick could be the key.

~

Despite all the protracted arrangements, the meeting with Duke Charles of Burgundy at Péronne did not have the best start. King Louis summoned Jasper to the rooms provided for him in a fine merchant's house in the town. To Jasper they seemed grander than the king's own summer residence, yet the king insisted on staying at the old castle.

King Louis led him to the window and pointed an accusing finger. 'There, you see?'

Jasper saw the castle, high on a hill overlooking the River Somme. The flags of France and Burgundy flew from its towers, in honour of the meeting, but even from a distance he saw tiles missing from the roof and piles of rubble where stone had fallen from the battlements.

'I made enquiries, Your Highness. It seems the castle is in a poor state of repair and is used as barracks for the duke's soldiers and a prison, which is why we've been accommodated here.'

'This is how Duke Charles plans to demean us, Tudor.' He gave Jasper a look of sudden suspicion. 'He treats us like merchants.'

Jasper saw little point in disagreeing with the king. 'I will explain to the duke's staff, Your Highness. It should be simple enough to resolve, as long as you have no objections to less comfortable surroundings.'

King Louis continued to stare out of the window. 'I know you think me petty, Tudor, but you must learn that such things matter.' He looked at Jasper. 'We all carry the burden of those who have gone before us. Your father was a servant, yet he was strong willed and married Queen Catherine of Valois. My father was a king yet he was weak. His men murdered the Duke of Burgundy, who trusted to meet him without armed escort. To this day they tar me with the same brush.'

Jasper left to make the arrangements, reflecting on the king's words. It had not occurred to him they could be in danger. Their escort of some eighty archers were camped on the outskirts of Péronne, and of little use if the king was attacked by Burgundian guards, who seemed to be in every doorway. It seemed unthinkable, as the king hinted, that one could be a paid assassin. Duke Charles would express his regret but Jasper could find himself caught up in a conspiracy.

Although he would prefer to remain in the comfortable merchant's house, he arranged a room adjacent to King Louis in the castle. Damp and draughty, little effort had been made to improve his accommodation. The furniture was a wooden cot with an uncomfortable straw filled mattress and a single, worm-eaten chair. He woke after the first night in Péronne Castle with the red bites of bedbugs on his skin, yet thought it a small price to pay for his proximity to the king, who could be heard snoring loudly.

As the negotiations progressed, Jasper took on the part of observer and intermediary, carrying messages between King Louis and Duke Charles. The duke refused to forsake other alliances and pledge support to a united France. He also added limitations that would make any agreement worthless. It seemed as if their position was weakening when the meeting was interrupted by a messenger with important news for the duke.

Duke Charles gave the king a cold, hard gaze. 'I regret, Your Highness, to inform you that the people of Liége are rioting. They have murdered the bishop and their governor, my representative.'

'I'm sorry to hear this, Duke Charles,' King Louis seemed unperturbed, 'although I fail to see why it merits interrupting our discussions?'

'Quite the contrary.' Duke Charles stood. 'It is said the instigator of this treachery was none other than yourself. I must therefore insist that you remain in your rooms here at the castle until the truth of the matter has been uncovered.'

'You are holding me prisoner?' King Louis slumped in his chair in disbelief. 'It's an insult!'

Duke Charles remained calm. 'Simply a precaution, Your Highness, for your own protection.'

Jasper detected a veiled threat in the duke's voice and realised the king was right to be concerned. It would be a simple enough matter to contrive a riot in the troubled city of Liége and people would be quick to believe King Louis, with his reputation for intrigue, could be at the root of it. He took on the role of the king's representative in the investigation and soon established that the allegations were false, as there was no evidence of the king's involvement.

This seemed to be of worryingly little concern to Duke Charles, who insisted the peace agreement was compromised, even when the bishop was found to be alive and well, as was the duke's representative. One of the few people allowed to see the king, Jasper found him in a black mood.

'I curse the day I ever thought to trust the Duke of Burgundy.' King Louis paced in his room like a caged beast and waved his fist in the air.

Jasper tried to be conciliatory. 'It seems, Your Highness, it's nothing more than a coincidence that the unrest occurred while we are here in Péronne.'

The king turned on him. 'That may be so, but does it warrant my confinement in this castle for three days?' He sat down heavily and held his head in his hands. 'How well is this place guarded?'

'Are you thinking of trying to leave, Your Highness? The duke has men at every gate, and the men we brought are archers, no use in this situation.' Jasper tried to placate the king. 'We need to take care not to play into the duke's hands. We both know you are innocent of any involvement in the rioting at Liége, yet if you leave it will make it look—'

The king interrupted him, his hands held up in the air. 'So what should I do?'

'I suggest we offer to conclude these discussions and remind the duke he has provided us with safe conduct in Burgundy.'

'Give in to his demands?'

'If we must, Your Highness.'

'It's an outrage!' King Louis began pacing again.

An idea occurred to Jasper. 'You could propose that we all travel to Liége to end the problems there, Your Highness.'

The king brightened. 'At last, Tudor, a sensible suggestion.'


The forty three pages of the peace treaty between Burgundy and France was prepared and sworn over a fragment of the true cross, supposedly once owned by Saint Charlemagne. King Louis agreed to pay a hundred thousand crowns in reparations to the duke and bells rang out across Péronne to celebrate. Watched by Jasper and King Louis, and supported by French troops, the army of Burgundy besieged the city of Liége and largely destroyed it on the pretext of quelling a rebellion.

# 14

## JUNE 1470

Jasper expected their diplomatic failure at Péronne to have consequences, yet King Louis placed none of the blame on his shoulders and granted him a pension of one hundred *livres tournois* a month. Duke Charles retained his allegiance with York, on condition it did not harm the interests of France, yet the peace was a fragile one. King Louis would find some clever way to avenge how he had been treated by the duke.

Their brush with danger was a timely warning and he sent for Gabriel, who had remained in Queen Margaret's household to help recruit and train more men for her personal guard. Gabriel arrived with a letter from the queen that confirmed the rumours which crossed the Channel to Jasper and King Louis at Arcis in Champagne of unrest and intrigue in England.

There were many frustrations of Jasper's long exile, particularly the unreliability of news from England and Wales. Rumours needed to be considered with suspicion, as York could easily spread them to his own advantage. Even the rare messengers, who travelled at great personal risk, could not be trusted to carry entirely accurate accounts. The letter, written in the scholarly hand of the queen's scribe, only added to his questions.

Queen Margaret praised God she and her son Edward were in good health and went on to explain that Edward of York's brother, George, Duke of Clarence, had married Warwick's daughter Isobel, against Edward's orders. Jasper knew little of York's younger brother, although he remembered meeting him once in Westminster and thinking him a drunkard and a gambler. Although he easily saw Warwick's plan, the latest pawn in his game appeared a far from ideal choice of husband.

It also seemed Warwick's simmering discontent with his treatment by York erupted into open rebellion. In an amazing reversal of loyalty he had mustered an army of two thousand men and seized London, holding the city for some weeks before York won the country back. Jasper read the queen's letter twice. Signed only with the letter M and bore her royal seal, it offered no clue about what became of Warwick afterwards.

'Tell me, Gabriel, there must be more. I want you to repeat every detail you've heard, rumour or not.'

'Sir John de Vere, Earl of Oxford, was the latest to arrive from England. He says your enemy Lord William Herbert is dead, sir, captured in a battle near Banbury with Warwick's men and executed in Northampton, along with his brother Richard.'

Jasper's mind filled with urgent questions. He had mixed feelings about the execution of his old adversaries by Warwick but a new concern occurred to him.

'What of my nephew? William Herbert took him to Harlech Castle. I pray he wasn't with the Herberts when they confronted Warwick?' Jasper prepared himself for the worst news. 'Have you heard anything of the fate of Henry?'

'I've not, sir. The queen's court is full of nobles fleeing from York but there's been no mention of young Henry.'

Another question occurred to Jasper as he struggled to see the implications of the news. 'When York regained control, did Warwick escape? Is he dead, or is he in the Tower with King Henry?'

'It's said that York was held in Warwick Castle, yet he persuaded Warwick to free him in return for a full pardon. The duke leads a charmed life, that's for sure.'

'I do wonder, Gabriel, what kind of hold Warwick has over Edward of York. There must be more to all this than we know.'

He cursed his isolation in France at such an important time for England. 'I must know what is going on across the Channel. It's my duty to do what I can for King Henry and my nephew—and I can't rely on rumours and gossip when they could both be in grave danger.'

'I could go, sir? I might learn where Henry is?'

'I would not ask you to, Gabriel. The country is full of York's spies, watching for anyone carrying messages from Queen Margaret. If they caught you—'

'I won't carry any messages, my lord, it would all be safe in here.' He patted his head. 'You've seen how little interest they take in Irish mercenaries?'

'I appreciate your loyalty, Gabriel, perhaps there is a way...' An idea formed in his mind. 'Lady Margaret Beaufort, Henry's mother, will make it her business to know what has become of her son. She might even rescue him from Herbert's household.' Jasper recalled his last memory of Lady Margaret. 'She is a determined woman, and her husband has influence.'

'How would I find her, sir?'

'Lady Margaret is married to Sir Henry Stafford. You might be able to find her at her mansion at Woking in Surrey.'

'I can but try, sir.'

'Good man, Gabriel.' Jasper shook his hand. 'Take care, and find out what you can. If you are able to see Lady Margaret you could kindly tell her I am well, and had no choice other than to leave her son at Pembroke. It would mean a lot to me.'

Jasper busied himself with continuing to act as a go-between, visiting the court of Queen Margaret and returning to the rambling palace of King Louis at Angers, while he waited for Gabriel to return with news from England. It was almost midnight when a messenger arrived and Jasper was roused from his bed for an urgent meeting.

A crackling fire blazed in the hearth and King Louis sat with his favourite hunting dogs, a pair of heavy-jowled mastiffs, looking unusually pleased with himself. For the past few weeks he had been withdrawn, yet whatever news the messenger brought had finally improved his mood. He held a goblet of wine in his hand and a red wine stain graced the front of his shirt. He called out to Jasper as he entered the room.

'A stroke of good fortune, Tudor.' He raised the goblet in the air like a trophy.

'What has happened, Your Highness?' Jasper rubbed his eyes. He had dressed hurriedly and sensed the months of waiting had finally come to an end.

'The Earl of Warwick has fled England with York's brother, the Duke of Clarence and landed at Honfleur. He sent a rider ahead to inform me he is on his way to seek my support.'

Jasper had to think quickly. 'You intend to agree an alliance with him?'

'I do, although not, perhaps, in the way he expects.'

'I expect he wishes to place the Duke of Clarence on the throne and make his daughter Queen of England.'

'Have you met the Duke of Clarence?' The king had a mischievous twinkle in his eye Jasper had not seen for a while.

'I have, Your Highness. He has a poor reputation as a drunk, with morals no better than his brother.' Jasper scowled at the thought. 'I would struggle to think of a worse person to have on the throne.'

'I must agree with you, Tudor. The Earl of Warwick would have done better to choose the younger brother, Richard of York, but I favour a different plan. One which will place me in advantage over the Duke of Burgundy.'

Jasper guessed King Louis planned to insist on the restoration of King Henry, yet there was something about his manner that suggested there was more to his scheming. He watched as the king refilled his goblet with red wine.

'Your support for Warwick will come at a price?'

'Of course, although I shall pretend disinterest when he arrives, and tell him to return to England,' King Louis smiled, 'after all, I must not break the terms of my agreement with Duke Charles.'

'So what does he have that you would want, Your Highness?'

'He wishes his daughter to be Queen of England?' King Louis didn't wait for Jasper's answer. 'Well, he has two daughters, and my cousin Queen Margaret has a son who is in need of a wife.' He gave the head of one of his mastiffs an affectionate rub.

'You will use Warwick's ambition for his daughters to bind him to the House of Lancaster, Your Highness?' Jasper stroked his beard as he tried to think through the implications. 'I find it hard to believe Queen Margaret would ever agree to such a thing. She would rather see Warwick's head on a stake.'

'You must bury your dislike of the Earl of Warwick, Tudor,' the king interrupted. 'As I must learn to tolerate those bastard dukes of Burgundy and Brittany.' He put a hand on

Jasper's shoulder. 'You must help my good cousin to see the virtue of this plan.'

'I think she could be persuaded, Your Highness.'

'Good, good. Your reward will be to see King Henry back on the throne, with Queen Margaret at his side, and your title and lands in Wales returned.' He clapped his hands for servants, despite the late hour. 'We must prepare this dog's kennel of a palace for our visitors. I shall order a banquet, to celebrate this sudden change of fortune.'

It was a weary and humbled Earl of Warwick who arrived at the palace, accompanied by his family and the Duke of Clarence. Like Jasper, Sir Richard Neville had lost everything except what he had been able to carry, and must place his future in the hands of King Louis. Despite his long journey, he was keen to get to business. King Louis set out his plan and while Warwick soon saw the advantage of it, his new son-in-law, George, Duke of Clarence, stormed from the meeting, cursing.

Jasper was concerned to learn that Warwick's eldest daughter Isobel had lost a child, born at sea during the voyage, and still looked deathly pale, her dress torn and fixed in place with pins. Warwick's other daughter Anne seemed barely more than a girl yet was excited at the prospect of marriage to the future King of England and wanted to know from Jasper what he was like.

'He is tall and handsome, my lady, and would surely be seventeen years old now.' Jasper refrained from adding that the prince was also an arrogant young man who seemed to have learned little from his tutors since arriving in France. Anne's mother, Countess Anne, was less enthusiastic and regarded both King Louis and Jasper with deep suspicion. He could see she had suffered great hardship since they last met, at a royal banquet in the great hall of Westminster which seemed a life-time ago. The countess had been the envy of the other ladies with her extravagant dresses and glittering jewellery. Now she appeared on the brink of a breakdown, her silk gown stained and creased, her face lined with worry for her family.

King Louis ordered a grand jousting tournament as part of the celebrations and arranged for Jasper to be seated next to Countess Anne. This was no accident. He had been left to win her over to their cause and now she regarded him with sad brown eyes.

'Tell me, Sir Jasper. Does Queen Margaret support this marriage of my daughter to her son as keenly as King Louis?'

'In truth, my lady, she has yet to learn of it.' He saw her eyes widen in surprise and felt he should explain. 'I am here as her ambassador, so I must leave in the morning to inform her of these developments.'

A trumpeter announced the start of the tournament to a cheer from the crowd of onlookers. Mounted knights rode in on gaudily caparisoned horses and saluted the king by raising and lowering their lances. As they made their way to the lists, Jasper saw King Louis was deep in conversation with Warwick.

He also noted one of the jousters wore the colours of Duke Charles of Burgundy, while another displayed the crest of Duke Francis of Brittany on his shield. King Louis had contrived to pitch the representatives of his great rivals against each other for his entertainment.

At the command from the master of the rolls, both knights lowered their visors and charged, bringing down their lances in a juddering clash as they met. There was applause from the crowd as the tip of the Burgundian's lance broke on impact. Both knights were handed new lances and turned to prepare for a second run. This time the Burgundian, a skilled jouster, struck the Breton full square, his lance shattering and unseating his opponent, who crashed heavily to the ground and lay still.

For a moment Jasper thought the Breton was mortally wounded, then he raised his visor and lifted a hand in salute to the victor.

The Countess of Warwick was more concerned with watching her husband's discussion with the king and shook her head. 'You seem to trust that man, yet my instinct tells me to be cautious.' She spoke softly, as if to herself.

'I should tell you, my lady, it was King Louis who persuaded me to set aside all that has gone before and place my trust in your husband.'

'And you have?'

Jasper nodded. 'He has agreed to risk his life to see King Henry restored to the throne, so can rely on my complete support, as can you, my lady.'

The countess didn't reply but for the first time Jasper saw a faint glimmer of hope in her sad eyes.

At the banquet that followed the jousting Jasper found himself seated next to Queen Charlotte. He noticed how she observed their guests closely yet with no sign of judgement. He leaned across to her and spoke in French.

'I understand you will soon be leaving for the Château d'Amboise to enter your confinement, Your Highness.' He smiled. 'With God's grace I hope all will be well for you and the child.'

Queen Charlotte returned his smile. 'That is most kind of you, Sir Jasper.' She eyed him conspiratorially. 'This time it's another boy, an heir for the king. We shall name him Charles.' She caressed her hand over her swollen middle, grown so large she could not sit close to the table. 'A mother knows these things.'

Jasper recalled King Louis telling him their first son barely lived two years. He raised his gilded goblet of wine.

'Your son is destined to one day be a great king, Your Highness.'

'I pray you are right, Sir Jasper,' she crossed herself, 'and you will soon be returning to the court of Queen Margaret of Anjou?'

He glanced across to where Warwick was enjoying a joke with King Louis as if they had always been great friends. He saw Countess Anne looking in his direction and was pleased to see her nod to him when their eyes met, the briefest of gestures yet a sign he understood.

'I must persuade Queen Margaret to embrace your new guests, Your Highness. The future of England depends on it.'


Queen Margaret stared at Jasper in tense, stern-faced silence as he gave her his account of all that happened in Arras, including the arranged marriage. He'd rehearsed his words many times on the long ride from Angers, and prepared himself for her angry reaction.

'King Louis summons me now, after all this has been settled?' She glanced at the empty chair at her side. The prince chose to go hunting in the woods rather than wait to hear the news Jasper brought.

'I can assure you his intentions are honourable, Your Highness. We've been searching for a way to win his support, and now he is asking for yours.'

'I think, Sir Jasper, you have been at the court of the universal spider for too long.' She spoke in French and her tone was harsh.

He tried not to show his dislike of her use of the king's nickname. 'I've done my best, my lady, to promote our interests. This offers the best opportunity, perhaps the only opportunity, to restore King Henry to the throne.'

'You trust Warwick?' It was more of an accusation than a question.

'You will find the Earl of Warwick much changed by his reversal of fortune, my lady.'

'I will never trust a man who put my husband in the Tower of London.' She stood, her eyes blazing at him. 'Do you forget so easily the pain and misery that man has brought upon my family?'

'I do not forget, Your Highness.' He needed to find a way to calm her. 'I too have suffered because of his actions, and know many good men who gave their lives for our cause, yet I must find it in my heart to forgive him, for the greater good.'

The sincerity in his voice seemed to have the desired effect and she sat down, looking close to tears. 'His daughter is the last person I would choose as a wife for my son. He should marry a princess, not the second daughter of an earl.'

'His daughter Anne is personable, my lady. She is young and pretty. I think she would be to the liking of the prince.'

'You went to the court of King Louis to see if we could turn Warwick's disloyalty to our advantage.' She seemed to be wavering for the first time since Jasper broached the subject. 'Your counsel is this marriage must take place?'

'It is the surest way to bind Warwick to our cause, Your Highness.'

'I will see this girl for myself, and you shall tell the Earl of Warwick he must bend his knee and beg my forgiveness.'


Queen Margaret wore a gold coronet and her royal robes, trimmed with ermine, for the meeting with Warwick at Angers, and sat flanked by Jasper to her left and her son, Prince Edward to her right. Both wore fine new armour, gifts from King Louis, with the gold-plated fleur-de-lis of France emblazoned in the centre. Jasper watched as Warwick approached, walking stiffly and trying to retain as much of his authority as he could.

Warwick bowed on one knee and waited for Queen Margaret to command him to rise before looking into her face.

'I hereby pledge my loyalty, Your Highness.'

Jasper saw the queen tense, pausing for an uncomfortably long time before she replied. 'You swear to restore King Henry to the throne?'

'I swear, Your Highness. I will not rest until he is once more King of England.' The conviction in his voice echoed in the room. He touched his lips to her offered hand and stood tall, with a little of the confidence Jasper had once seen.

The next morning a sharp knock at Jasper's door announced the return at long last of Gabriel, and he saw immediately from his friend's expression that the news he brought was good.

'It proved quite an adventure, sir.' Gabriel gratefully drank from the goblet of red wine Jasper offered him. 'England is in a proper confusion. Neighbour against neighbour, a good time for an Irish soldier of fortune.'

'Tell me, Gabriel,' Jasper tried to hide his impatience. 'My nephew Henry is alive and well?'

'He is, sir,' Gabriel grinned, 'yet he took some tracking down. You were right about Lady Margaret Beaufort, sir.' He took another sip of wine, nodding in approval. 'She has been to visit her son, who is well and living in Hereford under the protection of a Squire Corbet, the husband of a relative of Lady Herbert.'

'You gave her my message?'

'That I did, and she asked me to inform you that she remembers you in her prayers, sir.'

Jasper crossed to his window and stared into the courtyard while he composed himself. Lady Margaret would understand it could have cost him his life if he'd not escaped from Wales when he did.

'Did you travel to Hereford to see him for yourself?'

'I did, sir. He is older than I expected, some thirteen years now. The squire asked me to convey his promise to keep him safe.'

'You've done well, Gabriel, although I regret I have bad news for you.'

Gabriel's smile faded. 'What is that, sir?'

'I am returning to Wales once more, and wish you to accompany me.'

## 15

## SEPTEMBER 1470

The dawn sunrise glinted with amber and gold from the sails of a fleet of ships that stretched for as far into the distance as Jasper could see. He'd dreamed of this day and been told at least sixty ships had departed Normandy, escorted by the admiral of France. Each ship was filled with as many men and horses as they could carry on the crossing to the English coast.

Ahead of him in the flagship sailed Warwick, his son-in-law, George, Duke of Clarence and the Earl of Oxford, Sir John de Vere. The number of ships and men to be landed meant half the fleet would sail on to land at Plymouth while the rest would land at Dartmouth, where Jasper planned to head for Wales with Gabriel to raise a Welsh army. Warwick would lead the march on London, gathering men on the way.

Queen Margaret had decided to remain in France with her son and his new bride until it was considered safe for her to return to England. Jasper had been frustrated by the delay, as they needed to wait for a papal dispensation to be delivered from Rome before the betrothal of young Anne Neville and Prince Edward could take place. Queen Margaret seemed to accept her new daughter-in-law with good grace, yet Jasper predicted she would find a way to end the marriage soon enough.

A new danger lurked as they were about to depart, when the Burgundian fleet was sighted, waiting like a pack of hungry wolves for them to leave port. The Earl of Warwick swore they were keeping watch on behalf of their Yorkist allies. With typical bravado, he wanted to lead an attack on the fleet and use his cannons to blast them from the water, but nature intervened when a sudden storm blew the Burgundians safely up the Channel.

Gabriel declared this a good omen for Lancaster as he picked his way through the men who occupied every space on the deck, some sleeping, others gambling their pay with games of cards and dice. His mail shirt, made by craftsmen from thousands of riveted iron links was paid for by Jasper in thanks for the years of loyal service. The mail would protect him from most arrows and sword blows, although it was clear from the way he moved that it would take him a while to become used to the weight of it.

Jasper also commissioned new swords for them both, well-balanced with blades of fine artisan steel. More than simply weapons, the swords were a sign of status and could hold an edge sharp enough to shave with. Jasper's own was also engraved with his martlet badge, which his father once told him represented his quest for knowledge, learning and adventure.

'Message from the captain, sir. We should arrive in Dartmouth close to midnight.'

'Good. How are the horses?'

'Settled well, sir.' Gabriel studied the waves. Although the sky was as grey as slate the water was calm enough, with a promising breeze in their favour. 'These conditions have helped, although they'll be glad to see dry land again.'

'As will I. We have quite a ride to Wales, Gabriel, and I've no idea if we'll meet opposition on the way.'

'York could be waiting to give us a warm welcome?'

Jasper smiled. 'God is with us, Gabriel. Warwick's brother Sir John Neville has contrived a Lancastrian rebellion in the north to keep Edward of York and his army far from London until it's too late.'

'Surely York will see this diversion for what it is?'

'Let us pray he does not.'

'You think Sir John remains loyal to York?'

Jasper smiled to himself, Gabriel knew him well. 'I trust Sir John Neville will not rebel against his own brother. Even if he does it will be too late, for he will find his men all wear the bear and ragged staff badge of Warwick under their coats.'

They always understood it would be impossible to make the crossing in secret with so many ships, so Jasper hoped making landfall in darkness should give his men a fighting chance. Once in Wales he would soon find enough supporters to remain there in relative safety, at least until they received word from London of Warwick's success or failure.

Jasper looked up at the slender crescent of moon, surrounded by twinkling stars in an otherwise black sky, and said his prayers. The ship heeled in the wind and he nearly lost his footing, gripping the rail with both hands to steady himself. A stiff breeze tugged at the sails, adding an additional challenge for their captain as they approached the treacherous, rocky coast of southern England.

Gabriel had been talking to the crew and learned that the approach to the River Dart could be difficult at night, with the main landmark being a massive rock known to the locals as the Mew Stone. He pointed into the blackness at the indistinct shape as they gave it a wide berth.

'The waters here are a mess of rocks and shallows where ships can run aground.' He grinned at Jasper's frown. 'Sailors say it's not the sea that kills you, my lord, it's the land.'

He stared into the night and saw what Gabriel meant. A dangerous mass of rock rising from the water like a jagged castle, with another, smaller rock close by. His attention was caught by a distant light, which flickered then vanished, only to reappear in the same spot a moment later. He could see no other sign of life at such a late hour. They had timed their arrival well.

They watched as the ships sailing ahead of them cautiously entered the estuary, barely visible except when their masts and sails blocked the view of the moon. Their last obstacle was the old castle guarding the river entrance, connected to Kingswear by massive iron chains, which could be raised to prevent ships sailing upriver. If the chains were raised they would soon know. Jasper held his breath as the castle drew closer.

For once it seemed luck was on their side, as Warwick's flagship sailed past without incident and the others followed, until they reached the wharf used by merchant traders. Archers and crossbowmen lined the rail as blindfolded horses were unloaded, their hooves thumping rhythmically on the gangplanks. Once satisfied they had not sailed into a Yorkist trap, Jasper took his first step on English soil since being force-marched to Scotland after the defeat at Bamburgh.

He glanced across at the serious young man riding at his side and saw an echo of his long lost brother Edmund's features, although in character Henry was more like his mother, Lady Margaret. He shared her strength of spirit, evident despite his youth and slight build. The Beaufort steel merged well with his half-Welsh, half-French Tudor blood.

The loyal men of Wales gladly rallied to Jasper's call when word of Warwick's victory in London was trumpeted throughout the country. Edward of York and his brother Richard barely escaped with their lives to their allies in Burgundy, and a bewildered King Henry had been swiftly rescued from the Tower of London and returned to the Palace of Westminster. Jasper's first act had been to ride with a hundred men to Hereford to find his nephew.

'We must find you a good sword, Henry.'

'I would be grateful, sir.' Henry's voice sounded well educated and carried only the faintest trace of a Welsh accent. He looked confidently back at Jasper. 'My sword was lost at Edgecote...' His voice drifted away as he remembered. 'They made me watch while they cut off the head of Lord William Herbert. He went bravely to his death, may God rest him.'

Jasper bit his lip at a sudden memory of how they had said the same of his father. Secretly he was not sorry the man who murdered his father and other good men that day in Hereford market square met the same horrific fate, but he cursed Warwick's men for making young Henry witness the act.

'I thank God you were spared, Henry. Now we shall reunite you with your mother.'

'My mother told me to always have faith this day would come, sir. She used to tell me to be patient, although Lord Herbert said you were dead, and I was not to ever ask after you.'

'Well, as you can see, Henry, I am very much alive and your mother was right. There have been times when my faith was tested, yet I lived in hope of seeing your uncle King Henry restored to the throne, and I would one day keep my promise to your mother to see you safely returned to her.'

'I am too old to live with my mother, sir.' There was a note of protest in his young voice.

'I agree, Henry. We'll send for her when we reach London.'

He smiled. 'You are my ward again, and I look forward to getting to know you.'

London seemed a riot of noise and colour as Jasper rode through crowded streets, flanked by Gabriel and young Henry, at the head of his army of men from all over Wales. Church bells rang and the crowds cheered and cried 'God save the King!' when they saw his colourful standard, the royal arms surrounded by his badge of golden martlets, although he doubted many of them knew who he was.

Men in Warwick's livery with the badge of bear and ragged staff and armed with sharp halberds guarded each street corner as they reached Westminster. The duke had learned from past experience and would not allow York's supporters to pose any threat this time. Warwick himself was waiting to greet them on the steps of the Palace of Westminster, wearing a black fur cape and a heavy gold chain, his badge of office.

'Welcome to London, Sir Jasper.' The earl greeted him warmly, like an old friend.

'Thank you, Sir Richard, and well done.'

'London threw open the gates to us,' Warwick seemed pleased with himself, 'so my brother deserves congratulations, as not one man dared to oppose us.'

'You have informed Queen Margaret?'

'I have, and I've also written to our ally in France, King Louis, expressing our thanks.'

Jasper nodded in approval. 'And how is King Henry?'

'He is well.' Warwick lowered his voice to a whisper only Jasper could hear. 'His highness has not fully understood recent events, so I would be grateful if you would help him to appreciate what I've achieved?'

'You may count on it, Sir Richard.'

.   .   .

Jasper barely recognised King Henry. His once matted hair had been washed and cut, his beard neatly trimmed, and he wore a fine new hat and cloth of gold in place of the monkish habit Master Blacman encouraged. The greatest change of all was in his eyes, which had always been downcast and vacant, now studying Jasper and young Henry with keen interest.

'Your Highness,' Jasper bowed. 'May I introduce my ward Henry Tudor, son of your late half-brother, Edmund?'

'I am at your service, Your Highness.' Young Henry bowed as Jasper had done, his cultured voice confident, despite the awe-inspiring surroundings.

'We must have a special service to give thanks our little family is reunited here.' King Henry studied their faces as if seeing them for the first time. 'It is through the grace of God you have been saved, and I am truly pleased to see you safely returned to me, Jasper.' He turned to young Henry. 'And in you there is something of your father. He would have been proud to see how well you have grown.'

It was the most considered speech Jasper had heard from the king in many years, and it gave him hope all the hardship had been worth it. Good men and women sacrificed their lives to allow this day and it gave Jasper comfort to know they had not died in vain.

A messenger waited for Jasper in the hallway of Westminster Palace after his meeting with the king, and handed him a letter with the cross and portcullis seal of Lady Margaret Beaufort:

*Sir Jasper Tudor, Earl of Pembroke. I thank you heartily that you bring my beloved son Henry to London and beseech you to visit me at the house of my good husband, Sir Henry Stafford, as soon as you are able. Blessed be God, the King and the Queen, and with God's grace, whom I pray give you good speed in your great matters.*

Jasper understood why Lady Margaret was unable to

welcome him in person on his arrival and appreciated Sir Henry's nervousness. Although his mother was a Neville, like many who fought so bravely for Lancaster at Towton, he'd sworn allegiance to York in return for a pardon. Now he might be branded a traitor to the king by those less understanding.

Not wishing to delay reuniting Lady Margaret with her son, they followed her messenger through the narrow streets to an imposing house close to London Bridge. After announcing themselves to the housekeeper, they were shown into a richly furnished room with small leaded glass windows overlooking the River Thames.

Sir Henry Stafford had grown portly and his scarlet doublet, embroidered with silver braiding, drew attention to his bulk. He leaned heavily on a stick to support his weight as he stood to greet them. At his side stood Lady Margaret, dressed in a stylish gown of striking red velvet, the only reminder of her religious devotion a shining gold crucifix on a chain around her neck. Her eyes were bright as she studied her visitors, taking in every detail yet revealing nothing of her own feelings.

The sight of his brother's widow brought back a rush of memories. In Jasper's mind Lady Margaret had always been barely a woman, young enough to be his ward, yet nearly ten years had passed. He calculated she must be twenty-seven, and saw she now dressed as a woman of status. He had almost forgotten her great wealth from the Beaufort inheritance, as well as from Sir Henry.

'Welcome, Sir Jasper, to our home.' She nodded to her son. 'Henry. I give thanks to God that you are safely here.' Her eyes misted with tears as she fought to remain composed.

Henry seemed awkward in his mother's presence. He'd told Jasper she visited him on several occasions when he lived at Raglan Castle with William Herbert, although more than a year had passed since her last visit. They had never been left alone together, as Lady Anne Herbert was always required to keep a watch over them.

He gave a slight bow. 'It is my pleasure to see you again, Mother.' He nodded to Sir Henry. 'And I thank you, sir, for your hospitality.'

Sir Henry shook them both by the hand. 'It's good to see you. We've been looking forward to your arrival.' He nodded to a waiting servant. 'I trust you will be able to stay for some supper?'

Jasper glanced at young Henry. 'We would be pleased to. I am keen to learn what has been going on in London while I've been visiting France.'

He smiled at Lady Margaret. 'It warms my heart to see you looking so well, my lady.'

'And you, Jasper. It seems your life in France has suited you?'

'I've missed Pembroke,' he admitted. 'It has been difficult to be sure of news from England, with so many rumours, so I give thanks to God that, at last, we can meet as family.'

Sir Henry led them through to a large dining room with a polished walnut table set with four platters and goblets and invited them to sit. A log fire crackled in the grate to ward off the late October chill and beeswax candles cast their yellow, flickering light from a pair of tall silver candlesticks. Jasper sat in a carved and gilded crimson velvet-covered chair as fine as any in Westminster Palace.

Lady Margaret said a Latin grace, thanking God for the safe return of her son and brother-in-law, then a young maid-servant brought red wine for Jasper and Sir Henry, with mead for Lady Margaret and young Henry. Once their goblets were filled Sir Henry raised his and proposed a toast.

'To peace in this land, and the good health of King Henry.'

Jasper raised his goblet. 'To peace and family.'

Sir Henry sipped his wine and nodded. 'You've had some adventures since we last met, Sir Jasper, if only half the accounts I've heard of your exploits are not exaggerated.'

'In truth, I consider myself fortunate to be here.'

'We heard you had been killed fighting in the north.'

Lady Margaret crossed herself. 'I prayed each night the news was wrong.'

Jasper smiled. 'Well, my lady, your prayers were answered, as by the grace of God and with the help of friends I managed to escape the late Lord Herbert.'

He saw young Henry pale at the mention of the name and was glad the servants arrived with veal pie and a leg of mutton in a thick sauce. He waited while it was served, together with a trencher of freshly baked bread, still warm from the ovens.

Lady Margaret looked at Jasper. 'How is the king? It is some years since I saw him last.' She gave her husband a cautionary glance.

'You might ask your son?' He glanced across the table at young Henry. 'He was presented to the king and will be able to give you an opinion of his uncle's health.'

'The king is well, Mother. He said my father would be proud of me.'

Lady Margaret nodded. 'Your father would have been proud to see what a fine young man you've become.' She caught Jasper's eye and seemed keen to change the subject. 'I would be most grateful if you would help us to ensure my son's lands and title as Earl of Richmond are properly secured.'

'Of course. I will speak to Earl Warwick when I return.'

Sir Henry glanced up from his supper. 'Warwick runs the country?'

Jasper nodded. 'King Henry has little enough interest in matters of state, and the queen and Prince Edward remain in France.'

'So until we have a proper Parliament such matters fall to

Warwick?' Sir Henry's deep voice carried a note of concern. 'He is a vengeful man.'

Lady Margaret interrupted her husband. 'We must put our troubles of the past behind us, Henry, and pray good sense prevails.'

Jasper tasted the well-cooked mutton, seasoned with herbs, and dipped his bread in the rich wine sauce. 'Do you know what became of Henry's lands, my lady?'

'York granted them to his brother, George, Duke of Clarence.'

'That is a problem. Clarence had the promise of the throne snatched from within his grasp, so Warwick will be reluctant to also take the lands he had been given.'

Sir Henry signalled to the serving girl to refill their goblets. 'I heard he is to be made heir apparent, after Prince Edward, is that not enough to appease him?'

Jasper wiped his platter with a hunk of bread and took a bite while he considered the question. 'Prince Edward is a young man, and an ambitious one. In truth I doubt George Neville will gladly agree to relinquish an acre of land, unless he is forced to.'

'You will ask, on our behalf?'

'I will, my lady, although you must expect the answer may not be what we wish.'

He took another sip of wine and turned to Sir Henry. 'Will you tell me what I've missed while I've been away?'

Sir Henry laid down his knife with a clatter on the hard table. 'I must confess that life settled down well enough under York.'

Lady Margaret agreed. 'Edward was kind to us, Jasper. I think it important you know that.' She glanced at her husband, who nodded agreement. 'He granted us the manor at Woking and came to visit us there once. I asked his permission to visit King Henry and he told me if not for the Earl of Warwick he might have moved the king to a priory somewhere, to live out his days in peace.'

'Now we have to keep our wits about us.' Sir Henry helped himself to a generous portion of the veal pie. 'I can tell you it has not been easy. York's sympathisers opened the prison gates and bands of ruffians roam the streets, with nobody able to stop them.'

Jasper took a sip of his wine. 'I heard villages beyond the city walls have been ransacked.'

Sir Henry nodded. 'We plan to leave for the country as soon as we can.'

Lady Margaret looked at Jasper. 'I would wish for my son to travel with us, as it has been such a long time?'

Jasper smiled, recalling his conversation with young Henry, and nodded. 'Of course—and then he must return with me to Pembroke.'

'Thank you, Jasper.'

It was the first time he had seen her smile since she held her newborn baby in her arms at Pembroke Castle.


George Neville, Archbishop of York and Warwick's brother, led the service of thanksgiving in the cathedral of St Paul's, offering thanks to God for saving England and blessing what had become known as the re-adeption of King Henry. Choirs sang and every space in the huge cathedral was packed with nobles and their ladies, all keen to show their loyalty.

Although the idea of a service was the king's, Warwick quickly turned it into a public spectacle, a chance for the people of London to see their restored king with him, their self-appointed new Protector of the Realm. He made sure the streets were thronged with cheering crowds as they made the short ride through the city in procession, their horses followed by five hundred soldiers dressed in the blue, red and gold royal livery, with drummers and trumpeters adding to the noise and sense of grand occasion.

The king dressed in his full regalia and wore his heavy crown for the first time in many years. Warwick was right, as King Henry seemed not to understand what he had been through, yet looked happy enough as he waved to his people. It was as if Edward of York never existed. Warwick had even ordered all coins bearing York's face to be withdrawn, to be melted down and re-struck for King Henry.

After the service Jasper made his way in the slow procession back down the long aisle of St Paul's and froze as he saw Warwick's younger brother, Sir John Neville, dressed in his regalia of the Order of the Garter. In a flash of memory Jasper recalled they were knighted there together with his brother Edmund in the same ceremony by King Henry.

He also recalled the nightmare siege of Bamburgh, where he almost starved and nearly froze to death until John Neville chose to spare him. Their eyes met, only for an instant, yet Jasper saw acknowledgement in the eyes of his former captor. It was time to set aside their differences, although his memories would take longer to fade.

Jasper felt disappointed to see the king absent from the banquet. Instead, Prince Edward sat at the side of the queen, a gold coronet and fur-trimmed cape making him look older than his seventeen years. At his side sat Lady Anne, in a fine new gown. She caught Jasper's eye and the sadness he saw there told him all he needed to know. He made a mental note to keep watch over her, as although the marriage had not been his idea, he had helped to make it happen.

Also absent were George, Duke of Clarence and his wife Lady Isobel. Jasper took a seat next to Countess Warwick and enquired after the health of her eldest daughter. The countess had regained a little of her former grandeur, although her lined face told him how the hardship of the past months had taken its toll on her.

'I thank you for your concern, Sir Jasper. These things take time.' She glanced across at her husband, surrounded by minor nobles seeking favours. 'The Duke of Clarence has not taken kindly to his own misfortune but Isobel is strong willed, as must be my daughter Anne.'

Jasper glanced across to where Prince Edward was continuing to ignore his new wife. With a jolt he realised it was not entirely the boy's fault, as despite all his mother's attention and his long-suffering tutors, he needed a strong father to guide him in such matters.

'Never say that marriage has more of joy than pain.' He said it softly, thinking aloud.

'You surprise me, Sir Jasper.' She smiled. 'I thought you were a soldier—not a scholar?'

'My father was a self-educated man,' Jasper admitted. 'He taught himself to read and write, and insisted I studied both Latin and Greek, although it has thus far been of little enough use to me.' He saw her expression soften and smiled. 'I also doubt I'm destined to be a soldier, for I've never won a battle and it's only through God's providence and perhaps a little luck that I've escaped with my life.'

She looked again at her husband. 'Sometimes I wish he was less determined to be a soldier. You know he intends to declare war on Burgundy for sheltering Edward of York?'

'I did not, my lady, although the news doesn't surprise me.' A thought occurred to him. 'That is what King Louis was plotting, before we left France?'

The countess nodded imperceptibly. 'My husband treats this like a game of chess, always looking several moves ahead.'

Jasper wondered if Sir John Neville deliberately allowed York to escape to his allies in Burgundy. By now Duke Charles would be breaking the peace treaty by helping an enemy of France, giving King Louis the excuse he needed. He glanced at Queen Margaret and saw the satisfied expression on her face. He could only imagine how relieved she must feel to be returned to Westminster after so long in exile.

The Earl of Warwick may have kneeled before her and sworn fealty, yet he saw the queen as little more than a useful chess piece in his grand strategy. It seemed to matter little that, as in a game of chess, the queen could be lost, as long as he guarded his king. If the countess was right, to Warwick they were all his pawns.

The problem was Jasper witnessed for himself at Péronne how Duke Charles of was even more astute at playing this devious game with people's lives. A sharp mind worked behind the duke's engaging smile, and his resources seemed to know no limits. An old misgiving gripped at Jasper's chest. The war between Lancaster and York was not over while Edward of York still lived.

## 16

## DECEMBER 1470

The town of Tenby had prospered under York's benevolent rule. Jasper noted several new houses on the main street as he took his once familiar walk down the hill to the little harbour, crammed with merchant ships and more fishing boats than he remembered. His old friend Thomas White had ensured his house was kept safe and, once again, Jasper made the comfortable lodge his base in West Wales.

Gabriel happily accepted the appointment of Captain of the Guard at Pembroke Castle, where young Henry returned from his stay with Lady Margaret, to resume his studies. The men of the Pembroke garrison, once loyal to William Herbert, welcomed Jasper's return and swore fealty to King Henry.

There was also a new companion for Jasper's nephew Henry. Shortly before they set out on the fateful march that ended at Mortimer's Cross, his father confessed to fathering a child with a woman named Bethan, from Beaumaris. After his father's death, Bethan returned to the house his father bequeathed her in Beaumaris until Jasper sent for her, together with her son, his half-brother David Owen.

Two years younger than Henry, David Owen had the rugged Tudor good looks and humour of his father. His mother did her best to provide him with an education, and his tutors said he was doing well studying at Henry's side. The friendly competition between them was good for both, and they sparred with wooden practice swords in the castle yard, much as Jasper had long ago with his brother Edmund.

As well as being a fluent Welsh speaker, David Owen could ride a horse and sail a boat on the Cleddau as ably as men twice his age. His mother Bethan wished to remain close to her son and was appointed to oversee the castle servants, a responsible position, as most of the town of Pembroke worked at the castle in some capacity. Bethan was attractive and popular yet Jasper still found it hard to remember she had a relationship with his father, as she was some ten years younger than himself.

As he reached the harbour Jasper saw Thomas White at the quayside. Dressed in a long brocade jacket, a sign of his wealth, Thomas had recently stepped down as Mayor of Tenby, only to have his place taken by his son, John White.

'Good day, Lord Tudor.' Thomas raised a hand in welcome.

Jasper smiled. 'I've never seen this harbour so busy, Thomas.'

'Supplies for Pembroke Castle and all those men you've been recruiting.' He rubbed his hands together. 'What's the latest news from London, my lord?'

'The riots have ended and life there seems to be getting back to normal now the new Parliament has met.' He smiled. 'They declared York a traitor, all his goods and lands forfeit.'

'There's a story going around that Edward of York is dead?'

'It was rumoured I was dead yet here I am. I heard York fled to Burgundy. I won't believe he is no threat until I see his coffin.'

'Do you think he will return?' Thomas looked concerned. 'They say war is good for business—but I would settle for a few years of peace.'

'That's why I've been given a commission of array and am so busy recruiting men. We must be watchful, Thomas, and not only for Edward of York. His young brother Richard escaped with him and I've not forgotten men like Roger Vaughan are still at large, and here close by in Wales.'

Jasper didn't add that Vaughan, until recently constable of Cardigan Castle, had openly bragged about leading his father to his death in Hereford. He had not been able to confront William Herbert with his crimes but part of him hoped one day Sir Roger Vaughan would also be held to account.

Christmas and the New Year proved busy times for Jasper. A grand banquet filled the great hall at Pembroke Castle, which Bethan decorated with garlands of holly tied with red silk ribbons and more candles than he had ever seen. His guests of honour were Lady Margaret Beaufort and her husband, Thomas White and his wife, as well as the mayors and aldermen of Tenby and Pembroke with their wives.

Minstrels played and the local troupe of mummers entertained with songs and a Christmas play, with Bethan as Mary, Gabriel playing the part of Joseph, leading a real donkey, and young Henry and David dressed as shepherds. Fat 'golden' geese covered in butter and saffron were served with hundreds of woodcock, followed by Christmas puddings known as 'frumenty' of currants and dried fruit spiced with cinnamon and nutmeg.

Jasper gave a speech of thanks and proposed a toast to success in the New Year. He was in a celebratory mood, for in addition to recovering his former estates and title of Earl of Pembroke, he had been granted all the lands and properties of the Herberts in Wales and the Marches, and made a Justice of the Peace. Since his possessions were reduced to only the clothes he wore he appreciated what his new wealth could do, not only for him but for those dependent upon him.

He remained in regular correspondence with Queen Margaret in France, reporting on progress and developments in England and Wales, and sat at his desk by the window of his house in Tenby as he prepared another. Although he employed trusted men to carry his letters to France he was aware they could fall into the wrong hands, so chose his words with great care.

He sharpened the nib of his quill with his knife and dipped it in black ink, then began with the usual formality expected by Queen Margaret. He proposed it was time for her to return to England with Prince Edward without further delay, as with God's grace the country was now at peace. He re-read what he'd written, pleased with his letter's sense of urgency.

Jasper understood the queen's distrust of Warwick and had become increasingly concerned at how the earl controlled Parliament and acted in the king's name. He had personally benefitted from such favours, of course, and now effectively ruled the whole of Wales. Others had more questionable rewards, as Warwick replaced all the grants and appointments made by York to the family of his wife with those of his own choosing, not always on the basis of merit or ability.

He signed the letter and, satisfied the ink was dry, folded the parchment and melted red wax before pressing his personal seal to it. He held the letter in his hand. It looked ordinary enough yet could trigger a sequence of events that would change the country, and he wondered how the Earl of Warwick would react when Queen Margaret began to curb his power, as she surely would.

He worried about Prince Edward, who seemed to have grown even more unsuitable as the next king under his mother's care. He also worried about George, Duke of Clarence. Warwick's unstable son-in-law absented himself from Westminster and was also Edward of York's brother, a liability.

Jasper studied the middle-aged man before him, trying to decide if his story was a pack of lies. He'd heard many such cases since being appointed magistrate and had developed a good instinct for distinguishing fact from fiction. A wealthy landowner died intestate and without an heir. Now his family members argued and fought over the details as they divided their inheritance.

'He made promises to me, my lord. He said I should have his house and land after his days.' The man sounded convincing, although he avoided Jasper's eye.

'He left no will stating this was his wish?'

The man shook his head. 'He could neither read nor write, my lord, but I swear it's true.'

People muttered at this and someone in the crowded courtroom shouted it was a wicked lie. Jasper brought the room to order and frowned at how the townspeople liked to treat the magistrate hearings as entertainment. They were held in public for the law to be seen to be administered fairly, yet he found that often he must pass his judgement based on his instinct of what was right or wrong, rather than proper evidence.

'Swear what you tell me is the truth, in the sight of God.' He saw the man's hesitation and the flicker of doubt in his eyes. 'You know the punishment for perjury?'

Again, the man avoided Jasper's eye. 'I wish to reconsider my claim, my lord.'

Jasper waved for him to be dismissed. He could have the man imprisoned for wasting his time, yet he let him walk free. In truth, he was more concerned with the reply he had received from Queen Margaret, thanking him for his advice and saying she had decided to send Edmund Beaufort and Henry Holland ahead to ensure England was safe for her return.

He read the letter several times alone the previous evening at his house in Tenby, and could not ignore the thinly-veiled insult within her carefully chosen words. It was true he had been busy with his commission of array, raising a new army in Wales, and was a little out of touch with the finer politics of Westminster. He could imagine Henry Holland slyly suggesting to the queen that he should pave the way for her. Edmund Beaufort was a good man but not beyond reminding the queen of the many favours Jasper Tudor received from Warwick.

He called for the next case and tried to count his blessings rather than dwell on his lonely life since the sad loss of the woman he loved. He had his growing family in Pembroke, Henry and David Owen, and often visited to share meals with them. Bethan enjoyed arranging banquets and Gabriel was always good company with his stories, yet there was no one he could confide in and discuss his worries without feeling judged at times such as this.

The new plaintiff demanded the eviction of a tenant farmer for non-payment of rent. A swarthy bull of a man with deep-set eyes, he complained loudly and at length about how he'd been cheated from money owed to him, although his heavy, overweight build and fine clothes suggested he had not suffered unduly.

The defendant could not have been more different. He spoke plainly of the hardship he endured and how his requests for understanding were met by threats to his family. Jasper's eye strayed to the family, a thin, pale-faced woman with two young boys, waiting to hear his verdict. The boys reminded him of himself and his brother when the soldiers came. Although they wore ragged clothes and no shoes, they tried to stand straight and tall. Their mother wrung her hands anxiously as she watched her husband provide his testimony.

He waited until the farmer finished presenting his case, then took one of the papers in front of him and made a pretence of studying it.

'I have been advised a benefactor will settle this debt in full. The case is dismissed.'

He would instruct his agent to purchase the farm from the landowner and grant it to the farmer. There was no need for them to know the identity of the benefactor. As he watched the bewildered family leave he hoped this small act would improve their lives and offer the boys the future they deserved.

The first bright yellow daffodils of spring signalled an end to a long, cold winter as worrying rumours from London began to reach Pembroke, carried like the glowing embers of a bonfire in the air to settle on the dry tinder of the people's concerns. Bethan said she overheard them talking in the marketplace, then Gabriel was told in a tavern and decided he should repeat the story to Jasper, as that's what you did with rumours.

'They are saying Edward of York has landed in the north, sir. I heard he doesn't have an army but has returned to reclaim his title.'

'Which title would that be, Gabriel, King of England?' Jasper had heard so many stories about York he felt it difficult to take any too seriously now.

'Shall I ride to London and find the truth of it for you, sir?'

'So that's what this is about? You find Tenby a little tame after the big city?'

'The thing is, sir, if it was true, the first we would hear is rumours.'

'If York does land, we'll find out soon enough, as Warwick

will want our army, but to be certain, you can have your ride to London, and be sure to take some good men with you.'

After Gabriel left, Jasper continued working on his papers, checking the numbers of men, quantities of supplies, writing notes in the margins of things to be done, but he felt uneasy. He crossed to the window and looked out over the muddy brown estuary of the River Cleddau. The tide was out and the only sound was the haunting call of a solitary curlew, picking through stones on the foreshore.

Barely six months had passed since their midnight landing at Dartmouth. Although it seemed much longer, Jasper recalled how long it took to recruit men and find enough ships. There was no way Edward of York would be able to return before the summer and by then they would be ready for him. All the same he decided to double the guards as a precaution.

Gabriel had still not returned and Jasper's commission took him to Hereford when a rider arrived from London with the letter bearing Warwick's seal. He gave the man a silver coin and broke the crimson wax seal with a growing sense of foreboding. The letter was written in the earl's own hand, a hurried scrawl:

*We greet you well and desire and heartily pray that in as much Edward, the king our sovereign lord's great enemy, rebel and traitor, is now landed in the north of this land and accompanied by Flemings and Easterlings, and Danes numbering some two thousand persons, you will forthwith after the sight hereof make toward me with as many men as you can readily make. May God keep you. Warwick.*

Jasper called to his servant for his horse to be made ready. He would have to return immediately to Pembroke, over a hundred miles away, and rally his men. By the time they reached London it could already be too late for King Henry, although he was comforted by the knowledge Queen Margaret and her son were still safely in France.

He rode on through the night, almost losing his way in the darkness, and reached Pembroke Castle at dawn. Immediately summoning his officers, he ordered them to ready the men and wagons of supplies for a long march. Even though they had been preparing for this moment since he first came back to Pembroke it felt unreal. Edward of York had returned too soon.

Jasper found young Henry and David, woken early and wide-eyed as they saw him approach already dressed in his full battle armour.

'Will we come with you, sir, to fight?' Henry sounded hopeful.

Jasper shook his head. 'I need you here to keep this castle safe for the king.' He saw them glance at each other. 'It will be a one-sided battle. York has not much of an army, only a few Flemish men-at-arms, while we have our Welsh Army and the Earl of Warwick has ten times as many.'

Even as he said the words he doubted the truth of them. He wished to reassure the boys yet had seen how easily men turned from Lancaster to York. Even good men, loyal to King Henry, like Sir Henry Stafford, were quick enough to take a pardon to save themselves. He never said as much but knew in his heart the people hated Warwick, mistrusted Queen Margaret and had long since lost faith in King Henry.

Gabriel returned to Pembroke at noon, his face grim and his horse in a lather from being ridden too hard. He asked to see Jasper in private as soon as he dismounted. As they climbed the stone steps to his study he prepared himself for the worst news.

'York has taken London, sir.' Gabriel sounded breathless. 'The rumours were true—the Duke of Clarence has rebelled and left Warwick in the north to join his brother.'

'I wish I'd listened to you, Gabriel. Word reached me from Warwick when I was in Hereford. We've lost valuable time and lives could depend on it.' He saw from Gabriel's expression there was more bad news. 'What is it?'

'Queen Margaret has landed in the west, sir, at Weymouth in Dorset.'

Jasper looked at him in amazement. 'I hoped she would remain safe in France. Are you certain of this?'

'I am, sir. I saw the men of Sir Edmund Beaufort on their way to greet her.'

'Have something to eat and get your head down, Gabriel. We'll march at first light—and well done, I'm glad to have you back.'

Jasper knew what he must do. His first loyalty was to the queen and her son. Warwick would have to wait in the north, while he took his Welsh army to the west. He made one last visit to see the boys and remembered what his father told him, and his brother Edmund, when they seemed to face overwhelming odds.

'Be brave, boys, and remember you are Tudors.'

Q

When they finally reached the queen's army outside the market town of Dorchester, Jasper learned she had travelled to nearby Cerne Abbey with Sir Edmund Beaufort. He left the main body of his army and rode to the old abbey with his personal guard, to find her in the abbey guest house with a grave looking Sir Edmund.

'I thank God you are safe, Sir Jasper. Have you heard the news?'

'That York has taken London? I came as soon as I heard you were here.'

Queen Margaret shook her head. 'We have received worse news, Sir Jasper.' She turned to Edmund Beaufort to explain.

'I regret to tell you Warwick has been killed. His army was routed this morning at Barnet.'

'Are you sure he hasn't escaped?' Jasper found the news hard to believe.

'He is dead, Sir Jasper.' Queen Margaret's voice was cold.

Jasper sat heavily in a chair as he considered the implications. 'He sent for me, asked me to bring as many men as I could muster. If I had, Warwick might have lived. We might have beaten York.'

'And your stripped body might have been on display with Warwick's in St Paul's.' She answered sharply, her face set hard. 'We must deal with York without the Earl of Warwick, before he takes too firm a hold on the country.'

Sir Edmund sounded doubtful. 'It will not be easy to draw York out of London.'

Jasper turned to the queen. 'He will come for you. I found you easily enough, Your Highness, and if I can, so will York, and when he does we must be ready.'

'We need more men. We have my Frenchmen, as well as the men Sir Edmund has brought, and we are raising more from Devon and Dorset.'

'The men I've brought are only enough to ensure your safety, Your Highness, not to take on York. I have some four thousand men on their way to Chepstow from North Wales, including more than a thousand archers.'

'Then you must go to them, Sir Jasper. We will meet you once Prince Edward returns.'

'Where is Prince Edward, Your Highness?'

'He is helping to muster more men for our cause.' She sounded unconcerned.

'It would be better if he were with you, where we can ensure his safety.'

'He is a man now, Sir Jasper. One day he will be king, so I must let him learn to act as one.'

## 17

# APRIL 1471

Jasper marched his army back to the old Norman castle at Chepstow, the southernmost of a chain of fortresses built along the Welsh border, high on cliffs overlooking the River Wye. From the battlements they would have plenty of notice of anyone approaching and could control the old wooden bridge, the only river crossing for miles.

A strategic site since Roman times, the castle had a massive open courtyard within the high walls, and had been added to by each generation, as needs and fashions changed. Chepstow served well as a barracks, and he ordered his men to take a well-earned rest while they waited for the reinforcements from the north of Wales.

Days passed without any news, then a week. The worst thing about the waiting for Jasper was the feeling of powerlessness. He wished he had stayed with Queen Margaret and her son. His experience of mustering troops would have been invaluable and he worried about the reception young Prince Edward was probably receiving in the rural villages of Devon and Dorset.

Jasper also felt cut off from the outside world by the high castle walls and the fast-flowing River Wye. He posted guards at the bridge to question travellers and sent Gabriel into the taverns in the town of Chepstow to see what he could learn. So far no one brought him any new information, although as he feared, word of York's victory was already spreading far and wide.

He climbed the narrow, lichen covered steps of the high north tower and scanned the far horizon for his reinforcements. With a jolt he realised word of York's victory could have already reached the men of North Wales. They might have already turned back, or worse, joined York's army. The scrape of a boot on stone made him look round to see Gabriel had sought him out, a frown of concern instead of his usually cheerful expression.

'No word of the reinforcements yet, sir?'

'I regret there isn't, Gabriel, although it's too early to lose hope, as it's a long march here from North Wales.'

'You should know some of the men think our cause is lost and we should leave while we still can.'

Gabriel's words were no surprise to Jasper, as he had felt the same sullen mood which descended over them all, like ominous black clouds before a storm, following the news of Warwick's defeat. Despite his worries about deserters he gathered the men together and told them what had happened. They seemed to respect his honesty and there seemed little point in keeping bad news from them, as the rumours would spread soon enough.

'I understand how they feel, and I won't give them false hope, but we're going to need every man for the battle ahead. You've seen Queen Margaret's army.'

'All I saw was a few hundred French mercenaries, and Sir Edmund Beaufort's foot soldiers looked like beaten men.'

'They are poorly led,' Jasper shook his head, 'and if the truth were known, Edmund Beaufort fled from London to join the queen when a better man might have held the city against York.'

'He lost his nerve?'

'A good many of his best men defected to join York.'

'That's when Warwick's luck ran out, sir.'

'I never liked Sir Richard Neville, or his brothers, but I believed we could find a way to work together. If we had marched directly to him...' Jasper felt the sting of conscience, not only for the Earl of Warwick, but also for their cause, and the king, held prisoner once more.

'We were not to know, sir. We rode south to protect the queen.'

'You're right—there's nothing to be gained by worrying about what might have been.'

'I'll talk to the men, sir.' Gabriel patted the hilt of his fine sword. 'We're not beaten yet.'

Jasper watched him go and wondered if the loyal Irishman was right. The stakes had never been higher, as York would no longer be so generous with pardons for those who fought against him. Jasper had not told the men, but no quarter had been given at Barnet, even for the common soldiers. The only survivors of the battle were those who had been able to flee the field, and even they were being hunted down, as would all who rode under the banner of Lancaster.

He shared a meal of stale rye bread and salted pottage with his men, washed down with a tankard of watery ale, then retired to a restless sleep. In his troubled dreams he saw Warwick's sightless eyes, as he lay dead in St Paul's Cathedral where so recently they gave thanks to God. He saw the entire congregation turn to face him with accusing, deathly white stares, while Bishop George Neville's strident sermon accused him of being a coward, no better than Edmund Beaufort.

He woke to the sound of sharp hammering on his door and pulled it open to see the captain of the castle guard. A good-humoured local man, with an impressive grey beard, the captain had served under William Herbert and the Earl of Norfolk before him but now swore loyalty to Lancaster. Jasper had made a judgement to trust the experienced captain and his men of the Chepstow garrison, for as Gabriel observed, it was not their fault they had found themselves on the losing side.

'You have a visitor, my lord. A clergyman, Bishop John Hunden, of Llandaff. He's asked to see you.'

'What in God's name does a bishop want with me at this hour?' Jasper heard the irritation in his voice. He grunted as he pulled on his riding boots.

'He wishes to talk to you about a most urgent matter and asked me to wake you. He is waiting in the constable's tower, my lord.'

Jasper was already strapping on his sword. 'Let us go and see what is so important, Captain.'

Bishop Hunden stood as Jasper entered. A dark woollen coat covered his long, cleric's robes and grey stubble sprouted on his chin. Jasper knew Bishop Hunden, who had been a friend of his father and owned a house in Tenby. Forthright and influential, like many of the clergy, the bishop had to walk a tightrope of loyalty to both Lancaster and York.

Jasper tried to clear his head of unpleasant, troubling dreams. 'Good morning, Your Grace. What brings you to Chepstow at such an hour?'

Bishop Hunden studied Jasper with concern in his deep-set eyes and spoke in a soft Welsh accent.

'I regret having to wake you so early, Sir Jasper, but I've come to warn you that you and your men are in grave danger by remaining here.'

'York is on his way?'

Bishop Hunden shook his head. 'There has been a great

battle in Gloucestershire. I understand her highness Queen Margaret has been captured by York's soldiers and is being taken to London as we speak.'

Jasper felt a surge of guilt. 'Are you certain of this, Bishop? I was with her recently at Cerne, but she sent me here to wait for reinforcements.' A sudden and worrying thought occurred to him. 'Do you know if her son is safe?'

'I regret to tell you he died in the battle.' The Bishop made the sign of the cross. 'He is with God.'

'They killed the young prince?' Jasper's eyes blazed with anger. York had won and the House of Lancaster was finished. He formed a fist with his hand and clung to one last hope— this was yet another rumour, spread deliberately by York's spies to demoralise Lancastrian supporters.

'How did you come by this information, Bishop?'

'I visited the Abbot of Gloucester, who was told by the Prior of Tewkesbury that he saw the body of Prince Edward with his own eyes. There is no mistake, Sir Jasper, the prince is dead.'

Jasper struggled to come to terms with the loss, his mind a whirl of consequences. Now there was no heir, no more House of Lancaster after King Henry. He should have stayed with the queen, protected her or even persuaded her to travel with her son to Chepstow. If he had, the boy would still be alive. The guilt weighed heavily on his conscience and he felt his heart harden as he struggled to compose himself and fend off the overwhelming sense of loss.

'You said we are in grave danger here in Chepstow?'

'Sir Roger Vaughan of Tretower has been sent with his men to arrest you.' Bishop Hunden regarded him with sadness in his eyes. 'Your father was a good man, Jasper Tudor, as are you. I felt obliged to come here and warn you to leave while you can.'

Jasper placed his hand on the old man's shoulder, realising he must have ridden through the night at some personal risk to himself. 'I will forever be in your debt, Your Grace.'

'May God be with you, Sir Jasper, and keep you safe.' He made the sign of the cross.

'You must also leave, Bishop. Return to Llandaff and one day, God willing, I will come and find you there.'

After the bishop had gone Jasper called for the captain and told him the bad news.

'Sir Roger Vaughan knows this castle well, my lord, he is well aware of its weaknesses.'

Jasper knew the previous owner of the old castle had been William Herbert, who had done little to improve the defences. Chepstow castle had stood the test of time and had the oldest twin-towered gatehouse in the country, but there was no moat or defensible keep, as the original builders relied on the natural boundary of the River Wye to deter attackers.

'We don't have much time to prepare for a siege, Captain. Post your archers on the battlements with all the arrows we can find. I don't want a single man to cross the bridge. There is still no news of the men from North Wales?'

'No, my lord.'

'It could mean nothing—but I pray they have not been intercepted by York's army.'

'I have a suggestion, my lord. I am known to Sir Roger Vaughan from when he visited Lord Herbert here.'

'What do you have in mind, Captain?'

'We could choose to fight them, barricade the bridges and trust in your reinforcements arriving in time. The way I see it, my lord, is we could let them cross the river and come into the town.'

'Ambush them?'

'If you keep your men out of sight, with only the men of

the garrison to show themselves. I could tell them you had word and fled the country by boat from Bristol.'

Jasper hesitated, then realised the captain's plan could work. Vaughan would be unsurprised to learn they had fled or that the garrison at Chepstow had turned for York once more. This time he would use the Yorkist's complacency against them and rely on the element of surprise.

It was noon before men carrying Vaughan's banner of a golden lion were sighted by Jasper's scouts. His men were ready, having chosen hiding places within the castle and outbuildings, where they waited for the trumpeter's signal. Jasper told them the truth, holding nothing back, as all their lives depended on how well the captain's plan worked.

He chose a high vantage-point with a clear view of the bridge over the River Wye and the trumpeter at his side, ready to sound the alert. He expected Sir Roger Vaughan to stop with his men out of range on the far side of the bridge. He was wrong, as they continued marching he counted a dozen riders and some seventy soldiers.

The men approached the castle gatehouse with contempt for any danger from Jasper's men who could be within. He heard the shouted exchange, and the captain's voice inviting them in. Vaughan questioned the captain, then the clatter of hooves echoed in the castle yard as the riders entered then dismounted and allowed their horses to be led to the stables.

It seemed the plan was working, as he heard voices discussing something, but not raised, as Vaughan was led to the constable's tower. Jasper held his breath as he waited. Their plan was for Roger Vaughan to be seized and disarmed as he passed through the narrow entrance to the constable's room. He heard a shout, then a curse and silence.

Then he saw the signal he was waiting for, a white cloth waved from the constable's window, and he nodded to the trumpeter, who gave a long blast to alert the hiding men. Sir

Roger Vaughan's men outnumbered them, but were surrounded by archers, bows at the ready, appearing from their well-chosen hiding places.

'We have your commander!' Jasper bellowed from the high battlements, his stern voice echoing across the castle courtyard. 'Throw down your weapons!'

The tired soldiers glanced at each other, then there was the clang of a sword being dropped to the ground, followed by the clatter of another, then another. More of Jasper's men emerged with halberds and drawn swords to round up their prisoners.

'You can go. Go back into Wales, return home to your families!'

Jasper tried to contain the anger in his voice at these soldiers, whose only crime was to follow the wrong man. Without Vaughan to lead them they were simply Welshmen again. Some might make their way back to York's army, on its way to London, and tell of what happened in Chepstow but Jasper doubted it, and even if they did he would be long gone before anything could be done about it.

Sir Roger Vaughan was a different matter. Jasper watched the last of his men leave, many heading back into Wales, a few trying to cross back over the bridge, only to be turned back again by the guards posted there. He needed a little time. Not long, but long enough to do what he had to do.

Vaughan glowered at him, his anger barely contained. 'You are a traitor, Tudor. A coward and a traitor.' He struggled free of the men holding his arms and stepped forward.

Jasper stared into the dark, scornful eyes of the man who was said to have murdered his father. He had to be sure. Such things could not rest on hearsay and rumour.

'Tell me what happened after Mortimer's Cross.' He kept his voice calm and saw the puzzlement on his enemy's face.

'What do you want to know?'

'Was it you who marched my father to Hereford?'

'We spared the men but your father was their commander. I sent men to look for you, Tudor, but you ran like the coward you are.' Vaughan spat the words out, his contempt evident.

Jasper's fingernails dug into the palms of his hands as he fought to control his anger. Painful memories returned. His father pleading with him to head north, to march on through the night, away from the danger of ambush by York. He remembered the shock of hearing what happened to his father, and the guilt that haunted him ever since.

'Did you order my father's execution?'

Vaughan looked to the ground. 'We needed to make an example of them. Only ten were executed, the rest were pardoned.'

'I heard the River Lugg ran red with the blood of our countrymen, good men. Loyal to King Henry, the true king, chosen by God.'

Vaughan looked up at him, uncertainty in his eyes. 'I ask you to spare me, sir.'

'Would you have spared me, if we had been caught by your men?'

Vaughan didn't reply but his silence told Jasper what he already knew.

'I will offer you, sir, the same courtesy you allowed my father.'

If he let Vaughan go the man would not rest until he had his revenge and killed every one of them. Here, at last, was his father's murderer. William Herbert might have given the order but it was Roger Vaughan of Tretower who carried it out.

'Kneel before me.'

Vaughan sank to his knees, put his hands together and prayed for forgiveness, his lips mumbling the words.

Jasper did it for his father, for his brother, for the young prince who would never now be king. For poor King Henry, again locked in the Tower, for Queen Margaret who would soon join him there. He had never killed an unarmed man and would not ask any of his own soldiers to do so. His sword was the finest steel and the sharp blade had never been used. He doubted Sir Roger Vaughan knew the blow was coming.

## 18

# MAY 1471

Jasper felt certain York would soon come for them at Pembroke and began preparations for a long siege. He sent home as many men as could be spared, including Bethan and her son, David Owen, keeping only enough to garrison the castle. The less mouths they had to feed the better, despite the small mountain of supplies already stored in every available space.

Henry frowned as he studied a lengthy letter he'd received from Lady Margaret. His latest habit of dressing entirely in black made him look older, and was rarely seen without the sword Jasper had given him. It had seen some use, but was still a fine weapon. Jasper didn't tell him he took it from one of Vaughan's men, who had probably also taken it in battle.

Henry handed the letter to Jasper. 'What does this mean, Uncle?'

Jasper saw from the well-worn folds that the letter had been read several times, and felt an unexpected sense of loss as he recognised Lady Margaret's hand. This was a personal letter, but as he read it Jasper understood Henry's puzzlement. Margaret had been conscious of the danger of the letter falling into York's hands and took care to ensure it contained nothing that could be used against her.

She wished her son good health and said he was always in her prayers. Her letter went on to say, with God's grace, her husband Sir Henry Stafford would recover from the grievous wound he suffered fighting for York at Barnet. The letter ended with her praying to God her son would be safe.

'It means, Henry, that like all of us now, your mother has no choice. She had to swear loyalty to York for the sake of her husband, and to keep her fortune.'

'Will I have to swear loyalty to York?'

'I trust you will not, Henry.' He decided this was the time to raise an idea that had been on his mind since hearing of the death of Prince Edward. 'You remember we talked once that you have a claim to the throne? Well, now that claim is stronger than ever.' Jasper smiled. 'Can you imagine it, Henry Tudor, King of England?'

'I have no wish to ever be king, Uncle.' Henry answered quickly.

'A king doesn't have to fight in wars, Henry. If you were king, you could end wars, bring peace to this country, wouldn't that make your mother proud?'

Henry nodded yet remained silent for a moment, then gave Jasper a questioning look. 'Would Edward of York have to be dead, all his brothers and any sons, before I could ever be made king?'

'Edward of York took the throne by force.'

'As I would have to?' Henry shook his head. 'I don't think that would make my mother proud.'

Jasper was confident the thick walls of Pembroke Castle could be defended even if York brought his great cannons, yet he was less certain about the best course of action. There could be no new dawn for Lancaster now. Thomas White of Tenby visited with a merchant friend from London who brought the shocking news that King Henry had been found dead in his chapel in the Tower. Jasper listened with a sinking heart as the merchant repeated his story with the ease of one who has told it many times.

'We queued for half a day, my lord, to pay our last respects to his highness. He was laid out, you see, in the cathedral of St Paul's, and the line of people come to pay their last respects to him was more than half a mile long.' He held his arms outstretched to emphasise the point.

Jasper struggled to compose himself as he remembered his kindly half-brother, and how well Henry conducted himself, so recently in the same cathedral, despite his bewilderment at his sudden change of circumstances. He tried not to recall the nightmare he'd suffered at Chepstow where he dreamed a vision of the king's accusing eyes. The shocking news numbed his ability to think and he was too overcome to reply.

Thomas White seemed to sense this. 'Say what you saw,' he urged, 'tell Sir Jasper exactly what you told me?'

The merchant nodded. 'Only the part of the coffin over King Henry's face was open so that every man might see him, my lord, and on the pavement dripped his royal blood.'

Thomas White looked grave. 'You see, my lord, it's a sure sign he died not long before, and not from poison or being smothered in his sleep.' He shook his head. 'I know he was your kin but this puts the lie to any talk he died of grief.'

At last Jasper felt able to respond. 'The people showed King Henry proper respect?'

'They did, my lord, the king was dearly loved and many wept and mourned his passing.'

'He was buried in St Paul's Cathedral?'

'He was not, my lord. They took him to the chapel of Blackfriars, then to Chertsey Abbey for a proper burial.'

Jasper crossed to the window of his study and stood there for a moment, watching how the wind caused patterns of ripples on the tranquil river below. He doubted Edward of York would do such a thing but there were plenty of others who would, including his younger brothers George and Richard. Poor King Henry was no threat to anyone but, while he lived, there was always the chance of a rebellion. The price of York's peace of mind was the murder of an innocent, godly man.

He turned to his visitors. 'What of Queen Margaret? Does she still live?'

The merchant nodded. 'I was in London when York returned in a triumphal procession with Queen Margaret, my lord.' He glanced at Thomas White, who nodded for him to continue. 'The queen was shackled in a cart, where all could see her, on her way to a cell in the Tower.'

Jasper cursed York and remembered his father telling him how proud he had been to march behind the queen in 1445, when she arrived in London as a beautiful, radiant young bride on her way to her coronation.

'I imagine the people did not take so kindly to her?'

'York's guardsmen did their best to protect her, my lord, but I saw the people throwing mud, and worse, as well as shouting at her. I must say Queen Margaret took it bravely. She denied them the satisfaction of her tears.'

Thomas White nodded sadly. 'I've heard from a Breton merchant it's the talk of France. York has demanded payment of fifty thousand crowns in ransom for her life.'

Jasper found it hard to imagine anyone he knew in France being prepared to help her father, Duke René, to raise the ransom. The Duke of Burgundy always supported York, Duke Francis would say she brought it on herself, and even King Louis would see little to gain from the rescue of his cousin, now she had become a widow.

The hail of fire arrows fell harmlessly in the castle yard but the sight of them, smoking and burning within the walls, was a shocking reminder of the siege of Bamburgh and the danger they now faced. Jasper called for men with buckets to be ready to douse the flames with water as a second wave of burning arrows flew high and curved down into the heart of their sanctuary.

This was the second day of the siege and York's army began by attempting to storm the gatehouse. They were met by Jasper's archers and several of the attackers were wounded before they withdrew, a temporary respite, although one was captured alive. Gabriel dragged the soldier to Jasper and made him stand, his hands tied behind his back. The prisoner, a dark-haired man of no more than twenty years, was bleeding from a cut over his eye and clearly feared for his life.

'What is the name of your commander?' Jasper's voice was cold. Since the merchant's visit he felt little charity for followers of York.

The man hung his head in silence, then looked Jasper in the eye. 'Morgan ap Thomas.' There was a hint of defiance in his voice.

Gabriel nudged the man in the back. 'My lord.'

The man understood. 'Our commander is Morgan ap Thomas, my lord.'

'His father fought at my side, at Mortimer's Cross—' Jasper fought the bitter memories flooding his mind and turned his focus on the man in front of him. 'How many men does he have?'

The prisoner seemed uncertain. 'Two hundred, perhaps five, my lord.'

Jasper guessed it could be closer to the smaller figure. Morgan ap Thomas's men had swept into the sleepy town and promptly started evicting families from their homes. He'd watched from the battlements as women and children were ushered towards the castle. It had been a risky operation to allow them through the gate without enemy soldiers also breaking through. Now he had several dozen more to feed, although at least they had been spared.

He studied the young soldier in front of him, unluckily caught up in a war not of his choosing. He nodded to Gabriel that he had heard enough. As the men marched their prisoner off to the castle dungeons, Gabriel followed Jasper to the top of the high Norman keep where they saw a ditch deep enough to stop anyone entering or leaving the castle.

'You know this man, sir, Morgan ap Thomas?'

'I do, Gabriel. He married Catherine Vaughan, the only daughter of Sir Roger Vaughan, late of Tretower.'

The plan was risky but in the absence of a better one, their best hope. On the river side of the castle a natural limestone cave could be accessed by a stone stairway from within the castle walls. Used as a storeroom by the Norman builders, it would be a potential weakness in a siege and Jasper was planning to order the access to be blocked with rubble. Then he recalled his father mentioning it also once served as a boat-house.

Two sturdy rowing boats, complete with muffled oars, had been stowed secretly in the damp cavern. A false wall of stones blocked the opening to the river, where a sloping bank gave access to the water. The problem was that Morgan ap Thomas had posted archers on the opposite bank of the river.

'We need to distract them, Gabriel. I can't risk taking Henry unless this plan has a good chance.'

Gabriel scanned the enemy positions. 'There are a lot of them, sir, dug in deep as badgers, so they'll take some shifting.'

'There's a high tide after midnight, so we could try for the small hours and benefit from the cover of darkness.'

'I'll arrange a diversion at the gatehouse, sir. Make it look like we're making a break for it through the town?'

Jasper looked back out across the river. 'Good idea—let's give Morgan ap Thomas something to think about.'

The old wagon was loaded with buckets of tar, straw bales and most of the garrison's store of gunpowder. The axles were greased with fat and they practised pushing it around the castle yard under a canopy of tanned hides, to protect the men who had to run it into the ditch. Jasper nodded in approval as he studied it. The men besieging them had worked hard to dig the ditch as deep as they could, so the wagon would certainly draw their attention.

'I want it well alight before we open the gates, with plenty of archers to make sure they don't push it back at us.'

Gabriel agreed. 'Our archers and crossbowmen have been busy all day picking off any enemy soldiers who dare to show themselves, sir. At least a dozen have been killed and many more wounded.'

'What about our casualties?'

'Both should recover, sir.'

'Let us hope so, Gabriel.'

Jasper still had doubts about their plan but could see no alternative. At high tide they would pull down the false wall blocking the cavern, then slide the boats down into the river under covering fire from their archers on the battlements, while the wagon was lit and rushed into the ditch at the front of the castle.

Gabriel would be in the first boat with two crossbowmen, while Jasper followed in the second with Henry. A lot could go wrong, not least the danger from the remaining enemy soldiers watching from the opposite bank. They took the difficult decision not to wear mail coats or armour because of the risk of drowning under the weight. Instead they dressed in dark, ragged clothes, hoping to pass as sailors when they reached the old docks downriver, where they planned to find a more seaworthy boat, if they could board one without the crew raising the alarm.

Jasper helped Henry rub soot into his pale face. 'There's not much of a moon but you'd be surprised at how far off a man's face can be seen.'

Henry yawned. He was supposed to sleep early but had been excited by the prospect of escaping. 'I should not like to have a beard like you, Uncle. I shall be clean-shaven when I am older.'

Jasper was so used to his thick beard he didn't give it a thought. He smiled as he rubbed soot around his eyes, giving him the look of a pirate. 'When you are King of England?'

Henry nodded. It had become something of a joke between them, a game to pass the long hours of the siege. He had to think of new things he would do when he became king. Jasper embarrassed him earlier by suggesting that high on the list should be marriage to a beautiful and wealthy queen.

Men worked in the darkness of the cavern to slide the stones of the false wall to the ground as silently as they could. Moonlight flooded in and they peered across to the opposite bank where the enemy archers lurked. There was no sign of movement but it was hard to tell as the riverbank was a mass of shadowy shapes.

Jasper made a judgement. 'Now or never.' He gave the signal for the wagon to be lit and watched as Gabriel and his men pushed the boats out towards the river. They were heavier than they looked and needed a lot of strength to move. He turned to Henry, who'd been told to wait in the dark at the back of the cave. A sudden movement made him jump.

It was only a pigeon roosting on one of the ledges near the roof.

'Be ready when you see the boats reach the water.' He tried to keep his voice low and calm but heard the tension in his words.

Distant shouts and the clash of steel sounded on the still night air and they knew their diversion was underway. Gabriel pushed the first boat at the river's edge and was turning to check progress with the second when an arrow thudded into the long grass at his feet. Another struck him in the leg and he dropped, using the hull of the boat as cover.

His crossbowmen were ready to return fire and a yell of pain rang out as one of their bolts found its mark. More arrows from archers on the battlements flashed across the river and Jasper called to Henry to stay back. He dashed down to the river and grabbed Gabriel's arm.

'Can you make it back up to the cave?'

'I'll be glad of a little help, sir.' Gabriel grimaced with pain.

Jasper saw the arrow sticking from Gabriel's leg. 'We can't stay here.' He glanced across the water as an arrow struck one of the enemy archers in the chest. 'Quick, let's move.'

He helped the heavy Irishman back up the bank and into the cave, where the crossbow men still looked for targets. 'Take him to have that arrow removed, and be quick about it.'

Jasper glanced towards the river where the two boats still waited, tantalisingly close yet too far to risk. He remembered telling Gabriel that only those who actually rolled the dice could ever hope to win. Henry waited in the depths of the cavern and he was about to call him down when the horsemen appeared around the corner of the castle.

He shouted to Henry to run up the stone steps to safety and drew his sword. If he had to die to offer the boy a chance he was ready. Someone called behind him to hurry up the stairs and he realised it was Henry, refusing to leave him to his fate. The riders closed fast, swords drawn, and were met with a volley of arrows from high on the parapet. The leading rider fell from his horse and the others veered away, looking for cover.

Jasper ran up the narrow, spiral stairway and called for the entrance to be barricaded. Henry waited, his face still covered with soot and his drawn sword in his hand.

'We nearly made it, Henry.'

'We still have the boats. They won't expect us to try again tomorrow?'

Jasper looked at his nephew with new respect. It was easy to see his slim build and boyish looks and forget. 'You have Beaufort steel in your veins, Henry, and the heart of a Tudor.'

The wound in Gabriel's leg was deep and he'd lost a lot of blood before they could bind it. He needed better treatment than anyone in the castle could offer, adding yet another worry to Jasper's list. When Jasper visited him the Irishman looked feverish, his face pale and bathed in sweat, a serious sign.

'Hurts like hell, sir.' Gabriel's voice sounded hoarse, 'I'm sorry I stopped you getting away.'

Jasper called for a servant to bring Gabriel a cup of ale. 'It always was a risky plan, and it could just as easily have been me they hit.' He forced a smile. 'You need to rest—and I will pray for your recovery.'

He climbed the high keep with Henry, his constant companion since the night of their attempted escape. From the top they could see the trench had already been cleared, the ruined wagon cut into pieces to be burned for firewood. Morgan ap Thomas's army surrounded the castle on all sides, so there would be no more escape attempts. They had been under siege for over a week and supplies were already running low.

'What are we going to do?' Henry's question sounded as if it was as much to himself as to Jasper.

'In truth, Henry, I don't know.' Jasper looked east towards Tenby, with its harbour full of boats only ten miles away, so near yet so far. He pointed to where a group of enemy soldiers played cards. 'They are growing as bored of this as we are, and they're getting careless. Soon we'll not be able to feed the women and children we brought in for safety. It's me Thomas wants, so we could send them back, with you in disguise.'

'I won't do it, Uncle. I will not leave you here.'

Jasper felt touched by the boy's loyalty. It would be a risky plan, as Henry was a good prize for Morgan ap Thomas and could be sent to London, to the Tower, or worse.

'Our only other option is a mass break-out. They won't be expecting it and if we all head in different directions a good many could escape.'

'And a good many more be killed or wounded?'

'Yes. Morgan ap Thomas has used the past week well, as every road and path is barricaded and ditched to slow us down and make escape as hard as possible.' He saw Henry's worried frown. 'This castle will not be breached, Henry.'

'But soon we will run short of food?'

Jasper glanced down at the stables and remembered the siege of Bamburgh. He didn't tell Henry they could run out of water first. He should have dealt with the well, tainted and abandoned long ago, and their barrels of ale had gone far too quickly, despite the rationing. In another week or so they would need to slaughter the horses and the men would know it was the beginning of the end.

When the attack came it took them all by surprise. Jasper was visiting Gabriel on his sickbed, and relieved to see his friend seemed to be recovering from his wound, although still unable to put his weight on the leg. The arrowhead had been difficult to remove but he was strong and the risk of infection was hopefully passed, thanks to the poultice of herbs.

One of the guards came shouting for Jasper, and he rushed up to the parapet to look out across the ravaged town at a sight he thought he might never live to see. Morgan ap Thomas's soldiers were being beaten back into their own ditches by an army of men with halberds and spears, axes and scythes.

He heard a cheer from his men and realised, by some miracle, the new attackers planned to rescue them. 'Archers to me!' He yelled and beckoned with his arm. 'Choose your targets well!'

Jasper took a bow and grabbed a stack of arrows from a pile they had stored by the gatehouse. He had no idea who their rescuers were but they would need all the help he could give. As he notched the arrow he noticed from scorch marks on the shaft it was one of the salvaged fire arrows. He sighted on the men taking cover in the ditch below and fired, not waiting to see it hit before notching and shooting the next, then another. Archers to each side of him did the same, creating a hail of arrows onto the heads of their enemies.

As he watched, a huge bear of a man charged the soldiers trying to shelter in the ditch, swinging a deadly poleaxe. One of the soldiers threw down his sword and fled the battle, followed by a second. Morgan ap Thomas's men wavered. Jasper saw riders clash swords and heard the sharp ring of steel on steel as a battle raged, then more men began to desert, tipping the balance in favour of their rescuers.

At last, a thick-set, bearded man on a fine black horse bellowed up to him.

'Sir Jasper Tudor?'

He studied the man but couldn't recognise him in his armour and helmet. It could be a trick, but too many men lay dead and wounded for this to be an elaborate plot to lure him out.

Jasper cupped his hands and shouted back. 'Who goes there?'

'Dafydd ap Thomas, for Lancaster!'

Morgan's own brother, with the last remaining Welsh Lancastrian army, had arrived to lift the siege. Jasper couldn't believe his luck and signalled for the men on the gate to allow him to enter. Dafydd ap Thomas dismounted and led his horse through the great stone gatehouse and watched as Jasper clambered down to greet him.

'We made it in time, my lord!' His deep voice echoed in the castle ward.

Jasper shook him by the hand. 'I thank God you did, although it grieves me to see how York has turned brother against brother.'

'We cannot stay, my lord.' Dafydd ap Thomas glanced back towards his men, already busy looting supplies and gathering fallen weapons in the town. 'You must ride with us, before York hears of this and sends reinforcements, as he surely will.'

## 19

---

## JUNE 1471

Jasper rode the familiar back roads to Tenby through the night with Henry at his side. They dressed as commoners, in rough wool, their swords hidden in sacking bundles tied behind their saddles, containing all they owned in the world. Jasper chose to bring his precious armour, a gift from King Louis, as well as all the gold and silver he could carry.

He had thanked his loyal men and released them from any obligation, telling them to return home to their families. Soon the castle was deserted except for the wounded in the makeshift infirmary, the few remaining servants and those who had nowhere else to go. He regretted leaving Gabriel behind, as he'd wanted to leave with them but they both knew he would only slow them down. At least he should be safe enough when York's men came, and said he would track them down when he could.

Dafydd ap Thomas had offered them to ride with him back to his hiding place in the mountains, to continue to fight for a free Wales. Dafydd's men were, by his own admission, a rabble of farmers and adventurers. They were united only by their hatred of York and their desire to make life difficult for those the usurper king rewarded by granting them Welsh estates.

'If we had ridden with Dafydd ap Thomas we would have been choosing the life of rebels.' He glanced at Henry to make sure he understood. 'York's soldiers would have hounded us, and we would always be on the run.'

He didn't like to talk about the inevitable day they would be captured. He was under no illusions. They would both be seen by York and his ambitious brothers as a threat and would be hanged as rebels without even the need for a proper trial. At best they might be taken to London and put in the Tower but there could only be one ending to his story.

'Dafydd's men have shown they can fight, but they must hit and run, always looking over their shoulders, with no real hope of stopping York.' It sounded bleak, not the future he wished for Henry.

'What shall we do if we escape to France?'

'I'm half French and your grandmother, on your father's side, was a French queen of the House of Valois.' Jasper smiled as he recalled the stories his father told him about his grandfather's madness but decided to keep them to himself, for now. 'King Louis of France has been generous with his support and paid for our last expedition, so there is a chance he might be persuaded to do so again.'

'My mother is wealthy, Uncle. Could she not help us?'

'She could, but it's important we don't put her or your stepfather in danger of treason, for that is what they would call it.'

The sky was filled with glittering stars and a full moon lit the tall spire of St Mary's church as they drew close to the sleeping town. Once Jasper's sanctuary and stronghold, he had learned from Dafydd ap Thomas that Tenby was now sworn to York, so held new dangers for them both. They must reach the harbour without being spotted and find a merchant ship bound for France.

It would be an impossible task without the help of Jasper's good friend Thomas White, who seemed to know the master of every sailboat in the harbour. His house could be reached down the narrow back streets but the problem was how to rouse him from his bed at such a late hour without drawing unwanted attention to themselves.

'We have the advantage that they aren't looking for us yet, but if they do, my house is the first place they'll search.' Jasper kept his voice to a whisper as he glanced down the deserted street. 'I remember there are stables at the back of Thomas White's house. If we're quiet we should be able to reach them without waking anyone.'

A cat screeched from the shadows of a doorway, startling their horses as they led them down a narrow alleyway to the stables, which were fortunately not locked. Two of the stalls contained Thomas White's horses but there was plenty of room, so Jasper left Henry while he crept round to study the small windows at the rear of Thomas's house. Like many in Tenby they overhung the lower floor and were shuttered, although one was open to let in fresh air, an encouraging sign.

He tried the back door and it opened, so he slipped inside and waited until his eyes adjusted to the darkness. He found himself in the wine-merchant's kitchen, furnished with a well-scrubbed oak table. Red embers still glowed in the hearth and a brace of colourful cock pheasants hung from the low ceiling beams, alongside an assortment of burnished copper pots and pans.

Through an open doorway at the other side of the room was a small hallway and the stairs to the upper floor. One of the floorboards creaked loudly as Jasper moved and, aware that White could think he was being robbed, Jasper decided he would have to announce himself. He called up the narrow staircase as loudly as he dared.

'Thomas White? This is Jasper Tudor!'

He waited but heard nothing and was about to repeat his shout when there was the sound of someone moving around and a door opened. The glimmer of a flickering candle lit up the darkness of the hallway. Thomas White appeared like a ghost, wearing a thick cotton shirt, his feet bare on the wooden floorboards.

'My lord?' He held up the candle and peered down the stairs.

Jasper held up a hand in greeting. 'I am sorry to trouble you at this ungodly hour, Thomas, but we need your help.'

Thomas White descended the stairs and studied Jasper with surprise and interest. 'We all thought you were besieged in Pembroke. You know it's the talk of the town?'

'I managed to escape, thank God, with my young nephew Henry.' Jasper rubbed his eyes, realising he hadn't taken a decent night's sleep since the siege began. 'We need your help, Thomas. We must find a ship to France before anyone starts looking for us here.'

A frown crossed Thomas White's face as he understood the consequences of Jasper's words. 'I own a barque, the *Christiana*, that would serve your purpose. She would need to be provisioned and is moored high in the harbour so you would have to wait for the tide.'

Jasper produced his purse, heavy with gold and silver coins. 'There should be more than enough here. Would it be possible to stay in your house until she's ready?'

'I would have to ask you to keep out of sight, my lord. There is my wine cellar where you would be safe unless York's men made a thorough search?'

'After what we've been facing in Pembroke Castle a wine cellar would be like a palace, Thomas, and it would be wonderful to have one good night's sleep.'

Jasper woke from a disturbing dream in complete darkness and for a moment wondered where he was. The cellar proved to be dry and spacious, with a low, arched ceiling and whitewashed walls hewn from the solid bedrock. Barrels of wine lined one side, with smaller casks on the other, and the air carried a rich, heady aroma from all the wine stored there over the years.

Thomas White had provided them both with coarse wool blankets and fresh straw to fashion beds, and been generous with his wine. They had drunk more than they should, a welcome release after the tension of the siege, although what helped Jasper to sleep was the knowledge that for the first time since Chepstow he was safe, if only temporarily.

As his eyes became used to the light he saw Henry still fast asleep. The boy was looking more like his father all the time, although Jasper thought it fortunate he had his mother's temperament. They must find a way to let Lady Margaret know her son was safe and on his way to sanctuary in France.

He tensed at the sound of footsteps outside the door and his hand went to his dagger. Henry woke and gave him a worried look, then Thomas White appeared through the entrance. He carried a wooden tray with bowls of pottage and some crusty bread, which he set down on the small table.

'Good morning to you, sirs.' Thomas managed to sound cheerful.

'Good morning, Thomas.' Jasper stood and took one of the bowls. 'We appreciate the trouble you've gone to.'

Thomas was dismissive. 'I am sorry you find yourselves in such a predicament, my lord.'

'We are indebted to you, Thomas. After we escaped from

the castle you were our best hope.' Jasper tore a piece of bread and dipped it in the pottage, which was hot and tasty, flavoured with herbs and with good morsels of lamb. 'My only concern is that we put your good self at risk, so we must be gone from here as soon as we are able to. When do you think the ship might be ready to sail?'

'There is a high tide this morning, my lord, but it would be safer to wait until tonight when the harbour is less busy.'

'You are right, Thomas. We must take care, as we don't know who remains loyal to our cause.' Jasper shook his head. 'I know they have little choice, but it saddens me to know your own neighbours would turn me in to York's soldiers.'

Thomas agreed. 'These are difficult times, but you are safe enough here for now, and if there is anything else you need, please ask?'

Jasper glanced across at Henry, who was hungrily eating the pottage. 'Could I trouble you for ink and parchment? We need to send a letter to Henry's mother, as she will soon hear of the siege at Pembroke and be worried for his safety.'

'Would it not cause her trouble if we tell her where we're going?'

Jasper shook his head. 'I shall write it to her clergyman and find words to reassure her, without revealing too much.'

The wording of the letter occupied them both for most of the long morning, then Thomas White returned to tell them the captain of the *Christiana* and his crew would be ready for the evening tide, with just the horses to take aboard.

'And you have a visitor, my lord, a most insistent one.'

Gabriel appeared at the doorway, wearing a rough cotton coat over his heavy mail shirt and leaning on a stout wooden crutch. 'Good day to you, sirs.' He studied the cellar appreciatively, taking in the casks of wine and their comfortable beds of clean straw. 'I can think of worse places to hide than the cellar of a wine-merchant.'

'How are you, Gabriel.' Jasper looked at the bandage on the Irishman's leg. 'Are you well enough to sail with us?'

'Try to stop me, sir. It was a nasty wound but healed well enough, and I saw my chance to get out of the castle while I could. I've brought some of the men with me, sir, as well as your servants, already on board the ship.'

Jasper nodded thanks to Thomas White. 'I've been thinking about what happened. Morgan ap Thomas isn't the sort of man to flee at the sight of his own brother's army.'

'There's been no sign of him since, sir.'

'That's the thing. Dafydd ap Thomas was most insistent we should leave the same night, before York could send reinforcements.' Jasper cast his mind back to the battle. 'Although several men were killed and wounded by our archers, I didn't see any actually killed by Dafydd's men.'

'You think it could have been a plan to deliberately let you escape?'

Jasper smiled. 'We can't be sure but I suspect the brothers plotted the whole thing together, so they could be seen to be loyal to both York—and Lancaster. It's one way for Morgan ap Thomas to save his face and make sure their lands and family would survive, whatever happens in the future.'


Thomas White had one more surprise for them once the sun set and the people of Tenby took to their beds. He led them through a narrow passageway, barely high enough to stand upright, which led deep under the street, safe from prying eyes. They followed him through the dark tunnel, roughly hewn through solid rock and lit only by the flickering lantern carried by Thomas, which took them all the way down to the harbour where his ship was moored and waiting.

'I wish you luck, my lord, and God be with you all.' Thomas White shook hands with Jasper.

Henry stepped forward and also shook Thomas's hand. 'Thank you, sir, for all you have done for us. I will not forget it.'

They watched as Thomas slipped back into the tunnel entrance, so cleverly concealed it was impossible to see. Jasper studied their waiting ship, a black-painted, three-masted barque with square rigged sails, more than capable of a long sea voyage. He took one last glance back at the sleeping town that had been his home, then followed Henry and Gabriel up the gangplank to start his new adventure.

They headed out into the night and watched as the silhouette of the Tenby skyline, with the spire of St Mary's church and row of rooftops on the crest of the cliff, faded into the darkness. Jasper took a deep breath of the fresh sea air and felt a powerful sense of relief. The nagging uncertainty about what they should do was now resolved. He thanked God they had been spared the choice of starvation or the shame of surrender to Morgan ap Thomas, with its unthinkable consequences.

Gabriel joined him at the bows. 'I've checked on the horses, sir, all's fine below decks.'

'Henry is in the cabin?'

'He is, sir.' He looked out to sea, where a rolling swell was slowly building. 'He's no sailor though. He told me the only time he's ever been on a boat is on the Thames with his mother, so I told him to get his head down until morning.'

'He'll be right enough once he can see the horizon, and we should be round Land's End by then.'

'Is there a plan, sir, when we reach France?'

'No better or worse than last time, Gabriel. We need to stay out of trouble until I can secure an audience with King Louis, and I've no idea what mood I will find him in.'

Secretly Jasper worried that since he was last in France King Louis might have agreed a treaty with York's ambassadors. If he had, it could mean their arrest and imprisonment. There was no one to pay a ransom now, so the best they could hope for could be protracted negotiations for their exchange for his cousin Queen Margaret, followed swiftly by York's revenge.

The one glimmer of hope was the king's hatred of York's brother-in-law, the Duke of Burgundy. He also remembered how the king would listen to his wife. Queen Charlotte had shown him kindness last time he saw her, so might support his plight, despite the fact he had so little to offer. He glanced back down to the cabins where Henry lay sleeping. Henry had been right when he said his claim to the throne was worthless while Edward of York lived, and there were his ambitious brothers, George and Richard, as well as the sons Edward would undoubtedly have.

They had little money and no prospects, but Jasper hoped his Valois blood still counted for something. Perhaps it was time to find himself a wife, a wealthy heiress with a fine house and land where he could slowly build his fortune. Henry was also of marriageable age, and Queen Margaret's father, Duke Renee of Anjou, should understand they had done what they could to support his daughter.

After a sleepless night in an uncomfortable canvas hammock, Jasper clambered on deck to find the sea had turned into a foaming maelstrom. Strong winds buffeted the sails and the crew balanced precariously on the wet yard-arms as they tried to reef the flapping canvas.

There was no mistaking the angry dawn sky, so threatening, the sunrise barely penetrated the thunder clouds. As he watched, a surging wave broke over the bows, sending a sheet of salty spray in the air and nearly washing one of the sailors overboard. Jasper decided it was safer in the cramped cabin and returned to see Henry awake and discussing their future with Gabriel.

The Irishman grinned as Jasper entered. 'It's looking a little rough out there, sir.'

Jasper wiped his face dry. 'We are lucky Thomas White has let us take his best ship. I don't envy the crew having to climb out on the yards in these conditions.'

Henry's face was pale but he managed a smile, and showed Jasper a scrap of canvas with lines drawn on it in charcoal. It took him a moment to recognise it as a crudely drawn map of the south of England and the coast of France, marked with lines to show the territories of Burgundy and Brittany.

'Gabriel has been showing me where we are heading,' Henry glanced at the Irishman, 'and telling me about King Louis.'

Jasper studied the map. 'You see here?' He pointed to the black smudge which represented Paris. 'This is where your grandmother was from. Two days ride from Honfleur, where we will land.'

Henry nodded. 'Do you think the King of France will agree to see us?'

'I hope he will, Henry. He is our best hope and helped me in the past, but I must also tell you he is a complicated man, and I've not been able to repay his favours.'

'What do we do if he won't see us?'

'Then we must travel to see Queen Margaret's father, Duke

René.' He tried to reassure Henry. 'It won't be easy, but then anything worthwhile rarely is.'

A brilliant flash lit up the blackened sky, followed moments later by a crash of thunder, reverberating through the ship. Jasper looked up at the storm clouds as the deck pitched and another wave smashed into the bows, again sluicing the entire deck with sea water. They made slow progress in the stormy conditions and were well out of sight of land, their lives in the hands of the captain and his crew.

The helmsman battled to keep the *Christiana* heading into the rising swell as each wave grew larger than the last. Powerful gusts of wind buffeted the sails and Jasper heard the captain shouting orders to his weary crew. For the first time he realised they could be in real danger from the storm.

He'd not been able to think of Máiréad for a long time but he remembered her now, and thought how terrifying it must have been when the queen's fleet was sunk off Lindisfarne Island. Another wave splashed into his face, the shock of the icy seawater making him gasp. He promised himself that if they reached France in safety he would light a candle in her memory and say a prayer for her.

The storm still raged when darkness fell and the captain sought Jasper out to break the news that they had been blown far off course. They must now head for the island of Jersey and seek shelter in the harbour. They anchored offshore in the bay and weathered the storm until morning, when a cloudless, pastel-blue dawn showed the first signs of promise. Jasper joined Henry and Gabriel at the stern rail.

'We face a difficult choice. York's ships patrol the English Channel, so we could take our chances or land in western Brittany.'

Henry nodded. 'I would rather not go back out to sea.'

'We'll make a sailor of you yet, sir.' Gabriel laughed. 'At least you've survived your first long passage.'

Jasper looked towards the mainland. 'I'm in favour of making landfall in Brittany. I doubt Duke Francis has agreed an alliance with York, so at least we'll be fairly sure of a friendly welcome.'

## 20

# JUNE 1471

The bustling harbour at Le Conquet might not be their intended destination, yet Jasper said a silent prayer of thanks as they tied up between the battered old fishing boats laden with old wicker lobster-pots. Hard-faced crab and lobster fishermen were soon joined by an unwelcome crowd of curious onlookers as the whinnying, blinkered horses were led ashore.

Jasper sensed the mood of the local men and was keen to be on the road as soon as they were able to, although he now found they had an entourage of servants and soldiers. Gabriel, still leaning on his wooden crutch, shouted orders as he supervised the men, who had brought as many of Jasper and Henry's possessions as they could from Pembroke Castle in wooden chests.

'How are we supposed to carry this lot, Gabriel?' Jasper studied the heavy chests waiting on the quay.

Gabriel grinned. 'I know you didn't want me to burn your papers, sir, and the rest would have been looted by York's soldiers if we left them behind.'

'Your intentions were good, but it's going to slow us down.'

'I've thought of that, sir.' Gabriel pointed behind them with his crutch. 'I've already been haggling with the local merchants for a high-sided wagon.'

Jasper watched as a pair of rugged Breton carthorses were harnessed to the wagon. It would still make slow progress but at least there should be room for the servants to ride rather than walk. Gabriel was right, there had been no need to let York's men take his last possessions in the world, and some had more than sentimental value.

It was noon before they left the town and headed for the city of Brest. Henry rode at Jasper's side and peered down the stony, tree-lined avenue stretching for as far as they could see.

'How far is it to Paris from Le Conquet?'

'A long ride, Henry.' Jasper frowned as he calculated the distance. 'Paris is some four hundred miles to the east.'

'Do you think, Uncle, we will find King Louis there?'

'I hope to discover the king's whereabouts before we reach Paris. He has palaces at Angers and Chinon which are half that distance.' He glanced back at the slow, heavily laden wagon and the soldiers riding behind. 'My plan had been to travel light and fast with only you for company.' He smiled at Henry. 'At least now we look like the refugees we are, rather than having to travel in disguise.'

'Are we safe here in Brittany?'

Jasper glanced behind again. 'I won't lie to you, Henry. Duke Francis is a suspicious man and distrusts both King Louis and the Burgundians. He should welcome us as family, although he is as likely to arrest us once he learns we are here.'

'What good would that do?'

'York will request our return, while King Louis will endeavour to prevent it at all costs. We would become pawns, Henry, in the game of chess that's been played out between Brittany and France for generations.'

. . .

They were on the road for less than three hours when a group of fast-moving riders appeared in the distance. As they approached Jasper saw they were armed soldiers, one carrying a banner with the distinctive ermine badge of Duke Francis. He looked at the tired faces of his retinue, who stopped in their tracks at the sight of the advancing patrol.

For a moment he wondered if they could escape, rather than face possible imprisonment. He'd heard stories of men driven half mad in squalid cells while they waited for a ransom that would never be paid. His own father spent a long time in Newgate Gaol waiting for Parliament to decide what to do with him. He would never talk about it but Jasper remembered the haunted look in his eyes whenever the subject was mentioned.

Gabriel had brought a dozen armed men all the way from Pembroke but there was no question of fighting the duke's guards, and he had no wish to. Too late he realised his own soldiers should have stayed at home. It was time to risk placing themselves at the duke's mercy. He approached their commander, a distinguished looking man with a blue riding cape and a large grey moustache, and spoke to him in Breton.

'Good day to you, Captain. I am Jasper Tudor, a cousin of Duke Francis. I request an escort to meet with him.'

The captain studied them, taking in the mounted men, the overloaded wagon, and the servants waiting to see what he said. 'Good day, Sir Jasper. I remember you. We will escort you to Nantes, although I cannot guarantee the duke will see you.'

'I am grateful to you, Captain. That is a risk I am prepared to take.'

He rode at the captain's side as they made their way to the city. 'Tell me, Captain, what has happened in Brittany since I was here last?'

The captain sat back in his saddle and reflected before

answering in his gruff Breton accent. 'Brittany has prospered, and King Louis has learned to respect Duke Francis, as he should.'

Jasper appreciated the captain's loyalty but imagined this was not truly the case. 'Has the duke seen envoys from Edward of York?'

The captain replied sharply. 'I cannot say, sir.'

His reticence told Jasper all he needed to know. York had already sent ambassadors to negotiate an alliance against France, information which Jasper knew would be in his favour when he was eventually able to meet King Louis.

'Does Duke Francis know we are here?'

'I doubt he does, Sir Jasper. This is a routine patrol, so it was chance we happened to find you.'

Jasper nodded. Fate had blown them off course and brought them to the shores of Brittany. They needed time to recover from their narrow escape from Pembroke Castle and although Henry put a brave face on it, Jasper suspected he had been terrified by the storm and their perilous sea voyage. He would follow his destiny and make sure that by the time he met the king it would not be as a refugee seeking more favours.

Duke Francis looked a little older, and although he was Jasper's age his hair was already turning a silver grey. He dressed more like a king than a soldier, in a fashionable cap, a cloak of dark velvet and a heavy gold chain, studded with rubies. They arrived late in the evening at the magnificent Château de l'Hermine in Vannes after a full and tiring day's ride from Nantes, where they stayed the previous night.

The château was the duke's main residence and it was hard not to be impressed by its ambitious scale, from the towering walls to the glazed windows. As they entered they saw the former fortress had been transformed into a palace, with floors of decorative Italian tiles and colourful Flemish tapestries of hunting scenes adorning the walls, illuminated by hundreds of candles in gilded chandeliers.

A formal welcoming reception had been arranged for them, with a guard of honour and a gathering of Breton nobles with their colourfully dressed wives, civic dignitaries and church leaders. Trumpeters played a fanfare as Jasper and Henry, dressed in their best clothes, arrived looking more like visiting royalty than refugees. Jasper bowed in deference to the duke, who studied them both with interest.

'I am honoured, Sir Jasper, that you have chosen to seek exile in Brittany.'

'Thank you, Duke Francis.' He nodded to Henry who stepped forward. 'May I present my nephew, Henry Tudor, who will inherit his late father's title of Earl of Richmond when he comes of age?'

Duke Francis nodded, his face thoughtful. 'You are welcome, Henry Tudor.'

'Thank you, sir, for granting us your generous protection.' Henry spoke in perfect French and seemed to have a new confidence.'

'Did you know, Henry, that the first Earl of Richmond was a Breton?'

'I did not, sir.'

Duke Francis smiled. 'Alan ar Rouz sailed with William of Normandy, whom you will know as William the Conqueror, and was rewarded with the earldom of Richmond.'

'I will be honoured, sir, to continue his legacy.'

Duke Francis seemed pleased with Henry's response. 'You will both be granted safe conduct throughout my territories, and may rely on my protection for as long as you remain in Brittany.'

Jasper wondered if Henry had spotted the care with which the duke chose his words. He'd not forgotten how Duke Francis placed his own interests above all other considerations. He had given his word to protect them while they were in Brittany, but that could also effectively make them his prisoners, unable to leave for France without his consent.

He looked at the lavishly furnished Château and decided that, for now at least, there were far worse places to stay and plan for a new future. It would be good experience for Henry to learn something of the complex politics of France before he met King Louis, and Jasper had seen enough of what England and Wales had become under the rule of York.

Jasper gratefully accepted the duke's offer of an apartment at the château for himself and Henry but was concerned to be told that his servants must return home. It was another sign of the duke's real intention to control their movements. It was no hardship, as he had already provided them with servants from his household, although Jasper knew they were also spies, loyal to the duke.

They were permitted a final meeting with Gabriel, who was also under instruction to leave Brittany on the *Christiana*, which had been held at Le Conquet. He tried to remain cheerful as he came to say farewell, although Jasper knew him well enough to see his concern for them.

'Will you be heading back to Waterford, Gabriel?'

'I think not, sir. I plan to find work in Tenby with Thomas White and wait there for the day when you return.'

'You might have to wait a long time,' Jasper glanced at Henry, 'although you could do us a great service by helping to carry messages to Lady Margaret. It would be at some risk but we know how resourceful you can be, Gabriel.'

The Irishman brightened. 'It would give me cause to return here, and I can bring you news of developments in England?'

'That would be truly useful, Gabriel, for as pleasant as this place is, I fear the duke wishes us to be hidden from the world.'


Jasper's words proved prophetic when the duke decided to transfer them from Vannes to his fortified château at Suscinio. The isolated castle was a luxurious residence, with more than enough room for Jasper and Henry. With high, conical-roofed towers surrounded by a wide moat, the Château was next to a freshwater lake and surrounded by forests stocked with game for the duke's hunting parties.

Jasper's new room was a simple one compared with the extravagance of Château de l'Hermine, with whitewashed walls and plain, functional furniture. His window overlooked the open, high-walled courtyard, which housed the stables and kennels for the duke's hunting dogs. These gave plenty of warning of any new arrivals, although he had often been woken early by their persistent barking.

He walked with Henry to the wide, sandy bay of the Gulf of Morbihan, a natural harbour guarded by the island of Belle-Île, with its smaller sister islands of Houat and Hoëdic. The seafront was deserted except for a flock of small sandpipers hunting for shrimps and crabs at the tideline. The natural beauty of the scene lifted his mood and reminded him a little of the long south beach at Tenby in West Wales.

Henry picked up a seashell, bleached white in the sun. 'Why do you think we've be sent here, rather than staying at the duke's palace in Vannes?'

Jasper looked out across the tranquil blue Atlantic, so calm barely a ripple disturbed the surface. He was growing used to Henry's constant questions and encouraged him to learn as much as he could about their new home, although he didn't always have answers.

'Duke Francis said it's for our own safety.'

'Are we in danger?'

'York's agents are regular visitors to Vannes,' he saw Henry's worried look, 'and word of our presence here will surely have reached York. I suppose the duke wants to keep us out of the way, for now.'

Henry glanced back at the duke's armed guards, who followed them everywhere. 'I feel more like a prisoner, Uncle, than the duke's guest.'

'You are right. It's not going to be as easy as I thought to meet with King Louis, unless I can persuade Duke Francis there is some advantage for him in it.'

'What will we do while we wait here?' Henry pocketed the seashell and stooped to pick up a handful of the fine white sand, letting it trickle through his fingers. 'Time is precious. We must wait for the duke to decide our future?'

'I shall continue your education, Henry.' Jasper smiled. 'You can thank your tutors for your knowledge of the classics. Now you must learn how men lie and cheat each other, the complicated politics of this troubled land.'

'I would like you to teach me about the ways of women as well, for I must one day choose a wife.'

Jasper stopped in his tracks at Henry's request. It was the last thing he expected to hear. 'I don't pretend to understand women, Henry.' He recalled his failure to commit to Lady Eleanor and the deep grief he still felt at the loss of Máiréad. 'You are right, though. A favourable betrothal will be important.'

'You would agree for me to marry?' Henry sounded surprised. 'And what about a wife for yourself?'

'I would be happy to marry, if I could find a woman who would have me.' Jasper picked up a flat stone and skimmed it out over the water as his father had once shown him. It hit the surface and skipped twice, covering a good distance before disappearing below the calm surface. 'The thing is, Henry, you have youth on your side but I have little to offer a bride.'

The woods came alive to the excited baying and barking of the duke's hounds as they raced through the undergrowth in pursuit of the unseen boar. Jasper rode at the duke's side as his guest, with Henry following behind with a dozen minor nobles. These ambitious young men, eager to win the duke's approval, formed teams of flanking riders, ready to head off the boar if it tried to escape.

Riding dangerously fast, Jasper ducked, narrowly avoiding a low branch, his heart pounding with the thrill of the chase. He glanced back to check Henry had seen the branch and noticed he was falling well behind. Although Henry rode well, he had never hunted anything as challenging as a wild boar.

Duke Francis invited them both to join what they called his 'at force' hunt, the most strenuous and demanding way to kill a boar, which is why he surrounded himself with active young huntsmen. Jasper preferred the stealthier 'bow and stable' hunt for deer, taking his time and relying on the accuracy of his bow and stalking skills. Using dogs to drive their quarry to a woodland clearing for huntsmen to kill the boar at close range seemed unsporting.

The pine-scented breeze lifted Jasper's spirits and anchored him to the present. There was nothing like a fast ride in the woods to reconnect with nature and remind him he was alive. They were deep in the forest and Jasper lost all sense of direction, as the sun was directly overhead and the trees grew so thickly it was impossible to see.

His horse nearly stumbled on uneven ground and he struggled to stay in the saddle when he leapt a fallen tree, galloping onwards to catch up with the duke. As he drew alongside, Duke Francis glanced across at him as if reading his mind. He looked more like a soldier again, dressed in his hunting clothes, and had a glint in his eyes as he urged his horse even faster through the undergrowth.

The baying of the dogs sounded closer and changed to the frantic yelping that told Jasper their quarry was close at hand. Spurring his horse in pursuit he found himself in an open clearing where the duke's trained catch dogs had taken the loudly protesting boar by its ears and held it down. The animal was a fully grown male, with powerful curved white tusks and angry red eyes. He stayed in the saddle, aware the dangerous boar could break free at any moment.

He glanced behind and realised they had lost the rest of the huntsmen in the last rush of the chase and were alone in the clearing. He felt sudden pity for the boar, like him detained at the duke's pleasure. Duke Francis dismounted and drew his dagger, approaching the struggling beast from behind, then slashed its throat with an efficient swiftness, wiping the blade before returning his knife to the scabbard at his belt.

'You don't like the sight of blood?' There was a note of scorn in his voice.

Jasper realised the duke was talking to him. The bright spurt of red blood reminded him of the death of Roger Vaughan in Chepstow castle, a memory he still struggled to repress. It seemed long ago but was a moment he would never be able to forget, and it must have shown on his face. Now he worried the duke seemed to be able to read him so easily.

'I'm honoured to be your guest on this hunt, Duke Francis,' he forced a smile, 'and am grateful for your protection.'

'You have my word, Sir Jasper, although I hear you have taken to walking on the beach, out in the open?'

'Your men watch over us well enough, Duke Francis.'

The duke studied him for a moment, as if making a judgement. 'Take care, Sir Jasper. I've also made a promise to York that you will not return and cause him trouble.'

'Then it's your plan to hold us here?'

'For your own good, and also for the good of your nephew. What future do you think you would have if you returned to England?'

## 21

# JULY 1472

The blunt-edged sword sliced through the air where Jasper had been standing a moment before and struck his helmet with a resonating clang. He resisted the dizziness and fought back with increasing desperation, each of his blows being expertly parried. Sweat trickled down his face and he stepped back just in time to avoid another thrust. Exhausted, he dropped his sword to the ground and held up his hands in surrender.

'Well fought!' Jasper pulled off his helmet and wiped his brow. 'I'm getting too old to spar in this heat.'

Henry also removed his helmet. His hair, once cropped short, now fashionably long, not black like Jasper's but more golden brown, the legacy of his maternal grandmother, Queen Catherine.

'I think you let me win, Uncle?'

'Not this time, Henry. You know my tricks too well, and my weaknesses.'

Jasper picked up the fallen practice sword, grinning as he recognised their visitor, limping towards them across the court-yard. Gabriel had put on a little weight and his black felt cap and a cape made him look like a merchant.

He held up a hand in greeting. 'Welcome to Château Suscinio. It's good to see you at long last, Gabriel, and no longer needing to use a stick!'

'Good day to you, sirs,' he scanned the spacious courtyard, 'so where can a man get a drink around here?'

'We've been looking forward to hearing from you. Did you have a good journey?'

'The crossing was as rough as ever.' Gabriel scowled. 'I've been here for more than a week, sir, waiting for the duke to grant me safe passage.'

'He has more important things to worry about than us right now, Gabriel. I'm relieved your persistence paid off.'

Gabriel nodded to Henry. 'By God you've grown, sir.'

Henry smiled. 'I'm pleased to see you, Gabriel, and hope you have been able to see my mother?'

'Lady Margaret is well, sir, and sends you her best wishes,' Gabriel patted the worn leather saddle-bag he carried, 'as well as a letter.'

Jasper led the way to the refectory, where they could talk in private. The old stone walls were decorated with the duke's collection of stag antlers, brightly painted shields and ancient Breton weapons, including a massive broadsword, corroded with age. One of the duke's servants brought a jug of ale and pewter drinking cups. He poured them each a cup and discreetly left when Jasper thanked him.

Gabriel drained his cup and produced a folded parchment with a dark wax seal from his bag, handing it to Henry. 'For you, sir, from Lady Margaret.' He gave Jasper a meaningful look and they stepped over to the window while Henry broke the seal and studied the contents.

'I never thought I would see the day, sir, when Henry would be faster than you with a sword.'

'As you can see, he is no longer a boy. We've had plenty of

time on our hands here and Henry has proved to be a quick and capable learner. He is better than me with the longbow now, and has also mastered the Breton language.' Jasper smiled. 'He's more fluent than some of our dim-witted guards.'

'Lady Margaret will be relieved to hear he is well.'

'How is Henry's mother, Gabriel? Did you see her?'

'She is well, sir, although...' He glanced across at Henry. 'Her third husband is dead from his wounds, and she has married again, to Lord Thomas Stanley.'

'Lady Margaret knows what she is doing.' Jasper looked across at Henry, whose future had now become even more complicated, as Stanley had been married to Warwick's sister, Lady Eleanor Neville.

'She asked me to tell you she prays for you every day, sir, as well as for her son.'

'I am glad to hear it, Gabriel, for I wonder if I'm going to need divine intervention before the good Duke Francis permits me to meet King Louis.'

Henry finished reading his letter and joined them, handing it to Jasper. 'It reveals little enough.'

'I am sorry to hear of the death of your stepfather, Henry. He was a good man.'

'My mother writes that it was a blessed release for him, as he suffered greatly.' He looked at Gabriel questioningly. 'Lord Stanley is a Yorkist?'

Gabriel nodded and refilled his cup with ale from the jug. 'Everyone in England claims to be Yorkist now, sir, or must be ready to face the consequences.'

'Have you met Lord Stanley?'

'I have not, sir,' Gabriel sipped his ale appreciatively, 'although I understand he is a wealthy man of great influence, ten years younger than your late stepfather.'

'Tell me honestly, Gabriel, how did my mother seem to you?'

'In truth, sir, she misses you but is relieved you are here safe. She hopes you will soon be able to return and claim your inheritance and your father's earldom of Richmond.'

'Soon?' There was a note of hope in his voice. 'How soon, Gabriel?'

'That's a good question, sir,' Gabriel took another drink as he considered how to answer, 'as all I've seen tells me England is no place for a Tudor, or Wales, for that matter. York could grant you a pardon but he could be as quick to put you in the Tower.'

There was no denying Gabriel's words. The House of Lancaster was finished without an heir, and even Henry's slender claim through his mother's line was no use to them now. Edward of York had a healthy son and two younger brothers, all waiting to take his throne when their chance came. He would have to make the most of their new life in France with Henry and resolved it was time to confront Duke Francis.

The duke arrived at Suscinio, clattering into the courtyard with a noisy entourage of mounted soldiers—a sign to Jasper something unusual had happened. Worse still, he was flanked by a handsome, well-dressed man Jasper recognised as Lord Rivers, brother of York's queen, Elizabeth, and another, younger, English noble he'd never seen before. The Yorkist's presence spelt an end to Jasper's carefully rehearsed appeal and he felt a dark foreboding at what his visitors could mean.

Duke Francis broke the awkward silence as Jasper and Henry faced them across his heavy oak table. 'You know Sir Anthony Woodville and his brother Edward?'

Jasper nodded. He saw no malice in the eyes of either of the duke's guests, but there was no denying their air of superiority. Even the younger Woodville seemed to look down his nose at them both, now reduced to objects of curiosity, no longer any threat to York's dominance.

'In different circumstances, Sir Anthony, we might have been good friends.'

Duke Francis seemed amused at Jasper's reply. 'King Edward sent Earl Rivers and his brother here with a thousand English bowmen to help defend Brittany against attack from the French.'

Jasper couldn't hide his surprise. 'We weren't aware of any French invasion?' It was a double blow, to hear the duke refer to Edward as king and to learn that his relations with King Louis were at such a low ebb.

Sir Anthony answered in English. 'You needn't worry about the French, Sir Jasper. We soon saw them off.'

Jasper wasn't worried about the French. Instead he worried about Duke Francis, seated with one of York's brothers-in-law on each side. If what Sir Anthony said was true, the duke would owe them a favour, and they had not all travelled to Suscinio for the hunting. He glanced at Henry again and saw he had already reached the same conclusion.

Duke Francis spoke before he could reply. 'There was a price for King Edward's support.' He glanced at Lord Rivers. 'He wants me to return you to England, together with your nephew.' He looked across at Henry, who listened with increasing concern on his young face.

Jasper struggled to keep the anger and frustration he felt from his voice. He took a long breath, then spoke calmly. 'I know you as a man of your word, Duke Francis, and we are both here under your protection.'

'Which is why I've agreed a compromise with Lord Rivers. You are vulnerable in this isolated place, so you are to be transferred.'

'Where to?'

'Château de Josselin.'

Jasper glanced at Henry. 'What about my nephew?'

Duke Francis turned to Henry. 'You will be moved to Château de Largoet and placed under the care of the Lord of Rieux.'

'I respectfully request, Duke Francis, that I may be transferred with my uncle, so that my education can continue.' Henry spoke in perfect Breton, his voice confident and clear.

Duke Francis waved his gold-ringed hand dismissively. 'I've given my word to Lord Rivers. You must prepare to leave within the hour.'


It took little time to pack their few possessions. Jasper had to admit he would miss Suscinio, and Henry, who'd been his constant companion. He found Henry in his room, re-reading the letter Gabriel brought from Lady Margaret, apparently in the hope of finding some hidden meaning in her words.

He looked up as Jasper entered. 'I suspect Duke Francis has promised York we will be treated more like prisoners than his guests?'

'I agree, Henry. He's made a truce with York and it's only a matter of time before they persuade him to return us to England. The duke is a man of honour.'

'I don't understand, Uncle.'

'All they need to do is find an honourable way for him to hand us over.'

'Which is in the best interests of Brittany?'

'Yes, and when they do we must be ready. If they try to escort you to the coast, you must find a way to escape before you are put on board a ship, as after that it will be too late.'

Jasper peered down into the cobblestoned inner courtyard from Henry's window. A horse-drawn wagon was already loaded with his own luggage and a dozen of the duke's guards were saddled up and waiting to ride as his escort.

'It's time for me to go, Henry. You know what you must do?'

'Remember I am a Tudor, Uncle.'

'Your grandfather would be proud of you.' Jasper put his hand on Henry's shoulder, choking back unexpected emotion. 'Keep a lookout for Gabriel. He is going to try to bring you word from me, if Duke Francis will permit him.'

Henry forced a smile. 'Take care, and remember you are a Tudor.'

Jasper struggled to kneel, as his hands were bound tight behind his back with rope. He stared down at the wooden block, noting the dark stains and how it had been polished through use. The mournful drone of the priest's Latin prayers drifted across the silent crowd and he looked up at the faces of those who gathered to witness his death.

His eyes met King Henry's accusing gaze, a trickle of blood running down his cheek. A tearful Máiréad wiped her eyes, next to her stood the young Prince Edward, his face deathly white, contrasting sharply with the bright red blood soaking his doublet. He glanced around at the executioner and into the dark, glowering eyes of William Herbert before he woke with a jolt and sat up, bathed in cold sweat.

His room, in one of the eight imposing, conical-roofed towers of the château at Josselin was a prison cell, with a heavy iron door bolted on the outside. He lay awake as dawn broke and a shaft of bright sunlight revealed his only furniture, his low bed with a straw mattress, a rickety table riddled with woodworm and an old chair that creaked when he moved.

Two wooden chests, containing all he owned, sat against one wall. Most of his gold and silver was gone, although he had been allowed to keep his sword and armour, which were of little use to him. He was grateful, though, for the papers Gabriel had salvaged from Pembroke Castle. Letters and reports, bills and accounts, they helped pass the dreary months as he re-read them all, remembering happier times at home in Wales.

The duke's guardsmen brought him meals in his room and kept a vigilant watch over his every move. At first it irritated him when they peered through the iron grill in his door, but he soon came to know the men and discovered they had been warned to expect attempts by York's agents to carry him off to England. Since then he'd had the recurring nightmares, always the same.

He climbed out of bed and splashed water from a jug on the table over his face, gasping at the shock of its coldness. He stretched his arms and moved his chair to the window with a view of the River Oust far below. Taking his knife, he started to carve a new line, next to the others on the stone sill of his window. He had no idea how long this imprisonment would last so he had scratched the first one at the end of his first month.

Jasper brushed the stone dust away with his hand and sat back in his chair, fighting off the sense of despair. He should be glad to be alive and grateful for the duke's protection, even if it felt as if life was passing him by. He leaned forward and looked out of the window at the people coming and going over the old stone bridge, like busy wood ants, just as uncaring of his situation.

Josselin was at the heart of Brittany, a natural crossroads and busy with trade. Even this early in the morning, the bustling town seemed chaotic and noisy with its own dawn chorus of hammering stonemasons and shouting street vendors. Jasper missed the serene tranquillity of Suscinio, where they hardly saw anyone other than the duke's hunting parties.

On market days the old walled town became a buzzing hive of activity, with stalls lining the maze of narrow streets. Women haggled over the price of lace and linen and sometimes he heard musicians playing. Once he listened to a girl singing a tuneful but sad song of lost love, which served to remind him of his own loneliness.

He envied the freedom of the townspeople and often wished he could explore the market, talk to the merchants and have a drink in one of the lively taverns. The duke would not allow it, as it seemed he was determined to keep his promise to Lord Rivers and to make a show of treating Jasper as his prisoner, despite his kindness in the past. He hoped Henry fared a little better.

Limited to his daily walk in the inner courtyard, Jasper's only company other than the guards were the staff who kept the château in good order for its absent owners, the wealthy de Rohan family. Mostly simple Breton servants, when he was able to speak to them they knew little of the world outside the stone walls of Josselin. A mixed blessing, this meant news was hard to come by and he looked forward to the duke's sporadic visits.

There had been no sign of Gabriel or word from Henry, although the duke assured him he was well. At the duke's last visit Jasper took the opportunity to request his permission to visit his nephew. Duke Francis refused but grudgingly agreed he could write a letter and arranged for him to be provided with parchment and ink, as well as several good goose feather quills.

When he sat at his rickety table to write, he was reminded again of the difficulty Lady Margaret faced, as the duke or one of his men would surely read the letter before it was delivered. He chose the best of the quills and tested the nib, pleased to see it left a good mark with the black, ox-gall ink.

*To our well-beloved nephew, Henry Tudor Esq., We greet you well and pray that with God's grace you are in good health.*

He hesitated as he tried to find the right words to reassure Henry of his own circumstances. Inhaling deeply, he forced the suffocating despair of his imprisonment from his mind. In truth his situation was bleak, although it would help no one to put the facts so bluntly in a letter. He took his sharp knife and trimmed the point of his nib, then dipped it in the small inkpot and continued.

*We find our accommodation tolerable and wish to hear that you also fare well under the hospitality of the good Duke Francis. Keep the faith, your spirits good and remember you are a Tudor. We ask that you send us word as soon as you may, and of the health of your good mother, the Lady Margaret, as our trust is in you. God be with you.*

*Written at the Château Josselin.*

*J. TUDOR.*

He re-read the letter and hoped its brevity would serve his purpose. Henry's reply would no doubt be equally terse, yet he had made a start from which he hoped they could build more favours from their host in Brittany. It would be good to hear from Henry, and to learn if Gabriel had been able to return from his last visit to England, as he worried at what Gabriel's absence could mean. The duke could have him deported or, worse, arrested and imprisoned.

Seeing the ink was dry, Jasper carefully folded the parchment on itself. He had no wax to seal it but that was of no consequence. He took the letter when he went for his daily walk, and handed it to the guard at the gatehouse, together with a silver coin. A thin-faced man in faded livery, the guard listened attentively to Jasper's instructions about delivery of the letter to Henry at the Château de Largoet.

'I know Largoet. It's outside the town of Elven.'

'The duke told me my nephew was in the care of the Lord of Rieux. Do you know of him?'

'Lord Rieux is the duke's right-hand man. Your nephew has done well to be in his care.'

'I'm glad to hear that,' he fished another coin from his purse and pressed it into the guard's hand, 'and I'd be grateful if you can find a reliable man to deliver my letter and wait, if he can, for the reply?'

The guard pocketed the silver coin, one of Jasper's last. 'I surely will, sir.'


Jasper lay awake in his uncomfortable bed that night, pleased that at last he had done something to establish contact with Henry. He was also reassured by the captain's words. At least it seemed that Henry was well placed to learn something of the politics of Brittany and France. The Lord of Rieux could be a useful ally in the future if Duke Francis was persuaded to hand them over to York.

He wished for news of events in England and wondered if the duke would allow him to write to Lady Margaret. He had no idea how such a letter would be delivered, although there was a chance Sir Anthony Woodville might consider helping. Although he was the brother of York's queen, Jasper's instinct told him Woodville was a decent man.

He kept his eyes open, listening to the sounds of the night. He overheard guards talking somewhere, grumbling about the long hours and low pay. He heard the sharp shriek of a hunting owl down by the river outside his open window, then settled down as darkness again overwhelmed him and he drifted into a troubled sleep until the nightmares returned, as they often did.

## 22

### JULY 1475

J asper took his knife and began carving another line on the stone sill of his window. After half an hour of patient scraping he brushed the stone dust away with his hand and stood back, satisfied, counting twenty-three lines. His rituals helped him cope with imprisonment, like his routine of walking round the courtyard each day and the hard exercise, which kept his muscles firmer than they had ever been.

The second anniversary of his arrival in Josselin would soon pass and he'd achieved nothing other than to survive. At times his sense of hopelessness overwhelmed him, only his routine keeping him from despair. Like a monk, his world had been reduced to waking early, praying, taking his exercise and eating simple food, with only the briefest contact with the world outside.

He wondered how his nephew was coping and cursed at how the duke tricked him, for there had been no reply to his letters. He'd waited in hope for months before realising Duke Francis never had any intention of allowing communication between them. It had been an easy way to silence him or to see what he would write. Although the duke reassured him of his nephew's safety, a short letter would put his troubled mind to rest.

Jasper stood at the window, watching the bridge over the river. An endless procession of people made their way into the walled town, yet none were leaving. Something unusual was going on. His attention shifted to muffled noises from within the courtyard, of horse's hooves, shouted commands, the sharp clink of steel and the buzzing of many voices, like bees in a hive. The bolt on his door scraped and the door swung open to reveal one of his friendlier guards.

'What's happening?' He spoke in Breton.

'The King of England has landed at Calais with an army.' The guard seemed surprised Jasper hadn't heard. 'And the Duke of Burgundy has invaded France from the north.' He scowled at the thought.

Jasper followed the guard down the narrow stone steps. Groups of armed soldiers gathered in the usually deserted courtyard, some waiting in line for the kitchens, others sleeping or playing games of dice. The duke was obviously taking the threat from York seriously. Jasper had never seen so many horses crammed into the château stables and guessed they were preparing to defend themselves.

He sought out the captain of the guard, who was being helped to dress in his armour. The pieces looked mismatched and a poor fit, some showing the scars and dents of ancient battles. The captain questioned the parentage of the unfortunate man helping him, telling him not to pull the straps so tightly, as Jasper entered.

'Is Duke Francis supporting the English, Captain?'

'As you can see, Sir Jasper, he is moving men to defend the border. My orders are to take as many men as I can to him at the Château de l'Hermine.'

'What is to become of me?'

'I will leave enough men to defend this place.'

Jasper looked out into the courtyard and saw the soldiers preparing to leave. He'd not expected York to be so bold, although he guessed it could be a show of strength, rather than an invasion. If York was victorious, he could march on Brittany and Duke Francis would surely hand him over, as well as Henry. If he did not, Jasper felt the last place he needed to be was locked up in Josselin.

This was possibly his best chance of escape but he had no money left and nowhere to go. He returned to his room, noting there was no longer a guard to bolt the door behind him. Jasper looked at the two stout wooden chests containing all his worldly goods and an idea occurred to him. He unfastened the straps securing the closest one and took out his sword in its ornate, engraved silver and black leather scabbard. Underneath, wrapped in musty sacking and swathed with cobwebs, lay his precious armour, almost forgotten until now.

Buckling on the belt he drew his sword. The forged blade was in perfect condition and glinted as he turned it in the light, and he felt his sense of powerlessness diminishing. Jasper sheathed the sword and took his breastplate from the chest. It was impossible to fasten the stiff leather straps of his armour without assistance, so he carried it, together with his helmet, and rushed to find the captain of the guard before it was too late.

The captain was already mounted on an ageing grey horse, a long line of armed riders forming up behind him, ready to leave. Jasper saw he would have to be quick or his chance would be gone.

'Take me with you, Captain.' He tried to sound assertive.

'To Vannes?' The captain sounded doubtful. His eyes went to the sword and armour Jasper carried and he seemed unable to make a decision.

'Your orders are to bring as many men as you can,' Jasper

grinned, 'and you wouldn't wish to be responsible for me escaping if I was left behind?'

The captain shouted to the men waiting to leave. 'Bring him a horse.'

One of the soldiers helped Jasper buckle his armour over his doublet and he put on his helmet before mounting the horse and riding to the captain's side.

'Thank you, Captain.'

'You gave me no choice, sir, we must go.'

They rode out through the gates into the crowded streets, the people parting to make way as they clattered past in pairs over the old bridge across the River Oust. Small boys ran alongside, begging in shrill voices for coins and pretending to march like soldiers.

An attractive young woman waved to Jasper and shouted good luck to him in Breton. 'Chañs vat!'

He glanced over his shoulder in time to see her blow him a kiss and raised a hand in acknowledgement. The sight of the young girl reminded him of the time, so many years ago, when he rode from Pembroke Castle, leading his doomed Welsh army, his father riding proudly at his side. He missed having a woman to care for and decided he was finally ready to move on from Máiréad, if the opportunity presented itself.

The Château de l'Hermine had changed since Jasper last saw it, as an encampment of soldiers occupied every available space. Wood smoke from cooking fires drifted in the air and men were busy gutting a pig carcass, which dangled by its hind legs from one of the duke's ornamental trees. Jasper watched for a moment as a line of archers fired a volley at a straw target, their arrows thudding true and deep, as good as any English archer.

He asked to see the duke as soon as they arrived and was

surprised to be shown into the duke's study. Tall, leaded glass windows flooded the oak panelled room with late afternoon sunlight and the duke's collection of rare and precious books lined the walls. The duke sat in a high-backed chair by the stone hearth, looking pale, with dark shadows around his eyes.

At the duke's side sat a familiar ghost from Jasper's past, someone he thought he would never see again. The Duke of Exeter, Sir Henry Holland, was dressed in his full regalia of the Order of the Garter and wore a stylish velvet hat adorned with an iridescent peacock feather. On anyone else it would look ostentatious, but Henry Holland was able to carry it off.

Jasper nodded to Henry Holland and felt a sudden misgiving at the probable reason for his being there. Although Holland seemed pleased to see him, he guessed it meant York's invasion had already succeeded. He'd taken a great risk in riding to Vannes on his own initiative and could now face the consequences.

'I trust, Duke Francis, you will understand why I have travelled here from Château Josselin?' He held his breath as he waited for the duke's reply.

The duke seemed unsurprised to see him. 'A timely arrival.' His voice sounded weak and he glanced at Holland. 'Sir Henry has been sent by King Edward to secure my support for a new peace treaty.'

Jasper nodded to Holland. 'We heard you were badly wounded at the battle of Barnet, yet you look as well as ever.'

'As do you, Jasper,' Holland smiled. 'Your information was correct, as I was left for dead. They stripped me of my armour, and when they found I was still alive, locked me up in the Tower of London.' He shook his head at the memory. 'My wife divorced me and my estates were all at risk.'

'So now you serve as ambassador to York?' Jasper's old suspicions returned.

'I do,' Holland sounded unrepentant, 'although he isn't the man you would remember.'

Duke Francis was curious. 'What do you mean?'

'The king has lost the support of the people. His private life offends many and despite his unpopular taxes, he's emptied the royal coffers, which is why he made this foray to France with sixteen thousand men.'

'You make a fine ambassador for King Edward.' The duke sounded scornful. 'Does your master intend to claim the crown of France?'

'The threat he might do so would seem enough for his purposes.'

The duke coughed, a hacking, rattling sound that caused Henry Holland to glance at Jasper with a frown of concern. The duke's physician came forward and offered him a cup of steaming brew, which gave off an exotic aroma of herbs and spices. The duke took a sip, pulling a face at the taste. When he recovered himself he continued as if nothing had happened.

'I heard the Duke of Burgundy has disappointed King Edward?'

Holland nodded. 'Charles the Bold has his own problems. King Louis paid for an army of Swiss mercenaries, who are keeping him fully occupied in the north.'

Duke Francis frowned. 'I wonder where this will all end?' He coughed again into a cloth he held to his mouth.

'In peace, Duke Francis,' Holland smiled, 'King Edward has no stomach for a long fight through winter—and neither can he afford it. He has a peace treaty with King Louis and wishes to make his peace with your good self.'

'What was his price for peace with France?' Duke Francis sounded surprised.

'French gold. King Louis has agreed to pay seventy-five thousand gold crowns, and Queen Margaret is to be ransomed for a further fifty thousand.'

'Gold will win the day, as it invariably does,' Duke Francis seemed unsurprised, 'and what does King Edward ask of me?'

Henry Holland avoided eye contact with Jasper. 'King Edward wishes you to return Henry Tudor to England.'

After the duke left, Jasper found himself alone with Henry Holland. He felt at a disadvantage, as Holland held all the aces in his hand, except for one. Duke Francis was bound by his promise to keep Henry safe, while he remained in Brittany, at least. Despite his poor health, the duke was a man of his word and unlikely to surrender either of them as easily as York and his turncoat ambassador wished.

'You know you would be placing my nephew in great danger if you took him back to England?'

'You misjudge the king, Jasper. I am sure his intentions are worthy. He has great regard for Henry's mother—and could have had me executed, yet employs me as his ambassador.'

'You forget he condoned the shameful murder of my half-brother, the true King of England?'

'I don't forget, Jasper, although they say it was his brother's hand that ended poor Henry's life.'

'Richard, Duke of Gloucester?' Jasper struggled to control his surge of anger.

'I take some consolation from the knowledge he will never become king.'

'Let us be thankful for that, at least.' He studied Henry Holland, trying to guess what was going on under the peacock feather hat. 'We were friends once, Henry, which is why I feel I can ask a great favour of you.'

'You wish me to buy you time?'

'Not for myself. I fear for my nephew's safety if he returns now.'

'I will do what I can, Jasper. As for yourself, you might be able to return sooner than you think.'

'By bending my knee to York?'

'He wants peace, and has great capacity for forgiveness, even for his sworn enemies. You heard about the Earl of Oxford's little escapade?'

'I've been cut off from the world for a while, although I knew John de Vere's father and brother were executed on York's orders. His son still seeks revenge?'

'Oxford persuaded King Louis to let him and his brothers take a fleet of a dozen warships to invade England. They were nearly captured when they landed in Essex but escaped and became pirates, sending English ships to Scotland. Then they took the castle on St Michael's Mount in Cornwall.'

'What good would that do?'

'It served as a reminder to York that there are still some who are prepared to fight.'

'What happened to de Vere and his men?' Jasper could guess the answer.

'That's the thing. They held the siege for nearly five months and only surrendered on the promise of a royal pardon.'

'York spared them?'

'He had them locked up at Hammes Castle. If we could free them, we could build an army here with King Louis' French gold and prepare for an invasion.'

Jasper shook his head at the idea. 'I've been to Hammes Castle. It's close to Calais and easily defended. What you're suggesting seems a high risk while York's main army remains in Calais.'

'A plan is already in hand. We have friends in France and supporters of the House of Lancaster arrive from England all the time. God willing, a way will be found.' Holland studied Jasper as if making a judgement. 'Would you bend your knee to George, Duke of Clarence?'

Holland's question took Jasper by surprise. 'The last time I saw George was as Warwick's son-in-law. He struck me as hot-headed and unreliable.' Jasper also knew that Henry's lands had been granted to George by York, which would be a problem. 'George has no chance of the throne even if Edward were dead?'

Henry Holland nodded. 'Yes, the king has two sons, good strong boys, like their father, although you must have heard the rumours about Edward's parentage. They say his mother lay with a young archer and tricked her husband into thinking Edward was his child, even though they couldn't be more different.'

Jasper shook his head. 'I know Warwick spread such rumours but you've met Duchess Cecily. Does she strike you as one who would have a liaison with a common archer?'

'She does not, I will grant you, but they say when she learned of Edward's marriage to a commoner, she threatened to declare him illegitimate.'

'A dangerous thing for the mother of a king to say—if she did.'

'If she did or not, we need to rally round a claimant to the throne who is prepared to support our cause, and we have few options. No one has ever questioned George's legitimacy, and he will be with us, if we can raise the men.'

'It would be the last thing York expects.'

'Edward of York has grown fat and complacent,' Henry Holland flashed him a knowing grin, 'and he's had it his own way long enough.'

A shower of rain formed puddles in the courtyard of Château Josselin and Jasper wore his woollen cloak as he ran his fingers over the gouges marking the months on his window sill. He'd carved six more neat lines with his knife since Duke Francis ordered his return. The duke said he would be sent for when required but there had been no word.

Jasper felt in a different mood than before he left on his risky excursion to Vannes. He stood at his window watching the people of the town coming and going and no longer felt the overpowering sense of helplessness, which had gnawed at his mind like a hungry rat. Now there was more than a glimmer of hope, and it was simply a matter of waiting, as patiently as he could, until the right moment.

He had not expected to meet Henry Holland as York's unlikely ambassador, or to learn of the plan to replace York with his younger brother. The whole idea was deeply flawed, and Jasper scowled at the thought of the sort of king George would make, if he ever had the chance.

Jasper continually questioned his guards and the captain for news but there was no further talk of an English invasion. He hoped Holland had been as good as his word and managed to delay Henry's return to England. Despite whatever assurances and promises the duke was offered, it would be all too easy for his nephew to fall victim to those jealous of his slender claim to the throne.

He'd asked permission to visit Henry at the Château de Largoet and the duke seemed to be considering his request, but had not yet granted it. He wrote another letter to Henry, telling him of his visit to Vannes and the meeting with Henry Holland. He paid one of his guards, an insolent man, who cursed every time he opened his mouth, his last silver coin to see his letter was delivered.

Although he no longer expected any reply he took some comfort from the simple act of doing something positive. If there was any chance of a letter reaching Henry he must take it, as to give up trying was to give up hope. He wondered if the duke's illness had worsened, which would explain why his visits had ceased. The duke had no heir, so there could be unrest in Brittany if his condition didn't improve.

The rasp of the iron bolt on his door being slid open interrupted his thoughts and he turned as the door opened. Rainwater dripped from the brim of the captain's hat and he had a grim look on his face as he entered.

'You are to prepare for a ride, Sir Jasper. I have orders to escort you back to the Château de l'Hermine.'

'Do you know the reason, Captain?'

'I do.' The captain seemed to be enjoying his moment of power over Jasper. 'Duke Francis has been visited by another English ambassador and wishes to consult you about your nephew.'

## 23

## JANUARY 1476

Robert Stillington, Bishop of Bath and Wells, York's ambassador to Brittany and France, filled the chair he sat in. The crimson and purple chasuble worn over his robes was trimmed with glittering cloth of gold and around his neck a heavy, bejewelled crucifix looked more like a symbol of his status than a badge of his religion. The bishop's shrewd eyes shone with self-importance as he repeated King Edward's offer.

'His Highness wishes the Earl of Richmond, Henry Tudor, to accept his most generous offer of betrothal to Lady Elizabeth.' He spoke in a faintly patronising tone, as if giving a sermon in church, and his voice boomed in the duke's stateroom.

'His eldest daughter?' The duke sounded surprised.

'Indeed, Duke Francis.' The bishop leaned forward conspiratorially. 'A fine young girl, with her mother's beauty and her father's brains.' He chuckled at his own wit.

The duke raised an eyebrow in disapproval. 'Forgive me, Bishop. Do I not recall that the Dauphin Charles of France was to be betrothed to King Edward's eldest daughter?'

Bishop Stillington seemed momentarily flustered then regained his composure. 'There are many who seek the hand of the king's daughter, my lord.' He waved a podgy, gold-ringed hand in the air to emphasise his point. 'King Edward seeks to unite the Houses of York and Lancaster, which is why I've travelled here in person to see the matter resolved.'

Duke Francis glanced at Jasper, called in to witness the bishop's proposal. 'And why is the king so eager for such a marriage?' He barely concealed his distaste.

'King Edward wishes you to work with him to ensure a lasting peace, to which end he will provide a thousand of our best English archers to help defend your borders.'

The duke held a folded cloth to his mouth and coughed into it before continuing. 'I will need time to consider King Edward's proposal, Bishop.' He cast a glance at Jasper. 'You will appreciate why I don't share your sense of urgency. Having given my word to protect Henry Tudor, I would need to be sure it was in his best interests before I could transfer him to you.'

'What if we made it four thousand archers?' He leaned closer to the duke and lowered his voice. 'Perhaps we should discuss the sum of gold coin that would ease your conscience, my lord?'

'You insult me, Bishop?' The duke's weak voice had an acidic edge. A log on the fire crackled and spat, as if in agreement.

The bishop reddened. 'I have the king's authority to add that as well as his title of Earl of Richmond, Henry will be granted permission to inherit his mother's considerable fortune, including her Beaufort estates.'

'And if Henry Tudor does not return to England?'

'Then I am afraid, my lord, as the king's ambassador I must inform you he will lose his title—and inherit nothing.'

Jasper glanced at Duke Francis and saw he was seriously

considering his options. It pained him to see the once powerful man reduced to a coughing, hunched figure, particularly when his own future depended so heavily on the duke's good health. He hoped the duke's illness would not affect his judgement.

Before their meeting with the bishop the duke told him King Louis was also keen to discuss conditions under which both he and Henry could be transferred to France. Jasper knew if he could find a way to buy more time, this could be an ideal solution to all their problems. Although Duke Francis protected them better than King Louis ever did, there was no real future for them in Brittany, while France offered a wealth of possibilities. An idea occurred to him and he turned to the bishop.

'It would be helpful, Your Grace, if you could arrange for Lady Elizabeth to visit us here in Brittany, so that Duke Francis might make her acquaintance?'

'I regret that is not possible, Sir Jasper. Henry Tudor must return to England.' His voice sounded dismissive, more strident now. He turned to Duke Francis. 'I need your answer, my lord. I have a ship waiting to sail in St Malo and must return to England.'

Duke Francis looked tired and pale. 'You will have your answer tomorrow, Bishop. Now I must rest and recover my health.'

Bishop Stillington stood with some effort and bowed to the duke. 'I thank you for your time, my lord.' He gave Jasper a forced smile. 'With God's good grace and favour we will soon have an outcome that is satisfactory to all.'


Jasper waited alone in the duke's stateroom, his mind troubled by the turn of events. He threw another log onto the duke's fire and stared into the flames, doubting if anything would change the duke's mind. He'd taken an instinctive dislike to the corpulent Bishop Stillington, although he understood why Duke

Francis would be tempted by his offer of military support. Less easy to accept were the bishop's assurances that Henry would be well treated and his Beaufort inheritance restored.

Jasper imagined Lady Margaret was working hard on her son's behalf to ensure he could retain his title and might even be behind the proposed marriage. She would have found it easy enough to gain access to the king through her new husband Sir Thomas Stanley, Lord Steward of York's household. Once at court Lady Margaret could become one of Queen Elizabeth's ladies-in-waiting, and even carry her train, if it meant she could protect the future of her son.

The doors opened and Duke Francis entered the room, still carrying a cloth, which he held to his mouth when he coughed. Jasper noted how the duke shivered and pulled a woollen cloak around his shoulders as he sat at the other side of the hearth, warming his hands. He decided to try again, this time to appeal to the duke's sense of honour.

'I urge you to reject York's offer, for Henry's sake, Duke Francis. I swore an oath to his mother to watch over him, so I am bound to do what I can to prevent his return to England until we are certain it's safe.'

'Bishop Stillington assures me his proposal is supported by Lady Margaret.' The duke glanced across at Jasper with red-rimmed eyes. 'Henry is no longer a boy. I cannot hold him here in Brittany indefinitely.' He sounded apologetic.

'You have been as good as your word, Duke Francis, but once Henry sails there will be nothing either of us can do to protect him.'

The duke coughed, a dry, hacking sound, muffled by the cloth he held to his mouth. 'King Edward needs Brittany as an ally. He would be foolish to risk our treaty by allowing any harm to come to your nephew.'

'It's not something I would wish to risk.' Jasper saw the duke's mind was made up and it was time to produce his trump card. 'England is about to become a dangerous place. Sir Henry Holland informed me of a plan to replace York with his younger brother George.' He watched the duke's reaction and saw his frown.

'I am afraid Bishop Stillington told me Henry Holland fell overboard, returning to England on the king's flagship. I thought it odd.'

'He was drowned?' Jasper felt the chill wind of impending disaster as another of his chances slipped through his fingers. He'd not liked Henry Holland but he had been so full of life and eager to rid England of York, even if it meant the hapless George becoming king.

The duke nodded. 'The Bishop said no one saw it happen but he was not aboard the ship when it docked.'

'This is how York works.'

The light of understanding dawned in the duke's tired eyes. 'You think Holland's plan was discovered?'

'I am certain of it. We must rescue Henry before he meets the same fate.'

The duke held out a cautionary, gold-ringed hand. 'It is too late. He is already on his way to St Malo.'

'Will you let me ride with some of your men to see if I can bring him back?'

'I cannot allow you, of all people, to confront York's ambassadors.' He shook his head. 'I gave them my word you were not in a position to threaten anyone.'

The familiar frustration of powerlessness returned. 'Could you send one of your own men, Duke Francis?' He heard the pleading in his voice. 'The bishop will be keen to sail without delay.'

～

Jasper hardly recognised the hooded figure who rode into the château with the duke's personal guard. He watched the rider dismount and hand the bridle of his horse to the waiting groom. Pulling back his hood, the man scanned the courtyard as if looking for someone. Clean-shaven with long brown hair, he dressed like a French nobleman, with a black damask tunic. He carried a fine sword on a low belt and had an athletic, fighter's poise. His searching eyes met Jasper's and his face lit up in a broad grin.

'Henry!' Jasper stepped forward and shook him by the hand. 'By God, I thought we were too late.'

'So did I, Uncle.' Henry glanced back at his escort. 'The duke's envoy arrived just in time.' His voice sounded deeper and he spoke in English with the accent of one who has used only French for many years.

'Come with me. The duke has provided me with a fine room here. You must be tired and hungry after your journey, and I want to hear what you've been up to.'

Jasper didn't mention how they had been some of the most anxious days he could remember since the siege of Bamburgh Castle. Duke Francis finally agreed to send his most trusted advisor, Pierre Landais, to see if he could negotiate Henry's return, although it seemed an unlikely prospect, despite the heavy casket of gold he carried in recompense. Bishop Stillington had been worryingly keen not to return to England without Henry.

The same age as Jasper, Pierre Landais was good looking and successful. The son of a wealthy Breton cloth merchant, his relentless ambition saw him rise from being the duke's valet to become his treasurer and Prime Minister of Brittany. Charming and persuasive, he seemed the perfect choice for the challenging task and had experience of negotiation with the English.

St Malo was over a hundred miles away, a two-day ride

with an overnight stop in Rennes. Landais left within the hour with the duke's personal guard but there was nothing Jasper could do but wait for news. As Henry had more than a day's start on them, he could already have sailed, and Jasper urged the duke to authorise Pierre Landais to pursue them at sea in a fast ship. Duke Francis refused, pointing out such action would be seen as an act of war against England.

Jasper felt overwhelming relief as he led Henry to the duke's sumptuous great hall, where servants brought steaming onion soup, fresh crusty loaves and salted butter, as well as a jug of strong Breton cider. Henry ate hungrily, and watching him Jasper found himself remembering his older brother Edmund, whose life was cut so cruelly short in Carmarthen Castle twenty years before.

Edmund had the same lithe build and engaging smile, but there the resemblance ended. Edmund also had a selfish streak, and hadn't hesitated to secure his inheritance by fathering a child with his new bride, even though she was barely twelve years old. Jasper could never forget the anguish of Henry's birth on a wintry night in Pembroke Castle. Although she bore it with Beaufort courage, the dangerous delivery nearly killed Lady Margaret and she told him she could never have another child.

Jasper looked across at Henry and saw Lady Margaret's sharp eyes looking back at him. He hoped Henry also inherited something of her Beaufort steel, for he was going to need it. York would not take kindly to having been outwitted at the last minute and could even declare war on Brittany. Duke Francis was a sick man, no longer capable of leading an army as he had in the past, and Jasper was certain the self-serving Bishop Stillington would soon inform York of their vulnerability.

He calculated Henry must be nineteen years old and would be twenty in January. Duke Francis had been right when he said Henry was no longer a boy. He had been well tutored under the care of the Lord of Rieux during his captivity at the Château de Largoet and had a modest air of confidence that made him seem older than his years.

Henry finished his meal and studied Jasper. 'I remembered the advice you gave me all that time ago at Suscinio. You told me to find a way to escape before I was on board a ship.'

'As after that it would be too late.'

'You were right, but it wasn't easy. I remembered how superstitious sailors are about having anyone with fever aboard. I was able to convince them I suffered from a sweating sickness by pouring water over my shirt when they weren't looking.' He smiled at the memory. 'The thing was, although they kept me ashore, I was placed under armed guard, so escape was impossible.'

'Yet it bought you time until the duke's envoy arrived?'

Henry nodded. 'I was able to talk to Pierre Landais in Breton without my guards understanding, and tell him what was going on. He did try his best to negotiate my release but Bishop Stillington would have none of it.'

'So how did you escape?'

'Landais came up with a plan to distract the guards and told me to make a run for it to the cathedral.' He took a drink of the sharp-tasting cider. 'I was spotted and they chased me through the streets. I didn't know the way but I darted through a side street and kept heading for the spire. I've never run so fast in my life.'

'You claimed the right of sanctuary?' Jasper smiled as he recalled the stories his father told him of how claiming sanctuary in Westminster Abbey once saved his life. 'When the guards caught up with you they couldn't take you back.'

'Pierre Landais stirred up the locals, telling them the English were trying to violate the sanctity of their cathedral. In no time he had a small army of men with scythes and pitchforks, standing guard at the doors.'

'York is not going to forgive us. I hope he doesn't use this as an excuse to invade Brittany, as Duke Francis is in no condition to defend us.'

'That's the thing. Bishop Stillington forced his way into the cathedral. They couldn't stop him, as a man of the church. I thought he might try to threaten me but he thanked God for my recovery and promised to do what he could to explain to the king.'

'It seems I misjudged the man,' Jasper recalled his dislike of Robert Stillington, 'but I think we can rely on the bishop to concoct a version of events that will appease York, if only to preserve his own reputation.'

Henry placed his empty tankard on the table. 'I wrote letters to you from the Château de Largoet, Uncle, but they wouldn't let me send them.'

'I thought as much. Our host Duke Francis is a good man, and honours his word. He must have promised not to allow communication between us. I wrote to you as well. Twice before I realised,' Jasper smiled, 'it helped to pass the time.'

'Have you any word from Gabriel?'

'No. I haven't seen or heard from him since we saw him off. The duke was adamant about replacing my servants with his own, which is a pity. Gabriel would have been good company over those long years at Château Josselin.'

Henry sat in silence for a moment. 'What's our plan, Uncle?'

'Good question, Henry. We can't return to England, that's for sure.'

Jasper lay awake in the darkness, listening to the gentle patter of rain on the windows and pondering the answer to Henry's question. From the age of five, Henry had effectively been held prisoner against his will. Now Duke Francis seemed in a more favourable mood and might be persuaded to allow them both more freedom. He resolved to propose to the duke that the risk of either of them being abducted was reduced if they stayed at the Château de l'Hermine.

It seemed the duke's health was not likely to improve and he would need men he could trust to help manage his affairs. It made sense to keep them both close to him, ostensibly under guard, if he wished. Jasper stared up at the vaulted ceiling above him, decorated with gilded plasterwork fit for a king. If he must be imprisoned, this was the grandest of prison cells.

He said a prayer for the soul of Henry Holland, yet another victim of York's cruel regime. When the time was right, he would try to find a way to free the Earl of Oxford and his brother from the prison fortress at Guisnes, if they still lived. Together with other Lancastrians taking refuge in France they would assemble an army, and with the support of Duke Francis, one day return to England.

## 24

## APRIL 1483

The rumour spread like a wildfire through the Château de l'Hermine and, although he hardly dared believe it, Jasper rushed to find Duke Francis. He found him in his study, wrapped in furs despite the spring sunshine. His illness had worsened in the years since Henry's return, as the cough still troubled him and he had grown thinner. The duke also walked with a slight stoop, like a much older man, and his failing eyesight did little to help his often surly mood.

'They are saying York is dead.' Jasper searched the duke's face for any sign of confirmation. 'Is it true?'

Duke Francis nodded. 'I've yet to be informed officially but I have it from a reliable source. King Edward has finally paid the price for his excesses.'

Jasper sat heavily in one of the duke's comfortable chairs and tried to gather his thoughts, his mind a whirl of consequences and possibilities. Edward was some ten years younger than himself and had last been reported as being in good health, despite his life of debauchery. Word of his unpopular taxes and favouritism for the Woodville family reached as far as

Brittany, and there were still bitter Lancastrians waiting for their chance.

'Do you think it's possible he might have been poisoned?'

The duke grunted. 'Anything is possible with the English. I heard he'd become so fat he could no longer ride a horse.' He gave a wry smile. 'A man's deeds, good or bad, will repay him in kind, even if he is the King of England.'

'If York is dead, his son Edward, Prince of Wales, is heir to the throne.' He felt an old annoyance at the prince's title.

Duke Francis nodded. 'He will be twelve years old now, a fine and upstanding lad by all accounts, yet with a few years before he comes of age.'

'Richard, Duke of Gloucester, will be named Lord Protector.'

'There are no other candidates, after what happened to his brother George.'

Jasper recalled the rumours of Duke George's punishment for daring to wish the throne for himself. It was said that when York signed his death warrant he allowed his brother the choice of execution, and George chose to be drowned in a barrel of wine. Although such tales had a habit of being embroidered on their way to Brittany, it seemed a sad end for the man who could have been king.

'I've always suspected Duke Richard had a hand in the death of King Henry.' His anger rose at the thought and he struggled to control it. 'I know he's married Warwick's daughter Anne, and fought against us at Barnet and Tewkesbury.'

'Richard of Gloucester is intelligent, ambitious and power-ful, Sir Jasper, and is not a man to be underestimated.'

'What does this mean for Brittany, or for Henry and myself?'

Duke Francis sat back in his chair. 'It means I am no longer bound by my promise to York.' He regarded Jasper in silence for a moment. 'You no doubt think my treatment of you a little harsh, but it has probably saved your lives.'

'We will both be forever in your debt, Duke Francis.'

The duke smiled. 'You remember the first time we met, Jasper?'

'I was a little in awe of you, to be honest.' He smiled at the memory.

'I thought you looked like a dangerous pirate, with your Irish skirmishers.' The duke coughed into his folded cloth. 'I understand if you wish to visit your cousin, King Louis. Perhaps you will convey my best regards?'

Jasper felt unexpected pity for the once grand duke. 'We would wish to remain at your side until the time is right, and you can rely on our loyal support whatever the future holds.'

Henry fired questions like an archer loosing a quiver of arrows. 'Will King Louis welcome us at his court? Do you think it's safe to return to England? Will Duke Francis help us raise an army?'

Jasper held up his hands. 'Please, Henry, I don't have all the answers. The first thing we need to do is write to your mother and see what she thinks is best.'

'My mother?' Henry sounded surprised. 'Would she be able to visit us in Brittany?'

'I've no idea of her circumstances but it's bound to be an uncertain time for her. We must be careful with our choice of words in any letter and not put your mother in any risk.'

'How shall we raise an army with no money?' Henry frowned as he remembered. 'All my possessions were lost when I escaped from St Malo. There was a chest with my best armour, as well as the fine yew longbow you gave me.'

'Be glad you have your freedom, Henry. You still have your sword, and as for money, Duke Francis is a wealthy man. I think I can persuade him to pay for mercenaries, and we have King Louis if he will not.' He looked out of the window into the bright sunshine and felt a new day dawning. 'Henry Holland said there are plenty of Englishmen exiled in France, waiting for a leader to emerge, if only we can find them.'

Duke Francis stifled a coughing fit as they waited for his servant to pour them each a goblet of his best red wine. Candles flickered in silver candlesticks on his cluttered desk, casting dancing shadows on the walls and lighting his face with a golden glow. The shutters were already latched over the windows and Jasper and Henry were intrigued to know why he summoned them to his private study at such a late hour.

The duke sipped his wine and savoured the taste. 'I had a visitor, Dr Thomas Hutton, a clerk of the English Parliament and a senior cleric. He brought grave, if not unexpected news. Richard, Duke of Gloucester, has been crowned King of England.'

'What of the prince, young Edward?'

'You remember Bishop Stillington, York's ambassador?'

'Not a man I will forget in a hurry.' Henry shook his head at the memory.

'It seems the bishop found a way to earn the gratitude of the Lord Protector of England.' The duke's tone was scathing. 'He advised Richard of how he officiated at a betrothal between York and Lady Eleanor Talbot, widowed daughter of the Earl of Shrewsbury, before he married Elizabeth Woodville.'

'Rendering the boys illegitimate.' Jasper glanced at Henry.

The duke took another sip of wine and fell silent, lost in his own thoughts for a moment before replying. 'I've never truly understood the English, although I continue to be surprised by them.' He smiled at Henry. 'I'm sorry. I think of you as French yet you are half English.'

'And one quarter Welsh.' Henry returned the smile. 'Did the cleric mention us, Duke Francis?'

'He did, which was why I kept you from his sight. It seems the new king is no less keen to see you return.'

'What did you tell him?' Henry leaned forward in his chair.

'I told him he must send me the four thousand archers I was promised.'

'You would return us?'

'Of course not. I saw no need to cross England's new king, although I suspect he will find the price a little high in his present circumstances.'

Jasper tasted his wine, recognising the rich flavour of the duke's best claret, saved for special occasions. 'You've bought us much needed time, although I suspect there is something else behind calling us to see you so late in the evening?'

'Indeed there is.' The duke signalled to his waiting servant, who slipped through the door and returned with a man Jasper had never seen before.

A little older than Henry, he wore a fur-trimmed robe over his doublet, and a short, silver handled dagger at his belt. He would have been handsome if not for his prominent brow, under which deep-set, intelligent brown eyes fixed on Jasper and Henry for a moment, as if taking in details to describe later.

Duke Francis bid the man to sit and told his servant to bring wine for his new guest. 'Monsieur, I present Sir Jasper Tudor and his nephew Henry Tudor.'

The man bowed his head. 'I am Hugh Conway, servant of Lady Margaret, sent here to deliver this letter.' He spoke with a lilting accent Jasper recognised as from North Wales, and produced a folded parchment which he handed to Henry.

Henry broke the seal and held the parchment to the

candlelight to read the neat script, then handed it to Jasper. 'My mother commends you to our service, Master Conway. Am I to infer you have some further information for us of such importance it could not be trusted to a letter?'

Conway took a deep breath. 'We fear, my lords, that the young princes Edward and Richard have been murdered.'

Henry gasped and the duke shook his head, obviously already having been informed of the news. Jasper's mind raced with questions. It seemed inconceivable events could move so quickly after York's death, yet he saw Hugh Conway was no mere servant and spoke with certainty.

'How did it happen? By whose hand?'

'There is much speculation in London. A group of the late king's servants tried to rescue the princes, and there were riots in the streets until the guards were brought in to enforce a curfew.'

'How can you be sure the boys are dead?'

'Lady Margaret has been close to their mother, sir. If she thought they were still alive, they would not share a common cause and she would not have agreed Lady Margaret's plan.'

'Which is?' Jasper guessed their lives were about to change yet again.

Hugh Conway turned to Henry. 'Your mother plans for you to claim the throne, sir. She sent me to tell you to raise an army and overthrow the usurper—before it's too late.'

His words hung in the air like the wisps of smoke that come before the hungry flames of a forest fire, full of danger-ous, irreversible consequences. Even the usually subdued Duke Francis looked startled at the suggestion. Jasper knew Lady Margaret would not send this messenger unless she was certain such an outrageous plan would find popular support. He watched for the duke's reaction as he spoke.

'You must inform Lady Margaret we'll need time to raise the money for mercenaries and ships. It could be at least another year before we could be in any position to return to England.'

'I've brought a fortune in gold, sir, as much as I could carry, raised by Lady Margaret through loans from your supporters in the city. I would say it's enough for as many ships as you need.' Conway smiled for the first time since he entered the room. 'I should also tell you Lady Margaret has secured the support of the Woodville family through agreeing your betrothal to their daughter, Lady Elizabeth, and the Duke of Buckingham is preparing a revolt to coincide with your return to Wales.'

Henry turned to Jasper. 'You knew this could happen, Uncle?'

'I did not, Henry. We've always known of your claim on your mother's side, and talked of you one day becoming king, yet there were so many in line ahead of you it was hardly a consideration.' His eyes narrowed. 'What about you, Henry. Could you see yourself as King of England?'

'I hardly dare dream of such a thing, Uncle. You are right. Until this moment it has not been a serious consideration.'

'You can count on my support.' The duke's eyes flashed in the candlelight. 'Prince Edward was to have been betrothed to my daughter Anne. I can never forgive whoever has done this.' He seemed to struggle to compose himself. 'I've already spoken to Pierre Landais. You may use my château at Suscinio as a base, and you shall have as many men as can be spared—I don't want you having to ask King Louis for ships.'

'Thank you, Duke Francis. We must make contact with the men in France, and find a way to free those held prisoner in Guisnes?'

Hugh Conway answered. 'It is in hand, sir. Lady Margaret sent messengers to our supporters, telling them to make their way to Brittany.'

Jasper raised his goblet of wine in the air. 'A toast, gentlemen. To a new adventure, and may God be with us.'

News of the sudden and unexpected death of King Louis at the end of August brought a new urgency to their preparations. Jasper mourned the loss of the well-intentioned and often misunderstood king who helped him through difficult times. He worried that King Louis' young son and heir to the throne, Charles, would struggle to control France, despite the support of his elder sister, Anne, chosen to act as regent.

Daydreaming of what might have been, if not for Henry, he wondered if he could have become an advisor to the princess and live out his days in luxury at the French court. The Duke of Burgundy, once the thorn in King Louis' side, was long since dead, killed in a pointless war with the Swiss, his body so mutilated it could only be recognised by his valet. Duke Francis was ill and vulnerable to subjugation by France, yet Jasper would always remain loyal to him.

Looking out of his window at a thunderous sky he saw there was no time to waste if they were to reach England before the winter storms. Henry was no sailor and it would be foolish to risk five thousand soldiers and their precious ships by making the crossing too late in the year. As if to remind him, the skies opened up with torrential rain which drummed and rattled at his window like a bad omen.

Henry was in his makeshift study in one of the duke's unused state rooms, counting the latest tally of their expenses. He had been tutored well by the duke's financial controller, Pierre Landais, and developed a flair for understanding numbers. He dipped his quill in the silver ink pot and scratched some notes in the margin of the ledger he was working on, glancing up as Jasper entered.

'The gold brought by Hugh Conway is fast running out.'

Jasper's brow furrowed in a frown. 'More men arrived today, all needing food and lodgings. You might speak to Pierre about a loan from the duke? I will find the ships if you can raise more funds.'

'What progress is there with the ships, Uncle?'

'Good news, Henry. Duke Francis has provided five ships at his own expense, three of which are warships. The best is *La Margarite*, a good omen, I think. She will serve us well as a flagship.'

'If each is able to carry three or four hundred soldiers...' Henry made a quick calculation. 'We will need another dozen at least.'

Jasper was surprised at the change in Henry since his mother's letter. No longer content to listen in the background, he seemed fired up with a new resolve and sense of purpose as they worked together on the plans. It was easier now to imagine him on the throne of England, regaining control of the vast treasury squandered so carelessly by York.

Before he could answer they were interrupted by a sharp knock on the door and Hugh Conway entered and turned to Jasper. 'You sent for me, sir?'

'I would like you to repeat what you told me about the Duke of Buckingham.'

'Of course, sir.' Conway closed the door behind him and moved some papers to sit in the spare chair. 'The Duke of Buckingham's father and grandfather were both killed fighting for Lancaster, yet he married the queen's sister and became a great favourite of the late King Edward. Now Richard has made him chief justice and constable of all the royal castles in Wales.'

'Are you suggesting he cannot be trusted?'

'I am not, sir. I felt obliged to point out to Sir Jasper that I was present when Lady Margaret secured his agreement to assist you. I feel he has his own ambitions, sir.'

'What did he say to make you question his loyalty?' There was an edge to Henry's voice.

Hugh Conway shifted uncomfortably in his seat. 'The Duke of Buckingham is a powerful man, with influence enough to persuade others that Richard should be made king. He told your mother his own claim to the throne is at least as good as yours, sir.'

'Now it seems he is out of favour.' He looked from Conway to Henry. 'We would do well to be on our guard.'

A cruel wind whipped at the rigging of their ships as Jasper and Henry waited to depart. Soldiers sought shelter wherever they could and raised voices carried from where some had started a fight in the harbourside tavern. Others, mostly mercenaries, deserted while they could, slinking away rather than taking their chances with the angry waters of the English Channel.

The first day of November began with cold rain stinging their faces as if admonishing their failure to sail earlier. As Jasper feared, despite generous loans from Duke Francis, the necessary preparations took far too long. Only five ships were moored among the fishing boats in the tidal harbour of Paimpol, although they hoped many more would join them under the command of the Admiral of Brittany, Jean Dufou.

'We've missed another tide, Henry.' Jasper peered out to sea where his ships bobbed and tugged at their anchors. 'We face a choice—to sail in the dark or wait until dawn.'

Rainwater ran from the brim of Henry's hat as he studied the ominous clouds. 'There are dangerous rocks offshore. We sail at dawn, when we can see where we are going.'

Jasper laughed. 'You are beginning to sound like a sailor, Henry. How did you come by that information?'

'I listen, Uncle. I hear the men's concerns and learn what I can from them.'

'You will make a good king, if we can ever get you across this infernal stretch of water.'

The eerie autumn mist hovered over the sea as they made the most of a freshening breeze and trimmed the sails of *La Margarite* for a westerly heading. The plan was to meet the rest of the fleet in mid Channel but there was no telling if they also missed the tide or waited ahead in the glimmering dawn.

Jasper said a silent prayer that God would keep them safe. He glanced across at Henry, now grown into a man, and knew his brother Edmund would have been impossibly proud. He smiled as he imagined what his father would have had to say about a Tudor invading England to take the crown.

They had made some difficult decisions, which he hoped they would not regret. It had been his idea not to bring horses. As well as the difficulty of loading and unloading them, there wasn't the room, as every space was filled with men. Instead they carried the duke's gold and hoped to buy horses once they landed in Wales. If they could not, they would march all the way to London.

He reached out and gripped the wet wooden rail to steady himself as the ship lurched in the swell. 'Have you found your sea legs yet, Henry?'

Henry grinned, for a moment looking like the boy Jasper remembered. 'If these favourable winds hold up we'll be across in no time, but how are we going to see the fleet in this mist?'

'It will lift once the sun comes out.'

'We should post more lookouts. It wouldn't do to invade England with only five ships.'

Jasper scanned the horizon. The visibility was improving but the skies ahead looked dark and brooding. A shower of foaming spray splashed across the deck, soaking soldiers lining the rail. He smiled at their colourful curses, in English as well as Breton and French. This was more than a mercenary army. Good men came to support their cause from far and wide.

He studied the sails of the other four ships in the little fleet, already starting to disperse in the uncertain seas, yet close enough for him to see a man on the deck of one raise a hand and wave. Instinctively he waved back, a small act of reassurance. Some of those who sailed with him did so for the pay but many lived in hope of a new life under a king they would be proud to serve.

When the squall hit it was as if nature conspired against them. The rain seemed to come from all directions, with such force it took Jasper's breath away and forced him to seek refuge below decks. Although this was one of the largest ships, chosen as the flagship, the low ceiling meant he had to stoop. The hold was a dark, damp world of cursing, dripping men, their lives depending on the unlucky few with the task of weathering the storm.

He found Henry in conversation with Captain Derien le Du, master of *La Marguerite* and one of the duke's most experienced captains. A likeable, swarthy man, he wore a Breton cap and an oiled leather seaman's cape over his doublet. Some of the hardier sailors played a noisy game with dice and the others sang old songs in their deep, heavily accented voices, accompanied by someone on a shrill penny whistle.

Henry spotted Jasper and beckoned him to come closer. 'Captain le Du needs to know if we wish to press on or wait until we see the rest of the fleet.'

The ship shuddered as the bow crashed into another heavy wave and Jasper raised his voice to make himself heard. He realised they were both looking at him for confirmation of their plan.

'They know we're headed for Dorset so it makes sense to cover the ground while we can. I don't relish the prospect of waiting for this storm to worsen.'

The storm finally eased a little and they followed Captain le Du back on deck to shelter in the lee of the sails. Henry pointed to a dark shape off to starboard. With a shock of realisation Jasper saw it was *La Michelle*, one of the ships that had been at their side. Her mainsail was torn and flapped violently in the stiff breeze as they watched the crew struggle to bring it under control.

'Where are our other ships?' Henry searched the horizon in all directions.

As if in reply a wave broke over the bows, sending a foot of seawater across the deck. Jasper tasted the salty tang of seawater and looked up at the troubled sky. The storm may have passed but there was no sign of the other three ships.

Captain le Du was philosophical. 'They might have turned back.' He glanced at Henry. 'I was nearly minded to.' There was a hint of criticism in his voice, although as captain it was his decision.

Jasper cursed at the thought. If the other ships turned back their plans would be ruined. By the time they returned to Brittany winter would have set in and it would mean waiting until spring. Worse still, they had used most of the duke's loans. The crews and soldiers would still demand payment, as it would not be their fault they never set foot on English soil.

'We will sail on.' Henry pointed ahead. 'I can see land, there on the horizon. The rest of the fleet could be already off the Dorset coast, waiting for us to arrive.'

'That looks to be the Isle of Wight.' Jasper squinted into the gloom.

Henry turned to the captain. 'We could shelter overnight at

Poole Harbour and see if there is any sign of the fleet by morning?'

The captain grunted agreement and went to shout orders at his crew. Jasper looked at Henry and tried to recall the boy who shivered below decks on the outward voyage. He was learning fast, and knew how to command men with much greater experience than himself.

After sailing through a stormy, sleepless night, Jasper felt great relief as they made the narrow entrance into the safe anchorage of Poole in Dorset, with *La Michelle*, the one remaining ship, following in their wake. There was no sign of any others from their fleet. This was a disappointment but there was no danger of their being taken for an invading army. They looked like what they were, a couple of Breton ships seeking shelter from the storm still raging in the Channel.

The first light of dawn glimmered on the horizon as they set anchor and tried to have a few hours of sleep while they waited for the other ships to arrive. When Jasper woke there was still no sight of them, so he decided to take *La Marguerite's* skiff ashore. It would be useful to see if there was any news of the Duke of Buckingham's revolt, although he insisted Henry must remain on board, as landing was not without risks.

As they rowed closer to the harbour wall Jasper spotted armed men on the quayside, watching their approach and called up to them. 'We are Breton, in need of supplies!'

One of the men stepped forward. He cupped his hands and shouted back in a rich West Country accent. 'Come ashore, boys!'

They rowed to the stone steps and tied up to an iron ring set into the harbour wall. Jasper's instinct told him something was wrong. This was where they had arranged to meet the other ships but too many men waited for them on the quayside. Too many to fight, if they had to. An idea occurred to him and he called up again.

'Is there any news of the Duke of Buckingham?'

'We are the Duke of Buckingham's men. Come up and we'll tell you!'

The relief he felt was immediately replaced by alarm as he heard some of the soldiers laugh. He had heard that laugh before, the laugh of men who shared a joke at someone else's expense. They had unwittingly sailed into a trap at their first landfall. Two of his men had already reached the top and a third was half way up the steps.

'Come back!' He glanced back at their ship, silhouetted at anchor a surprising distance away. 'We have to get back!'

His warning came too late. His men at the top of the quay were seized by soldiers and a third was caught in a scuffle as he tried to return to the boat. More soldiers scrambled down, but the narrow steps were slippery, giving Jasper an advantage and he managed to wrest his arm free of their grip. He leapt back into the boat, nearly causing it to capsize, and cut through the mooring rope with his knife.

'Row, as fast as you can!'

The remaining two sailors grabbed the oars and pulled the boat away from the quay as Jasper slashed with his knife at the hands grasping for their boat. One of the soldiers cursed loudly at the wound on the back of his hand and staggered backwards in surprise.

The oarsmen found their stroke, but as they sped away from the quay, Jasper could see his two men left behind still struggling, despite being hopelessly outnumbered. He looked at *La Margarite* and wondered if there was time to bring it alongside the quay to rescue his men but it was too late. Once again he'd escaped capture by running away from a fight and the knowledge left a bitter taste in his mouth.

## 25

### DECEMBER 1483

The choir sang in Latin, a haunting, ethereal sound that echoed in the chill air of Christmas Day in Rennes Cathedral. To Jasper it sounded more like a requiem than a celebration. He raised his eyes to the life-sized figure of Christ and prayed for his nephew Henry Tudor. They were there for the exiled nobles to formally swear allegiance to Henry as the rightful King of England, and for the blessing of his betrothal to Princess Elizabeth, York's eldest daughter, whom he still had never set eyes upon.

As the self-important priest began a long sermon Jasper found his mind wandering to the recent failed invasion that so nearly cost them their lives. He thanked God they were both safe and well in Brittany but the near disaster cost them a fortune in loans from Duke Francis. He doubted they would ever now be in a position to repay the money owed to him or keep the promises they had made.

After his narrow escape from the soldiers in Poole they had no choice other than to return to Brittany. Another savage storm caught them in the Channel and took them so far off course they made landfall on the Cotentin Peninsula near Valognes in Normandy. He understood when Henry had no wish to return to sea, so they secured safe conduct down the coast of France to Vannes. When they finally returned it was to a welcome from an army of refugees from Richard's purges, led by Thomas Grey, Marquess of Dorset, Queen Elizabeth's son by her first marriage, and Sir Edward Woodville, the queen's younger brother.

Jasper smiled to himself as he recalled Henry's reaction. Instead of accepting defeat, the disaster strengthened his resolve, despite news the Duke of Buckingham was dead, publicly executed for treason after his Welsh retainers deserted him at Brecon. They had learned some hard lessons and would be better prepared next time.

He glanced across at Henry's serious face and calculated it would be his twenty-seventh birthday next month. He was pleased Henry was committing to a good marriage, rather than let the years slip past as he had. He remembered Bishop Still-ington commenting that Princess Elizabeth was a fine young girl, with her mother's beauty and her father's brains. It was meant in jest but by all accounts the truth.

Lady Margaret knew what she was doing by arranging this marriage. If it ever took place it would be a fresh start, uniting the Houses of Lancaster and York. Only one obstacle stood in their path. Jasper scowled at the thought of Richard declaring himself king. He couldn't understand how the good men and women of England could accept the disappearance of the two young princes, yet by all accounts it seemed they had.

His eyes returned to the painted figure of Christ, which seemed to glow in the light of a hundred candles, and swore a private oath to do everything in his power to see Henry on the English throne, with Elizabeth of York at his side as queen. He had not come to the cathedral expecting to find his faith restored, yet now he felt all the hardships and apparently wasted years had prepared him well for what lay ahead.

Christopher Urswick carried a letter from Lady Margaret that confirmed him as her priest and confessor, her most trusted man, and recommended him to Henry. The thin-faced priest looked at Jasper with dark eyes that seemed to read his mind, then turned to Henry. He spoke quietly, in a voice that sounded older than his years and made his words all the more chilling.

'Pierre Landais is plotting to return you to England.'

Jasper cursed and Henry stared at the priest as the consequences of this news sank home. Eight months of hard work unravelled in an instant. Duke Francis had retired from public life because of his failing health and Landais now effectively governed Brittany. The arrangement suited them well, as he had been generous, extending further loans for the ships at anchor in the harbour of St Malo.

'He saved my life.' Henry turned on the priest. 'I find it hard to believe he has betrayed our trust. How did you come by this information?'

'Lord Stanley overheard the story by chance at Westminster Palace. He felt obliged to inform his wife, Lady Margaret, who sent me secretly to Bishop John Morton, who is currently in exile in Antwerp. The bishop provided me with a letter of introduction to the Regent of France, Duchess Anne de Beaujeu, who has granted safe-conducts for you both, my lords, and bids you to make haste. There is little time to be lost.'

'What of the loans, the ships, and all the work we've done?' Henry sounded shocked.

'Praemonitus, praemunitus. Forewarned is forearmed, my lords.' The priest gave the ghost of a smile. 'I believe divine providence is at work. Bishop Morton has also provided money to help your escape.'

'We must leave right away.' Henry's tone softened a little. 'I thank you for risking your life for our cause.'

Jasper agreed. 'We must also alert Duke Francis. He has been good to us. It would not be right to desert him.'

'You must take care not to alert Pierre Landais and force his hand.' The priest glanced towards the door. 'I understand he is an ambitious man, and close to concluding his negotiations.'

Jasper cursed again. 'How could we be so blind? Ever since Duke Francis took to his sick bed Landais has been plotting.'

'That's why he agreed the loans, to keep us here as his pawns?' Henry glanced at his papers, accounts and detailed inventories, now useless.

'And it explains why there have been so many delays. Our ships should be ready now, yet there is always some problem, some reason not to set a date for the invasion.'

'Pierre Landais has good reason.'

Jasper heard the bitterness in Henry's voice. 'We must prepare to leave while we can, Henry. With God's grace there is still time. He has no reason to suspect.'

'Will Landais not come after us, when he hears we've escaped?'

'We must deceive him. I will leave with a small group of hand-picked men on the pretext of visiting the duke. You could leave shortly afterwards and meet us in Angers?'

'What about all our supporters here?'

The priest spoke again, his voice unexpectedly authoritative. 'You can't tell anyone of our plan, my lord. We need them to continue as if nothing has happened, at least until we are safely in France.'

.  .  .

No one paid any attention to Jasper as he rode out from the Château de l'Hermine with the sombre priest at his side, followed by half a dozen trusted nobles. They said they were visiting Duke Francis, and would be away for a few days. Instead, they galloped hard for the border, avoiding the main roads and staying away from towns and villages.

They needed to rest the horses, but continued through most of the following day before the distinctive twin spires of Angers cathedral appeared on the skyline. Henry followed shortly afterwards, stopping only to meet the wagon carrying their possessions, where he changed into the plain clothes of a servant. After an anxious wait, Jasper spotted an exhausted Henry, still disguised, with a straw hat shading his face.

'Henry!' He waved to catch his nephew's attention.

'Praise God I've found you!' Henry glanced back behind him as if expecting to see Landais' soldiers in pursuit. 'We had to leave the wagon, although I hope it will be here soon.'

Jasper smiled. They had amassed few enough possessions in all their years in Brittany. Even Jasper's precious armour showed its age, the leather straps gnawed by rats, and fitted poorly around his broadening middle. He tried to keep himself fit and although he was over fifty, he reminded himself how his father had a son, David Owen, when he'd been even older, and had willingly ridden into battle with their Welsh army.

The thirteen-year-old King Charles wore a black felt hat too large for his head and a heavy gold chain around his neck. Jasper suspected their invitation to his court at Montargis, south of Paris, had been prompted by the young king's shrewd and attractive sister, Duchess Anne, who at twenty-two would certainly realise the value of Henry's claim to the English throne.

'We are grateful for your generosity, Your Grace.' Henry

spoke in French and sounded confident. 'Let us mark this day as a new beginning between France and England.'

'You speak for England?' King Charles' voice betrayed his youth.

'I do, Your Grace. With your help and support, we will take the throne.'

Henry's words hung in the air while he waited for the young king's reply. Jasper gave the princess Regent of France a barely imperceptible nod. They had rehearsed this moment earlier. The future security of both their countries was too great a prize to leave to chance. He saw the flash of acknowledgement in her eyes. She would have made a fine wife for Henry, had she not already been married to the Duke of Bourbon at the age of twelve.

'If we provide the support you need, will you relinquish all claim on the crown of France?'

'I will, Your Grace.' Henry addressed himself to the fledgling king, although his sister asked the question. 'I give you my solemn word all loans will be repaid in full, and we will agree terms of peace with France.'

When he was finally alone with Henry they looked at each other in silence for a moment as the enormity of what had been agreed dawned on them.

'All those months of planning have not been wasted after all, Uncle. Now we can fund as many ships as we'll need, instead of limiting our men to those we can carry.'

'It's not such a bad thing to have another year of preparation, Henry. We will let Richard think we've failed and are no longer a threat.'

'Surely he won't believe a word of it?'

'People hear what they wish to, Henry. Richard and his advisors are no exception.' Jasper smiled. 'All the same, we can ask Christopher Urswick to take a letter back and ask him to see it falls into the wrong hands.'

. . .

So many of Henry's supporters arrived in Montargis it was necessary for Jasper and Henry to arrange a special court to welcome them, and agree what part they might have in the preparations for invasion. One of the first men they met, Sir Thomas Grey, Marquess of Dorset, had put himself forward as a spokesman for the men they had been forced to abandon in Brittany.

Jasper instinctively disliked the thick-necked son of the former queen, an alienated Yorkist who showed little respect for Henry. His brother, Richard Grey, had been executed for his part in the Duke of Buckingham's rebellion, but Jasper's instinct was not to trust him. The trouble was they needed him for his Woodville connections, and he knew it.

Henry welcomed him to Montargis. 'It's a great relief to see you here, safe and well, Sir Thomas.'

'We feared you had both been abducted by York's agents when you failed to return.' Sir Thomas gave Jasper a questioning look. 'You didn't even take Duke Francis into your confidence?'

'We could not, Sir Thomas.' Henry's voice had a defensive edge. 'Pierre Landais was close to handing us over. We had to act as soon as we found out, without alerting him.'

Sir Thomas snorted. 'You've heard what happened soon after you left?'

'No.'

'We found out from the duke that one of your servants betrayed you. He told Landais, who sent men after you, but he was too late.'

'What has become of Landais?'

'They say he's escaped into exile,' Sir Thomas shrugged, 'where I don't know.'

'What did Duke Francis have to say about all this?'

'He is frail but well enough to be furious at Landais. He granted our full expenses to travel here, although frankly I think he was glad to be rid of us.'

'Thank you, Sir Thomas. We've many new men arriving every day, so it would be most appreciated if you will take responsibility for those who came with you from Brittany?'

'It would be an honour, my lord.' It was his first acknowledgement of Henry's new status yet Jasper remained unconvinced.

After Sir Thomas Grey left, a white-bearded knight, dressed in battle-worn mail with a tattered and stained surcoat, introduced himself as Sir John de Vere, Earl of Oxford. Jasper struggled to recognise him as the same man he had last seen setting sail for England with Warwick.

'You've been released from Hammes Castle?'

Sir John gave a wry smile. 'Escaped, more like it, after ten years.' The smile vanished as he remembered. 'I tried jumping from a high window into the moat once. Nearly did for me that time. They thought I was trying to kill myself.'

Henry was curious. 'How did you escape, Sir John? There was talk of rescuing you once, but the castle was too well defended.'

'I owe my freedom to Sir James Blount, Captain of Hammes. He told me he could no longer live with his conscience after what is rumoured to have happened to the Princes in the Tower.'

'He helped you?'

'He is here, Your Grace, ready to swear to serve you.' Sir John glanced at Jasper, as if making a judgement. 'We have a request, my lords.' He looked at his boots. 'Unfortunately we had to leave Lady Blount behind. She is safe enough, as she has the garrison to protect her, but...'

'You want us to rescue her?' Jasper was already thinking how useful it would be to their cause to have a Lancastrian military commander with Sir John de Vere's experience, even though, like them, he would be learning from his mistakes.

'Not only Lady Blount, Sir Jasper. I believe the entire garrison of Hammes Castle could be persuaded to join our cause.'

'That would certainly win us the attention of the garrison in Calais,' Jasper smiled, 'I must consult Duchess Anne before we can consider your request, Sir John, although I must admit it does appeal to me.'

As the next man entered both Jasper and Henry were checking the lists to see how many more remained to be seen. Jasper looked up to see a hooded man, wearing an old sword that seemed familiar. The man pulled back his hood and grinned.

'Gabriel, by God!' Jasper leapt to his feet and shook his old friend by the hand. 'What took you so long?'

'It's been a while, I will admit.' Gabriel bowed with exaggerated courtesy to Henry. 'Your Grace, I would hardly recognise you, that's for sure.'

Henry also stood and crossed to shake Gabriel's hand. 'It's good to see you, Gabriel. We need men who are good at choosing horses, and you always were one of the best.'

'Well, thank you, Henry, I mean, Your Grace.'

'Where have you been? What have you been up to, Gabriel?' Henry gestured for him to take a seat.

Gabriel sat heavily and studied the two of them. 'Duke Francis wouldn't let me in the country, or allow me to send you any letters, so I returned to Waterford for a while, then found work with your old friend Thomas White in Tenby.'

'So, you're a wine-merchant now?' Jasper smiled at the thought.

'I've been skippering his ships, sir, from Tenby to Cork and back.' He returned Jasper's smile. 'The best of both worlds, although I often spared a thought for you here, while I was working hard.'

'Well, it's good to have you back.' Jasper glanced at Henry. 'You heard we made the mistake of trying to invade last winter?'

Gabriel nodded. 'There was a story you were shipwrecked, but I know it would take more than that to stop you, sir.'

'We won't make that mistake again. We won't set sail until the weather is set fair.'

'You seem to have enough men, but I've heard them talking. Some are wondering if you have the money to pay their wages?'

'We're keeping our cards close, Gabriel. There could be spies for Richard among them, so it would be no bad thing for our enemies to think we've no money for an invasion.'

Henry agreed. 'The Regent of France promised us forty thousand livres, and we will raise further loans when we need them. We have more than four hundred English exiles, including Sir John de Vere, Sir Edward Woodville and Sir Thomas Grey.'

'And we've agreed to take French soldiers,' Jasper added, 'as well as artillerymen, together with their guns, which we can hire for the invasion.'

Gabriel rubbed his hands together. 'There's a lot of men in Wales waiting for your call, if what I've heard in Tenby and Pembroke is true, sir. Which reminds me—you mentioned Sir Thomas Grey, Marquess of Dorset?'

'What of him, Gabriel?' Jasper wondered if his instinct had been right.

'It might be tavern talk but some of the men are saying his half-sister, Elizabeth, is to marry King Richard.' He saw Henry's frown. 'Forgive me, Your Grace, her uncle Richard, who has usurped the throne.'

'But Richard is married to Anne Neville?' Jasper struggled to understand.

Gabriel shrugged. 'They say his queen is gravely ill and might not last the year.' He looked from Jasper to Henry, seeming not to appreciate the significance of his words. 'You could find, sir, you have more than one enemy in your camp if the Woodville family are restored to favour.'

## 26

# AUGUST 1485

J asper watched as the effort of the men heaving on the capstan was rewarded and the rusting iron anchor emerged dripping from the water. He felt the dull thump as it banged into place against the tar-painted hull and the ship lurched with sudden freedom. Flapping canvas sails filled with a freshening southerly breeze and at last, after more than a year of preparation, their fleet was leaving Harfleur for the open sea.

He looked up at Henry, high on the raised afterdeck. Dressed in black he made a striking figure, flanked by Sir John de Vere and their arrogant but capable captain, Guillaume de Casenove. No one seeing him would suspect Henry's fear of the sea after the near disaster of the last storm. His secret was safe. From now on Jasper would be Henry's shadow, watching his back, advising and protecting their future king.

His own shadow spoke in a cheerful Irish voice. 'Now isn't that a sight, sir?'

At first he thought Gabriel meant Henry but realised he was talking about the fleet of thirty crowded ships following in their wake. Jasper studied them with the critical eye of one who has borrowed money for their hire. They sailed as one, arrayed like a flock of migrating geese behind the *Polain of Dieppe*, with its proud red dragon pennant flying from the main mast.

'We've waited so long it warms my heart, Gabriel.' He looked to see they could not be overheard. 'There were times when I doubted we would ever see this day.'

Hard lessons had been learned in their earlier attempt. This time they waited for clear blue skies and were ready for the perfect tide. He watched the fleet begin to break formation. Bellowed commands carried across the water as each captain sought to make the most of the light winds which would carry them on to Wales.

He breathed the fresh sea air and felt a huge sense of relief after all that had happened. In January, Sir John de Vere returned triumphant with thirty-seven members of the Hammes Castle garrison and Lady Blount. The trained men-at-arms were all professional soldiers, a welcome addition to their invading army. Although many had been York's men, Jasper was satisfied they were loyal to Sir James Blount, former Captain of Hammes.

At the end of March they heard that the usurper's queen, Anne Neville, had died in Westminster, on the same day as an eclipse of the sun, a bad omen for Richard. Rumours reached France that he now planned to marry Elizabeth of York, as if to spite Henry's ambition. Elizabeth had been released from sanctuary and was enjoying the freedoms of the king's court, together with her mother and sisters. It was said the match was viewed with suspicion by the people and had done nothing for Richard's reputation.

Jasper was already considering alternative candidates for Henry's queen, including Lady Katherine Herbert. Although the daughter of Jasper's enemy William Herbert, Henry spent his childhood with Katherine at Herbert's Raglan Castle in

Wales, and she would serve to keep former Yorkist supporters in the fold.

Another of Gabriel's concerns proved right when Sir Thomas Grey slipped away in the night from Montargis, taking several of his close associates. Jasper had ordered a watch over all those with Woodville connections and sent men in pursuit. They returned with Thomas Grey as prisoner and Henry ordered him to be left in France as security until their loans were all repaid.

Their benefactor Pierre Landais had been caught in Nantes and publicly hanged in July, although it saddened Jasper to learn his confession was extracted by torture. Jasper said a prayer for the soul of the clever and likeable man, who had saved Henry's life and was guilty only of ambition.

The need to take a wide berth around Land's End meant a full week passed before they entered the shelter of Milford Sound on the western coast of Wales. Although it remained light until late into the evening, the sun burned low in the sky with an amber glow, turning the sea to molten gold. Men shouted orders and ropes were hauled to reef the sails as they approached the rocky, pebble strewn shore.

Jasper felt a powerful surge of emotion at the thought of setting foot on Welsh soil after so many years in exile. As they drew closer, he could make out the familiar headland and the sheltered cove of Mill Bay. Chosen for privacy rather than practicality, the hidden cove was only accessible by ship at high tide but it would be a long march to the nearest village at Dale.

A figure appeared high on the path, waving an arm and calling to them. Jasper strained to hear what he was saying, mindful of the cruel trickery they suffered on their last landfall. He needn't have worried, as more men appeared, cheering and waving in greeting. Boats were lowered and the small bay crowded with ships, some dropping anchor, others sailing right to the shore. There were splashes as the more eager men jumped into waist-deep water and waded ashore, rather than waiting their turn for the boats.

Jasper agreed to go ashore first and signal to Henry when he was sure it was safe. Thick rope netting was lowered over the side and he clambered over, followed by Gabriel into the already crowded longboat. The oarsmen were ready and at his nod pulled hard towards the shore, crunching the keel on the hard pebbles of the beach. He leapt out and cursed at the cold shock of water soaking his boots.

A handsome young soldier wearing shining armour stepped forward and reached out a welcoming hand to steady him. 'You don't recognise me, brother?' The man had the soft local accent, and there was something familiar about his intelligent dark eyes, which fixed on Jasper's as he waited for an answer.

'Praise God!' Jasper shook him by the hand as he saw the striking resemblance to his father. 'David Owen, the boy who sparred with Henry in Pembroke Castle?' The memory returned as if it were yesterday, instead of half a lifetime ago.

'I am, and I've brought a dozen trusty men-at-arms from Pembroke to welcome you home.'

Jasper drew his sword and turned towards the *Polain of Dieppe*, raising the blade high in the air, he gave the sign they waited for. They watched as Henry's boat approached and he stepped ashore to a rousing cheer from the growing crowd of men. Henry acknowledged them with a raised hand. He bent on one knee and lowered his head.

'Judge me, O God, and plead my cause against an ungodly nation: O deliver me from the deceitful and unjust man.'

Jasper recognised the words of Psalm forty-three, which Henry once said carried a particular truth for him. The crowded bay fell silent as Henry stood and addressed the men, his new army. He said a prayer of thanks for their safe arrival and for God to witness their victory over their enemies.

'I thank you all for your support, which will never be forgotten. There is much to do before we lose the light. Let us unload the ships and make for Dale, where we will set up camp.' His voice echoed from the high cliffs, clear and confident, the voice of a future king.

As they began the long march up the steep, narrow path from Mill Bay, Gabriel pointed out to sea. 'Our fleet is already trimming their sails, sir, ready to turn for home.'

'There's no going back now, Gabriel,' Jasper admitted, 'it was my idea, just like the skirmishers.'

'Sail in and out fast, before anyone has the chance to spot them?'

'We've no further use for those ships, and the crews have earned their pay.'

He looked behind to where teams of men followed. Some carried wheels, others shared the weight of the cannons, already straining as they clambered up the steep slope. The wagons they brought were designed to be dismantled for manhandling, although it was clear the burden of supplies they carried was already slowing them down.

'We'll need you to find us horses, soon as you can, Gabriel.' Jasper grinned. 'If we have to drag those guns all the way to London we'll still be doing it at Christmas.'

After the first full night of sleep for a week in their temporary camp at Dale they set off at first light on the march to the market town of Haverfordwest, where they hoped to be greeted by a Welsh army. The skies were clear and scouts sent out at dawn returned with no reported enemy sightings. The air was filled with the sounds of men talking and laughing as they prepared for the day's march.

Henry appeared, followed by David Owen. 'We've had grave news.' Henry's earlier confidence seemed to be wavering. 'Rhys ap Thomas has been made Lieutenant of South West Wales, as reward for not supporting Buckingham's rebellion. There are rumours he is mustering more than a thousand men.'

'Does he know we're here?' Jasper shook his head. 'I can't believe he would turn against us, Henry. His grandfather died at the side of yours at Mortimer's Cross.'

Henry looked concerned. 'We need him on our side, Uncle.'

'I'll ride ahead to find him. Gabriel will buy horses and we'll travel faster than your men can march. We will meet you at Welshpool, God willing.'

'We wish you God speed. Our future depends on it.'


Armed with a purse of gold coins Gabriel returned with half a dozen horses for the men Jasper had chosen, all loyal Welsh speakers from good families. If Rhys ap Thomas was Richard's man, at least they might dissuade him from standing in Henry's way. Better still, Jasper hoped to persuade the Welsh army to join them.

Gabriel handed him the reins of a fine Welsh cob. 'She's no destrier, sir, but she'll do.'

Jasper turned to his waiting men, all mounted on Gabriel's horses. 'Follow my lead, and keep a sharp eye for the enemy. I don't want to be caught in an ambush.' Even as he said the words he had a flashback to the fateful day at Mortimer's Cross.

As they were about to leave another rider joined them and he recognised his half-brother under the shining sallet helmet.

'You don't think I'd miss the chance to ride with you, Sir Jasper?' David grinned.

'You're welcome, David. You know these roads better than I do.'

'Word has it that Rhys ap Thomas is no longer in Carmarthen. His army marches to Llandovery. I can take you there by the shortest route.'

They rode at a fast pace through the Welsh countryside. Jasper was glad of the excuse to avoid the long, slow march, and to be doing something that could turn the tide for Henry. Stopping to water and rest the horses, they risked a meal in a tavern where the innkeeper was in talkative mood. He told them riders recently passed through on their way to join Rhys ap Thomas, who occupied the castle at Brecon, where he was mustering a great army.

Jasper smelt woodsmoke on the still night air before they even reached Brecon. They turned a corner and saw the lights of a hundred campfires. An army occupied the town, their tents lining the street on both sides far into the distance. Henry had been right. If they could not win over this Welsh army, their invasion would be at an end. He dismounted and turned to his men.

'I will go in alone, and send for you when I know it's safe.'

David also dismounted. 'I should come with you,' he handed his reins to Gabriel, 'I know these men.'

'You know they could arrest us as rebels?'

'We have no choice. There must be over a thousand men here and more on the way.' David looked Jasper in the eye. 'I will come with you.'

Gabriel looked unhappy at the idea. 'And if you don't return?'

'Then you must ride to Henry and warn him.'

.   .   .

They crossed the old drawbridge of Brecon Castle, guarded by two towers, and up to the main gate where they announced themselves to the guards. The captain of the guard soon appeared and led them through the noisy courtyard filled with soldiers to the great hall, where Rhys ap Thomas sat surrounded by his commanders. Jasper saw they had been drinking for some time, judging by the look of them.

A handsome, stocky man with long dark hair, Rhys ap Thomas wore a white surcoat with his distinctive badge of a black raven over a finely-made mail shirt. One of the richest and most powerful Welshmen alive, he looked every inch a knight. In England he would have been made an earl but because he was Welsh the English regarded him as a commoner.

Rhys ap Thomas studied them both as the guard commander introduced them, then gestured for them to take a seat at his table. 'Welcome, Sir Jasper Tudor. I am honoured you've come all this way to see me at such a late hour.'

His strong Welsh accent was cultured and the buzz of conversation in the great hall fell silent as their attention turned to their visitors. Few of them would be old enough to have even heard of Jasper, and even those who did might fail to recognise him now his hair and beard were turning grey.

'Too much rests on this to entrust it to a messenger. We've come to secure your support for my nephew, Henry Tudor, the true and rightful king.' Jasper sounded more confident than he felt.

'You know I refused to support Buckingham's revolt? I've promised that Henry Tudor will only reach England over my dead body.'

Some of the men around Rhys ap Thomas laughed but Jasper knew everything they worked for depended on persuading this man to follow Henry. If he chose to, Rhys ap

Thomas commanded enough men to drive Henry's small army back into the sea.

'I understand why you chose not to follow the Duke of Buckingham, an Englishman.'

Rhys ap Thomas nodded. 'And now I am charged by another Englishman, King Richard to stop you,' he glanced at the men flanking him, 'and we've taken payment from the crown.'

'We cannot do this without your support.' Jasper looked at the men flanking Rhys ap Thomas and saw he had their full attention. 'We are descended from the true princes of Wales. Henry marches under the red dragon of Cadwallader and they call him *Y Mab Darogan*, the son of prophecy. Your grandfather, Gruffydd ap Nicholas, fought and died at Mortimer's Cross,' he glanced at David Owen, 'at the side of our father, Owen Tudor. How proud would they have been to know their deaths were not in vain, that one day Welshmen would defeat the English and claim the throne?'

Rhys ap Thomas looked back at him, unblinking and impossible to read. 'A fine speech, Sir Jasper, but I must remind you the stakes could not be higher. King Richard is rallying a great army of thousands in the north. If I follow Henry Tudor he must win, for if he loses, I will surely lose my head.'

Jasper had one more ace up his sleeve but if it failed to win Rhys ap Thomas over all would be lost. He took a deep breath. 'I bring you Henry Tudor's offer of the position of Chamberlain of South Wales, with a pension for life and a knighthood, in return for your loyal support.'

The great hall fell silent again as Rhys ap Thomas considered Jasper's offer. With a glance at the men on either side of him, he called for another jug of ale. They waited while a servant filled a pewter cup with ale in front of each of them, then Rhys ap Thomas raised his cup in the air.

'We are with you,' he drank then raised his cup a second time. 'To victory, for Wales!'

Henry's men cheered when they saw Rhys ap Thomas ride into their camp at Long Mountain, outside the town of Welshpool, flanked by Jasper and David Owen. The black raven standard flew at the front of an army of over nearly two thousand men, the bright sunshine glinting from their weapons and armour, the finest soldiers in Wales.

Henry rode forward to greet them. A fine silver helmet replaced his black hat and a new breastplate gleamed on his chest, a dark riding cape flowing in the breeze behind him.

'Praise God, we have doubled our numbers on the march through Wales, and now have an army worthy of the name.'

Jasper felt a surge of pride at what he'd accomplished, despite suspecting Rhys ap Thomas intended to support them all along. 'Where now, Henry? What news is there of our enemy?'

'Richard's army is on the move. We'll take the old road and cross the River Severn at Shrewsbury. Now we can no longer keep our presence secret I've sent word to my stepfather, Lord Thomas Stanley, and to my mother.'

'Do you think Lord Stanley will join us?'

'In truth, I doubt it. He has five thousand men, but I believe he will not fight against us.'

Jasper made a calculation. Including the men who followed Rhys ap Thomas, Henry must have around four or five thousand soldiers. If Lord Stanley had five thousand, Richard would surely have double that, perhaps fifteen thousand or more. They would be outnumbered more than two or even three to one, even with the new men arriving every day. Henry was still talking but he wasn't listening, his mind numbed by the scale of the challenge they faced.

He had allowed himself to believe they had a fighting chance. The truth hit him like a splash of cold water in the face. It would take a miracle. They had come too far to turn back. Their ships had sailed and the consequences of losing too dreadful to contemplate. They could not rely on Lord Thomas Stanley to stand by, he must join them for Henry to have any chance of victory.

Jasper leaned back in his saddle and muttered encouragement to steady his horse. Flanked by David Owen and Gabriel, he closed his eyes for a moment and said a prayer, not for himself but for Henry. He felt strangely calm for someone facing death. All his worries slipped away with the certainty that, one way or another, he would meet his destiny at last.

He opened his eyes again. He had never seen so many men so still, so silent, as on that morning, on a broad field south of the market town of Bosworth, in Leicestershire, bordered by the River Tweed. Sir John de Vere, chosen as commander, had persuaded Henry to form his army in a wide line, archers to the front. Jasper glanced across at Henry, who decided to remain on foot with his guards.

He remembered the words of Marcus Aurelius: *The twining strands of fate weave together our existence and the things that happen to us*. He'd had enough of running, and Henry was old enough to be his own man, make his own decisions. If it was his destiny to die in this summer meadow, then so be it. He fastened the thick leather strap under his helmet and pulled it tight, then pulled on the black leather gloves he'd chosen instead of steel gauntlets, in deference to the heat.

Across the field the deadly ranks of King Richard's army shimmered with a dreamlike quality in the sunshine. Jasper shielded his eyes with his hand and made out Richard's standard bearer, with the long pennant of the white boar. Richard could not be far away. He glanced across at Henry's standard, the red dragon of Cadwallader, carried by William Brandon, surrounded by loyal Lancastrian mounted knights.

With a shout, Sir John de Vere committed them to battle. The air filled with arrows, spurring the enemy into action, as they returned an equally devastating volley and closed the ground between them with alarming speed. The clash of steel and cries of wounded and dying men brought deeply buried memories back for Jasper and he drew his sword. The blade flashed in the sun as he held it high, the signal for the next wave of men to attack.

His horse spooked at the sudden boom of their cannon and he stroked its withers to calm it as he watched the shot blast deep into the enemy ranks. Men fell dead without even knowing what hit them, the price of the deadly new warfare. For some reason the enemy cannons failed to reply and Henry's men pressed forward to exploit their small advantage.

From his position at the rear of the battlefield Jasper could see they were outnumbered by more than two to one. He scanned the horizon in vain for Lord Stanley's men, their only hope of salvation. The ground under him vibrated then his ears rang with the booming thunder of Richard's guns. With a jolt he realised they had been holding their fire until Sir John de Vere's vanguard was at close range.

Cannonballs cut swathes through the ranks of Henry's mercenaries, killing and maiming in an instant. Men cried out and one gave a blood-curdling scream but the ranks closed and continued to press forward as if nothing had happened. The sun, which had been behind their enemy, moved overhead and the savage, hand-to-hand fighting ebbed and flowed like a tide as fighting men gained ground then lost it as others pressed forward.

Jasper felt a hand on his shoulder and tore his gaze from

the carnage. Gabriel wore a sallet helmet with a guard that covered most of his face, causing him to shout over the noise of the battle.

'They're routed, sir!'

Jasper stared into the melee. Gabriel was right. The enemy vanguard parted, split in half to let them charge through. 'Is it a trap?'

'No, sir. Look!' Gabriel pointed with his sword.

Jasper saw Richard's men deserting, some being cut down by their own side, while others dropped their weapons or stood aside. Unlike Henry's loyal Welshmen and mercenary soldiers, Richard's army would be mostly working men, northerners, with little training, and now it seemed he would pay the price.

'Praise God, Gabriel! There is hope for us yet!'

David Owen yelled a warning, pointing to a figure on a white horse fighting savagely through the knights around Henry's standard, slashing with a broadsword onto the head of Henry's standard bearer. The flowing banner fell as William Brandon died without letting go of it to defend himself.

The swordsman unhorsed one knight and thrust at another before looking directly at Jasper. The brave knight was close enough for him to see the gold circlet on his helmet. It must be King Richard, fearlessly taking the battle into his own hands, and he was heading towards Henry.

Jasper called out the order they had planned for such an emergency. 'Pikemen, take position!'

The hand-picked Frenchmen formed a circle around Henry, their long sharpened pikes linked in an impenetrable forest. Henry drew his sword, and stood ready, his face pale and his lips moving in silent prayer as the rider on the white horse closed the ground between them.

Then with pounding hooves, and a fierce battle cry, came the men carrying the banner of the black raven. The mounted men-at-arms of Rhys ap Thomas surrounded the usurper king.

Richard raised his sword defiantly, refusing to surrender, and charged the man nearest to him, hacking without mercy at the man's head. On a shouted command from Rhys ap Thomas, the Welshmen cut him down with swords and axes, showing such savagery Jasper felt a sudden shock of pity.

King Richard lay dead, his body twisted and bleeding, while the Welshmen cheered at their easy victory. Jasper heard a distant roar and looked away across the battlefield in time to see Lord Stanley's men swarming from the hills, driving Richard's routed army back the way they came. Incredibly, the tide of the battle had turned.

'We've done it.' He spoke to himself, his voice low and choked with emotion. My God, we've done it!'

The fighting stopped as suddenly as it started, the yells and clashing steel replaced by an unexpected, unnerving silence as they surveyed the field of dead and dying men. Jasper loosened the strap on his helmet and pulled it from his head, letting it fall to the ground with a hollow thud.

One of the men near to Henry called out. 'God save the King! God save King Henry!'

Jasper joined in with a thousand others, tears of relief streaming down his face, raising his sword high in the air and shouting at the top of his voice.

'God save King Henry! God save King Henry!'

# AUTHOR'S NOTE

The skyline of the picturesque seaside town of Tenby in Pembrokeshire, Wales, close to where I live, is dominated by the towering spire of St Mary's church. Inside lie the tombs of Thomas White and his son John, both Mayors of Tenby, who helped Jasper Tudor fund the raising of the town walls 'to the height of a man'. Thomas White later hid Jasper and the young Henry Tudor in his cellar and enabled their escape to Brittany through secret tunnels under his house.

When researching this book I was shown the cellars and tunnels by the manager of Boots the Chemist in Tenby, which now occupies the site. We started in the basement cellars and it's easy to see how Jasper and Henry could have remained out of sight for as long as they needed to.

As we entered the tunnels, deep under the street, we were plunged into darkness and had to rely on torches. I saw the roof of the tunnel closest to the entrance had been rebuilt with bricks, and the remains of a fireplace, complete with chimney. This could be further evidence for its use to hide people who might need a fire.

Further down the tunnel the roof was roughly hewn

through bedrock, with several other exits bricked up. After emerging back into the winter sun of Tenby I went to pay my respects to Thomas White. Visiting the church and looking into his sculpted face reminds me he was a real person, who left his mark on the town and helped change the history of Britain.

Jasper Tudor doesn't seem more than five centuries away as I walk in his footsteps from the church in the high street, down the same narrow lane with uneven stone steps. I pass the timber-framed Tudor merchant's house, now a Tudor museum, and see men preparing their boats in the sheltered harbour. It was from here that Jasper and Henry sailed into their long exile, to return to claim the English throne.

Two years of research led into this book, so the names, dates and locations are based on the best sources I could find. Only the characters of Gabriel and Máiréad are fictitious. Gabriel represents the loyal servants who shared Jasper's life, risking their own by riding with him into battle.

Máiréad is intended to represent the possible relationship Jasper might have had before the siege of Bamburgh Castle. Some writers suggest he was infatuated with his brother's widow, Lady Margaret Beaufort, although the only evidence I found is of their shared concern for Henry's welfare during such dangerous and troubled times.

Thank you for reading this book, which I hope you enjoyed as much as I did writing it, and please consider leaving a short review. You can find out about my other books at my website www.tonyriches.com.

**Tony Riches**
**Pembrokeshire**

## OWEN - Book One of the Tudor Trilogy

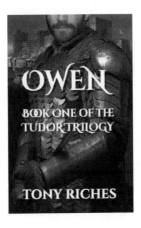

England 1422: Owen Tudor, a Welsh servant, waits in Windsor Castle to meet his new mistress, the beautiful and lonely Queen Catherine of Valois, widow of the warrior king, Henry V.

They fall in love, risking Owen's life and Queen Catherine's reputation, but how do they found the dynasty which changes British history – the Tudors?

This is the first historical novel to fully explore the amazing life of Owen Tudor, grandfather of King Henry VII and the great-grandfather of King Henry VIII. Set against a background of the conflict between the Houses of Lancaster and York, which develops into what have become known as the Wars of the Roses, Owen's story deserves to be told.

**Available as paperback, eBook and audiobook**

**MARY ~ Tudor Princess**

**Book One of the Brandon Trilogy**

**Midsummer's Day 1509:** The true story of the Tudor dynasty continues with the daughter of King Henry VII. Mary Tudor watches her elder brother become King of England and wonders what the future holds for her.

Born into great privilege, Mary has beauty and intelligence beyond her years. Her brother Henry plans to use her marriage to build a powerful alliance against his enemies – but will she dare to risk his anger by marrying for love?

Meticulously researched and based on actual events, this 'sequel' follows Mary's story from book three of the Tudor Trilogy and is set during the reign of King Henry VIII.

**Available in paperback and eBook**

## DRAKE - Tudor Corsair
## Book One of the Elizabethan Series

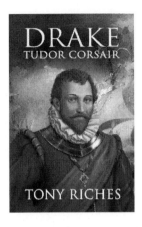

1564: Devon sailor Francis Drake sets out on a journey of adventure, and risks his life in an audacious plan to steal a fortune.

Queen Elizabeth is intrigued by Drake and secretly encourages his piracy. King Philip of Spain has enough of Drake's plunder and orders an armada to threaten the future of England.

Drake – Tudor Corsair continues the story of the Tudors, which began with Owen Tudor in book one of the Tudor trilogy.

**Available in paperback and eBook**

**GRANDMOTHER WILLOW** You understand the natural order of the world. You listen before speaking and are good at getting others to open up and share what's on their minds and in their hearts. Kind and wise, you help people find their own answers by asking the right questions. When focused, you dislike distractions and make sure everyone respects your need for silence.

**Magical Gifts:** Grandmother Willow bestows the gift of intuition, mystery, and individuality. She teaches you how to cultivate your inner wisdom to benefit yourself and others.

**Keys to Your Success:** Teaching others to hear nature's spirit talking.

**Grandmother Willow's Story:** *Pocahontas* (1995)

HONEST
CONSCIENTIOUS
SELFLESS

**BAMBI** You have a special role to fill, and you need time to acquire the skills necessary to fulfill your destiny. At a young age, you learned how to take care of yourself, and you admire those who taught you survival skills. You remember every kindness shown to you by others, and they fuel your ambitions. You are intuitive and your dreams provide you with poignant and prophetic information. A powerful defender, you earn the respect of your peers.

**Magical Gifts:** Bambi bestows you with the gifts of bravery, tenderness, and devotion. He teaches you how to walk alone as well as with others.

**Keys to Your Success:** Growing into the great person you were meant to be.

**Bambi's Story:** *Bambi* (1942)